IT SHOCKS! IT SHATTERS!
TINSEL IS...

"A PAGE-TURNER. . . . IF HOLLYWOOD HADN'T EXISTED, GOLDMAN WOULD HAVE INVENTED IT. IN A WAY, HE JUST HAS."

—*Philadelphia Inquirer*

"A HOLLYWOOD—MAYBE *THE* HOLLYWOOD—NOVEL."

—*Cue*

"A FAST-MOVING TALE. . . . GOLDMAN GETS OFF SOME ZINGERS."

—*Variety*

"A SKILLFUL, FUNNY, INFORMED . . . APPROACH TO THE REAL TINSEL IN AN INCREDIBLE BUSINESS . . . COULD BE THE HOLLYWOOD NOVEL OF THE '70s. ABRASIVE ENTERTAINMENT."

—*San Francisco Chronicle*

"ONE OF THE GOOD ONES . . . THE INSIDE STORY. . . . JULIAN GARVEY, THE PRODUCER, IS WORTH THE BOOK. HIS RAPACIOUS SCHEMING, HIS DEVIOUS DEVICES, HIS SMARMY CHICANERY, GIVE *TINSEL* ALL ITS ENERGY, PROVIDE IT WITH THE SORT OF MAD, STRAIGHT-AHEAD DRIVE IT NEEDS TO GO."

—*The Wall Street Journal*

TINSEL

WILLIAM GOLDMAN

A DELL BOOK

For Ilene

Published by
Dell Publishing Co., Inc.
1 Dag Hammarskjold Plaza
New York, New York 10017

Dell ® TM 681510, Dell Publishing Co., Inc.

ISBN: 0-440-18735-4

Reprinted by arrangement with Delacorte Press.

Printed in the United States of America

First Dell printing—July 1980

Grateful acknowledgment is made for permission to re-print from the following material:
"Mister Tambourine Man" by Bob Dylan: © 1964 Warner Bros. Inc. All rights reserved. Used by permission.
"A Hard Day's Night" (John Lennon and Paul McCartney): Copyright © 1964 Northern Songs Limited. All

I

DIXIE

1

Dixie was daydreaming over coffee waiting for Mr. Balducci to arrive. She sat alone in the breakfast room, dressed in her tennis whites, and lit another True from the butt still burning in the ashtray. She was closing in on three packs a day now, triple what she used to smoke in her good old Camel Unfiltered days. Dixie had tried, in between brand-switching, to stop cold turkey and, to her astonishment, succeeded.

She also gained twelve pounds in fourteen days so, telling herself that there were some things worse than cancer, she went back to smoking.

"Ethel," Dixie called then, "is there any more—" but she stopped as the black maid entered with the large coffee pitcher in her hand. "Thanks, Radar," Dixie said, referring to the character on *M.A.S.H.* who always managed to appear with whatever anybody wanted before they had finished the requesting. Ethel, a tv freak, laughed, poured the cup full, and left.

Dixie rubbed her eyes, picked up a packet of Sweet 'n Low, tore it open, poured it in. Down the hill now, she got a glimpse of Mel lugging the ball machine onto the court, looking as he always did, like Robert Duvall: balding and powerful, decent and plain. He was bare from the waist up, and pale. He worked too hard to ever get much tan, and watching him till he was blocked from view by some shrubbery, Dixie marveled at his energy.

He was forty-two, four years more than she, and they had gotten stoned the night before. He loved to do that on weekends, and he paid top dollar for the best Hawaiian seedless. It was really the only time he ever relaxed, after grass, and even though Dixie could take it or leave it alone, she liked what it did for him. She was always after him to slow down, even though she knew it was not about to happen. If he ever slowed, he'd stop. Mel should have been the messenger at Marathon.

When they were both very high they had, as they always did, sex, and he was, as he always was, strong. By one in the morning Dixie was wiped out, so she kissed him good-night and flaked, ordering him to do the same.

At half past two she sensed his absence, so she got groggily up, tracked him to the library where he sat with the headphones on, listening to the second Brandenburg, a half-empty bottle of Mondavi Cabernet in one hand, a half-filled wine glass in the other. "You trying to kill yourself, it's two-fucking-thirty."

He lifted one ear of the headphones off. " 's late," he told her. "Don't want you missing your beauty sleep."

She could tell from his slurring he'd had a few extra tokes. "You know I get nervous when you're not there, now c'mon."

"I will, Dix; soon as I finish this." He lifted the bottle.

"Cork it up; you can finish it tomorrow."

Like all enormously successful medical men in the Bel-Air vicinity, Mel was deeply into California wine. Now the look on his face told Dixie she had committed some gaffe of unpardonable proportions. "Cork it up? Jesus, this is a sixty-eight. I cork it up, it might not be all airtight, it might be vinegary tomorrow. Word of that gets around, I'm finished at Pearson's," that being where he bought his wine. He nodded up at her. "Get a glass."

"Mel, what if I found it flinty? Or flabby?" She loved to zap him about wine. "What if I thought the bouquet was off or the finish a little on the short side?" He was laughing now; he never laughed enough and when she could bring it on, it always pleased her. She gestured with her index finger for him to follow her to the bedroom.

He sat very still, just stared at her. "You are just so goddam gorgeous," he said finally.

Certainly he meant it. Maybe it was true. "Especially at two-thirty-six in the morning. You should see me at four; I'm really ravishing then. By dawn I'm a dead ringer for Maria Ouspenskaya."

"Why can't you just say 'thank you'?"

Dixie shook her head, shrugged, said nothing. She could sense her nipples against the satin of her nightgown.

"You don't need beauty sleep; never have, never will."

"Look out, Dixie, he's horny again."

Mel smiled. "It's true, I can't help it."

"Solly, Cholly."

"Even if I let you tie me up and whip me first?"

"I've got to admit that's tempting, only my rubber suit's still at the cleaners. Now g'night." She left the room, starting down the corridor, letting him yell, "Hey, Dixie, please" a few times before he fell silent.

She got back into bed and lay alone for a while. She didn't want any more sex, the first time had been plenty, so she closed her eyes, rolled over on her right side, got the pillow fluffed, and took several deep breaths.

Who was she kidding? He was a good man and he cared and all she owed him was everything, so she got up, took off her gown, went into her bathroom, brushed her teeth, dabbed some Joy behind her ears, beneath her breasts and, after a moment's hesitation, in her pubic hairs. Then, naked and silent, she walked to the bar, got a wine glass, entered the library, kissed his bald head.

He started to move for her but she said, "Freeze." Then she lit the gas log fireplace, turned off the overhead light, and said, "Hit me with the Cabernet, Baldy."

"I'll cork it up, let's go to bed."

"Every drop gets finished or you don't cop a feel." She took the bottle, filled her glass to the top, moved carefully back, sat with the firelight glowing against her skin.

"You're driving me crazy."

"I do hope so," Dixie said.

Mel started to chug-a-lug his glass.

"You do that, you'll be too drunk to enjoy anything later."

"Who said I enjoyed it?"

Dixie smiled on that, sipped her wine, the fire behind her, her husband in front, and she felt so goddam secure. Eventually she let him sit beside her where they kissed for a while, two people total ages eighty still getting turned on by necking, and after that they wandered to the bedroom where she undressed him slowly, which he liked a lot, taking her time with each pajama button, easing the top off his body, pretending to be unable to untie the bottoms, and when their games were done they went to bed quickly, where he was a little lacking in control from the wine and the grass but his heart was pure and after he came she held him gently until at last he was able to find sleep and even then Dixie kept right on holding him, her own bald baby, in her arms. . . .

2

"The Eye-talian has got here," Ethel announced from the breakfast room doorway, the news catching Dixie with her coffee cup in midair. Ethel always referred to Mr. Balducci as that, "the Eye-talian," because she was the kind of maid who insisted on *totally* running a household, for which she was paid two fifty per week and worth every penny, and it frosted her that Dixie handled Mr. Balducci herself.

Rising quickly, Dixie asked would Ethel please tidy the breakfast dishes. Then she hurriedly left the room, moved through the butler's pantry and enormous kitchen just beyond. Opening the back door, she walked down the steps toward the wonderful blue truck and the little round man waiting beside it, cap in hand.

Mr. Balducci had lived into his legend.

If, as insiders suspected, the richest people in Southern California were the Chandlers, who ran the *Los Angeles Times,* Stein and Wasserman, who ran MCA-Universal, and Smitty, the head doorman who ran the car concession at the Beverly Hills Hotel, then Mr. Balducci was not far down the line. Simply put, he sold the finest and undoubtedly the most expensive produce in the world. And more than that, if you lived in Bel-Air and a few of the better streets in Holmby Hills, he brought it all to your door in his ancient blue truck for your selection.

One side of the truck was for fruits, the other vegetables. Nothing was priced. You simply walked around and made your choices and Mr. Balducci would nod his ancient head. He never wrote anything down but when you were done, bags of merchandise would be left by your back door and once a month a bill was sent to your accountant.

"It's-a da beaooo-ti-full Mrs. Kern, I'm-a can die now," Mr. Balducci began, his more or less standard opening.

"Why is it," Dixie wondered, "that you say you've lived in this country for over sixty years, and each month your accent gets thicker?"

"I'm-a confoosed myself," Mr. Balducci replied, following Dixie around to the vegetable side of the truck.

Dixie looked at the display and, as always, it thrilled her because nothing else in this world, not October at the Plaza Athénée or the charge at Giorgio's or the perfect place on Stone Canyon reinforced how far she had come from the crappy little grocery back in Lake Forest, Illinois, that had belonged forever to her father.

"What's-a fo' dinner?" Mr. Balducci asked, since he always liked planning the menu. "An' how many?"

"Just maybe six; I think we're going to do something different for a change and barbecue steaks."

Mr. Balducci held up a bean sprout. "Fo' salad."

Dixie wasn't all that crazy about bean sprouts, and said so.

He kept holding it out. "Sniff. Nibble."

Dixie did, then looked at him, surprised. "What are they?"

"Fo' you special, Japanese mushrooms. Goes great-a wit dis—endiv-a from da Belgian." He looked at Dixie. "You want me to help?" She always did, so while she watched he indicated some tomatoes the size of artichokes and artichokes the size of melons and red-tip lettuce and also arugula and giant red onions plus some fresh dill and Dixie couldn't take her eyes off the avocados so how could he deprive her of them and then they moved around the truck to the extraordinary piles of fruit and Mel loved the Turkish figs and my God, where did he find the wild strawberries—"frezz-a da bois" he called them—and there were bunches of giant hothouse grapes from one of the European countries that Mr. Balducci had trouble pronouncing, but God they looked beautiful and Mel loved them with Brie and whatever the wine was he'd been standing up for several days now so the stupid sediment might settle.

Dixie wandered with the little old man for really too long; she always did that. He'd been coming five years now, since they first moved into the place, and he never much seemed to mind their time together. He liked her and obviously she reciprocated. Eventually, though, the shopping spree was over and Dixie flashed her smile, as she always did at the end, and he doffed his tweed cap. which was his return signal, but then he did something he'd never done before, something no one had done for over three years now, and probably it was because she was so unprepared that it rocked her so.

What he did was, he asked her for her autograph.

Dixie had never handled the situation with ease. Even when it was difficult for her to walk a block on Rodeo without getting stopped at least once, she always flushed and wanted almost to run, convinced that once she'd said yes whoever asked would point to her and laugh and cry out "April Fool."

She had good reason for the paranoia; her first fifteen years had been that sad. If you lived in Lake Forest in the 40s and 50s you were either very rich or you worked for them. The town was still small and remained, along with Kenilworth, one of the two gentile strongholds along the North Shore outside Chicago. If you worked for the rich, you were either staff or shopkeeper. But the shopkeepers needed places less fancy than the rich could afford, and Dixie's father's store was such a place. Crowder's Grocery was dark, hot in summer, chilly the rest of the time, and Dixie—Dorothy Crowder then—helped out with her parents in her spare time.

She had a lot of that. School was drudgery, she had no hobbies, no friends; she daydreamed of being Judy Garland but told no one.

Her parents were a sour team, and at nights, after the meager store was shut, they would jab at each other through dinner until, bruised and weary, they slept.

Dorothy was slight and average, with hair that was almost blonde and a face that was almost pretty, would have been pretty if she had felt better about herself. At fifteen she was five foot two, still with braces and without her period, a trailer.

The next year made all the difference. She got the curse, spurted four inches, lost her braces, gained a shape. Boys flocked. In corridors they watched her move. Her breasts were large now, her hips rounded. She made her hair lighter in tone. It helped.

Everything helped. She was still a mediocre student, still hated home, but she tried out for the school musical her junior year, 1957, and almost got the part of Laurie. The next year she got the lead, Julie in *Showboat*, and she sang "Bill" and sat on a piano, and her voice wasn't much but nobody cared. When you looked the way Dixie looked —she was Dixie now—people found it in their hearts to forgive you.

She tried Lake Forest College for a semester, or almost a semester, because at Christmas she eloped with a senior who played, naturally, the trumpet, and just as she wanted to be Judy Garland, he wanted to be Harry James. He was a Jew and her parents never spoke to her afterwards, but that didn't bother Dixie as much as it might have since they hadn't spoken to her all that much before.

The trumpeter's name was Benny Durbin and he called his group "The Durbinaires," and they scrounged the Middle West a couple of years, grabbing Lodge work and small conventions whenever they could, which was often enough to eat but not eat well. There were five of them, piano, drums, guitar, trumpet, and vocal, and they had one car to stuff themselves into, and they weren't bad, they just weren't very good.

Except people liked looking at Dixie.

She was twenty in 1960, and she couldn't sing much at all, but she tried, her thin voice at least on pitch, and she wore white silk blouses and white slacks and her hair was quite blonde now, her body as good as a body had to be. She looked like one of the Al Capp heroines that menaced Li'l Abner on Sadie Hawkins Day and for the Middle West, that was enough.

In '61 The Durbinaires tried Vegas and that was the end of them. The piano player ran off with the drummer —they'd been fighting it for two years now—and the guitarist went to Dealer's School, eventually landing a job at the New Frontier. Benny got mean as his dreams faded, but Dixie hung in with him, tried to make it work. He discovered, one night, both hash and Zen, and since he didn't want an unbeliever like Dixie hanging around the Seattle commune he was headed for, they divorced.

Dixie would have been more destroyed than she was by these events if she hadn't been discovered by a Universal talent scout who tied her to a seven-year contract. The studio dropped her as soon as they possibly could, six months later, when they decided she acted a little bit worse than she sang. But the contract got her to L.A. and she actually did a bit part in a feature film, a sun-and-sand epic, where she played a handmaiden and was chosen to say one line, "If only the Prince was here," which she delivered properly on the second take and it nearly broke her heart when the scene was cut.

Even though she was out of work and broke, it never occurred to her to leave L.A. If you were a performer, it was either New York or the coast, and if you were a performer with Dixie's looks, New York was a washout. So she hung around, modeled a little at Robinson's, did spiels at conventions, waiting.

The break came so fast it surprised even her. In '62,

Beverly Hillbillies got the worst reviews and the best ratings of any show ever on the tube. And immediately the spinoffs and the ripoffs started. *Green Acres, Petticoat Junction,* and *Dogpatch.*

Dixie became Daisy Mae. *Dogpatch* premiered in the fall of '63 and though it never went through the roof, it managed to stick around four seasons and in January of '66 Dixie was on the cover of *Life.*

And was, for that blink, a star.

But a lot of people made the cover of *Life* around that time, Ina Balin and Brenda Vaccaro and Nicole Maurey, and even though Dixie had fan clubs (three) and supposedly, according to *Movie Mirror,* was unofficially engaged to Bobby Darin and absolutely, according to *TV Exclusive,* broke Sal Mineo's heart, the end was coming too too fast.

Dogpatch got canceled.

It was as simple as that. Dixie was, of course, upset, but she had a good agent at the Morris office and he easily booked her into the Dunes. Dixie spent a lot of what money she'd saved for her act. She got lovely costumes and decent choreography and a number of funny-enough one-liners from a San Francisco comic who had a crush on her.

She just couldn't sing very well.

She was a stunner, good natured and kind, and she couldn't figure out why people kept walking out of the act. She busted her hump to please, but the Dunes foreclosed her, and after eight days she was replaced by Joey Bishop, who owed the hotel a favor.

When it goes, it's gone, and Dixie tried like hell to change that, but she wasn't cut out, like Zsa Zsa, to be a tv "personality," someone famous for being famous. She did guest shots on a few series, but she wasn't any better at acting now than she had been at the beginning, just a little less camera shy.

And she was twenty-eight.

Old.

The twenty-year-olds kept coming, busloads of them, each one prettier than the next, some of them hungry too. Dixie unloaded her small house in the hills above Sunset, rented a semidetached place near the Beverly Wilshire Hotel. She pestered the Morris office and they were decent to her as long as they could be, but then they cut her loose. Dixie understood, even said "thank you" as the conversation was terminated.

That night she tried to call Benny Durbin.

No luck.

The next day she tried to hustle up another agent.

Solly, Cholly.

Dixie entered what she came to refer to as her "bad patch." It lasted three years, a sharply descending line, and ended, miraculously, with a toothache.

"Doctor Kern?"

"That's right."

"Well, listen, you don't know me but my name is Dixie Crowder and I really honest to God hurt."

"Who referred you?"

"My dentist, Doctor Gumble."—(Lie, he wasn't *her* dentist, he was just *a* dentist, a guy she'd met someplace, a party, maybe at the Marina, and she'd called him at home and described what she was going through and he said it sounded like root canal and that Doctor Kern was the best if you could get him, Doctor Kern in Century City, and then he'd hung up fast because his wife was calling from the background)—"He said you'd help me, can I see you now?"

"I'll cancel lunch, come by at twelve—"

"I can't wait two hours—"

"Miss Crowder, you sound like an actress," he replied and before Dixie could acknowledge the fact he said, "I don't like actresses," and gave the phone back to his secretary.

Dixie arrived a little before noon, devouring a box of Tic Tacs because she'd belted down too much Scotch from ten till eleven-thirty to cope with the pain. She looked like hell, taut and drained, dark under the eyes, but he wasn't all that much either, a ringer for Robert Duvall, definitely not her type, except that by half past one she would have eloped with him practically if he'd asked, because her pain was gone. She wanted to thank him, do a gratitude number, started it even, but he cut her off, said he'd see her again on Friday at noon to finish off the job and be careful chewing until the Novocain wears off.

He was even more romantic on the last appointment, saying precisely zip, so Dixie was more than a little surprised when he asked if she liked chamber music and she was about to say either, "Shit no" or, "What the hell is it?" but instead, thank God, she managed "Oh, yes, ever since I was a child."

"There's a concert at UCLA tomorrow night. Are you busy?"

She was. "Nothing planned," she heard herself say.

"Starts at seven-thirty, shall we eat after?"

Dixie nodded, wondering why she was getting into this, but the answer was easy—too bad this Kern wasn't blue eyed like Newman, and sure it would have been nice if he'd been funny like Woody Allen or cute like Cavett. The fact was the man was a rock. Or seemed that way.

"I'll stop by at seven."

Quick head-shake from Dixie. "I live way out in the Valley, I'll meet you at the concert."

He was looking at her funny. "The address you gave my secretary," Doctor Kern said, "wasn't in the Valley."

Dixie tried for a laugh. "Did I say *lived* in the Valley? —weird—I meant I was going to *be* in the Valley, at Universal, auditions and stuff."

"Saturday at seven?" He looked at her and waited.

"I'm living with a guy," Dixie said finally. "I don't think he'd be crazy about you jingling the front door."

"Is it serious?"

Dixie shook her head. "He's an actor."

"Then you were busy."

Dixie said nothing.

"Let's bag the whole notion, okay?" he said. "It sounds like it might be complicated."

"There's nothing goddam complicated about it." He was, she could tell, a little surprised at her anger. "You asked me out, I said fine, now have we got a deal or don't we?"

The concert was a snooze. But brief, thank the Lord, and Dixie got through it wondering should she put out for him later or not. She looked, considering she was a thirty-one-year-old woman who had just had root canal work, pretty fucking sensational, so there wasn't much question he'd try a move, hit on her a little, see what happened. And he didn't look like the kind who took rejection easily, so she was running a risk if she shot him down. But she was running a risk the other way, too, because he didn't look like the kind who wanted a triumph without a struggle; he was a fighter, this one, so what she decided was split it down the middle, turn aside the pass but let him know she was desperate for a chance at a return match. She'd say it was her period but she'd say it with evident regret, and she'd graze her body accidentally across his a couple of times, an old ploy, sure, but one she'd always had success with.

What followed didn't exactly buoy her confidence because after a quick dinner at a French place she'd never heard of, he not only didn't make a pass, he didn't ask her out again. He just said, Good night, Miss Crowder, and drove off in his car, leaving her to drive off in hers.

It made Dixie crazy—for fifteen years, *everyone* had asked her out again. Usually it was just to try for a roll in the hay, but at least they tried. And why shouldn't they? She had a wonderful body and there wasn't that much wrong with the head, and maybe she wasn't up on the latest chamber music, but at least she wasn't mean, never castrated anybody.

Good night, Miss Crowder, for chrissakes.

Some rock.

It made her so crazy it took a couple of days for her to

put the incident completely and totally out of her mind, where it remained for almost a week, at which time she drove to his office at the close of working hours and waited—lurked—in the hall, telling herself all the while that the boys with white suits and butterfly nets were going to be on her tail if she didn't watch it. My God, she was great looking and she had been on the covers of over forty-seven different magazines and now she was pursuing a dental surgeon.

It was close to seven when he finally walked out into the corridor and she was very frayed by that time, confused over which opening to try and what to follow up with if it didn't work. He stopped only briefly when he saw her and Dixie was surprised he didn't seem surprised.

"I moved out," Dixie said suddenly.

From the good doctor, not a word.

"On the actor, I mean."

Now a nod.

"I live alone again." She didn't know what to say further, but it had to be something because she was obviously carrying the conversational ball alone. "You can pick me up is the point, don't you see? If you want to, that is, do you want to?"

She could almost not endure the silence.

Finally, at goddam last, he pushed for the elevator and muttered, "Come on, you can walk me home," but Dixie wasn't sure she'd heard him right so it wasn't till they were on the sidewalk she said, "You can't walk home in Southern California, it's against the state laws or something."

He didn't smile or shrug, just pointed to the twin condominiums down the way. They walked awhile before Dixie asked how come he'd never called.

"You're a desperate lady is why."

No point in arguing that.

His apartment was nice enough, a couple of bedrooms, a living room, terrace, twentieth floor so the view was terrific. He went into the kitchen while she stood staring out the window. All of Century City was once the back lot of Fox, and he had that view. *Dogpatch* had been shot there, and looking down now, Dixie was hit by memories. He came out of the kitchen, carrying a couple of glasses of white wine, followed her glance toward the studio. She was tempted to tell him she'd shot there for four years back in the sixties.

But something told her not to.

After a few minutes he said, "Bring that into the bedroom, why don't you," indicating her wine glass. She did obediently what he said and they undressed quietly. Then they showered together, and he soaped her body with great care. Dixie didn't know what he thought of the merchandise because he wasn't a talker, but from her point of view, she was pleased, since he wasn't tall, an inch more than her maybe, and didn't seem all that powerful in clothes, so the muscles of his body came as a definite surprise. She soaped him next, hoping he wasn't some kind of weirdo who got off on Fels Naptha.

He wasn't.

Fucking was okay, as far as Dixie was concerned, but she usually had a miserable time reaching orgasm which always presented problems, because unless she faked it, the guy sooner or later began feeling it was all his inadequate fault, so she usually made sure, once her partner had come, to act up a storm and end things happily, if not forever after at least for a while.

"Quit that!"

She had been panting away, building to the pseudo-inevitable when he spoke so sharply it almost made her afraid.

"I wasn't—" Dixie began, the finish to be "doing anything" but one look at him and she clammed, because she could see on his face he knew.

The son of a bitch knew she was faking.

Why would a goddam dentist know a thing like that?

"Okay," she muttered, quieting.

He began to work her then, patiently, with great care and before too long she actually began to relax and from then on, it was easy street.

"What, do you give clinics or something?" Dixie asked after she'd come.

For the very first time, she made him laugh.

The next weekend he said, "It'd be a lot less hassle if you moved in." They were having dinner at some Chink place in downtown L.A., a dumpling house for chrissakes.

Dixie hesitated, not because what he'd said wasn't the most lushly romantic proposition she'd ever heard—she was already resigned to the fact that Mel was never going to drink champagne out of her slipper—but because in their hours thus far together, he'd never once yet said he even liked her. "You sure?" she tried.

He nodded. "Less hassle all the way around."

"You make me sound like a utensil or something. 'Take the hassle out of housework with Dixie Crowder.' The way you talk, I could be a goddam trash compactor."

He looked at her awhile. "Hey listen," he said finally. "I'm very direct and I hate bullshit. If I didn't want you around the house, I wouldn't ask. Now yes or no?"

"What would you do if I said no?"

"I'd be very sorry."

"I'll settle for that," Dixie said.

That Sunday morning they read the *Los Angeles Times* together in bed. He pointed idly to something in the Calendar section. "Look; there's a show of Klee drawings at this gallery on La Cienega; I wonder if it's any good."

Dixie, busy with the society pages, made a grunt.

The next evening she had a glass of white wine ready for him when he got home. He kissed her, sipped it, inquired about her day which she told him was mainly shopping for a bathing suit and a few phone calls, and he said only, "I guess you didn't have time for the show then," and he said it quietly, but Dixie suddenly realized, *omichrist, omichrist, I shouldda gone.*

The next day she was at the gallery half an hour before it opened. She spun her car around, drove to a Tiny Naylor's and had a couple of cups of coffee with Sweet 'n Low, fended off a couple of passes, only one of which was unpleasant. When she got back to the gallery it was open so she took off her sunglasses and walked inside.

Squiggles. The whole goddam room was full of nothing but squiggles by this Klee. *Omichrist, omichrist, what am I gonna say about it?* She walked around and around the place, and being early, she was alone at first, but then when other women began coming in, she made her move, hurried to the fag who ran the establishment. "He's really something, isn't he, this Klee," Dixie said.

"Oh, yes, wonderfully amusing," the gallery guy replied.

"Wonderfully amusing," Dixie said to Mel that night as they sipped their Chardonnay. (He had taught her what the wine was the night before.) She was surprised then, when he took her in his arms. "You're really very sweet," he said.

Coming from him, Dixie decided, that had to be good.

She had never, of course, heard the myth of Galatea and Pygmalion. She really wasn't all that sure who George Bernard Shaw was. But the night *My Fair Lady* had won the Oscars, Dixie had been at the ceremonies, being her agent's date for the evening, and seeing Rex Harrison in the flesh spurred her into going to take in the movie later that week, even though she never much cared for musicals where people stood around and jabbered all the time and no one could really *sing,* the way Garland could.

During the first month with Mel, Dixie found herself reflecting a lot about the poor dumb flower girl who learned to speak properly, because Mel was always saying things like, "I wonder if the new Graham Greene's up to snuff?" or along those lines which meant off she went to Martindale's the next morning. He was really kind of relentless with her time, shipping her to this museum or that gallery, casually making sure the bookshelf on her side of the bed was always bulging.

The crazy thing was Dixie enjoyed it. She wasn't stupid in school, she just hadn't given much of a crap about logarithms or *Lorna Doone.* Now she cared and she busted her hump to please, and she couldn't tell if he cared back or not, but she assumed he had to, at least a little, otherwise he'd have booted her out. Besides, the consequences of his not caring was something she was just not strong enough to deal with.

She was terribly in love with him before she found out he was rich, a tidbit that came her way when she was on a cattlecall out at Universal for a secondary part in a Movie of the Week. The casting director had been her pal since *Dogpatch* days, and tried to work her in for old times' sake whenever possible, and in the few brief moments they'd had to chat he asked what she was up to and Dixie said she was kind of living with a guy and he asked was the guy a civilian and Dixie'd nodded, said Mel's name and boy did she get a reaction.

"You fucker," she said to him that night, handing him his properly chilled glass of Heitz '69 Chardonnay. "Why didn't you let on you were loaded? It would have given me a better reason for sticking around than just plain pity."

"Who said I had money?"

"Pat Mulcahey—he's this sweet gay casting buddy I have and he said your father was an honest to Christ *financier*."

"He worked at a bank."

"He *owned* the bank according to my sources."

"He owned stock in it, does it matter?"

"Bet your ass it matters, dummy; I'm gonna start putting out for you now." Dixie thought that was pretty funny but she was the only one in the vicinity who did.

They drove to Musso Frank's for dinner, Mel's favorite place, and usually it put him in a good mood, but not tonight. He wasn't angry, just unusually quiet, and the drive back was accomplished in total silence.

Dixie was in a panic.

When they got back and began undressing, she reached to unbutton his shirt, which was one of the more obvious ways she let him know she wouldn't mind a little action, and he was cordial, didn't slap her hand away or anything like that; he just stepped slightly back, continued undressing while he explained he had a monster of an operation coming up tomorrow, a jaw reconstruction on a black kid out from one of the clinics he spent time at, and he wanted to go over some of the procedures in his head, a habit of his.

Dixie showered and started to put on her nightgown. Instead she took a white half slip, raised the elastic to just above her breasts. It was a look of hers that he liked, a lot, and she stopped in the bedroom long enough to let him see her, explaining she was going to read in the living room on the sofa. Except when she got there, she couldn't concentrate on the Turgenev, so she put it down, switched out the couch light, and curled up, staring at the Fox lot lit below by moonlight, the giant *Hello, Dolly!* set still standing, white bones from another time.

She heard Mel in the kitchen after a while, rummaging around, cabinet doors opening and closing, then the sound of a cork being pulled, the scratch of glasses against shelving. Then his voice, starting when he was still hidden from sight. "What are we, the end of May? All right, listen to me now"—he moved into the room, holding the bottle of red wine, a couple of glasses—"the way I see it there's *three* big ifs involved." He poured her a glass, did the same for himself, went to the window, stood with his back to the night. "If we go to Vegas and marry now, the most I'll be able to take off is a long weekend, but if we wait till August, I'll book out the month and we can travel and—"

"No contest," Dixie said. "Now"—and she started to rise and move toward him but before she could really move he said, "I told you there were three ifs, Dixie, now sit the hell down!"

Dixie felt panic again.

"You've got to give it up," Mel said finally.

"Give what?"

Mel gestured with his thumb behind him toward the studio.

"Jesus, you don't mean my career?"

"That's the subject under discussion."

Dixie sipped her wine. "Naturally, if the situation was the other way around, you'd give up yours."

Mel watched her silently.

Dixie shook her head. "Give up my career, give up my career, God, what a thing," and she was going to go on awhile longer with her voice soft and serious except when something struck her as really funny, she was never able to sustain control, and she broke up now. "That's like asking Esther Williams to give up dancing, Mel, you know what I mean?"

Still he watched her.

"Mel, baby, there ain't no career. There is no call for my talents at this particular point in time. The reality is I am thirty-one years old and the day before yesterday's news."

"I don't give a fuck for the reality."

Dixie blinked.

"It's the daydream I'm talking about."

Dixie finished her wine, held out her glass for more.

Mel poured, then sat on the far end of the couch from her. "You remember almost the first thing I said to you? Over the phone?"

"You hated actresses."

"And you remember our first date, you poor bitch when you were trying like hell to stay awake during the chamber music concert? I was thinking then should I screw you or not?"

"I would never have put out on the first date."

"That's not the point. The reasons I didn't make a move even though you were this undeniable sex object were (A) I didn't want to deal with the guilt of waking up the next morning and (B) you're in show business. If you'd been a stewardess or a grad student, I'd have handled the guilt all right, but the two together made it a no-no."

"What's so terrible about show business?"

"Just one thing: the bullshit. Show business has cornered the world supply of bullshit and Southern California is the world center of show business."

Dixie lit a Camel Unfiltered and took a deep drag.

"My father wasn't just a stockholder in that bank we talked about earlier, he was chief stockholder. And his particular specialty was in lending money to studios for production. My mother was once a Metro starlet. At the age of fifty, she was still a starlet. We entertained all the time, and I saw this pathetic creature stroking everyone in sight because she just knew she was going to break through one of these days. She died when she was sixty-three and she still knew on her deathbed that if she just got the part it was all gonna happen. They fucked up their marriage, they fucked up their lives, and I was witness to it all." He stopped then, nodded toward her.

"What do you want me to say? What are you putting me on the rack for?"

"I'm not."

"Then why do I wanna cry?"

"Why do you?"

"Because," Dixie said, and that was all she said, because suddenly she was crying, surprising him probably, certainly surprising herself. She barely had time to get her glass down to the table. She turned her face away, buried it in the sofa pillow, clung tight, until she got control again. "Because I'm a joke." Her voice was quiet now. She didn't have much energy and there was only him, close by, to hear. "See, what I wanted was to sing. I had almost everything going for me: not bad musical instincts, not bad looks on the bandstand. Crowds didn't make me nervous, I got almost perfect pitch. I love songs, I love singing. The only little problem was my voice is shitty. So I lucked out onto the tube and I jiggled my boobs for four years, but people were laughing, I knew it, I didn't blame them once I got used to it, I was the standard-brand dumb blonde, the Sheena Queen of the Jungle of the sixties. I hate the star trip, because when I think about it what I think about is that I'm a wipeout. You're looking at a failure, baby, and that's why I hate the fucking daydream —just give me a different one to fill my time like you've been doing; I'll go to the galleries and I'll sit through the concerts and I promise I won't sleep and I'll read till I think I understand what the hell I'm reading and I'll never claim a headache any time you want to screw and if that's not enough, too bad, it's all I've got to offer, go find somebody else, you son of a miserable bitch."

Thus ended the longest speech of her career, evidently a good one, since they were married in August with just the Lorbers, Gus and Jill, in attendance. Mel took, as promised, the month, and they did Europe, where Dixie had never been except for two days at the Dorchester on the start of what was to be a two-week publicity push for the program, only she got really sick on arrival and ended up with nothing much in the way of knowledge of the Continent that didn't exist in the bathroom of her small suite where she pitched a good deal until they sent her home.

Their honeymoon was pretty much flawless and a little bit confusing; she had never been rich before and it took some getting used to. She had never been pregnant before either, but she was by the time they returned to L.A., or at least Dixie thought she might be, a suspicion confirmed by her obstetrician in early fall. They were both jubilant and Mel found the house on Stone Canyon just below the Bel-Air Hotel and was deep into negotiations when Dixie miscarried. But by then he was hooked on the place so he bought it anyway, because clearly she was going to get pregnant again and it wasn't *that* big, three masters only, on two acres, flat ground, unusual for that part of the world.

Her next miscarriage was her last, and a toughie, because she lasted well into the fifth month before the same thing happened again, the muscles in the uterine wall collapsed from the child's weight and there wasn't a whole lot you could do about that, and Dixie was willing to give it another whirl even against her MD's say-so, but Mel wasn't, good doctors took risks but not dumb ones and he was very very good. They chased the blues in Hawaii awhile, the Kahala for a fortnight, and after that he started

Dixie off on Twain, Poe, and Melville while he became obsessed with building what he came to refer to as The Big C, his tennis court, the best, in its own strange way, that money could buy.

And the last five years had been, for Dixie, full ones, replete with book knowledge and a growing confidence that she wasn't a dummy, clothes and concerts, her husband's affection, a little charity work now and then, and a quiet parade of professors Mel had picked up here and there, lawyers and tennis players, plus having to learn to deal with maids and gardeners and specialty butchers and visits to the wine merchant and twice-weekly visits from a tiny Italian who sold mushrooms from the Orient and "frezza-da-bois" and who stood before her now, asking, for God only knew what reasons, for her to sign the name of Dixie Crowder on a piece of white paper with a proffered yellow stub of Ticonderoga pencil.

"Mr. Balducci"—she was flushing terribly now—"why in the world would *you* want my autograph?"

"Notta me—my granddaughter—she's watch-a da tube wit' me yesterday anna we see Lucy—she's-a funny, Lucy —anna da buncha Bradys—not so funny—anna next comes you inna da yellow top—"

"Omigod," Dixie said. "They must be rerunning *Dogpatch*. Mel's gonna have a field day." The last time had been over three years before, the show lasted two weeks, but he insisted on watching the episodes with a copy of Aristotle's *Poetics* in his lap and after each half hour he would dissect the symbolism as if the hillbilly talk had been written by James Joyce at his most intentionally obscure. "What channel?"

"I'm-a don' know channels." He handed the pencil and paper over, gestured for her to use the truck hood to write on. "Please to say, 'fo' Louisa' anna sign yo' name."

Feeling like the jerk of all the world, Dixie filled the request, waved, started off.

"One-a ting mo?"

Dixie turned toward the tiny figure.

"You much prettier lady now."

"Not without make-up," Dixie said, giving her best smile, then turning again, heading for the tennis court to spread the news.

3

Mel was murdering overheads.

He had the ball machine set so that it lobbed high just past the service line and Mel positioned himself each time at net, so that with every lob he had to backpedal, time his swing with his left hand pointed toward the sky, then cream the ball. Afterwards he would race back to the net to be in place when the next lob came.

It was exhausting just watching him but Dixie did, quietly sliding open the glass doors to the tennis house, pulling a swivel chair into view. The chair was heavy but on casters so it moved without sound. The machine held a hundred and fifteen balls and he looked to be about two thirds done when she got there. He was alternating the direction of his smashes, first to the forehand, then the other corner, back and forth.

When he was done, he turned off the machine, came over to the tennis house, and gave her a kiss, being careful to lean way over as he did it, since he was dripping sweat and she was as yet unstained. "Morning," she said then, went to the towel pile, tossed him a couple. They had not seen each other since the night before, because he got up every morning of the world at seven and jogged for an hour down Stone Canyon, across Sunset to UCLA, circling there awhile, then the hard part, back up the hill to the house. "You sit," Dixie told him. "Rest while I gather up the balls." She started out onto the sunlit court.

"What is this Stepford Wife routine today?"

"I just don't want you having a stroke before the Lorbers get here. If I'm stuck entertaining the twins alone all day *I'll* have one." The Lorber twins were twelve and a half now and had been troubled by adolescence for the past fifteen years, the girl being a tub who ate only junk food, the boy thin but with a stammer and the habit of constantly standing around talking and playing pocket pool in what he thought was a surreptitious manner.

Dixie grabbed the ball retriever, started filling it.

"She wants something," from Mel.

Dixie picked at a few more balls, slowed.

"Here it comes," Mel said.

"If I tell you something you've got to promise not to harass, embarrass, humiliate me, or be a general pain in the ass, is it a deal?"

Mel waited.

"*Dogpatch* is back on syndication for a little I think maybe. So says Mr. Balducci anyhow."

"You mean your performance as Daisy Mae is going to be visible again to the human eye? Those nuances of human behavior, those subtle illuminations of the soul?"

Dixie nodded. "Yup."

"I imagine Katharine Hepburn will go into permanent retirement on hearing the news. Glenda Jackson will retreat to some rep company in the provinces rather than face the competition."

"It wasn't so goddam easy, buster. The best line I had to say in four years was 'I'm gonna git him come Sadie Hawkins Day, I just knows it.' The Abner was queer, Mammy Yokum was drunk, and the Pappy had just had the operation where your intestine comes out your side so he stunk more often than not. Let's see Olivier emote under those conditions."

" 'Yer beautiful in yer wrath,' " Mel said. "John Wayne to Susan Hayward in *The Conqueror*." He pointed for her to get her racquet. "Let's hit a few."

"Promise not to zap me publicly?"

"Word of honor."

"Then I'll give you a break and volley with you," Dixie said, hurrying to the tennis house, grabbing her blue Head, moving quickly back to the court. They scraped the remaining balls aside and Mel opened a new can of Wilson Championships. Then they began to hit.

Dixie had only taken up tennis since she'd met Mel, and seriously only from the time they had the court of their own; she was not a natural athlete by any means, but with Mel across the net she felt like Bueno who Mel said was the most graceful of any of them. He was a superb player, of course, and when they volleyed he played customer tennis, always hitting the ball low and crisply, always returning them so she could reach them easily without having to run far or fast. He was practically teeing them up for her to belt, and that she had learned to do, under his tutelage. It was really a sign of his feeling for her that he had unending patience as far as her game was concerned. He didn't like playing with women, disliked mixed doubles more than a little. But he always gave her more time than she needed each weekend morning, and whenever a mixed doubles opportunity came about, most often with Lorbers, he never hedged.

The phone rang.

"Let me," Dixie said, and she went quickly to the tennis house, picked up by the third ring, gave a hello.

It was Gus on the other end. "Give me the bald one," he said.

"Gus for you," Dixie said, and put the phone down, half smiling because Mel was *very* sensitive about his lack of hair and no one dared mock him about it except Gus, who was forever sending anonymous hair transplant articles to the office or mailing wig ads to hotels when they were on vacation. Gus was six four and a powerhouse, which gave him courage in the face of danger; besides, he and Mel had been roommates through four years at UCLA and best friends the twenty years following.

Dixie put the phone down and went back onto the court,

grabbing up a few balls to practice serves. She was big and strong enough to serve with power except that Mel always said—

—she turned toward the tennis house where Mel was talking, talking loudly and with anger—

—Mel always said that women, because of the way they were built and God bless that, couldn't really cream a serve the way a man could, it all had to do with the musculature around the breast and—

—and now he slammed the phone down, stood over it a moment, then wheeled back onto the court.

Steaming.

"What?" from Dixie.

Mel just stared at her.

"They cancel?"

Mel shook his head. "Fucking Garvey," Mel said.

Dixie didn't get it.

"Gus invited Julian Garvey over for a quick doubles game. Garvey pressured him about the court. Had to see our court, it was crucial."

"Who's this?"

"You don't know Julian Garvey? You never met Mr. Three-by-Five himself?"

"I've heard of him, sure. He was a big producer even when I was working. Why the nickname?"

"Because," Mel said, "Julian Garvey has only screwed every decent looking broad to hit Southern California since the gold rush. And afterwards he writes down their names and particularities on three-by-five cards. In graphic detail."

Dixie started laughing.

Not Mel. "It's true. Anybody gets their hands on his private files could blow the roof off half of Beverly Hills. I could kill goddam Gus."

"Maybe this Garvey's good."

"He stinks. I saw him all the time when I was growing up. He was at my mother's parties. People always lost to him, people that should've wiped up the court with him.

It's like today, you don't want to beat Dick Zanuck bad. Used to tick the hell out of me."

What he did next made Dixie realize just how angry he really was, for with no warning he brought his metal racquet down with all his power, the edge hatcheting into the net. The net took the blow of course, but Dixie had never until that moment seen Mel do anything that might remotely damage The Big C. Because, from the very beginning it was clear that the court was Mel's baby.

It was black, and it had cost over eighty thousand, but that wasn't what made it special. And it had extra-wide boundaries and perfectly placed mercury-vapor lights, five on each side, for night play, but lots of places had lights of similar quality.

But no place matched the quality of the players.

For that was what Mel had built: a court for players. It was lightning fast and he had supervised every minute of the five days it had taken to get the concrete foundation to settle perfectly so that the court would have no cracks, no places where a crummy bounce might decide what should only be decided by skill. The cyclone chain link fence was thirty feet high surrounding the playing area, and the black canvas, the identical shade of the court, reached to the fence top, so that wind was minimal.

And over the years the court had become, in its own way, famous. Never in *Los Angeles* magazine or in Haber or *New West,* it was like a great little restaurant that you stumble onto and tell no one about, because that would spoil it.

Only players were welcome at Mel Kern's court. Every kid that rated one or two in the Pac-8 conference knew about it, and some of them had been. Olmedo came over after finishing his daily chores at the Beverly Hills Hotel Courts. And touring pros, the best ones, arrived often without even having to call first. During the Pacific Southwest tourney, the court was jammed eighteen hours a day.

Mel had no strict laws against show people playing. Gus himself worked in legal at Fox. And Dunas and Cantor came, Ron Preissman too. But they were players. No Hollywood hacker was welcome, not Heston or Eastwood or any of them.

And now Julian Garvey was coming to sully the place.

Mel rocketed the ball at Dixie. She tried to get her racquet back in time but it was impossible. He hit another. Harder.

"Give me a break, huh?" Dixie said.

The third ball was the hardest yet.

"Goddamit, Pancho, go easy."

For a moment or two he did go easy, or at least easier, the balls coming back at a more returnable pace, but then gradually he began to place them further away from her, swinging her across the court, side to side, and Dixie thought she really wasn't all that crazy about Mel this particular morning, because so what if a *schlepper* was coming to play, it wasn't for forever, it wasn't something to be rotten to your wife about, and then she realized it wasn't just the guy's coming that ticked Mel, it was the business with his mother, and maybe his mother had fawned all over and made an ass of herself—

—and then Dixie's mind was going *omichrist, omichrist,* and she dropped her racquet and walked silently off the court into the tennis house and sat, staring flushed and hurt into the bright sunshine.

"I'll slow down," he called from the court.

She didn't budge.

He moved closer, looked in at her. "I apologize, it was childish, let's play."

Dixie said let's not and say we did.

"I said I was sorry, didn't I, isn't that enough?"

Finally Dixie was able to say it, looking dead at her husband while she did: "You think I screwed this Garvey."

"Oh, come on."

"You do, admit it."

"Jesus, Dixie—"

"Tell the goddam truth Mel please!"

He hesitated. "No, it's not that, it's just, you had to be

there to think I'm not crazy, but my mother used to make
an ass of herself and. . . ." He hesitated again, then finished
quietly. "And that's it."

"Tell me the goddam truth I mean it."

". . . Yeah. . . ." he said finally. "Yeah. Okay. You're
right."

"Why, Mel? I never met the son of a bitch. I told you I
never met the son of a bitch, so why?"

"I don't know. I just saw the image of the two of you in
my head."

"Have I ever lied to you?"

He tried for a smile. "I've never caught you, I'll admit
that."

"Have I ever-ever-ever-ever lied?"

"No. You don't."

"Then why are we going through all this?"

"Couldn't begin to tell you. I just really hate him a lot."

"Hate him?"

"Oh, sure, Dix, it's easy. You've just got to understand
one thing: Julian Garvey is the worst man in the
world. . . ."

4

The Lorbers arrived screaming.

Dana, the girl twin, had wanted to stop at the Pizza Hut on San Vicente which her mother said was ridiculous since it wasn't even eleven which started Dana crying which made Gus junior start to laugh which really increased her tears so he hit her which made Gus senior tell his son if he ever hit her again he was not only going to lose his color tv set but also his pushbutton phone which started the boy sobbing which made their mother jam in her *Saturday Night Fever* cartridge and turn it up full blast which sat less than well with her husband who hated noise which was their general family condition when they tumbled from the Mercedes and opened the gate where Dixie and Mel were quietly volleying.

"Hit the pool," Jill gestured to the twins, Dana obeying instantly, Gus junior doing the same a moment later after he'd taken a look at Dixie's breasts full in the white tennis top she was wearing.

"Listen, I'm sorry as hell about Garvey but what could I do?" Gus said as Mel walked toward him.

"Say no."

"When the biggest producer in town wants to meet and he trumps up some cockamamie thing about seeing your court, I'm not about to say no. It won't be so terrible. He's bringing a caddie with him, the Beatty kid who's number one at Berkeley this year. Anyway, you're psychotic about the court, we all accept that as part of your charm." He held out a beautifully wrapped package then. "Here. By way of apology."

Mel eyed the package, then shook his head. "I know you, there's a wig in there, I'm not opening it."

"It's not a wig, take it."

"I'll bet you anything it's a wig—you always give me a wig when I'm ticked—I feel like Charlie Brown when Lucy claims this time she'll hold the football so he can once really kick it only she never does."

"I promise you it's not a wig." Gus obviously meant it.

Mel looked at the big man. "You don't have to give me anything, it'll all pass." There was a pause. "It is a wig, isn't it?"

Gus started screaming—"I swear to Christ it isn't a wig now open the damn thing!"

Mel opened it.

It was a wig.

Gus started laughing and clapping his hands together.

"The Rover Boys," Dixie said.

"Why don't you girls go join the twins," Mel said. ."Homicide needs privacy."

"And miss seeing what this Garvey guy looks like? You've got to be out of your mind."

Julian Garvey looked like Leslie Howard. Tall, impeccably groomed, he contemplated the world with pale blue eyes that shouted sensitivity. He entered through the gate shyly a few moments later, accompanied by a tall lithe young man with acne.

Dixie hurried up to him, hand out, saying, "Hi, we haven't ever met but I'm Dixie Kern and don't worry, it'll all be strictly stag, but I have to do my hostess number." She shook Garvey's hand, the young boy's too, then pointed to the tennis house. "Towels in there, showers if you need them, salt tablets in the medicine cabinet, beer and soft drinks in the fridge. If you need anything else, give a holler."

"My son Noel," Julian Garvey said, staring at Dixie,

"is so deeply and permanently in love with you there are no words."

"How so?"

"He came to puberty when that show of yours was first on. He had pictures of you all over his room. What John Travolta is to the libido of young girls today, you are to him." He studied her a moment longer. "And who's to say he's wrong?"

Dixie made a little curtsey, said, "See you anon" to Mel, then headed with Jill for the pool. "He didn't seem like such a monster," she said when they were far enough away.

Jill was related to the Zanucks and she knew the business about as well as anybody. "He would suck," she said, "and happily, your eyeball for a grape if it could get a picture going."

Dixie shrugged, and they walked the rest of the way in silence. The twins were splashing each other in the pool when they got there. Jill was in her tennis clothes and didn't want to change but Dixie wanted as much sun as she could get, so she went into the poolhouse and put on a white bikini, came out again, pulled a lounge parallel to Jill's, and stretched out, her hands above her head.

"Have you got any Shake 'n Bake?" Dana asked from the pool.

"Mel would kill me," Dixie said.

"Shit," Dana said.

Jill pointed a finger. "Watch your mouth." She lay back again and closed her eyes. "Hey?"

"Yes ma'am?" Dixie answered.

Jill started talking quiet and fast. "I don't want to say anything or anything, but Jesus, Dixie, did you have to wear a bikini, Gus junior's going to start sneaking looks down your front and I can really do without that." She was a small woman, Jill, and dark, and everything that could be done for her had been done for her, the nose, the ears, the hairline, so when she was young she was cute like June Allyson, but at forty she had aged sadly, like so many ingenues, and cellulite had taken control of her thighs.

Dixie started to say that she wasn't trying to lure the child toward madness but simply to get a decent tan, except Jill always frightened her whenever sex was the subject, because Jill was positive that her husband had the hots for Dixie and if given the opportunity, would bed down.

And of course it was true.

The week before she married Mel, Gus had made a pass at her in Mel's kitchen. He had pretended to be drunk and it was all disguised reasonably well, but Dixie had had enough men hit on her to know. And she thought it was a genuinely rotten thing to do. But she let it go, never mentioned it to Mel, what gain could come of it? Except that sometimes it got hard, 'cause Gus watched her too much, dropped too many signals.

Only Jill sensed it and distrust was always in the air between them. So now Dixie said nothing at all, just went back into the poolhouse, found an old one-piece, and changed, making very sure her breasts were discreetly covered before reentering the sun.

On the court, meanwhile, the men were ready to play. Garvey and his caddie won the racquet spin and though the kid offered Garvey the chance to serve first, Garvey shook his head and took position at the net.

Mel played the forehand side, as he had with Gus for almost a quarter of a century. They had been Pac-8 doubles champions and once had gotten to the finals of the national intercollegiates. Part of their success was due to skills, part to their Mutt and Jeff qualities. Gus, big and powerful, seemed like a killer whereas actually he was a tireless retriever, and Mel, all five seven of him, had the most vicious shots of anyone around.

Now he waited for the kid Beatty's serve, betraying nothing. The kid was lithe and whippet quick but he didn't put out too much at the beginning, and his first serve, while accurate enough, had neither particular pace nor spin, and Mel stepped into it perfectly and, with the startling power he'd always had, rocketed the return directly toward the teeth of Julian Garvey standing in front of him across the net.

A lot of things happened then, some of them simultaneously. Garvey gave a cry of surprise, totally involuntary, Gus screamed, "Mel!", the kid screamed "Jesus!", and Garvey, ducking, managed to salvage his profile by just getting his racquet up to his face in time. The ball smashed into the racquet and went over the fence and Garvey, all balance gone, fell backwards on his ass in the doubles alley.

The kid, probably sensing his future film potential going down the tubes, ran to Garvey, helped him up. Garvey dusted himself a moment, then looked at Mel. "I have neither forehand nor backhand but I sprawl magnificently."

Gus took the next point with a lovely cross-court return, and at love-thirty they were back to their starting positions.

Mel waited for the serve.

Garvey moved a few feet further from the net than before.

The kid threw in a big twist serve to Mel's backhand, followed it to net but Mel lobbed deep over Garvey's head so the kid, hollering, "Got it, got it, mine," had to chase it down and lob it back.

Mel stood in the middle of the court, waiting to bury the overhead, looking up toward the ball, then a quick glance to see which way Garvey was ducking, then back at the ball, back one final time to Garvey and once it was clear that Garvey was in flight toward the back of the court, Mel drop-shotted lightly over the net for a winner.

The sense of drama held for the rest of the set, but Beatty, better than any of them with his young speed, protected his partner from serious injury. Mel and Gus won easily enough, 6–2, the second game a gift from Gus who double-faulted twice.

"Another?" Mel asked dutifully as they finished, knowing the time had come for the purpose of the day, Garvey's talk with Gus, whatever it was about. But Garvey surprised him by saying, "Plenty for me, why don't we let young Beatty play some singles," and then he paused. "With Gus."

"Fine with me," Mel said, as he and Garvey walked off the court, sat in the swivel chairs set up on the patio of the tennis house. By the time he was comfortable he had managed to sort out why he shouldn't have been surprised because it was really a good move on Garvey's part, delay things, keep Gus on the hook as to what it was all about.

"I deserved what you did to me," Garvey said quietly.

Mel turned his head. "What did I do?"

"What have we known each other, Mel, thirty years? No point in prevarication now. You humiliated me and I cannot find it in my heart to blame you."

"You must be on something," Mel said.

"I came here this morning—bludgeoned my way, if you will—because. . . ." He stopped, hesitant.

Mel waited, surprised again, because if there was one thing you had to admit about Julian Garvey, it was that the son of a bitch could put together an English sentence. "You don't know Noel, do you?"

Mel tried remembering about Garvey's son, but there wasn't much, other than he had been badly hooked on drugs once and had badly cracked the year before last. "Supposed to be a good kid."

"Oh God he is that, a wonderful boy—not really a boy, he's twenty-seven now and. . . ." The hesitancy again.

The kid from Berkeley was slaughtering Gus.

"Fragile. Noel's one of the permanent victims of the 1960s, I think. He never got over that time, it hit him when he was at his most impressionable and he did some minor experimentation with drugs and he let his hair grow and lived in San Francisco when that was essential and. . . ."

And suddenly Garvey was blinking back tears.

Stop this! Mel wanted to say. Don't you goddamit go get human on me.

Garvey spun from the chair, went inside the tennis house. Mel heard the bathroom door shutting a moment later.

"This kid's got no respect for his elders," Gus called, as they changed sides of the court.

Mel made a nod.

"It's one–four, get ready for your turn."

Mel nodded again, watched half the next game when Garvey was back, dry eyed, embarrassed, in control. "Let me finish this quickly and then shall we both do our best to forget about it? Noel had some personal problems, he was away for a while, we recently brought him home but he doesn't do much, doesn't do anything really, and last night my good wife thought what if we built a court, we have the acreage, because Noel used to play beautifully when he was a child and if we could interest him in taking over the project, well, it would be a start, and this is the best court and I needed to see it and how it was done except the minute I got here I realized it was all too silly because even if we forced it on him, it would end soon and there we would be with a court that no one played on and a son who hasn't really been happy since he sat last in the mud at Woodstock."

"How much of this was bullshit?" Mel asked idly.

Garvey took it well. "Some, certainly. Parts."

"Which?" Mel asked.

"No one *ever* knows with me, Doctor Kern." He paused a moment. "Which I suppose, when you come right down to it, is the secret of my success. . . ."

As Gus Lorber slumped perspiring into the chair beside him, Julian Garvey said, "Query: Would you or would you not be interested in perhaps a bit of *hypothetical* conversation?"

Gus rolled the Coors can across his overheated forehead and looked out onto the court where Mel and the Beatty kid were warming up. "Julian, I was valedictorian of my high school class; I was Law Review at UCLA. Not only that, I've been in the ring with Dino and Ray Stark and even held my own once with Joe Levine. But I don't delude myself that I'm about to outwit you. So please delete the 'hypothetical' part and cut to the chase."

"All right then: I read last night the most brilliant in all ways piece of movie material I've come across in my thirty-year career. Query: Do you want to talk about it?"

"Does a bear shit in the woods?"

"I assumed your answer would not be in the negative." He stared at the court where Mel was starting serving. "He just kills the ball, doesn't he?"

"What's the material?"

"Don't rush things; one wants to maintain a sense of climax in sex as well as life."

"All right, I'll ask something else. I'm in legal at Fox, why bother with me; why not call Laddie?"

"Because in the first place, Laddie's out of town at the Board of Directors meeting, and as you'll see, there are some legal ramifications to be dealt with.

"Is the material a book? Screenplay, what?"

"Screenplay. Original. Owned, happily, by me."

Gus sipped his Coors, waiting. Garvey was famous for orchestrating meetings and he'd made a kid's mistake rushing things before.

"Whenever I discuss a movie, I always wear two hats," Julian Garvey said then. "My artist's hat and my hooker's hat. When I did my Eastwood film, all those dreary John Wayne shitkickers, I was aware going in that the product stood little chance of being Shakespearian. When I worked with Fellini, finance was not uppermost in my mind. Rarely, very very rarely, does one have a shot at both. I loved *Annie Hall, Godfather I,* perhaps *Cuckoo's Nest,* certainly what Lean did with *Lawrence,* surely *Gone With the Wind*. This script that I just read, if the gods are kind, has that kind of chance."

"What's the name of it?"

"Tinsel."

"Can you tell me a little more?"

"Just this: If I do it properly it's going to be the first great sex film ever made."

"I don't mean to be disrespectful, Julian, but sex ain't exactly virgin material."

"True. We've had eighty million movies from *Ecstasy* to *Deep Throat* which are one kind of garbage, and eighty million more where, just when Grace Kelly is about to consummate her wild passion for Cary Grant, we either cut to fireworks exploding in the sky or horses kicking down stable doors. I'm talking about a movie where sex— fucking if you will—fantasy—the kind of thoughts that flash through my mind and I do hope still flash on occasion through yours, are an integral decent crucial weave of the fabric of the film."

"I think Fosse wanted to do something like that once but there was trouble with the financing."

"Hypothetically, pretend I've got the financing, five million, from German tax-shelter money."

"You know there's always been interest in this out here —Ernie Lehman said years ago if somebody could make a really explicit classy sex film the money would be coming in over the transom."

Garvey nodded.

"Who wrote this *Tinsel*?"

"A brilliant young television director slash writer named Robert Schwab."

"I've seen some of his stuff, it's very good. Chubby guy. Known I think to one and all as Schwab the Slob." Gus tried very hard, but unsuccessfully, not to smile.

"Tell me what's so funny?"

"Well, Jesus, Julian, you come on about this fucking masterpiece blockbuster like it's the Sistine Chapel under discussion, and then it turns out that the writer happens, if I'm not mistaken, and I'm not mistaken, to be married to your daughter."

Garvey nodded. "The son-in-law also rises; a grand and noble Hollywood tradition."

Gus started laughing then, got up for another Coors, came back and sat down. "In one sentence, what's this *Tinsel* about?"

"That's a ridiculous and insulting question, asking a major piece of film literature to be encapsulated, but since it's also a question I ask a lot of myself, I'll answer you: Marilyn Monroe's suicide."

Gus thought awhile. "Schwab the Slob wants to direct I imagine."

"That point is automatic."

"First feature, Julian."

"The boy is brilliant, and the point of who is to direct is not open to discussion now or later."

"And you'd produce."

"I'd exec, of course, but actually I was giving some thought to perhaps letting my son Noel be the producer."

Gus started laughing again. "What are we into, a five-million-dollar vanity production? Who's gonna play Marilyn Monroe, your wife or your daughter?"

Garvey made a smile, waited for Gus to quiet. "Shall we, for a moment, downpedal the levity? Because you've raised a serious point, the casting of the central role, and I am convinced, when one speaks of sex symbols, that there is only one lady alive to play our part. Obviously, when I said it was about Monroe's last hours, I didn't mean that literally—the legal ramifications I mentioned earlier would be overwhelming. So our lady doesn't have to look like Monroe, but she *has* to have a fabulous body, and she *has* to have been in the public eye consciously as a body for enough years to give us what Swanson gave Wilder in *Sunset Boulevard*. I ask you, sir, who has been for the past dozen years the leading and arguably the only American sex symbol?"

"Gotta be Raquel Welch."

Garvey nodded. "Hypothetically, pretend I've been in

contact with her representatives and they are more than a little bit interested."

"You just read the screenplay last night, when'd you talk, this morning?"

"I get up early. And hypothetically, again, there are no dealbreakers on the horizon."

"Can she act it?"

"A lot of people think she's enormously talented. Besides, she's going to be bare assed the last half of the picture, who cares if she can act it? And when was Monroe Duse?"

"You hustling porno at your age, Julian?"

Garvey watched the two men slugging the ball across the net for a moment. Then he stood abruptly and moved into the shade of the tennis house and when Gus joined him, started talking very low and very fast. "No, it isn't pornography, you microcephalic, it's something new fresh and different, and I'm about to indicate just *how* new fresh and different I mean, but try to realize this: The movie shows the last hours of a sex symbol but that's not what it's about; it's about us, out here, and what this town does to women, how it raises them up and dashes them down, skins them and discards them because the truth is and we know it out here—there's always a new pair of tits on the horizon."

"I'm still waiting for fresh and different," Gus said.

"Okay—okay hear me and pay mind because I do this once and only once—the opening of *Tinsel*—we open on a shot of something only we can't tell what—but there's a glisten to it, a sheen—and we hear a woman groaning but not pain groaning, sexual is what we're thinking—and this man's voice says, 'God, you're beautiful, you're really incredibly beautiful sometimes, it's illegal how goddam beautiful you are' and then the camera shifts and we realize we're not watching a sex scene, we're watching a woman being given a massage in a classy looking room and she's naked but covered with towels and what he's doing is he's working on her back and she loves it because she's under this incredible tension, she can't sleep, and this is one of the only things that can ever get her close to relaxing, and she's the Monroe part and she looks sensational and we can almost but not quite see her breasts as she rolls over and is covered and the guy starts working on her neck and her skin is glistening with oils and she says, 'What are you up to tonight?' and he says, 'Nothing, I'm gonna be home alone most likely watching the tube'—and then we flashcut to a different scene—remember this flashcut will take no time at all and we'll keep hearing the conversation between the star and her masseur but what we'll see is the masseur's apartment and it's got pictures of her all over but he won't be alone watching the tube, he'll be there and he'll be dressed kind of exotically and there'll be another guy there, young and they'll be watching each other in that way fags have and they'll be holding a fag drink like a mai-tai and as they clink their glasses we'll end the flashcut and go back to the massage. And that device, the flashcut device, we'll use throughout. You understand what that does."

"I think but go on," Gus said.

"Well, it makes their sex lives, the fantasy part, it brings it right into the real lives of the characters, just like it's in our lives."

"How so exactly?"

"Well, obviously, when you meet someone like Mrs. Kern you wonder what she'd be like in bed, that's natural enough, wouldn't you agree?"

"Bad example," Gus said quickly. "I know Dixie too well; I mean, she's my best friend's wife, I don't day-dream about humping her. But I see what you mean."

"See, in *Tinsel*, Monroe's fucking Jack Kennedy. And Bobby. And various Vegas headliners. All those people at one time or another. Disguised, of course, so we don't spend the rest of our natural lives in litigation. But what the device of the flashcut does is it makes the sex real. Makes the thoughts of the characters real."

"What can I tell you, I like it; in theory anyway. But

what difference does it make if I like it, I don't run the decision-making process at the studio, just, I like to think, the canons, edicts, and commandments."

"Where are the twins?" Garvey said then.

Gus pointed in the direction of the swimming pool. "Why?"

"I make it a point to be kind to show-business children. I sent Jane Fonda birthday presents for years and when I snookered her into working for me, I did very nicely. I listened to Blake Edwards' youthful laments, and when I nailed him to direct for me, that did nicely too. Your kiddies may grow up to be useful." He stood, called out to the court. "Destroy the Doctor quickly."

"He's doing just fine," Mel called back between points, his bald head splotched from sunlight and overexertion.

There was a wide path of perfect lawn that led from the court to the pool and poolhouse on the other end of the property. "Be back in a little," Gus said as he and Garvey headed back out into the sun, moved quietly toward the path.

"We come now to the legal problems," Garvey said. "Since this is a movie about Monroe and her last day, we obviously have to deny that fact. One way, which we've done, is to have the movie taking place today, not fifteen years ago when she died. But crucially we've got to *always* have her aware of what happened to Monroe. She *refers* to Monroe constantly. She's determined that what happened to Monroe—the final disintegration—will *never* happen to her. That helps legally, don't you agree?"

"Well, if somebody wants to sue, you can sue the Pope for bastardy. But if you make it clear you're not Marilyn Monroe and the Kennedys aren't the Kennedys it helps a helluva lot."

"Most people don't realize this, because today it's all different, but Monroe was a Fox star. The last twenty movies she made, I think sixteen or more were Fox pictures. Including the reason we are together: *Something's Got to Give.*"

Gus shook his head. "That's one I never saw."

"No one ever saw it—it's the one she was suspended from when she died—it's the one she was naked in, she had a swimming pool scene and in the few minutes they shot of the picture, she got naked. Well, in order for *Tinsel* to work, I've got to have that film, and since it's owned by Fox, and there's no way they're going to lend it out—"

"—highly frigging doubtful," Gus said. "How does it fit into your flick?"

Garvey stopped halfway between the court and the pool and again started talking softly and fast. "Remember, it's about this last day, and she's falling to pieces, she's under suspension, and she *knows* what happened to Monroe, she's *haunted* by what happened to Monroe, and she's waiting from the beginning of the movie for some footage to be delivered to the house for her to screen and she's drinking and she's on pills and anyplace else in the world she'd be a traffic stopper but here, in this business in this town, she's panicked she's slipping down the iceberg, and her lawyer comes and says go back to work and it's a nightmare building for her and Kennedy's delivering a speech in L.A. and she fucked him two weeks before at his birthday party in New York only now he's supposed to call her but he hasn't and the time of day goes on and it's starting into dusk when *finally* she's alone in her house and boozed up and the film she's been waiting for comes with this kid projectionist—think of a Ronny Howard type for the kid —and she lets him in and he sets up the film and starts to run it and—"

"—and it's the nude swimming scene Monroe did!"

"Right, my friend. And our girl watches Monroe sitting in the darkness of her small screening room and then we cut to the kid and he's bug eyed over what he's screening and we stay with him watching Monroe on the screen and then from the dark room comes the command, 'Freeze it' so he does and then we cut to Monroe, naked on the screen, frozen, and then the voice again and this time it says, 'Come out here now' and the kid does and he's standing in the dark screening room with just the image of Monroe lighting up the place and then—and then our star moves alongside the Monroe image—and she's naked, Gus—for the first time we see her naked and she stands alongside the image and she says, 'I'm better, tell me I'm better,' and the kid doesn't know whether to pee or go blind and he says finally, 'Yes, ma'am,' and she says then how old is he and he says twenty ma'am, and then she screws him, right there with the image of Monroe watching them, and she says, our girl says, you must tell everybody this happened and in fifty years you must still be telling everybody because that way I'll still be beautiful, won't I—it's a fantastic Tennessee Williams kindness-of-strangers scene—and after the kid goes, and she's alone, she never gets dressed again, she just stays naked and goes bonkers and can't get anybody on the phone and that goes from the President down to her masseur who's too busy screwing his boyfriend to answer—is the irony of all this getting through your cranium, Gus—*the most wanted body in the world and she can't get anybody on the phone.*"

"I get it, I get it."

Garvey started walking toward the pool then. "I'll keep you posted on the project as things move along."

"I would imagine you would, since if we don't make it, you're not going to be able to make it with anybody else."

Garvey nodded glumly. "Tell me something I don't know."

Dixie was sunning alone by the pool. "Where's the brood?" Gus asked.

"I think the kitchen."

"Back in a sec," Gus said, hurrying toward the house as Garvey moved toward Dixie, held out his hand. "Mrs. Kern, thank you for allowing my intrusion on your morning," he said as they shook, followed by, "What was all that 'happy to *meet* you, Mr. Garvey' charade when I arrived?"

Dixie glanced quickly toward the house, then back. "It was best; Mel wasn't in the most sensational of moods."

"He's always loathed me, nothing new." He smiled at her. "Don't look so nervous, I'll be gone shortly."

Dixie nodded.

"He doesn't know?"

"About us? Not thing one."

"Dear God let us keep it that way," Julian Garvey said. . . .

"What a weird morning," Dixie said a little later, as she and Mel sat in the sun, watching the Lorbers volley.

Mel drank deeply from his can of Gatorade. "Nothing weird about it; I guarantee you the same thing happened at a hundred courts and pools today."

"What happened, do you mean?"

Mel shrugged. "Probably a deal got made."

II
GARVEY

1

The Garvey place stood on Sunset, west of the Beverly Hills Hotel. It was a mansion, of course, worth over a million before the recent Arab invasion, with only the high wall visible from the street. The style was that bastard Mediterranean so common to the area, and as native to Spain as Vasco da Gama. The property was just over three acres of garden and shade trees and lawn, impeccably kept. But the unique thing about it, and probably the leading reason for Julian's having bought it close to a quarter century before, was this: No movie star had ever owned it. It could never be referred to as the old Garbo house or Gable's home. Bogart could not have slept there.

It was now and forever the Garvey place. Period.

As he parked his El Dorado convertible, he noted that the catering staff had already arrived for the evening's "do," as Estelle always referred to *her* parties. "Julian and I are thinking of having a little do Friday week and we'd love to have you join us." For a "do," the average age of the gathered would be high sixties, the average religion high episcopal. And no one outside of the hosting family would have any remote connection with show business.

A trifle uncomfortable in his still-damp tennis clothes, Julian started for the house, altered direction quickly, and headed for the pool where his assumption that Estelle would be taking some sun proved correct. She lay, lightly oiled, in a brown one-piece, eyes closed, the copy of *Tinsel* he'd given her earlier on a table nearby.

"You have a chance to finish?"

She half sat, looked up at him. Then she nodded, lay back down.

"That bad?" Julian said.

"I don't remember making a judgment."

"Estelle, your entire life is spent in continually making judgments. Some silent, some of a more verbal variety. Most all of them disapproving."

"Don't start."

"You just have the capacity to anger me, as you well know. I mean, our son-in-law hands in his first hopefully major work for the screen, I thought it might be worth more than a nonverbal nod." He waited for her to speak then. Estelle didn't much like the picture business and she especially didn't like his pictures very much. Still, he dutifully gave her every undertaking at the earliest possible moment because she was a dazzlingly smart woman whose opinions, however painful, had value.

"Nods are by definition nonverbal."

She said it with her eyes closed in that schoolteacherish tone she sometimes assumed to nettle him, which it did, always. Garvey said nothing, just sat on the neighboring lounge chair waiting and watching. Estelle had always been caught between plain and homely, but these last years she'd been staging a comeback, and vaguely that nettled him too.

"Schwabby's very talented," she said finally. "I mean, the boy writes wonderfully well."

"Agreed."

"And he has a gift for characterization. And I think a sense of structure."

"But?"

And now she opened her eyes. "Julian, isn't it dirty?"

" 'Isn't it dirty, isn't it dirty?' " Garvey mimicked. "My God, your brain is truly antediluvian. We live in a world where the word 'shit' was used on the front page of the *Yale Daily News*, where the word 'prick' was spelled in its entirety in *Sports Illustrated,* where the word 'fuck' is allowable in parental guidance pictures, and all you can say about a screenplay that has the courage to deal honestly with the subject of sex for the first time in the history of the world is that it's dirty." Garvey paused then and lowered his voice. "I'm not sure if it's dirty or not, Estelle."

"You've yet to do a memorable picture—"

"—thank you, beloved—"

"—but you've also yet to do a smutty one. I wouldn't like this to be the first."

"Agreed. Let me assure you that when there are rewrites we will add nothing salacious."

"I suppose that's comforting. Julian?"

"Madam."

"It's very commercial, and you know I don't usually say that. And the Monroe part I should think someone would kill for. Anything else?"

Garvey pointed toward the poolhouse. "What did Noel say?"

"Only that he'd looked at it."

"He didn't seem at all interested in working on it with me?"

Estelle shook her head.

"How did he seem?"

Long pause. "I don't really think he's improving, Julian." Another one, longer. "And I'm not all that sure he's holding his own."

Garvey turned his face to the sun.

"I'm afraid he's getting obsessive again. Increasingly so."

"Query: Might you be mistaken?"

"Very possibly. He was up most of the night, he said, on the phone to everywhere. He's on the verge of a major breakthrough and it all could be excitement."

"Let's hope so," Julian said and he stood, started for the poolhouse.

"I don't think he needs any pressure just now, do you?"

"Christ, Estelle, give me credit for something! I'm not a stupid man—"

"—but you like to get your way—"

"—don't we all—"

"—yes-but-not-all-the-time—"

Garvey was the first to get control. "Query: Do you think we'll be delivering body blows like this forever?"

From Estelle now, the schoolteacherish tone. "I should think so." She dabbed some lotion to the area around her eyes, then returned her concentration to the sky.

Garvey moved on to the poolhouse. It was really more than that, he had converted the main room into a screening room by adding a projectionist's booth and had turned the large vacant storage space a floor below into an at-home office. Noel had asked for the use of the office upon his most recent return and both parents had more than gratefully agreed.

As Garvey hesitated by the poolhouse door, the sound of Bob Dylan doing "Mr. Tambourine Man" was almost too much for him to bear. But he forced himself into the maelstrom, and as he crossed the room, the dreadful sound began edging close to his pain threshold. "Noel!" he shouted down below. "Noel *dear God!*" but it was futile. Placing his hands over his ears, he plunged downstairs toward his son.

> *I'm not sleepy and there is no place I'm*
> *going to.*
> *Hey! Mr. Tambourine Man, play a song for me,*
> *In the jingle jangle mornin'*
> *I'll come followin' you.*

Noel Garvey did not look remotely fragile. If anything, he resembled Smokey the Bear: stocky, powerful, cherubic, and covered with body hair. He smiled now and said, "Didn't hear you come in," after he'd turned the sound down. "That better?"

"I'd prefer off, but I'm thankful for small favors."

"Why do you think Dylan used 'jingle jangle' to describe the morning, Daddy? I'm convinced that's the goddam key to the whole song, symbolically speaking. Does the phrase conjure up anything special to you, image-wise?"

Garvey shook his head. "I'm sorry. I wish I could help you."

"Don't worry, I'll get it sooner or later."

"I'm sure," Julian said, watching his son. The boy seemed agitated, but more than usual? Hard to say, hard to say. "Query: did you have a chance to look at *Tinsel*?"

"I wouldn't want to take an exam on it or anything, but I flipped through it some."

"And?"

"Really good, Daddy. Schwab the Slob's a super writer. Excuse me." He turned away as the telephone rang. "Yes, speaking," he said into the receiver. Then to Julian—"it's London, this may take a while."

Garvey nodded and sat in a chair to wait.

"Yes, fine, go ahead," Noel said, and a moment later, his voice louder, "Okay, it's a rotten connection but I can hear enough, shoot." Pause. "No, I don't need either Lennon or McCartney's, I've got photostats of both here and I've got a decent verification on Harrison. It's Ringo Starr that's got to be dealt with."

Garvey tapped his fingers on the arm of the chair and looked around the room. It was strewn with papers and phonograph records. Noel's charts covered the walls. Dates: "9 Feb '64—Beatles on the Sullivan Show." "8 July '69—1st reduction of troops in S.E. Asia." "11 Sept '65—1st Dylan makes it to number one." This last entry was crossed out and underneath it was written: "11 Sept '65—1st Dylan *performed by Dylan* makes it to number one. (Don't forget The Byrds.)"

Greek, Garvey thought. All, all, all. Some new virus had swept the world fifteen years ago infecting the young.

And now Noel's voice was starting to rise: "Are you sure it's Ringo's birth certificate you're reading from? Are you positive it's an authentic reproduction? Because I was told on excellent authority that he was not born July seventh of 1940 but '41. And that would be, I'm sure you agree, rather fucking significant."

Garvey stood and began to pace. When they brought Noel home this time and he said he wanted to try his hand at writing, Estelle would have wept if she'd been allotted tears. Then he told them he wanted to do a giant historic survey of the sixties centering on the symbolism inherent in the songs of Bob Dylan and the Beatles.

That dampened the enthusiasm somewhat.

"Could anyone have tampered with it, do you think?" Noel shouted. Pause. "I don't know who. Somebody. Anybody."

There was a whole nest of them, it turned out. Biographers, music mavens, whatever you called them. And they would talk on the phone and write one another. "Can you be sure that medical report on Dylan's motorcycle accident hasn't been Xeroxed." "Have you got proof of the exact time when John first saw Yoko."

Sometimes at dinner Noel would bubble on about the discoveries of the day. Sometimes he would pick in silence at his food. Then he wanted a hi-fi. Was it all right if he had a hi-fi for the office?

Anything you want, don't even ask, Garvey assured him.

But he didn't realize it was going to take a week to get it installed, two weeks more to get the sound balanced *perfectly*. The speakers were by Beverage, eight and a half feet high, five thousand per. The tuner was by Sequerra, another twenty-five hundred gone.

It was Noel's money, so there was no trying to stop him. His grandfather had left him five million dollars when the boy became legally of age, so if he wanted a twenty-thousand-dollar hi-fi for his office, it eventually was there.

Crushed, Noel hung up the phone.

Garvey waited for the boy to say something.

Noel just sat there.

"Want to talk about it?"

Noel didn't.

"I've got nothing else on the agenda."

"You'd think it was silly."

"Perhaps I wouldn't."

"I know you. You would."

"Query: Why don't you trust me?"

"I do, it's not that, but see, from where I sit, there's no one more important this *century* from a cultural and sociological point of view than Dylan and the Beatles. If you accept that, and frankly, a lot of people have trouble doing it but I can't help their ignorance, then the fact that Ringo might have been born in a different year than was originally thought, well, you can't imagine the repercussions. Only just now I found out I was on a false trail." He shook his head very sadly. "And I really thought I had it that time."

"Honey? The world continues to spin."

"Huh—whazzat?" Sharply spoken. "Come again?"

"I just meant . . . it depresses me to see you upset yourself over something—"

"—something unimportant, that's what you're gonna say, isn't it?"

"Not at all. Something *beyond your control* was my thought."

"I knew you wouldn't understand. That's why I could never work for you. You just see what you want and fuck anybody else's vision. No way I'll work for you."

"Query: When were you asked?"

"Oh, cut it out—don't you think I hear the whispers in the corridors. You want to get me off this, something really goddam earthshaking, for a flick. Well, it's not gonna happen."

"I fail to see the earthshaking qualities inherent in the birth date of Ringo Starr, Noel. I know I'm old, but I'm not, at least common wisdom has it that I'm not, senile." And he was about to go on, but then he realized he shouldn't, shouldn't have said what he'd already said, shouldn't have challenged the boy, because now Noel was up and pacing, his hands going through his thick curly brown hair. Distraction growing.

"Well, get this then—just try and get this—everyone knows there's got to be a connection between Dylan and the Beatles—a *deep* connection because genius always clusters—look at the Greek dramatists and the Elizabethan dramatists and the nineteenth-century Russian novelists— well, if Ringo had been born in '41, and you'd then averaged the birth dates of the Beatles, *they would then come out to have been born in just about the same month and day and year as Dylan.*"

Nod, Garvey thought. Nod and smile and ask for time to ponder. And leave the boy quietly. "Honey," he heard himself saying, "you can't average birth dates."

"You can. People do it all the time."

"What people?"

"Smart people—wonderful people—you can do it, Daddy."

Agree with him, Garvey thought. Tell him he may have something. And leave the boy quietly. "Noel, shall we have a quiet lesson in logic?"

"*I—hate—the—quiet!*" Noel screamed and then he ran to his turntable and then Dylan was singing again—

> . . . *play a song for me,*
> *in the jingle jangle mornin'.* . . .

Noel turned the knob and the music began to build.

> . . . *I'll come followin' you.*
> *Take me on a trip upon your magic*
> *swirlin' ship.* . . .

Louder now. Louder and the walls seemed as if they would give. The sound bombarded off the walls and Noel kept on turning and turning the knobs.

. . . My senses have been stripped,
my hands can't feel to grip. . . .

Garvey pressed his own hands over his ears, tried to holler for forgiveness but Noel only moved closer to one of the giant speakers.

Garvey ran. Up the stairs and through the screening room and across the lawn to the main house and, slowing lest the servants pay attention, straight to his bedroom suite and the shower beyond. He stripped, adjusted the sprays to their most intense, and let the water sting his skin. After a few minutes he softened the power, shampooed, trying to replay the scene with his son in his mind and make it come out perfectly. No. Forget perfection, settle for anything, anything at all that would have maybe a *soupçon* of dignity.

He finished, dried himself in his terrycloth robe, stepped on the scale. 159. He had weighed that for twenty years or more. Five eleven and a half and one fifty-nine. No variation. Garvey began to dry his hair when his reflection in the mirror was replaced by the sight of Noel in his office, standing close to rigid, turning the record louder and Louder and LOUDER and Garvey grabbed the robe and threw it around him and rushed to Estelle's suite for contrition, intending to say, "I bitched it up, Estelle, I didn't mean it, I swear" but before he could even begin, she whirled on him cutting through with, "You-must-always-knock!"

She stood in the center of her room, naked.

Garvey muttered apologies while she hurried for cover, returning a moment later in a robe of her own. And Garvey, in her absence, wondered if it had been a year and a half or two since he had last seen his wife without clothing.

"Now what is it?" she said, tying her robe around her.

Julian told her about his chat with Noel.

She punished him with silence.

"I can outlast you," Garvey promised. "I can stand here an hour if I have to."

"Now you want to pick a fight with me, is that it?"

"No, that is not it, but I'm worried about the boy, Estelle. Don't you think we might do something, alert Slesinger perhaps, keep him abreast of events?"

Estelle nodded, picked up the phone, dialed Massachusetts, but Doctor Slesinger wasn't at Riggs, it being Saturday. She managed to track him to his home and from there to the card room of his country club, where she told him succinctly of Noel's lack of progress.

"It is that bullshit Beatles thing?" Slesinger wanted to know. He was a brilliant analyst, but permanently influenced by Ben Casey.

"That's right," Garvey said, standing close beside his wife, talking into the receiver.

"Afternoon, Julian," the doctor said. "Or I guess it's still morning out there."

"I was thinking of perhaps trying to interest him in another sort of endeavor. Perhaps the picture business."

"Couldn't hoit," from the phone.

"Do you think Noel's up to working alongside his father?" Estelle wanted to know.

"The truth, Estelle, is that Noel's a lot stronger than *some* people give him credit for."

"You've always felt we've babied him, I'm aware of your opinion. I happen to think you're wrong."

"Oh, Christ, Estelle, you and Julian crumble every time Noel throws a snit. How many times a month do you bug me?"

"We're just concerned parents," Estelle said.

"I appreciate that," the telephone told them. "But there are times, as I've said to you before, that I think Noel's troubles are half of what keep you two together."

"Ridiculous," Garvey said, but of course it was true, and he'd known it for quite some time now. Estelle, being brighter than he was, had undoubtedly reached the same conclusion long before. . . .

2

Lunch that day was cold salmon and sliced cucumber salad and iced tea. Garvey and Estelle waited at the table by the patio for the Mexican girl to alert Noel. She returned eventually with the news that Noel wasn't hungry.

Estelle took up the cause.

Garvey waited at the head of the table, the large umbrella shielding him from the sun. There was no doubt in his mind that Estelle would return triumphant, prey in tow, for when it came to entreating their son, her ploys were infinite, it was only a matter of time. The games they could play upon each other were really, Garvey thought, undoubtedly quite dull to anyone outside the family, but if you had an emotional stake, really remarkably complicated. It was like a basketball game played at the very top level—many players, all of them aware of the enemies' moves and feints, yet at the same time always susceptible to humiliation if a foe decided surprisingly to go backdoor on you when you were denying him the ball out front.

Noel was cheery. He had wanted a swim, he said, and hadn't felt particularly hungry. He sat at the table in a madras bathing suit and Garvey was aware of the terrible body scars. There were scars of less severity, of course, across the boy's face too. But those, being familiar, were of no moment. But the welts across the chest and shoulders were, no matter how Garvey tried to prepare himself, always fresh and new and shocking.

"I think your father has something to tell you," Estelle said, once the servants had departed.

Noel tried to head it off with "No, it was just a thing that happened, forget it."

"I can't."

"You could be brief though."

"I love you very much. I hate to cause you pain. And I'm totally sorry. There; done."

"Good salmon," Noel said.

"It looked good," Estelle replied. She turned to her husband. "I'm not sure about the cucumber dressing. It's from Gourmet, but sometimes they're a little unreliable on salads."

Garvey picked at his plate. "Since I am known by one and all to loathe cucumbers, I'd hardly place much stock in my opinion."

"I was hoping this might get you to like them," Estelle said. "They're so healthy."

"Your concern is continually amazing."

"What's the party for tonight?" Noel asked quickly.

"The usual," Estelle told him. "More visiting cousins."

"From Philly or the Texans?"

Estelle's father had been a maverick Claiborne who had broken off and headed for California shortly before the First World War. For a while neither the Philadelphia branch nor the group that settled in Texas admitted to his existence. But then, when it turned out he had plunged into the Southern California real-estate market and done rather nicely, rapprochements were successfully made. "The Eastern contingent," Estelle replied.

"What are we screening?" Noel asked his father.

"I have managed, with more than a little arm-twisting, to secure *F.I.S.T.*"

Estelle looked at her husband. "Isn't that supposed to be dreary?"

"Shit, Estelle, you bitched when I got *Godfather II*, that was 'awfully long' if I may quote you. I don't know if

F.I.S.T. is dreary since it hasn't opened and no one's seen it yet. I only know that Jewison has only had one failure in fifteen years and that Stallone is the biggest star in America as of now and UA is very high on it. Forgive me, I should have booked us a fucking Mickey Mouse Festival."

"What in the world," Estelle said at her most schoolteacherish, "prompted that?"

"I can't ever fucking please you and sometimes it gets to me just a little!"

"Shall we say it a few more times and all get it out of our systems, Julian? 'Fucking, fucking, fucking.' "

"I loved *Rocky*. I thought it was just so great, I'm really looking forward to this one, Daddy. You say the studio thinks it's a real winner?"

Garvey managed to nod.

Noel turned to his mother. "It's about the labor movement—this Hoffa type of guy. I'll bet all your cousins love it 'cause they hate unions. I don't think Daddy could have made a better choice."

Finally Estelle said, quietly, "He does try."

"Really fabulous salmon," Noel went on.

Estelle managed to nod.

Then they all picked at their food for a while.

The Mexican girl returned with a fresh platter of salmon but only Noel took more. He hadn't finished his firsts yet but it was too good to pass up, he said.

Both his parents managed to nod.

"I saw," Julian began, but he had to stop and get his throat clear. "Today, Noel, I saw someone of interest."

"Who's that?"

"Doctor Kern's wife. Mrs. Mel Kern. Mean anything?"

Noel shook his head.

"She acted once under the name of Dixie Crowder."

Noel shook his head again. "Dixie. . . ." And then he had it—"Omigod, you mean, oh Christ, Daisy Mae? Does she live around here? Daisy Mae lives here?"

"Up on Stone Canyon."

"Is she old and fat? Don't tell me, lie to me, she was the most fantastic-looking woman."

"Age and being rich and spoiled has only made a good thing better, let me assure you."

Noel put his fork down. "She would be fabulous for the Monroe part, don't you think?"

Garvey nodded, wondering was it imagination or the sun or were Noel's eyes, at least momentarily, alive . . . ?

Estelle was, alas, right: *F.I.S.T. was* dreary. Garvey stood it as long as he could, seated in the rear by the intercom to the projectionist. But before the second hour was close to completion, he silently stood, stepped over his lawyer, his doctor, and his accountant, seated in a row with their wives, and made his way to the door. They were three overburdened and enormously successful men, but Garvey never had to wait when he wanted their services, and the reason he knew was simply that whenever he had a screening, they were there. It made good cannon fodder for their wives the next day at their various clubs. Screenings were one of the great weapons ever invented. No one got to Julian Garvey's by accident.

Pausing by the door, he beckoned for Noel to follow him into the night. The boy nodded immediately and stood, preceding his father outside. "Anything wrong?" Noel asked when they were alone.

"Not a great deal, other than Mister Stallone."

"I didn't think he was so bad."

"He wasn't bad, I don't think I said that. Wrong is different from bad. One can, of course, be both—Brando in the Chaplin picture comes to mind—but that is really, when you consider talented performers, quite a rare thing." They wandered to the pool, which was lit below, and sat.

"Query," Noel said then. "Am I supposed to think we're here by accident or will the other shoe drop soon?"

Julian Garvey smiled at his son.

"The Million Dollar Smile," Noel said. "Who wrote that about you, wasn't it *Newsweek*?"

"Just so that it wasn't the *National Geographic* I don't see that it matters much, do you?"

"I guess not." Noel waited only a moment before he said, "I'm still waiting for that other shoe."

"Why are you angry with me tonight?"

"Lot of bad vibrations going around lately," Noel said. "I'm sensitive to that kind of thing, I like to think. Little pops of anger, spurt here, spurt there. Then the quiet and the wonderful peace we all know and love. There's secrets running rampant. Don't misunderstand me, you love secrets more than anybody in the history of the human race, that's a given. But I get edgy when in the middle of a flick I'm tapped on the shoulder and taken for an aimless walk to the pool. 'Cause I know you pretty good, and 'aimless' isn't in your lexicon."

"What I want—the purpose of our being here together just now—obviously, it's not accidental. But you know what I'm after going in."

Noel nodded. "You can't see my sixties book for shit, can you?"

"Don't become abusive, please."

"I'm sorry. I'm just not cut out to be a movie producer, so strike it from your list of objectives."

"Four weeks, Noel—I swear—give it a month and see if you're interested—if not, go about your own work unencumbered. One month isn't such a much."

"If I give in to you you'll figure out a way to make it two. And then three and a half. Sorry."

"I've spent thirty years of my life learning how to do what I do. It's not so dreadful to want to pass the knowledge on. I've built something and I'd just as soon see it survive."

"Let's go back to the movie. Save a lot of bloodshed."

"Christ, Noel—a fucking month isn't going to kill you."

Noel turned and started away.

"*Please.* One *week* then. Seven goddam days; how can you turn that down?"

Noel whirled. "Easy—easy—because *my* work's going great and my work *matters*—" His voice was rising but he took a deep breath, got control. "Okay," he said finally. "We'll compromise. You said a month but you'll take a week. I said no but I'll shift to maybe. If my book ever starts going sour and God knows it may—if that happens I promise I'll tell you and we'll work something out. How can *you* turn that down?"

"I'm not really all that anxious to wait, Noel."

"Too bad about you."

"I can't wait, Noel. I don't, more than likely, have that luxury. Do you understand?"

Noel shook his head, stared at his father. Waiting.

"They didn't find it in time," Julian Garvey said finally, and suddenly he was blinking back tears. He turned away, wiped his eyes, slowly turned back. "Don't say anything to your mother, she doesn't know."

Noel stood as before, staring.

Garvey managed a smile. "I believe the other shoe was just dropped," he said.

"Why did you want to sit exactly here?" Noel Garvey asked. It was shortly after eight the following morning, and they were having coffee at Nate 'n' Al's on North Beverly Drive.

"Before the day is out you will know," Julian answered. "Before the morning, in fact."

"You won't tell me now?"

"I don't think it's best. Let me explain. We're now into the general subject of feints and thrusts, parries and counterparries. It's all very obvious to some of us. But for someone like yourself, an apprentice, I think it should be viewed first as an outsider. So bear with me?"

Noel sipped his coffee and nodded.

Garvey took the manila envelope from the seat beside him and took out the blood-red copy of *Tinsel.* He opened the screenplay at random, left it open on the table. "There are two steps—oh, one could consider this from any point of view, but just now let's pretend that there are only two steps until this"—he touched the screenplay—"appears on this." He mimed a motion picture screen. "What are they?"

"Don't know."

"Financing and casting. They are, more often than not, intertwined. Today we are financing."

Noel looked confused. "I thought you told me on the way here that when you played at Daisy Mae's court there was a Fox guy there and you hustled him the picture, because they have the Monroe footage from that last film and you can't make the movie without it."

"Noel, Noel, how can I say this without risking the loss of you forever?" Garvey flicked to another part of the screenplay. "I have been known, on not so rare occasion, to fiddle a bit with the truth."

"You mean the earth isn't flat?" Noel said.

"I love you a great deal," Julian replied. And then, to the waitress who had suddenly appeared, "Lox and cream cheese, please. A bagel lightly toasted. And if you could refill my cup I would remember you in my will."

"You got it, Mr. Garvey."

"I'll have the same I guess," Noel said. And when they were alone again: "How did you lie?"

"I don't need the fucking Fox footage. I told them I did because that will, logically, make them particularly hard-nosed when they come to deal with me. Then when they've found I'm talking elsewhere, a sudden panic may well set in because they'll be losing something they thought they had set."

"When are you going to go elsewhere?"

"Yesterday afternoon at Giorgio's."

Noel started to laugh. "I wondered why you suddenly went shopping."

"You see, one of the present honchos at Warner Brothers gets drunk at Giorgio's on Saturday afternoons while his wife buys trinkets. He drinks Bloody Marys and plays pool and I challenged him to a game and conveniently lost and while doing so, I dropped a few well-chosen words about *Tinsel.* I was very passionate, I whispered a great deal, and I pledged him to secrecy knowing he would be on the phone to his colleagues by nightfall. This is, my darling, a *very* small town."

"But why don't you need the footage?"

"Oh, it would be nice, no question. But we can shoot around it. We can shoot it so we never see the screen. Or we can use footage from other films where she's clothed—*The Misfits* or *Some Like It Hot*—those weren't Fox films and the crucial thing isn't that Monroe is naked, it's that our star is naked."

Noel blew into his coffee. "Will you go to other studios?"

"If it is remotely solvent, it will hear from me."

"Why?"

"Turmoil is essential for success in Southern California."

"Why?"

"Because my dearest, and this that I am about to say and have you repeat after me is Roman Numeral Uno of the picture business: *Nobody knows.* Say that for me."

" 'Nobody knows.' Okay, what don't they know?"

The waitress brought their bagels then and Garvey took a bite, followed with a sip of coffee. "All right, follow this now: a very good writer, Carol Eastman—*Five Easy Pieces* was hers—wrote a sex comedy. Now sex comedy is very hard to direct, maybe Mike Nichols does it best—remember *The Graduate*? Okay. He agrees to direct. Now this movie has two male leads. Would you settle for Jack Nicholson and Warren Beatty? And wait—this was Nicholson after *Chinatown* and Beatty after *Shampoo*. So total it up: two hot stars, a hot director who understands the *milieu*, a hot writer. All intent on doing a commercial piece of material. Let me assure you that Columbia practically *killed* to get that picture. It was called *The Fortune* which is precisely what it lost, maybe five million dollars, maybe over ten. And the kicker is this: *Today,* if you took that *same* package back to the *same* studio, *they'd make the same fucking deal all over again.*"

Noel broke out laughing.

"I know it's funny but it's true. Because movies are always a search for past magic, and nobody knows what will work." Abruptly he closed the script of *Tinsel*, shoved it back into the manila envelope as a large open-faced man in golf clothes moved toward them. "Morning, Julian," the open-faced man said.

"Philip," Garvey returned. Then: "Could I make an introduction, please. My son Noel, this is Philip Schwartzman."

"How do you do, sir," Noel said as they shook.

Schwartzman started off toward the large booth in the rear corner. "All work and no play," he said casually, indicating the manila envelope.

Garvey sighed. "These contracts I have to go over drive me insane, Phil. I don't think there's a decent lawyer left in town."

"They're all running studios, I guess," Schwartzman said, and with a wave, he joined four other men in the rear booth.

When they were alone, Garvey stretched and quietly asked his son, "What just happened?"

Noel shrugged. "I don't know. Not much. Nothing, really. You introduced me to some guy and you bullshitted him that *Tinsel* was legal stuff."

"Baby, honey, listen and listen good," Julian Garvey said then, reaching across the table, taking Noel's hands in his own. "*Everything* just happened."

"Where was I?"

"Back story: Common wisdom has it that the important men in the town, the men with 'go' power, are a bunch of droolers. Alas, that belongs with the myth of 'Hollywood the Destroyer.' There are Rhodes Scholars running studios now, and there will be more of them in the future. However, since nothing comes from nothing, there were, once,

droolers, and Philip Schwartzman is one of the last. Armed
with nothing but a glorious golf swing and the fact that
he was a fraternity brother of a cousin of Abe Lastfogel—
a name unknown to you and the great unwashed but let's
just call him perhaps the single most powerful agent in the
history of sound—with no more weapons than that in his
arsenal, Philip Schwartzman has failed upwards as well as
anyone of recent note. He became a mediocre agent with
ease plus a scratch golfer. Eventually he was offered a
middle-management job at a studio, a post he filled with
ineptitude. But he is charming and he has that golf swing
and he managed to survive several purges until for one
chaotic period, he ran a studio. He ran it for several years
and almost into receivership. When he was fired he was
rewarded with his present post: He heads about the biggest German tax-shelter investment group there is. He
comes here most Sundays and sits with that group back
there—The Refugees, they call themselves. A bunch of
expatriate New Yorkers who sit around and make L.A.
jokes to each other. Like 'No matter how hot it gets in the
daytime in Los Angeles, there's nothing to do at night.'
That kind of thing. Except with my back turned I can tell
you one thing that's certain: Philip Schwartzman is not
smiling."

Noel glanced back. "You're right, at least for the moment."

"He is thinking, with that small square mind of his,
'Why did Julian Garvey lie to me? Why did he lie, we've
done business together before. *What was that script?*' "

"You think he saw what it was before you hid it away?"

"Honey, sweet, I didn't hide the fucking thing until
after I'd made sure he'd seen. That was a practiced move,
believe me. I want Philip Schwartzman to finance our
movie."

"More than Fox or the others?"

"Oh yes. He's about to lose his job—a lot of clinkers of
late—he's on the ropes and he needs someone to throw
him a preserver. He'll offer us a better deal than anybody.

'What if it's *Star Wars?*' he's thinking back there. 'Forget *Star Wars*—what if it's *Smokey and the Bandit?*' "

A burst of laughter from The Refugees.

"He's just sitting there," Noel said.

"Um-hmm," Julian said.

"What happens now?" Noel wondered.

"Nothing yet. Anxiety builds. He tries to figure out a way to casually let me know he might be a little bit interested if I should ever happen to find a promising piece of material. He can't come up to me now because that would be too soon and would show he was desperate, which, since he is desperate, naturally he cannot do."

"Well, when will he do something?"

"Do I detect a certain note of interest?"

"You know goddam well you do, now come on, tell me, I really want to know."

"I'm a cautious man with a reputation to uphold, I can't go around making wild ludicrous predictions, but let me just hazard the totally unfounded guess that the next move will happen tomorrow, Monday, in Los Angeles, California, at thirty-three hundred West Sixth Street, at one-twenty-two in the afternoon." He paused for effect. "Approximately. . . ."

At precisely one-fifteen P.M. the next day, Garvey parked his Eldorado on Sixth Street and headed up to Cassell's at 3300 West, Noel at his side. They went inside where Garvey ordered for both of them, then sent Noel on ahead to the patio to secure a table. Because he was so obsessive about his weight, food meant relatively little to him. But he was knowledgeable enough to realize that no matter how much the locals would rave about the gravlaks at Scandia or the sherbets at L'Ermitage, the simple fact was that none of the famous restaurants in town would stay solvent for a week in San Francisco, New Orleans, or New York.

Only Cassell's was supreme. Junk food was truly the area's only culinary claim to fame, and Cassell's made, without room for the least argument, the finest hamburger on the face of the earth. It was a bizarre place, open only from seven in the morning till three in the afternoon, and relentlessly uncomfortable. But glorious. Unmistakable. Worth a detour in any Michelin.

When their lunches were ready, Garvey paid, took the trays outside, spotted Noel off by himself. Looking neither right nor left, he joined his son and sat, as Noel leaned forward and whispered with excitement, "He's here. Schwartzman. Just like you said."

"There was never any doubt, my darling." He took a small forkful of the potato salad and ate with pleasure. "Just as *he* attends Nate 'n' Al's, *I* am known to frequent Cassell's on Mondays. Not only is it a pleasant way to begin the drudgery of the week, it is also not unhelpful to have a spot where one can be accidentally found. Usually, as he knows, I am here at half past twelve. I want you to pay particular attention to the slight discoloration of his face when I mention that I've been to the Valley."

"Because?"

"Both Warner's and Universal are in the Valley. And he will know that I've been to one or both. Plus, he must already have heard that I've already chatted with Warner's. So he will go mad wondering have I closed. And with whom. Have faith, it will all come true, trust Nostradamus." He smiled then. "That poor bastard's been sitting here for forty-five minutes wondering if I'd show. At this point I imagine his ulcers have ulcers."

"He's getting up," Noel whispered.

"I ask you, Noel, is there a better hamburger? I deny the possibility. Surely this must be the Platonic ideal."

"Afternoon, Julian," Philip Schwartzman said, as he passed their table. He nodded to Noel. "Fabulous day."

"Truly."

Schwartzman looked at his watch. "Christ, I'll be chasing my tail all afternoon trying to catch up."

"Best you be on your way then," Julian said, picking up his hamburger, studying it with genuine affection. "Oh, Phil—leave plenty of time for yourself if you're heading

for the Valley—traffic was murder just now. Both ways."
He took a bite of his hamburger and began to chew.

Schwartzman nodded, left, took a few steps, stopped.
"Oh, by the way, Julian, one thing."

"Did you try the potato salad, Phil? They make their
own. It's beyond compare."

"I did, yes, Julian, but—"

"—and the lemonade?"

"Huh?" Schwartzman said.

"They make that too. On a par with the potato salad,
wouldn't you agree, Noel."

Noel nodded.

"Promise me next time you'll try the lemonade, Phil,
will you?"

Schwartzman was back at the table now. "Yes, Julian, I
will make a note to absolutely have the lemonade, but we
made a lot of money together on that Bronson picture and
I thought we had something of a relationship."

Garvey appeared confused. "What has the one to do
with the other?"

"Julian, I would consider it remiss on your part if there
was a piece of material in your possession and everyone
had a crack at it but me. We made a bundle together and
I thought we both came out of it as good acquaintances."

"I'm very fond of you, Philip—"

"—then if a piece with real potential came into your
hands, I would of course have my turn."

"You're putting me into a terrible squeeze, Philip, but
then you've always been good at that."

"We all live with pressure, Julian, and what I want is
your word. An equal shot. Do I get it or don't I get it?"

"Ease up, Phil."

"Have you made a deal elsewhere?"

Garvey hesitated a long time. "Nothing legally binding,"
he said softly.

"Do I get my shot then? Are we moral people like I
thought we were or just plain piranhas like the rest of
them?"

"I promise I'll call you tomorrow, Phil."

"What's wrong with today?"

"Nothing. But you said how fiendishly busy you were and how you'd never catch up and I certainly didn't want to add to your burdens."

"I'll be in my office at five, call me at five."

"You have my word." Schwartzman hurried off then, and Garvey turned to Noel. "Time?" he asked.

Noel looked at his watch. "One-twenty-three."

"Truly, I am a force of nature," Julian Garvey said.

Schwab the Slob, at half past four that afternoon, said, "Are you all set?—are you really *really* all set?—because the killer idea of the century is about to be laid on you."

Garvey sat behind his desk in his intentionally oversized office and contemplated his son-in-law with considerable affection. Robert Schwab was physically most noticeable because of his fat cheeks—he had been almost tweaked to death by doting grandparents when a child. He was bright, with dervish energy, and had been, for five years now, a faultless husband to Sissy Garvey. They had three children, none of them as yet fatally spoiled. All in all, he was a decent and attractive young man except that no clothes had yet been created that proved a remotely proper fit for him. "Tuck in your shirttail please before going on," Julian said.

Schwab the Slob turned to Noel on the sofa. "Can you believe him? The notion of the millennium is about to be uttered and he's fussing about shirttails."

Noel laughed. He did at almost anything Schwab the Slob said. Noel and Sissy had been inseparable since childhood, she being one year older with natural maternal instincts. When she brought Robert Schwab home for parental approval, Noel was so overjoyed at actually *liking* his prospective brother-in-law, he sometimes carried it to extremes.

Schwab the Slob tucked himself properly, paused, then said, very loudly, " *'The Music!'* "

"What about it?"

"Well, I've been working a little, 'cause I know I wrote the fucker and I know I'm directing the thing, but Jesus, can a broad with no clothes on carry interest going bonkers for forty-five minutes? And then last night, came the dawn."

"The killer idea, as you put it."

"Yes. Listen—*the music will actually be a character in the film.* How, you wonder. That's what I'm here to explain. See at home, I bought Sissy a pretty good stereo for her birthday last week—nothing like yours, Noel, but fairly hotsy totsy if I do say so—and the amplifier's a Beomaster 2400—"

"—nice equipment," Noel said.

"I am lost and forlorn," Julian said. "I don't care about stereo equipment, I care about *Tinsel.*"

"It's got remote control tuning, Julian. Like some tv sets. You understand that. Okay, well what I realized is that Monroe, in her house, she's got a bunch of these set-ups, the music keeps her company, right? Okay, now get this— these things change stations automatically and get louder and softer by remote too, so when she's wandering—say from the bedroom to the bar to refill—she's got these remotes all over and she goes 'click' and the station changes instantly, from one kind of music to another—a snippet of this, she doesn't like it, click, she's got another station, the song's half over, she likes it, click, she makes it louder as she pours her booze and when it's done, click, another station, classical maybe, it stays on as she leaves the bar area and goes to the living room and click, changes that station around, but the one in the bar is still on classical so when she goes back to the bar for her next refill, classi- cal's what she hears, so we can connect *each part* of her house with a *special* music—this room can be placid, that room can be hard rock, the bedroom can be a Sinatra-type middle-of-the-road song. In other words, the music is part of the life that's disintegrating. It can get louder toward the end, harsher, more driving, sexier, dirtier, whatever we want and she can click and click and click as she gets worse, *the music is her companion.* It becomes *crucial. Essential. Integral.*"

"Stop underlining," Garvey said.

"Julian, I'm not getting through—here's the point, keed —if the movie works, with music that memorable, we can have maybe the biggest album since *Saturday Night Fever* in which the music was also crucial, essential and integral and which also, I might add, has sold over one hundred million dollars' worth of albums as we speak."

"I think Stigwood has the Bee Gees sewn up," Julian said.

"I don't want them, I want an American, an educated-type composer who can write every kind of music. And I've got the guy. Name of Small. The guy I won the Emmy with. Which is really why I'm here. Would it be out of line if I had some preliminary meetings to see if he's interested?"

"It would be premature."

"When can I call him?"

"When I have five million of someone else's dollars and Miss Welch's name on a telex."

"How long do you think?"

"I'll know a lot more by the end of the week," Julian said.

"I'll settle for that." He tucked in his shirt again, turned to Noel. "I think it's wonderful you're working on the picture."

"Giving it a whack is all," Noel said.

"Sissy thought it was kind of more or less definite."

"I'll know a lot more by the end of the week," Noel said.

"By the way, she sends you both her love, Sissy," Schwab the Slob said as he started for the door; then abruptly he whirled toward Garvey. "Hey, you bastard, didn't you like it even a little?"

"Truly a killer idea," Julian told him. He paused. "If it works. . . ."

At exactly five he had his secretary Matty put in the call to Schwartzman. She buzzed when Schwartzman was on the line. "Noel's with me, Phil, so if you don't mind, I'll put us on the speakerphone."

"Fine with me; I'm taping things here."

Garvey laughed and switched the speakerphone on, reached for a yellow pad, wrote *Stay close* and showed it to Noel who moved alongside his father, sat on the corner of the desk. "You wracked me up pretty good at that accidental lunchtime rendezvous we had, Phil. I'm not like those other piranhas out there and I'd hoped you knew that."

"I do, Julian. But you're so goddam rich and famous that a little zap every so often is something I can't resist."

"Shall we stop circling the wagons and get down to it?"

"I'm just here waiting, Julian."

"The reason I didn't come first to you, Phil, and I'm sure you must credit me with thinking of you initially, is simply this: Those rich krauts you represent only want violence pictures—they want bang-bang epics because, as we both know, there is a market for them worldwide—action is visual, I don't have to tell you that, and this is certainly a visual picture, but it isn't action, it isn't an Eastwood bloodbath, and I just naturally thought that rather than begin with a rejection, I'd take it elsewhere."

"My guys are getting a lot more flexible, Julian. *Turning Point* and *Annie Hall* have changed a lot of minds. We're broadening our interests."

"Well, since the movies you back have the largest corpse-per-picture average outside of Kung Fu films, I'd have no way of knowing that."

"Exactly what's your flick about?" Schwartzman asked.

On the yellow pad, Garvey wrote *He knows.* "Hmm," he said, as Noel took a pencil and wrote *You sure?* underneath. Garvey nodded and said, "It's always hard for me to encapsulate the entirety of a project into a sentence, Phil."

"Where the fuck did you get 'encapsulate,' Julian? You make me feel like a moron."

He is *a moron,* Garvey wrote.

"You can tell me a little, Julian. You say there's no violence."

"We are definitely not dealing with a bloodbath, Phil."

"Well, is there any sex then?"

Garvey nodded to Noel before he said, "Nope, not a bit of it."

There was a pause now from the other end.

His small square mind is trying to function, Garvey wrote.

"No sex at all?"

"Not a foot of it—I mean, it's just the story of these two kids who run away from home and they find this giant panda who's either lost or escaped from a zoo and it's sick so they get it healthy and then we're into the really dramatic part—should they return the panda or not, because if they do they'll get caught and if they don't, the panda might die. I won't spoil the plot by telling you what they do, but the title's one word, *Boopsi* with an 'i' at the end. Boopsi's the panda's name. I hope you can see why I didn't figure your Nazis would find it up their alley."

Noel was on the floor by now.

"One sec, Julian—one little mo'—you've got a lot of material, I'm aware of that, so I wonder if maybe we've crossed a few wires here or something."

"You asked me at lunch if I didn't have something with potential, Phil—" Garvey's voice was up a notch now. "Are you telling me you don't like the Boopsi story?"

"No, Julian, not at all—"

"—I mean shit, Phil, have you checked out the *Benji* grosses?—"

"—tremendous, I know, but—"

"—my fucking panda will out-cute that fucking mutt

any fucking day of any fucking week outside of Rosh Hashanah, and if you think I'm crazy, call the Disney people and ask if they're crawling all over me or not—"

"—hey, buddy, easy—"

"—there's sequel potential, *Son of Boopsi*'s a natural, there's possibilities for a tv series, the toy tie-ins could outdo *Star Wars*, Mattel's on my phone night and day as it is—"

"—Julian—Julian listen—it's very hard to stop you once you get generating, Julian, but haven't you got maybe a story kind of about, like, say, a sex symbol?"

"Oh, Phil, you're talking about *Tinsel*—that's my old age pension, that one. But it's taken."

"Taken?"

"Well, more or less—"

"—has money changed hands?—"

"—not exactly—"

"—nothing's been signed then or agreed to?—"

"—not legally, no, but—"

"—get me the script, I promise you an answer by morning."

Garvey hesitated, watching as Noel, up again, wrote *How did you know he knew?* on the yellow pad. Garvey wrote back *This is a* very *small town*.

"Julian, I'd like an answer please. If I get you a yes by lunchtime, have we got a firm deal?"

"Read the script first, Phil, let's not get premature."

"Is casting set?"

"Let's not get premature."

"I'll have it picked up in half an hour."

"Noel's driving by your office on his way home now, Phil. I'll have him bring it in. Be good for him, checking out a real mogul in the flesh."

"We'll talk, Julian."

Garvey grunted, hung up. "You don't mind dropping the script off."

"No problem."

"Have Matty get you a copy and the address on your way out."

"Hey?"

"What, honey?"

"You did good on the phone."

"Minor-league action, but thank you. Go on home from Phil's. We'll chat over dinner on the events of the day."

"Do I have to bullshit this Schwartzman or what?"

"You're not nearly ready to take my Bullshit One course. Just ask him for a few pointers on your putting stance and try to stay awake while he answers. We want him to give us five million dollars, don't insult the man, *capiche?*"

Noel smiled, saluted smartly, did an about-face, and was gone. Julian, alone, rubbed his temple for a few moments. It was coming up to half past five and he shouldn't have been as fatigued as he felt. The tension of trying to intrigue Noel probably had a lot to do with it. More than a lot. All. He pushed down the intercom, said, "When you have a moment," and sat back, awaiting Matty.

She had been with him going on ten years—Estelle had selected her personally—and she was the envy of executives all over town. Bright, energetic, enthusiastic, with a marvelously retentive mind. Matilda Brown. A sweet enough black face. A body of three hundred pounds.

"Sire," she said from the doorway.

"What oddments remain?"

"Wanna do birthday gifts and anniversaries and all the other special days?"

"I suppose. What do we have coming up?"

She opened a large notebook. "One of the Bronson kids has a birthday."

"I don't feel Charley's as valuable to me as he was in days of yore. Send a card."

"Frank Parenti, birthday."

"I thought he might happen but alas, nobody's even heard of him any more. He's lucky to get tv commercials. Cross him off the list."

"Barbara Eden?"

"An appropriate card."

"Richard Harris?"

"I think he's coming back. Send whichever wife he has now something middling dear from Giorgio's."

"The Newmans?"

"Very key. Matching trinkets from Tiffany's—a car motif for him, dancing for her."

"Remick?"

"I like her even though she's not worth a whole lot. Be brilliant for me."

"Last name—Taylor."

"Elizabeth?"

"That's the one."

"Cross her off the list."

Matty nodded. "That about does it for the day. Want me to lock up?"

"I'll do it when I go."

"Be in at half past nine," she said, and closed the door behind her.

Garvey stood, rubbed his eyes, moved down the office to the adjoining room he'd had set up as a gym. He exercised twice daily, early morning before leaving home, and late afternoon before returning. He turned on the lights, moved to the jogging machine, got it started. The room had mats and a massage table with a phone and notepad beside it and jump ropes and a dressing area and shower. Garvey stripped, carefully hung his clothes on a hanger, put on boxing trunks, lay on the mat, and did twenty quick sit-ups. Then he stretched his muscles, gradually increasing the effort. When he felt loose he went to the jogging machine and fell easily into rhythm. He ran two miles in the morning along Sunset, one mile here. He liked to time out at not much more than five minutes but that was getting harder with the years. He perspired easily, a burden at formal parties, an aid here. He was drenched before the mile was up and when it was, he gratefully disrobed, stepped naked into the shower, soaped his body clean.

From beyond now, he heard someone calling his name. "Mr. Garvey? Hello? Mr. Garvey, are you here?"

Julian turned off the spigots, grabbed a towel, moved toward his office. A redheaded woman was standing alone in the center of the room, tall, discreetly dressed, with a model's figure.

"What is it?" Garvey said sharply.

She spun toward him, looking surprised. "Oh, holy cow, has there ever been a goof-up."

"What is it?" Garvey repeated.

She stumbled over her explanation—"I'm—my name's —I cleared this with your secretary—I set it up for today, I swear—"

"Set up what?"

"The interview."

"I don't give interviews generally. Now what is all this, Miss. . . ."

"Hoffman. I'm with a little paper out in the Valley and we're doing a movie series—and I thought that you, well, it would be kind of a coup to get you on tape and I called and set up and everything."

"I'm sorry," Garvey said. "Try selling me the Brooklyn Bridge why don't you, 'cause I'm sure not buying this."

"It's true—I swear—"

"—then show me your tape recorder," Garvey said quietly.

She looked very flustered now.

"Or your notebook, either will do," he went on as before. She had nothing to say.

"Miss Hoffman, I'm afraid you're a rotten actress."

She flared at that. "I'm not—I'm goddam good—I could really be somebody, Mr. Garvey—"

"Why in the world are you here with such a pathetic ploy?"

" 'Cause you've made more stars than anybody. I photograph great."

"Go see Ray Stark. He's on a hot streak."

"I'm a great lay, Mr. Garvey," she said then.

Garvey just shook his head.

"I am. It's true. I can do things you never even dreamed of. That's got to appeal to you."

"Why, pray?"

"Everyone says you've balled more people than anybody."

"Would that it were so."

"And you're hung like a goddam mule."

Garvey smiled. "Would that it were so."

She took a step toward him.

"You can stop right there," Garvey told her.

She did.

"How old are you?"

"I can photograph twenty-five easy with decent lighting—"

"—how *old*?"

"Thirty-one. I was thirty-one I mean. I'm thirty-two now."

"And I am almost sixty. And not anxious, after a difficult day, for cardiac arrest. So now please turn around—" He made the gesture with his right hand.

She hesitated, finally obeyed.

"Good-bye, Miss Hoffman."

She never looked back, just ran.

Garvey watched till she was gone and a good deal longer. Then he went back into the gym, dropped the towel, looked briefly at his body in the mirror. Pretty good nick for a man of his years, as the English would say; excellent nick. His face was remarkably unlined. And he resembled now more than ever Leslie Howard. He went back into the shower, got the spigots to the right temperature, began to shampoo his hair. It was salt and pepper, with the hairline barely receding. He rinsed, added soap a second time, massaged vigorously, and was standing eyes closed letting the water pound at his scalp when she burst naked next to him, her red hair wet and long, and her hands had found his penis and begun to rub and he tried to push her off but she continued to rub and he could tell he was firming up, but not yet hard, and she tongued his mouth fiercely and then they all but fell from the shower, groped for the massage table where she knelt and blew him and he wasn't hard yet as he mounted her and she spread her legs as he quickly dialed the phone and when Estelle answered he said, "I'm about to close up shop here" and Estelle said, "And you're coming straight home?" and Garvey said, "Those are my plans," and now he was at last hard and the redhead guided him deeply in as Estelle said, "We're having cucumber salad as a starter" and Garvey put his hand over the mouthpiece and shot his wad, biting into his wrist as Estelle said, "That was a joke, Julian, it was supposed to be anyway," and Garvey said, "I understood," and after they hung up the redhead rose and got a towel and turned out the light as Garvey lay on the massage table and she returned and cleaned his penis of the last drops of sperm while he just lay limp with his eyes closed until she said, "I can't make it next Monday, Julian" which made him wonder aloud "Why," and she explained that it was her kid's birthday and he said "Fine, Tuesday then," and pointed to his trousers and she went to them, took out his wallet, handed it over and waited while he gave her the hundred, and she left him alone in the dark where he stayed, listening to her dress in the next room, the slide of cloth against firm skin, and then the sound of the office door closing and still Garvey lay there in the gathering dark, filled with the self-loathing that always followed the enforced game-playing he so needed nowadays, and when that emotion left him, as it always did, he was left with the perhaps ultimate irony that of all things, his cock had been what betrayed him. . . .

There was no question in his mind that it had been what won him Estelle. Not alone, certainly. She admired his appearance, she said she enjoyed his company, his way of expressing himself, what a lot of people thought of as his charm. But ultimately, the battle was won on a dozen different mattresses. His constant ardor, his reassuring her of her particular beauty, these helped. But the clincher was always his cock, the way the sight of her made it splendidly perform.

Oscar-caliber work on Julian's part since Estelle was nothing if not plain. They met at a dance at the Riviera Country Club that Julian had finagled an invitation to, a formal affair, and although he was always handsome, nothing brought out his looks quite as much as a tuxedo. He could have lived at Gatsby's parties; more than that even —flappers would have followed him discreetly with their eyes.

Estelle was dancing when he first saw her, her escort for the evening being one of the less-than-bright Chandlers that no one much liked to talk about.

Julian could not take his eyes off Estelle.

The orchestra was playing "Mam'selle" and after that it segued into "Confess" followed by "Everything I Have Is Yours" and Julian stood on the outskirts of the dance floor, elegant and alone.

And watching.

Eventually she had to become aware, and she did, and then quickly looked away and made it a point not to look back. For a while at least. But finally she glanced casually in his direction.

He was gone.

She was standing alone an hour later by the pool, watching a bunch of terribly intoxicated young men act out a semivulgar USC football cheer. From behind her Garvey said, "Never have I felt so far from New Haven." And after that, "Julian Garvey." He reached for her hand then, and led her toward the music.

She half resisted.

"One dance; if you don't I promise to expire promptly and you must have other things you'd rather have on your conscience." He paused. "Oh come along, Estelle."

She began slowly to accompany him.

"I've spent the last hour gathering information on you. Claiborne—fancy name. And you're quite a catch, or so a drunk at the bar informed me. I've never danced with a catch before."

"You look like a Yale man."

"We all have our crosses," Julian said.

Estelle smiled. "And you have that oh-so-carefully cultivated air of nauseating superiority."

"Advanced Superiority is a required freshman course."

"You find us prehistoric out here, Mr. Garvey?"

"Not at all—I just wish you all weren't so ruggedly healthy. I'd love to see a pimple on an adolescent chin. I miss those things."

The orchestra was butchering "Ballerina."

"I have to tell you something myself, Miss Claiborne, because if it came to your ears from lips other than mine, I would be distraught. There is a dark side to me. I am lower than a swindler. My prestige ranks beneath that of a slum landlord." Julian paused. "I am an agent, Miss Claiborne, may God have mercy on my soul." He spun her gently in his arms as she smiled. "But not forever; by 1950 I plan to be a producer, and within a year or two of that, there is no doubt I shall be solvent for life. So you can see, I trust, what makes me different from all the other men in your life." He pressed his body close against hers.

"What makes you different?"

His cock was hard against her as he said, "I don't want marriage, Miss Claiborne; I only want to go to bed with you." And he held her tightly and spun her body to the music until she broke free and left the floor without looking back.

Of course he sent her a gift along with a note of apology and of course she did not reply. The next week he sent another gift, more expensive, and did the same the week after that and the notes kept getting more sincere as the gifts escalated in cost until after a month and a half she called him at his small home on the beach south of Santa Monica and said, "Look, this is really very silly, you must stop."

He assured her he had no intention of doing so.

"What do you *want?*"

"Oh, come now, that's already been established."

"Ass!" and she hung up.

But contact is more than half the battle and there was no doubt in Julian's mind concerning eventual victory. If anything, it was too easy. Here she was, rich and homely, brown and plain with nothing to shield her from life but a sharp mind, and here he was, anxious only to prove one unassailable truth: She was sexually irresistible. Deny it as she might, she had to want to deep down believe it was possibly true, and so within another month and a half they had dated, and talked, and on occasion even laughed together.

"You're something of a catch yourself," Estelle said, standing by the window of Julian's living room, watching the dark ocean beyond.

"Am I now?" he said, handing her the refill of Scotch and water. He was still on his first, nursing it carefully, now and then sipping.

" 'One of the hottest young agents in town' I think was the exact phrasing."

"The hottest," he corrected. "With no one in close pursuit."

"I really hate your ego," Estelle said.

"Do you now."

"Yes. You're insufferably confident."

"It's all show." He was standing behind her, close behind her, and he could feel her body starting to tense. It was understood that they were to bed down for the first time that night. Earlier he'd suggested casually that she might like his view and she'd said casually that she'd always had a thing for the ocean and he'd come back with a mocking remark about her use of the phrase "Having a thing" and on and on they went, feinting and verbally thrusting, when all the time they both knew what they were talking about was would they fuck later or not.

And now it was later.

Estelle was more tense now than ever. Garvey moved

right up behind her, establishing contact, and she was practically rigid when he said, softly, "Estelle?" and she managed "What?" and he replied, "I hate your goddam sensible
shoes, why must you go clumping through life, it's laughable," and that surprised her as intended, for the word
"laughable" made her turn and Garvey went on, saying,
"And you must stop trying to dress as though the only
clothes in the civilized world came directly from Lane
Bryant."

. She looked at him now and probably if she hadn't been
holding the glass she might have bolted, because he had
been so flattering, so continually complimentary, and now
it was all changing or seemed to be, and what would follow
after, and Garvey, well aware of where he'd suddenly put
her, chose that moment to strike, and she clung to him
because he knew her past had been no hiding place, and
suddenly he was taking away her future, and moving her
to the bedroom was no problem and once they were naked
he was home.

She hid awhile behind a sudden drunkenness but he let
her play, caressing her constantly, touching her deftly,
seeming always to care; she was square shouldered and
flat chested and heavy legged, but he nursed her along like
Nefertiti and slowly she began to give to him, to soften
and respond, and he left her momentarily to open the door
so they could hear the ocean and when he came back he
said he knew it was gloriously corny, the pounding of the
waves, but please would she be able to forgive him, and
her arms went around him tight in reply and her legs went
around him too and he was hard and she knew it but he
held off entrance just short of cruelty and then he was in
and moving and telling her what a glory she was and how
he, Julian Garvey, was indeed the most fortunate of men,
and in a little while he had her really moving and wild
and a little after that he could sense her bunching for her
orgasm and she began to make sharp intakes of breath
and as they increased he knew it was drawing closer and
it was then that he pulled out of her and she said, "What

is it?" and he said, very calmly all things considered, "Say you're pretty."

"Come back inside me."

"When you've said it."

"I'm not, though."

"I think you are. Say, 'Julian thinks I'm pretty.' "

" 'Julian thinks I'm pretty.' Please come back."

"When you've said it."

"I'm pretty. I'm pretty."

"Louder and mean it."

"I'm pretty, you son of a bitch!"

He reentered her then, and she'd gone a long ways back but he had nothing but time, he was a master of many situations, none more than bed, and eventually she was close again, on the verge, and he brought her slowly to climax and held her there for as long as he could before she exploded.

An hour later he began to caress her again. They were lying in each other's arms with fresh drinks on the bedside table and Estelle said, "Oh, baby, don't."

"I must."

"I'm a little sore," she said, but she didn't totally push his hand away.

"Too bad about you, what about me?"

"What about you?"

"Feel."

"Are you always hard?"

"Only around you, Estelle," and his hands were roving her body.

"What are you going to do?"

"First I intend to fuck your brains out, my sweet; after which I plan on sleeping like a baby. . . ."

The next morning at his office he made a few notes about the encounter on a three-by-five card. Nothing graphic. Just standard material mostly: name, place, date, any idiosyncrasies worth remembering either physical or mental, and an overall rating.

It was a silly habit, most likely, but he'd been at it ever since when, at twenty, he could no longer summon up the memories of all his conquests, and at twenty that seemed important to him.

Julian finished with Estelle's card, put it alphabetically in place in the card box, placed the box in his bottom desk drawer, and locked the drawer securely. There were times when he considered pitching the whole collection, but that was most likely silly too. After all, some men collected postage stamps, others bubble gum cards. . . .

Estelle was petrified of her father, a fact which only became important in August (she had met Julian in April). She was painfully in love with Garvey and he kept her in that state, seduced her often, bought her presents unexpectedly, never sought anything permanent.

They were wandering along the beach late one afternoon near Garvey's tiny house when Estelle asked, idly, if he had any Italian clients.

Garvey ran the tip of his finger along her tanned arm. "That may simply be the most loaded question I have ever heard in my life. You cannot conceivably be curious about the answer."

Estelle said she was only making conversation.

"Why don't you ask me about my Tibetan list, then? Ah, I have many sherpas who are box office in downtown Lhasa. There's been a tremendous revival of moviegoing interest throughout the Himalayas of late, and we at MCA have, I am happy to say, cornered the talent market."

"There's a very fine art school in Florence is all I meant," Estelle replied.

"Are you just making conversation again?"

"I may be going there in the fall."

"Very sensible," Garvey allowed. "Especially since you have been sneaking up on your doctorate in art history at UCLA since before California achieved statehood."

"Be serious with me, Julian!"

He took her arm, guided her up toward the house, sat

her in his living room, fixed her a Scotch. "What are we into?"

"Father thinks it might be broadening for me to attend Florence. Or so he said at dinner last night."

"Well, if the legendary art connoisseur Stanford 'Sonny' Claiborne, who ranks Norman Rockwell only slightly above Michelangelo, thinks Florence might be for chrissakes broadening, we must all pay heed."

"Don't mock him. He can be very powerful."

"Only to his children, child."

"I'm probably going to Florence is the point."

Garvey started laughing. "In practically the middle of the twentieth century, Estelle? Because Daddy says so? It's fucking Dickensian."

"Still. . . ." She let it dribble away.

"Estelle, Jesus, you're twenty-four—frankly I think it's a little weird you're still living at home. Just say no and go about your business."

She sat on his sofa, turning her Scotch glass around and around with her short fingers. Even her hands were homely. "I've got to know, you see."

"What, pray tell?"

"About . . ." She let it dribble away again. ". . . you. In connection . . . with me."

"It's back to Dickens again—are you asking if my intentions are honorable? Nothing about me is honorable, Estelle—that's a State of California law. No practicing talent . agent is allowed anything that might be termed honorable."

"Shit, Julian, do you love me? You've never said one way or the other and you've never mentioned marriage one way or the other and Father says no, Father says it will not happen and I'm so homely, you don't know what that feels like but it's with you in the morning and it never goes away and at night before sleep you're homely and you pray for something to work its miracle so you won't have to face it again the next day, and you're my miracle, Julian, I'm pretty with you, please let me stay pretty, I'll do anything, I'll do anything, I'll do anything to be pretty with you, why aren't you answering me?"

How could he speak with his eyes so filled with tears? He wept and held his arms out. She sought refuge there . . .

Stanford "Sonny" Claiborne resembled a road-company William Howard Taft. He lived alone with his spinster daughter in a gigantic stone pile in Hancock Park. When Julian arrived for his evening appointment, the butler, who resembled a road-company Arthur Treacher, showed him into the library. The room was enormous and book lined, with ladders that wheeled along the walls. "The Master will be down presently," the butler said. Julian could not believe that these words had ever actually been uttered before, but there it was.

The door closed. He was alone. He glanced at his watch. Nine o'clock. The set hour. He guessed the old man would appear by nine-fifteen. It didn't matter. Time was a game agents were good at playing. The books were mostly leather bound, collections of Walpole and Pepys and Twain, and Julian opened a few volumes at random, noted that the pages had, in the main, not been cut. It was a library not for readers. All show. He had no idea if that would come in handy or not, but any information was worth something, if not today, tomorrow.

At nine-thirty Stanford Claiborne entered, somber and ponderous, and before he could say anything Julian said, "I'm sorry I got here so early."

"Early?"

Julian hurried on apologetically. "Nine-thirty was the appointed hour. You, of course, are punctual. I must have written it down incorrectly in my date book. Stupid of me."

Mr. Claiborne had a great white walrus mustache and his right hand went to it now, brushed it as he studied Julian in silence. "You're a very handsome fellow," he said finally. "I fully understand Estelle's attraction." He went to a large desk and sat heavily behind it, gesturing for Julian to take the chair across.

Julian, of course, sat quickly.

"You enjoyed New Haven?" the old man said then, and after that, interrupting himself—"I could offer you port and a cigar but I don't think we're here to deal with amenities, do you?"

"The ball," Julian answered, "is in your court."

"You enjoyed New Haven, I ask again?"

"Good times and bad."

The great head nodded. "Hm-hmm. Um-hmm." Again, the mustache-fingering. "A third time, sir: You enjoyed New Haven?"

"Some days more than others."

"Odd."

"Why so?"

"You must understand, Mr. Garvey, that it is not unusual for a man such as myself to have contacts in many places, east as well as west."

Julian waited.

"You never went to Yale."

"How much have you checked on me?"

"Enough for my purposes. You lied, sir, to my daughter. You never went to Yale, true or not true?"

"I never said I went to Yale."

"My daughter told me—"

"What *I* told your daughter," Julian interrupted, "and I am quite capable of quoting myself, was this: 'I never felt so far from New Haven in my life.' She later said I looked like a Yale man. I never felt the need to go into it deeply. If she'd told me I looked like a Princetonian, I would not have done ten minutes explaining that I'd never set foot in New Jersey. And as you surely must know from your research, I was born and brought partially up in New Haven. I attended, for a year as I'm sure you know, business school near New Haven. Quinnipiac was the name of the institution. I left, among other reasons, because I couldn't pronounce the name."

"And to get married."

"Also that."

"You never told Estelle?"

"She also is unaware of my having had whooping cough. I was married at eighteen and divorced within a year. The general feeling was the marriage didn't take. I hope you have me down for no children."

"You are very charming," Stanford Claiborne said. "You are a *most* charming fellow. But I think you will not marry my daughter."

Julian said nothing.

"A most mellifluous name, Julian Garvey."

"I rather think it has a ring."

"More than Julius Garfinkel surely."

Julian said nothing.

"You never told Estelle that either, did you?"

"No sir, I did not."

"It's rather a Jewish name, isn't it; Garfinkel. You don't look remotely Jewish."

"I have my horns trimmed weekly," Julian explained.

"Wonderfully charming; do you work at it?"

"I'll be serious, not that you care: I *invented* myself when I first hit Southern California. I am not an easterner who scorns it here. I love the place. I love the leisure, I love the mood of the people. But I suppose most of all I love the fact that in New York, while certainly being above average, I don't stand out remarkably, whereas here, I find myself in the altogether enviable position of being smarter than practically anybody."

"Are you so certain of that?"

"I'm sure as shit smarter than you," Julian Garvey said. And then, after a beat, "Yes, I work at it."

"I would not be too quick to underestimate me, Mr. Garfinkel."

"You poor prehistoric fart, you don't even know the

name of the game we're playing. You think you control Estelle—"

"—that has always been the case—"

"—I've got news for you, Sonny, they've invented the wheel, there's even talk of gravity being discovered in the not too distant future—why don't we get down to the true subject of the evening."

"By all means. And what is that?"

"Estelle's money—you've got it tattooed somewhere deep inside that I'm some scummy kike come from the ghetto to steal the family fortune—"

"—are you saying it hasn't crossed your mind?—"

"—of course it's crossed it—"

"—and of course the thought caused you pain—"

And then Julian was on his feet, trembling as he screamed across the desk—*"I don't want your Gentile gold!"*

"Then what is it you're after?"

"Estelle." He sank back into the chair. His voice abruptly softened. "I want Estelle." And now his pale blue eyes filled with tears. "But with your blessings. . . ." he managed finally. And then he wept. . . .

Julian had many secrets but perhaps his most cherished was this: He could cry at will. He had read once that the great Gielgud could do the same thing, it was a family trait. Weak lachrymal glands. The whole Gielgud family could weep when they wanted to. So it was with the Garfinkels of New Haven. All you had to do was blink a few times sharply and lo here came the tears. Stopping was the problem.

Another problem was when to use the weapon. Nothing gave you a leg up in any sincerity derby as much as weeping to prove a point. But you had to be careful. If the news got out, you became a joke, and Julian had wept in front of Estelle very recently in his house on the beach. He would have to risk the old man would not bruit Julian's emotions to his daughter.

Because the truth was, Julian didn't give a shit for Estelle's money. He knew his capabilities in Hollywood, and earning bread had never once bothered him.

Power was the problem.

To have power, real power, you had to be in the rat race but out of it too. Above it and beyond. Marrying a Chandler would have been ideal. All in all, though, a Claiborne wasn't so bad. But it had to be with the old man's good wishes. Estelle alone was just a dog. Estelle with her family along meant plenty and then some.

Julian averted his head, dried his eyes, looked at the aging ogre across the desk. "I am marrying your daughter but there has to be one condition and I'm about to tell you what it is."

The old man watched him.

Was he, Julian wondered, convinced of Julian's sincerity? Had the tears washed away doubts? He took a breath and said the words: "No money."

The old man still watched. More than watched. Studied.

"You're going to lift up the phone in a while and you're going to call one of your fine goy lawyers, someone deeply Protestant and therefore totally trustworthy, and you're to instruct him to draw up a premarital agreement for me to sign. And what it will say is this—under no conditions am I to be allowed *ever* to touch a penny belonging to Estelle. And if we have children, and I plan very much on doing just that, I will not legally be allowed to touch their money either. And on through as many generations as you think safe. If you choose to give money to Estelle or our children, you may do so without loss of sleep."

"I think you think I won't do it. I think you plan on my relenting. May I promise you you're wrong?"

Julian smiled and shook his head. "You're dead but you won't lie down—the war is over, you've lost, Estelle is no longer in your possession. What we're talking about now is do you lose your daughter brutally, or do the three of us walk slowly toward the sunset. You see, I think that once this messy scene is over with, you and I will likely get along. We have something quite rare in common."

"That being?"

"We are the only people ever born who truly love Estelle." His final salvo fired, Julian sat and waited for some sign.

"Perhaps we are," the old man said finally. "It could be so."

Julian was never noisy when a victory came his way. Personal preference. Quiet savoring was more his style. He looked at the wreck across from him. "I hope you serve a decent port," was all he said. . . .

The wedding, which took place on a dazzling October day, was an immediate success. The marriage was an eventual disaster. The first few years went well enough. Sissy was born in 1949, the year Julian produced his first film. Noel came along a year later, the year of his first hit, a John Wayne western. He tended to work on one film at a time so he rarely had more than two in a calendar year. But it was enough to make him very rich, for he had a wonderful eye for new talent—he was one of the first to use Martin and Lewis, one of the first to grab Sinatra after the *Eternity* comeback. Eastwood he had early, Lemmon, McQueen, MacLaine.

He was good with script, had a sense for popular taste before it quite became popular, knew enough about stars' insecurities to be able to deliver in a room. He kept a profile so low as to be nonexistent. He didn't give interviews and never, at the Bel-Air Country Club, talked show business.

He became, carefully, a quiet legend. Always handsome, he grew increasingly distinguished looking as he aged. In a land of blue jeans and jogging clothes, he dressed totally English. Lobb made his shoes, Turnbull his shirts. The suits and jackets and slacks were primarily the work of H. Huntsman & Sons, though lately he'd been drifting toward Doug Hayward.

And he was relentlessly unfaithful.

If it moved and was young, chances are he'd seduced it. Even if it wasn't so young. Probably it wasn't all that crucial if it moved or not. And he was not always, particularly when he was younger, as discreet as he might be. News of his card file began being whispered. It wasn't so terrible, at least to Julian's mind, to be known as the man, in this town, who had had more than anybody.

The only time his cards almost got him in trouble was once when he was incontinent enough to screw his secretary, a bubble-headed girl named Bumpstead. She was attractive and probably as skillful as Elizabeth Ray when it came to stenography. She also became attached to Julian, and took it badly when he dumped her. He caught her with the key to his drawer where the card file was kept and if she'd gotten it out, he might have been vulnerable to blackmail for the rest of his natural life. But such did not turn out to be the case. He fired her, gave her two extra weeks' salary for loving him, and sent her on her way.

Julian's time for loving happened later, when he was pushing fifty, and he came in contact with Ginger Abraham, the one and only.

She wanted nothing to do with him, which only inflamed him the more. He could not believe that after all the successes the failure would come when it counted. But it did, and he was a bruised figure for quite a time after Ginger left his life. But being a survivor he, of course, survived, and at the start of '78 Julian had his health, his hair, his unchallenged position in the industry, and probably close to twenty million dollars in the bank.

It didn't seem so much that January morning when, after a brisk shower, his fingers found the lump in the area around his groin.

He visited Doctor Riley later that day and Riley said that it was probably just a swollen lymph gland and the logical thing would be to watch it closely for a month before acting. Julian, in his best 'don't say yes until I finish talking' tone, answered that (A) he didn't much want to wait a month or half that long and (B) could it be done in

San Francisco, the biopsy, because he didn't want anyone in town having a leg up on him.

Riley replied that it could indeed be done, so Julian got himself booked into a Frisco hospital under the name of Garfinkel, told Estelle he was off to New York for an overnight attempt to nail down the new Michener. It was a perfectly safe subterfuge—he knew she'd never try to call him; in the past, she had, often, and her disenchantment in finding him not to be wherever he told her he was going ended her dialing habit.

Alone and unknown and awaiting the result in San Francisco Julian stared at the hospital ceiling, the proverbial drowning man. He began to fiddle with the headline he would get in the *Los Angeles Times*. "Julian Garvey, 58, The Last of the Giants." "Julian Garvey, 58, Noted Movie and Charity Figure." But as the day wore on, his fantasies wore down. By noon it was "Julian Garvey, 58, Stroker of Stars." By dinner, "Julian Garvey, 58, and No One Will Mourn." By nightfall he had arrived, alas, at the truth:

JULIAN GARVEY, 58, FAILURE

For he was that. He had failed terribly as a father, even though, at times, he had tried. There had never been any attempt at success as a husband. He had failed as a lover —no one had screwed more and gotten less out of it emotionally, and the one time he had allowed his emotions to surface, with Ginger Abraham, he'd failed again. But worst of all was this: He had failed as a producer.

What he had given the world, for three decades, was shit.

Abbott and Costello and Martin and Lewis—shit. Eastwood and McQueen—shit. Over forty features, over twenty-five hits, and not one would tax the mentality of a ten-year-old. Even when he went foreign, it was shit foreign. Shit Fellini. Shit Truffaut. It was like the Updike stories published in *Playboy*—shit Updike. The good stuff went to *The New Yorker; Playboy* simply paid. He understood the world's need for shit and he set about filling that need, but never once when art and commerce came into conflict did art stand a chance. Not in a Julian Garvey picture.

He lay in the hospital, the despair relentless, and he wished that he could cry honest tears, but of course he couldn't—even his tears were shit. Here he was, at fifty-eight, an immaculate dissembler. That was really the one thing at which he was truly world class: He could prevaricate with the best; his right hand had not nodded to his left hand since before the Second World War.

He lay in the hospital, the despair relentless and now building and he understood, perhaps for the first time, the possibility of madness. If you stayed in movies long enough, you met madness and got to have a decent acquaintanceship, but it was always the affliction of the weak, and Julian had banished the possibility of weakness when he created, out of the usable pieces of Garfinkel, the great shining slabs of Garvey. To be a great Producer, what you had to have was knowledge, not just of the business but of everything outside the business. Selznick, his idol, read voraciously, and not just for deals, he enjoyed the act of reading. And looking at paintings and listening to music without wondering would it do for background scoring someday. Selznick *knew*. Garvey was ignorant. Oh, not totally, there were some things—

—like Hollywood, he knew Hollywood—but big deal, you hang around long enough, you learn it, lots of people knew Hollywood; but there were other things—

—like women, God knows he knew women—hold the phone now, hold the fucking phone.

Garvey sat up in his hospital bed and almost at that moment shrieked with joy.

> *—and he knew the corrosive effect*
> *the one had on the other*

His mind went back to Monroe, he'd fucked her a lot in the days that everyone was fucking her a lot, the days after she'd left the sweet cop Dougherty and before DiMaggio, the late 40s early 50s time when she was still more Norma Mortenson than Marilyn Monroe and she was just a dippy hunk with an itch and not much talent, and they'd gotten on, she'd liked his manner, he liked her build, and they'd stayed in contact through the years as he watched her madness build, all the booze and all the pills, the mandatory equipment for self-slaughter, and—

—and straight from the hospital Garvey flew down to Schwab the Slob who was talented and sick of television and they made the deal that day, Schwab to write and direct the story, but Julian would tell him what story to write and how to shape it properly, where to build, where to elongate tension. And speed, Julian said, speed must be part of this operation, for this was a picture that needed to get made and made *now*.

What's the rush for? Schwab the Slob wanted to know.

From Julian in reply: what else but his enigmatic smile . . . ?

4

"Why does it have to be Raquel Welch?" Noel asked his father as they were tooling along Sunset toward the Beverly Hills Hotel. It was shortly after noon, Friday, and they were heading for a luncheon meeting with her agent in the patio outside the Polo Lounge. "It just seems weird. You don't like her all that much, but you're just the producer. What's crazy is Schwab the Slob not only doesn't like her all that much he told me yesterday he's never even been able to sit all the way through one of her pictures. And he's got to direct the damn thing."

"I told him the day we made the deal it was going to be Miss Welch, we're all going to have to live with it."

"But is she even that big a star anymore?"

"She is in Europe, baby. She made a flick with Belmondo this year, *The Animal*, and it cleaned up. People outside the business don't understand but movies are international now. Who's Bud Spencer?"

"Never heard of him."

"Well, believe me if I tell you that Bud Spencer is bigger than Paul Newman. Worldwide. Does Terence Hill mean much to you?"

Noel shook his head.

"Terence Hill, my child, is bigger than Bud Spencer. And the two of them together are retirement money."

"Are you making these guys up?"

"They're Italian action stars, baby. They took American

names, and they don't mean much in the English-speaking world, but in Italy and France and Japan and South America and any other country you care to come up with, they are Steve McQueen. Do you know who would have been the biggest star of the 70s and was the biggest star—no question—in the world when he died? Bruce Lee."

"And we need Welch because of the foreign?"

"We really need her because our German financing, which should be set-set by the end of the week, *insists* on her. They don't know who Diane Keaton is abroad. No Welch, no deal. But there's another reason too."

"Hit me with it."

Julian glanced at his son. "You're very frisky today, aren't you?"

"It's been kind of a looney-tunes week, but not in a bad way."

"Terminal boredom has not set in?"

"What's the other reason?"

"This is not virgin territory, baby. Chayefsky kind of covered it in *The Goddess* which was a disaster at the box office. Major writer and major talent—Kim Stanley—in the lead. But one didn't want to bed down with her. *You* may not fantasize about Miss Welch, but a lot of people have in the past decade. And having her naked for the first time—that's not only commercially blockbuster, it will have a value on screen. Monroe got famous, remember, for going naked. The present and the past entangled. That gives us texture." He drove into the hotel and parked under the portico. Several uniformed boys said, "Hey, Mr. Garvey," and he politely nodded and moved on into the hotel itself.

Noel looked at his father awhile as they walked. And then he said, "Are you worried?"

"Very."

"Why?"

"Because this meeting is only crucial to our enterprise, and I didn't know that Harry Brennerman was her agent.

As far as I know he's never been remotely associated with her in the past and it's not to our advantage that he is for this particular project."

"Is he a crook?"

"If only he were we'd be home free, my darling. He is a bore and a plodder. But he is honest and cannot, absolutely *cannot* be bullshitted." Julian paused at the entrance to the Polo Lounge. "Also, he hates me. For reasons you're too young to understand."

The maitre d' led them along and Garvey, preoccupied, made only a few quick smiles as he passed the filled green booths. Ordinarily he could take ten minutes to run the gauntlet, but now he didn't once pause. Just followed along to the booth in the rear of the patio where Brennerman waited.

"My son Noel," Julian began.

Before they were even seated, Brennerman said, "Keed, I've read this *Tinsel* and I'm not so sure we can do business."

Julian looked at Noel. "Mr. Brennerman is famous in the industry for beating around the bush." He looked at Brennerman now. "We're going to do business, Harry, and we both know it. You could have said no on the phone. I know you're washed up in town, but you can't have sunk so low you'd endure an hour of me for a free lunch."

Brennerman turned to Noel now. "I've known your old man since he hit town. We worked MCA together in the 40s. 'Silver-tongue' I used to call him." He winked at Garvey. "Right, keed?"

"You always had a gift for imagery, Harry."

They ordered drinks first. Brennerman took a vodka gimlet, his drink even before *The Long Goodbye*. Noel took a Virgin Mary, Julian a Perrier with lime.

As soon as the waiter left, Brennerman said, "I'm getting director approval or there's no deal."

"Miss Welch is one of God's glories, Harry; and she has been a major figure in the industry for fifteen years. But where is it written that she always must get director approval?" He paused. "Do you mind if I explain something to Noel, he's thinking of learning the business?"

Brennerman shrugged, ate a breadstick.

"There are, remember, no secrets in the business. Harry knows exactly what she has gotten, and he knows I know exactly what she has gotten. The trick is, he doesn't know how badly I want her, and I don't know if she is particularly interested in the project. So it's a matter of probing. Am I clear?"

Noel shrugged eventually.

Brennerman said, "I'm not a hard-nosed type fella. I'll withdraw my demand for approval. I'll just insist on an experienced director, how's that?"

"Does television experience count?"

"Not even in horseshoes."

"Well, then you're asking the same thing as approval, aren't you Harry, since you know I'm morally committed to Robert Schwab directing his own screenplay."

Brennerman stared around the room. "Something crazy's going on," he said. "Julian Garvey hid behind a moral commitment and the walls are still standing."

"Are you suggesting I fuck my own son-in-law, Harry? May your bleeding ulcer shift into overdrive."

"Silver-tongue; I love this guy."

Noel nodded, made a quick smile.

"Shall we come back to this point, Harry? Perhaps move into some areas of agreement?"

"It's not gonna evaporate, keed."

Their drinks came. Julian sipped his Perrier while Noel toyed with his Virgin Mary. Brennerman downed his gimlet, signaled for another. "Do you want to begin with a discussion of salary or move up to it?"

"It's not gonna evaporate, keed."

Julian took out his reminder pad from his inside suit pocket. "I assume she would like her choice of still cameraman."

"Of course. And hairdresser and stand-in and make-up."

"Fine," Julian said. "What about a bodyguard?"

"Not necessary for a studio shoot. On location, of course."

"Car and driver?"

"Twenty-four hours a day. Caddy limo. I'll take a Lincoln. Mercedes. Whatever."

"Two thousand living expenses should be satisfactory."

"Gotta work in cost of living, keed. Twenty-five hundred will be even more satisfactory."

Garvey made a note. "All right, Harry—now about salary—"

"—Julian, I'm not going to allow my client to go into a dicey project like this with an inexperienced director, now believe that."

"The boy's won an Emmy—"

"—he may be Ingmar Bergman, I hope for your sake he is Ingmar Bergman, but this is a delicate operation that could turn into pornography, it could be a genuine career destroyer if it goes sour, you know it and I know it, and there's not much point in not facing up to it now. I want someone whose taste I can check out from a track record. I'm sorry, but there it is."

"Harry—"

"—let the boy debut his next time out, Julian—"

"—he would never have written it without my promise that this was his shot—"

"—a broken promise has never made you blink in the past, Julian—"

"Harry, I want her—I won't consider any other actress just as I won't consider any other director—she's a major talent and this can alter her career and it has always been one of my ambitions to work with her—"

"—cut the bullshit!" Brennerman said, as his second vodka gimlet arrived.

Quietly Julian Garvey said, "It is not tactful to call a bullshitter a bullshitter, Harry."

"You don't want my client for her talent—you've probably got some deal where she's lumped into the financing—"

"—the financing is not your area of expertise, Harry, so keep your very evident nose out of my business. The fact is I think your client is a brilliant performer—"

"—signal for a check, Julian, I can't stand your lying." He turned to Noel. "I'm sorry you were here for this. Sometimes we actually behave like humans."

"He was bullshitting you," Noel Garvey said then. "You were right, Mr. Brennerman, my father doesn't think she can act all that wonderfully—"

"—that's enough, Noel!" Julian said.

"—but Mr. Brennerman, please—"

"—Noel," Julian said with more heat. "That is really quite enough from you."

Noel reached out then and took Harry Brennerman's hand. "You've got to do this one thing, Mr. Brennerman, and I'm begging you, please—give my brother-in-law a chance—let him meet Miss Welch, let them be together in a room, that's all I ask—give him his chance in court, Mr. Brennerman, because he *is* talented and he *is* going to be a major figure out here but most of all, he is the greatest fan of Raquel Welch in the world so help me God."

Harry Brennerman said nothing.

"And I don't mean just as a beauty, everybody admits that; no, he thinks that she's a rare and special talent and that's why he's been working on this *Tinsel* for her for over seven years, off and on."

Brennerman sipped his vodka gimlet.

Noel looked at his father. "Daddy, do you remember when I was in the hospital? The one outside Saigon?"

Julian nodded.

"I was broken up kind of bad, Mr. Brennerman, and this was five-six years ago now, and my only interest, all that really kept me ahead of the pain—"

"—oh, shit, you got shot up bad, that's right—" Brennerman said.

"—it wasn't rifle fire, it doesn't matter what it was, I was hurting, and these letters from home were all I had to concentrate on and Schwabby was really terrific, he wrote me a lot, as if nothing specially bad had happened to me, and it was show-business stuff—I've got them still, I'll show you the letters someday—and it was during these letters that he first started talking about this thing he was writing called *Tinsel* for Miss Welch, because he saw her in *Bedazzled* and he said, My God, she's just like Monroe before *Bus Stop*, all people see is the beauty, nobody's shown the vulnerability yet, and he's been to everything she's ever made since then, and he's in this fear that he won't get his shot at showing the world what he knows is true, that what happened to Keaton this year can happen to Miss Welch next, and of course you're right to want a man with experience, Mr. Brennerman, but no man alive has the conviction about her talents that Bobby Schwab has and at least let them be together in a room."

Brennerman sipped his drink in silence. Finally he said to Noel, "Okay, I'll set up the meeting." He looked at Julian. "If your son-in-law is half as convincing as your son, we may have a movie after all."

"Life is full of surprises," Julian Garvey said. . . .

III

PIG

1

"You're hurting them!" Pig cried out in the darkness.

"Sorry," Johnny said, trying hard to hold her as she twisted her body sharply so that her breasts were no longer near his mouth.

Pig moved to the edge of the round bed and got into a sitting position, feet on the carpeted floor, feeling her right nipple. It really hurt and she could not avoid the quick intake of breath.

He rolled toward the sound, reached out, found her body, began stroking it again. "Carried away by the moment, Pig."

"Tishlubb," Pig replied, a Santa Monica word from her childhood, "bullshit" spelled backwards, only you had to cheat a little to make it come out right. She stood then, getting away from his soft hands.

"What are you saying, I meant to hurt you?"

Pig let her silence be her answer, because there was no point to going into it more deeply, at least not now. But she had known before they started lovemaking it wasn't going to be one of your more magical interludes. He was always rough when things weren't going just so, and less than an hour before, twenty-six floors down, he had blown fifteen thousand at the roulette table in less than half an hour. She started across the bedroom toward where she remembered the bathroom was, except the place was so damn big that even after a week of living there, she still got lost at night.

The best suites in Vegas, the very best suites, were not for rent. Most of the time they stood empty, awaiting high rollers. Whenever Johnny Small came to the Grand, he got one of the six top suites, usually the Ben Hur, with the multicolored Roman decor. He came every couple of months, played mostly roulette with a little 21 thrown in, quit when he'd lost around fifty, left with handshakes, tips, and smiles all around.

Pig found the bathroom door and a moment later flicked on the light switch. She blinked at the sudden brightness, blinked longer than most people, because her pale blue eyes were always sensitive. Then she walked to the full length mirror and slowed, studying her famous bosom. Her breasts, never less than thumping, were almost silly now, what with her period only a day or two away. Always at this time Pig thought she resembled nothing so much as a Schmoo.

Carefully, with both hands cradling her right breast, she raised it slightly so she could study the pink nipple. It was, thank God, not bleeding; but it was still sore, so when Johnny appeared behind her, she was in no mood for much of a reconciliation.

Neither was he. "What are you saying, I meant to hurt you?"

"Snooze," Pig said.

"You're really fucking weird."

"He loves me," Pig said.

"Why do you always refer to your tits as 'they' or 'them'? You make it out like they're past participles or indirect objects."

"Gee, I love the word 'tits' a lot. It really lets me know you respect me." She brushed past his thin naked body, handed him a towel. "Please; cover yourself—I can see your *whang*. Your *dong* is visible, Johnny," and she headed out into the semidarkness for the living room far beyond.

"Where you going?" she heard from behind her.

Pig kept on the move.

"Christ, Pig, don't do this, I apologized, didn't I?"

Pig whirled. "You called me 'fucking weird' and since when does that constitute an apology?"

"Well, you knew I meant I was sorry."

For a moment she almost slowed, because he was truth-telling now. Apologizing was very hard for Johnny. He had been very big very recently and sometimes his ego still got in the way. But he had been malicious with her in the sack, chomping down on them all under the guise of passion, so she decided to let him suffer awhile longer.

She entered the living room as behind her she could hear him getting back into the round bed with the round mirror above it in the ceiling. Pig closed the living room door good and hard, to let him know he wasn't winning, and turned on the lamp by the oversized sofa.

Then she reached for her copy of *Who's Who in Baseball* and began, happily, to read.

This was the sixty-third edition, covering the current year, 1978, and it was new, the pages still stiff and clean. By the time the Series came, her copy would be dog-eared, torn beyond use. Pig licked her index finger and turned to her three favorites, James Augustus (Catfish) Hunter, Stanley (Steamer) Higgins, not to mention Albert Walter (Sparky) Lyle, and began to commit their new lifetime marks to memory.

Johnny came running naked into the room, wild with excitement. "I know why I lost!"

Pig looked up from her baseball stats. "Huh?"

He dropped to his knees by the couch. "At roulette, my God, just now at the effing tables, you were there."

"You lost 'cause you bet the wrong numbers, Johnny."

"Obviously, but *which* numbers was I betting and *why*?"

Pig was good at remembering that kind of thing. "You blew it on twenty-seven and thirty-one but I don't know why."

"Birthdays, Piglet—those were birthdays—the two greatest songwriters that ever lived, Schubert and Mozart, don't you see?"

Pig didn't.

"I was betting *their* birthdays because I wanted *their* luck. I should have been betting nine, Pig. Nine's *my* birthday, and *I'm* the only one can bring my luck back, praying to Mozart for help or Franz ain't gonna do it. Now do you see?"

Pig didn't.

Johnny handed over a ton of bills.

"What's this for?" Pig said, not taking them.

"Listen carefully now—a mistake could be fatal—we're talking about my future, Pig, and how my life is going to change back to its old and proper course—this nine hundred dollars must be taken immediately down to the casino where one must carefully go to the ninth roulette wheel one passes—not the eighth or the tenth, only the ninth will do—and then a hundred dollars must be bet on number nine for nine consecutive times."

"Good luck," Pig said, and she went back to *Who's Who in Baseball.*

"You've got to do this for me, Pig."

"Oh, come on, I don't gamble, I'd probably goof it."

"Please. I can't."

"Sure you can."

"I can't and you damn well know it!"

Pig knew what was coming now.

"I just can't take everybody bugging me right now." He put the money in her hand and stood, walking to the bar way across the enormous room.

Pig watched him. He was six feet tall but looked more, because he was so emaciated, and she sometimes wondered where his strength came from, the overabundant energy.

He opened the icebox and rummaging around in it said, "You've got to save me from the hassle, won't you at least do that?"

Moved, as she always was at this, Pig said, "Sure," carefully took the money, put down her statistics annual, and stood. "I'll just throw on some things."

"Let me check you out before you go."

Pig nodded and left, heading for her closet. Her own preference in clothes ran to ordinary jeans and loose cotton tops but in the year she'd been with Johnny, all that had been put aside. Pig put on seamless pantyhose and kind of a no-bra bra, which gave her a little support—she didn't need much—so that when she wore blouses or sweaters, it appeared she was not wearing undergarments at all and accounted for what Johnny favorably referred to as her ladylike jiggle. She picked baby blue for color, took out the silk blouse and the matching slacks she had to lie down to pull on, and the high-heeled sandals which, when her hair was even reasonably teased, made her six feet tall.

Pig did a final tuck-in job on the blouse, looked at herself in the mirror, shrugged, and went back to the living room. Johnny was sitting naked in a chair in the half-darkness far from the couch lamp. He was playing his guitar, chording in that way he had. Pig pirouetted. "Do I pass or what?"

He was very nervous. He watched her a long time before he said, "This is very important, you know that."

Pig did and said so.

"Everything rests with you; it all changes when you win."

"Tishlubb."

"It's all gonna change, Pig."

"Okay, okay. Just trying to lighten the atmosphere."

He studied her. "Turn around one more time slow."

She followed orders, knowing he was going to say, "That's mine" or some variation, which probably wouldn't please the feminists much, but what the hell.

"Son of a bitch, that belongs to *me*."

Pig made a Japanese curtsey of obedience, turned, headed for the suite door.

"Hey?" from behind her.

"Quoi?" from Pig, who knew ten words of French.

"I shouldn't have bit you."

With the door half open, Pig said, "Goddamn right you shouldn't—I mean, I'm getting to be maybe the world's oldest groupie, I deserve a little respect," and she flashed her smile for him, closed the door and let the smile die. Heading for the elevator bank, she wondered only how bad he was going to take it when she lost.

Probably very. That was pretty much the way he was taking everything lately. But Pig really couldn't find it in her heart to be too hard on him. Considering.

Every year there's someone in pop music who sells more records than anybody. Today it's the Bee Gees and a decade ago it was Herb Alpert and in between there's been Carole King and Simon and Garfunkel and Cash, Denver, and Diamond but none of them skyrocketed quite like Johnny Small. He'd been a successful songwriter for a number of years—"Today Is Just Yesterday Tomorrow" had been top ten for the Fifth Dimension and "That Was Then, This Is Now" had gone all the way to the top in Streisand's version.

Then Clive Davis, in one of the last hunches he played at Columbia before his fall, had Johnny record the Streisand hit himself, and when it was ready for release, finagled Johnny a spot on a Glen Campbell special where he sang it.

Every twelve-year-old girl in America went crazy.

It was clearly a freak occurrence, and nobody knew how long it would last, but everybody knew why it was happening which was obviously the contrast between how Johnny looked and how he sounded.

Physically he was so thin as to seem clearly a victim of *anorexia nervosa,* and his eyes were deeply set and shadowed, haunted eyes. There was nothing haunted about the voice. It was, as *Rolling Stone* wrote in their review of his first album, a voice that belonged in Robert Mitchum's body. A rough baritone, big and commanding, blatant and strong.

Johnny's first album, with just two words on it, *Small* and *Giant*, went gold inside a month. His second album, just four months later, *Titan*, shipped platinum. Columbia knew they had something that was selling like crazy so they sold it, pumping out tunes by Johnny Small, and inside fifteen months after his appearance on the Campbell show, Johnny earned seven million dollars, sold out Madison Square Garden three nights running, won two Grammys plus an Emmy for his own tv special.

The next year he earned half of what he'd done previous, his second tv show with a different director/writer stiffed in the ratings. He still sold out his personal appearances but that softened the third year. Johnny pulled out of them once that happened. His last albums were, as they say in the trade, "disappointments." He had earned a lot of money, had kept an enormous amount of it, was rich for life. He still made plenty from his catalogue, but it was different and gone and everybody knew and accepted that fact.

Not Johnny.

He still had a chauffeured Mercedes to take him around, and he traveled in a private jet. More often than not when he went to dinner he had a bodyguard along. And on occasion he sent his mistress out to make crazy bets for him, because he couldn't bear the hassle of the crowd. . . .

Pig entered the casino as quickly and surreptitiously as she could and started noting the roulette tables she walked by, keeping careful count, and she was past the third before a bunch of soldiers began tracking her one aisle across and she was at the fifth when the old fart from Oklahoma who'd tried propositioning her by the pool the other morning moved into her path saying softly that he'd really like to fuck her and Pig smiled and thanked him, promising him they absolutely would as soon as he grew a penis and two more guys made moves in her direction but she picked up the step, made it to the ninth table which was, thank God, busy with just one seat open so she sank into it, opened her purse, took out the nine hundred dollars.

The wheel was already in spin and Pig watched as the ball slowed, praying that nine wouldn't come up a winner because Johnny would never forgive her if she'd been too slow.

The ball dropped into double zero briefly, bounded, and landed finally in twelve, directly across the wheel from the nine.

Was that a sign? Pig wondered. You couldn't do worse than twelve, it was 180 degrees wrong. Maybe what she should do is get up and go back to the Ben Hur Suite and explain that the ninth table she passed was closed and rather than settle for a substitute she decided not to bet at all. She played the scene briefly through, realized it would only anger him more, and her right nipple was sore enough as it was.

"A hundred dollars please on the nine," Pig said, giving the money to the lady dealer who spoke quickly to the pit boss standing behind her, who nodded. The lady dealer gave Pig some chips and while Pig placed the bet, she took the ball in her right hand, the wheel in her left, spun the wheel counterclockwise, tossed the ball the reverse direction, and then everybody waited.

This time the ball landed in double zero and stayed there.

"Will you give the wheel a decent goddam spin," an angry man to Pig's right said.

The whole table was angry; double zero was nobody's friend.

"A hundred on the nine please," Pig said.

"Just place your bet," the dealer said.

"Sorry," Pig said. She hated roulette, always had.

"It's very stupid betting so much on one number," a drunk woman to Pig's left told her.

"I guess it is," Pig said, watching as the dealer spun the wheel, harder, it seemed than before.

Seventeen won. Closer to nine by half. But still many numbers away.

The man to her right won on seventeen. "You see what

happens when you spin it good?" he said to the lady dealer.
He bet seventeen again while Pig put her hundred on nine.

Nine won.

"Holy shit," Pig said as the lady dealer gave her thirty-
five hundred dollars in chips.

Pig put the fourth hundred on nine.

The woman on her left reached out and took her hand.
"I realize that you are winning whereas I am behind at the
moment, but please don't bet that number again. The odds
are one thousand four hundred and forty-four to one
against it coming up two times in a row."

Pig hesitated. "What do you think I should switch to?"

"I feel confident about fifteen," the lady said. She was
even drunker than Pig thought at first, but still and all,
very well mannered and she spoke distinctly.

Pig put her hundred on fifteen, then, at the last moment, switched back to nine.

Nine won again.

"Cocksucker," the lady on her left said. She glared at
Pig. "You are living in shit."

"I'm sorry about fifteen," Pig said, as the lady dealer
gave her her winnings and a container to put them in.

Pig put the next hundred on nine.

The drunk lady did the same.

Fifteen won.

"I don't find this fucking funny," the drunk lady said.

Pig just put the next hundred on the nine, but it didn't
win, didn't even come close. It came close the next spin,
but it didn't win again until the eighth time. The lady
dealer gave Pig a larger container and Pig bet the last
hundred without paying much attention because what she
wanted to do was just scream with excitement but she
couldn't because she felt so guilty since the drunk lady to
her left had started to cry.

Twenty-two came up a winner and Pig said, "Thank
God" almost out loud and hurried across the casino floor
to the cashier's window and handed in her chips. The
gentleman inside counted awhile and then said, "I get ten

thousand five hundred, does that check out with you?" and Pig said, "Fine, fine," and when he asked how she wanted it Pig told him that hundreds would be fine and when he handed them over she didn't bother seeing if he was right or not, she just shoved the bundle into her purse and headed fast for the elevator banks.

There was an empty waiting so she got right in and pushed the top floor and half a minute later she was hurrying down the corridor toward the Ben Hur Suite and just before she put her key in she tried for a Sense Memory, got it right off, and then she unlocked the door and moved inside, going in a very soft voice, "Honey, I tried just so hard."

The living room was empty.

Pig heard the guitar sounds coming from the bedroom then. He was chording "That Was Then, This Is Now" quietly, and she went in and saw him sitting there in dim light, naked, on the round bed beneath the round mirror. "Honey, I tried just so hard," Pig managed.

He stared at her.

The words poured out. "I wanted it you'll never know how much, Johnny, but we put our money on the wrong number, fifteen is the number that won, twice fifteen came up and this drunk lady sitting on my left she won a fortune practically and when I was leaving she said how stupid I was betting a number like nine and I asked her why she kept on with fifteen and she said she always bet fifteen because it was the year Liberace was born." Pig paused, shaking her head. "We shouldda bet Liberace, Johnny."

"Bet Liberace?" he exploded, standing suddenly in the center of the bed, gripping his guitar by the throat. "I don't bet Liberace—I went to the Juilliard fucking School of Music, I don't make asshole bets on candelabra freaks. . . ." His voice drained then and he shook his head. "You mean we didn't win anything? Not anything at all?"

"You never listen to me sometimes, what do you think I've been saying."

He sat back down on the bed again. "I just felt it so strong, we must have won a little."

"Oh Johnny, Christ I tried, I wanted it so bad for you."

He stared at her for a long time. "You must have done it wrong."

"No, I swear I did it perfect."

"You never were any goddam good at following instructions—"

"—I did what you said exactly, you gotta believe that, I took the nine hundred dollars and I bet the number nine, nine straight times. I sat right down at the first table I came to just like you said. I've got a head on my shoulders when it comes to numbers, you know that."

He tried for a smile. "You're very sweet, Pig; but it was supposed to be the ninth table, not the first."

"You mean I goofed? I feel just so horrible."

He was hard to hear now. "Listen, it doesn't matter, we would have lost anyway."

"You're not mad at me or anything?"

He barely shook his head no.

Since it was clear things weren't going the way she'd wanted, she quick took out the bundle of bills, waved them around.

He watched her.

"We won three times, dopey. Here." She handed the money over.

He sat as before.

"Lazybones," Pig said and she placed the money carefully into his hands.

He just sat there, deeply and terribly moved.

"You wanna go out or anything? Celebrate maybe?"

He didn't much.

"So we'll stay right here then?"

That was more or less the plan.

"You're not drugged, are you? You didn't take any stuff while I was downstairs?"

He'd promised her he wouldn't, hadn't he? And he

never went back on a promise. Or as rarely as possible.

"I'll just get comfy then," Peg said, anxious to leave him alone for a little. She undressed quickly, dropping her blouse over a chair arm, kicking her slacks toward a sofa, coming pretty close. Her undergarments she left in various spots as she headed for the bathroom, poured some bubble-bath powder over the drain, spun the spigots on full. Then she got in and soaked lazily, got out eventually and started toweling off, moving quietly to the doorway so that she could get a peek into the bedroom.

"Get in here."

"In a sec."

"Now."

"When I'm dry, gimme—"

"—Pig, move it!"

"Okay, okay," she said, wondering what was up now, but she couldn't tell much from his face as he lay on the bed watching her approach.

"Pitch the towel."

She let it fall.

"Come lie down."

"I'm still wet."

"Flat, I want you. Legs together, arms at your sides."

Pig squinted. When he said for her to lie down, she thought he wanted a little action, but not in that position. Still she followed orders, lay straight, staring up at her body reflected in the glass.

Johnny knelt alongside her.

"What are you up to?"

"Shut up. Don't move. I mean it." He began slowly, starting at her ankles, to cover her with hundred-dollar bills.

"Oh cut this—" She started to sit.

He pushed her back down. "Move one more time you're in big trouble." He strung the bills in a row up each leg. "Some supergroup did this once, I think the Mamas and the Papas after their first big payday. I've been wanting to ever since I heard about it. I always wondered if it was a turn-on." He carefully took bill after bill from the stack, placing it above and touching the one next to it, and when he reached her vagina he started putting the bills across her body, at right angles to the single green lines up her legs.

"I'll tell you, Johnny, it doesn't do a whole lot for me, does it do anything—" She stopped then because he was getting an erection. "Is this a perversion do you think?"

"Nothing's a perversion if you only do it once." He knelt closer now, making even green rows across her stomach, concentrating fully on his task until he went, "Shit" as the telephone rang.

"Yeah," Johnny said into the receiver, and then a second later he was shouting, "Schwab the Slob!" A moment after that he said, "What the fuck's *Tinsel*?" Johnny listened some, then said, "Well, if you wrote it, it's gotta be moronic and tasteless and that's just the good scenes."

"Can I move?" Pig whispered.

He waved her quiet.

"I've gotta sneeze."

He shook his head no and said, "Sure, I'll talk to you about it, come on up tomorrow morning, what plane, I'll have my lady meet you. The nine Western, you got a deal. Just please do me a favor and bathe before you come." He hung up, turned back to Pig, shaking his head happily.

"What was all that?"

"The writer/director who did my first special—the one that got the Emmys—he wants me to do an original score for a picture he's got."

"Will you?"

"I'll sure listen." And then he was shouting out loud, "The wheel is always in spin, don't forget that, never you forget it, huh?"

"You talking to me?" Pig asked.

"To them," Johnny answered, and he nodded toward her breasts. Before he covered them with money, he bent slowly down and kissed her right nipple.

Gently.

2

Pig, wearing her white bathing cap and Speedo goggles, swam around and around the Grand Hotel pool. She had a powerful four-beat flutter kick and her right arm pull was fine but her left was never quite as strong as she wanted it. The giant pool was otherwise empty. No one was around except for the lifeguards who were stacking towels and unstacking deck chairs and generally getting ready for the ten o'clock morning opening. Pig always got down a little after nine because that way she could get her daily half mile in fast, without having to worry about bumping into a lot of kids. And nobody bugged her, either, no Chevy executives on the lam for a week from their wives or suntanned singles from San Francisco who figured they were God's gift. Johnny *schtupped* the head lifeguard a bundle each trip so that she could get her exercise alone.

As she switched to the backstroke—which she didn't like doing but someone had once told her it gave a stronger workout to your pectorals—one of the girl lifeguards waved at her. Pig stood in the shallow end, pulled her bathing cap loose so she could hear. "You said to tell you when it was coming up nine-thirty," the girl said.

"Thanks," Pig nodded, walking out of the pool, grabbing her beach robe, throwing it around her, hurrying toward the hotel then down along the corridor past all the shops to the elevators.

Johnny was all scrunched up in the round bed when she

got to the suite, his arms clutching a pillow. Pig dropped the robe on the floor, shook him with her foot, saying, "I'm off for the airport to get this Schwab, better wake up."

She moved to her closet, picked the peach ensemble that Johnny liked her to travel in, grabbed a bra, struggled in, started buttoning the silk blouse over it.

Johnny was asleep again so she gave him another boot, then lay across the bed as she slid her way into the slacks. That woke him finally, and once she was sure, Pig ran her hands through her hair a couple of times, put on one pair of sandals, decided they were the ones that hurt, kicked them across the room, found another pair and her purse, and left the suite on the fly for the front of the hotel where the limousine driver was sure enough waiting. He made it to McCarran in no time and Pig got out after telling him to wait, it wouldn't be long, and then she ran inside, checked the proper gate, got there two minutes before the ten o'clock arrival.

Bleep, Pig thought when she saw that the plane was late. "How late?" she asked a Western guy.

He looked at her for too long a moment before he said, "Ten, maybe fifteen minutes."

You like Vegas so far? Pig predicted to herself before the guy said, "So how do you like Vegas?"

She shrugged, decided not to make a smile, walked nervously away from the arrival gate looking for a corner to nestle down in. She knew from long experience that when she was waiting she was in trouble; when she could keep on the move, she was all right, it was hard for people to hit on her. There were some chairs with a view out toward the flat field and the flat desert beyond, and she headed for them, but before she got there she could see the Shriner type moving alongside. You look like a lady who'd like a little fun, Pig predicted, as the paunchy man smiled, shrugged the shoulders of his polyester jacket, and went, "First time in Vegas?"

"Naw," Pig told him, "me and my husband come here

all the time when he's not wrestling," and that stopped him good, at least good enough for her to get to the chairs and sit staring by herself toward the smog-covered mountains, wondering if the day was ever going to come when people would leave her at last the hell alone.

She was just one of those California blondes.

Her coloring came from her mother, known always as The Finn, after her nation of origin. The Finn worked as a script girl at Metro and was, in all ways, punctual and precise.

Her size and athletic ability were a likely inheritance from The Vampire, her father, and so-named because he was one of the best special-effects men ever to work at Paramount and whose forte was blood. Eventually he fell in with Hitchcock when the master shifted over from Warners, and the responsibility for much of the gore for everything from *Rear Window* through *Psycho* was the direct result of that collaboration.

Pig herself was just plain Patsy Higgins until she was five.

Then one Saturday her mother simply could not tolerate the mess in her room any longer and said, in that distinct way she had, "Your name should not be Miss Higgins, you know, it really ought more properly to be Piggins and that is what I shall call you whenever I find your room in similar disarray."

She was Miss Piggins from then on, the inevitable shortening process bringing it within a year down to its final form. Pig was clean, she just wasn't tidy. There simply wasn't *time* to be tidy, not if you wanted to make it out to the Santa Monica beach after school and then in from there to get your baseball glove and out to the back yard with one-year-younger brother Stan. She was much the better athlete in those days, the one who followed the Pacific Coast League as if it were the Majors.

They lived in a nice enough house on the wrong end of Kingman and spent a lot of time, grudgingly, at Metro or

Paramount. Both kids hated it, being around the studios, because unless you have something to do there is no place more boring. They used to take baseball mitts when they were seven and eight and Pig would make Stan play catch with her on some deserted back lot street or other.

Movies had no romance for either of them, since what they heard day in day out was always technical. Gable had not hit his marks and had lifted a glass with the wrong hand and ruined a take or Elisha Cook, Jr., had moved too quickly before Jack Palance had a chance to fire and the blood had spurted too soon; shoptalk.

Pig had given Stan his nickname when they were nine and ten, and his astounding southpaw power was just beginning to make itself known. He was firing the ball harder and harder now, and it hurt sometimes as she knelt to catch his stuff. Feller, they wrote in all the papers, threw smoke. Stan, Pig said one night at dinner, threw steam, because she had seen a picture of the old car in a magazine once, and her memory was always remarkable. Stan became the Stanley Steamer from then on, Steamer alone, once he made it to high school.

In 1957, when Pig was a fourteen-year-old freshman, she stood close to five eight and weighed an even one hundred thirty pounds. Her hair, fresh from a summer of surfing, was long and white blonde and her eyes, set off by her tan, were never as baby blue. Her skin was clear, her profile clean, her measurements 35-22-38 reading, thank God, from bottom to top.

She didn't have a whole lot of girlfriends.

Rumor had it that she was either a lesbian or the town pump or both. And shatteringly stupid. The facts were that she was a rather healthy virgin who got A's. This last bothered her a little. She knew what people said about her, and she really couldn't help her figure, it just happened and if you were a health nut who exercised constantly, it would probably continue to happen. But it seemed logical that she should be stupid. Dumb blondes were a great American tradition and she didn't even like school. So her grades made her guilty, which she handled by deciding that she wasn't smart, just lucky, she was able to outguess her teachers about what they'd ask on tests, they were right, the other girls were right, she was stupid after all. Or if not stupid, then undeserving.

But the bottom line was it really didn't matter what the other girls said. Or what anybody said, not that particular year. Because in the last spring of '58 the Dodgers were moving to town.

Over seventy-eight thousand fans flooded the Coliseum to see the first home game, in April against the Giants. Pig and the Steamer listened to Vince Scully doing the play by play, and it seemed almost too much to bear. Pig knew every Dodger stat of value and the Steamer was already a local phenom, even though he wasn't much over thirteen. He stood six feet and weighed in at 165 and nobody ever dug in on him at the plate because not only was he Koufax fast, he was southpaw wild. And best of all, as they sat transfixed by the radio, was the knowledge that in early June, less than two months off, the mighty Braves of Milwaukee, the World Champeens, were coming in and The Vampire already had tickets for the family. Aaron would be there, Hank the Hammer, and handsome Eddie Matthews and Spahn and Burdette, all of them sleek and ready to face Duke and Moon and his moon shots and Sandy and Johnny and Don.

Pig never got to go.

The day before the June game, her mother simply bowed her neck and would not give to pressure. Pig's room was beyond description and there had been a deal—the room was to be "suitable" for a week prior to game time or no game.

"It's suitable," Pig wailed. "Please please please."

"Let the kid for chrissakes go," The Vampire said.

The Steamer put in a good word for his big sister too.

But The Finn was having none of it. "Suitable, in this case, was agreed upon to mean that shoes would be in closets, clothes would be in drawers or neatly spaced on hangers. If you will look in the child's room you will see that the bedspread is not visible beneath the debris. There are sneakers on her desk, three sneakers I might add, not four, not two, and one moist bathing suit is drying on a bedpost. I'm sorry, but that is not and never will be, suitable."

The night of the game they left her alone in the house and drove off. Pig knew for sure they'd circle around and come back.

They didn't.

Pig wept for an hour and was good for a great deal longer, but Spencer T. Murtaugh came knocking at the door. Spencer (*everybody* in Santa Monica, it seemed, was named after *somebody*) Murtaugh was, from Pig's point of view, almost too beautiful to be real. He was the best surfer in sophomore class, and the best baseball player in the school. He had gone to bed with, according to reputation, not only all the cheerleaders in town, but over half of the girls who spurred on Beverly Hills High. He stood six three, weighed one ninety-five, and had the darkest tan in Santa Monica.

"Who is it?" Pig called from her upstairs bedroom.

"Puh?" came the answer. "Puh? Puh?" Then, finally, gratefully, "Pig?"

He also stuttered.

Pig dried her eyes. "Oh, hey, Spence. Hi." She started down then stopped suddenly, because why had he come now, when she looked all puffy and red. "One sec," she called to him, then ran back to her room, waded through the debris to the bathroom, and looked at her face in the mirror.

Not so hot.

But there wasn't much she could do on short notice, other than grab for her largest pair of sunglasses and push them up tight. Barefooted, she went downstairs and looked at him through the screen door. He was wearing faded khakis cut off at the knee and his T-shirt was slung casually over one shoulder.

He should be made *illegal*, Pig thought, as she opened
the door and said, "What brings you a-callin' " as casually
as she could.

He pointed toward her sunglasses. Spence did that a lot.
Pointed at things. Anything to avoid the speech thing.

"The doctor thinks I may be getting some kind of pink-
eye," Pig said, wondering why he had come by now, what
had she done that day to at last bring him around. They
had been in the same group surfing the weekend before
and she'd worn her new white two-piece. Probably that
was it.

"Kuh—kuh—can I see the Steamer? Guh—guh—got to
have a tuh-talk."

Shit, Pig thought. Ordinarily she never thought slang,
only *bleep*, a word her mother allowed, the *only* word her
mother allowed, but right now she wasn't all that high on
her mother. Shit shit shit, why didn't he come to see ME?
"Whole family went to the Milwaukee game."

He nodded.

"Can I get you anything?"

He shook his head.

"Me, I'm in the mood for a Coke," Pig said then. "Sure
you won't join me?"

He shrugged, followed her to the kitchen. "Guh-guess
you'll keep your room kuh-kuh—neat from now on."

"How do you want your Coke?" Pig said when they
stood in the small room. Her tone was idle but she was
watching him closer now.

"Wuh-wuh wuh-hat do you mee—?"

"I mean with lemon or lime or just plain old ice or
how?"

"Luh-luh—"

"Coke with lemon coming right up."

"Don't duh-do that."

"Do what, Spence?"

"Fuh-finish my suh-sentences."

Way to win somebody, Pig told herself, saying quickly
that she was sorry, really sorry. She smiled at him, figuring

he couldn't be *too* angry at her since she could tell from the bulge in his khaki shorts that he was getting an erection. She turned quickly toward the icebox, saw there were no cold Cokes, grabbed a lemon and an icetray, then went to the pantry and grabbed a couple of bottles from the half-full case on the floor, moved to the sink, opened the bottles, took down glasses, and turned on the hot water so that the ice cubes would come out easier. Her back was to him when he slammed his body up against hers and his hands went around and up under her blouse toward her breasts as he said, "I luh-luh-love you so much, Puh-Pig, I've always luh-loved you," and she knew it was tishlubb but so was what she came back with: "Oh Spence, you must stop this, I thought you had respect for me, Spence, I'm not one of those, I'm not what you think, I'm asking you as a friend, Spence, you must stop this now," and he went, "Oh yes, duh-deep love is wuh-what I feel," and he was roughly massaging her breasts but as she started to turn toward him he abruptly let go and his hands went to his trousers and he was half bent over saying, very loudly, "Oh no, no, son of a bitch shit Jesus," and then he was as embarrassed as anyone Pig had ever seen and he whirled and ran out to his car and was gone.

She learned two things that night and that was the first —she could make men come with her breasts.

She cleaned up the kitchen, put the Cokes back—she never drank them except for social reasons, they weren't healthy, and if you took care of your body now, it would take care of you later, at least that's what Adelle Davis always wrote and—

—and did that just happen, was he here, Spencer Murtaugh? Forget about Adelle Davis, what about him? Did he always behave that way with girls? Had he had an embarrassed orgasm in front of all those cheerleaders at Beverly Hills High? Doubtful, Pig decided. I don't think he's experienced at all.

She wandered out of the kitchen and slowly up to her room. It really was messy. She pushed the clothes from the bed onto the floor and lay down. What a few minutes that had been, what a lot to think about, Spencer Murtaugh here and gone. Pig reached out to her bedside radio and listened to Vince Scully describe Koufax escaping barely in the third. He had just the most wonderful voice. The man she wanted to marry should look like Spencer Murtaugh and sound like Vince Scully. Pig rolled up on one elbow and surveyed her room.

It was a zoo.

She sighed, got up, picked everything from the floor, everything on her desk and dresser top, all the clothes scattered in corners, dumped it all on her bed, and began to fold things neatly into piles. By the bottom of the sixth, the room was almost perfect.

That was when Spencer returned.

"What do *you* want, Mr. Murtaugh," Pig said from the top of the stairs. "I would think you'd be too ashamed to come back around here." She hoped she didn't sound too severe.

"I am—kuh-can I come in?"

"To assault me again? No thank you, Mr. Murtaugh, you can say whatever you have to say from just where you are."

"Puh—puh—please."

Pig hesitated for what she hoped was a tormenting amount of time before going oh all right.

He was wearing a clean white shirt now, and jeans and loafers, and his long hair was partially combed. He looked up at her from the front door. "You got to not tell."

"Too late, Mister Rapist," Pig shot down. "Donny Santana called me when I was in tears after you left and I couldn't help but explain what you'd done. He said he was going to thrash you within an inch." Donny Santana was football captain, a lineman who weighed 255 and was scholarship at USC in the fall.

"How much you say to Donny?"

"Just that you arrived asking for Steamer but let slip that you knew my room was a sight, meaning you knew all along Steamer was gone and rape was on your mind from the start. And how you grabbed my bosoms like they were sponges off a supermarket shelf and bruised me and would have done worse except you shot your wad too soon. That's all I told him."

"Tuh-tuh-true?"

Pig hesitated, then shook her head. "I have too much respect for you to ruin your reputation, Spence." She paused. "*Had* too much."

"I'm juh—just so embuh—barrassed."

"You got every reason and right."

"Friends?"

Pig shrugged noncommittally "What made you do it?"

"I guh-guh got to sleep with somebody soon."

"Oh, I see," Pig said. "So you came to the expert."

From down below, he nodded.

"What about all those cheerleaders you're supposed to have been with?"

"People say things."

"Well, I wouldn't know about that." She turned away. "I just know I got to get my room tidied before the enemy returns or I'm dead for sure." She went back to where she'd been, flicked off the radio, continued folding clothes.

"Kuh-can I help?" he said from the doorway.

"I don't see how, since you don't know where things go. *I* don't know where things go and I live here." She crossed the room to the dresser, carefully put some blouses into the second drawer.

He watched her.

"If you're thinking of trying to rape me again, just don't, all right?" Pig said, returning to fold more clothes.

"Why do you say I'd even tuh-try?"

She pointed toward his jeans. "Go play pocket pool someplace else."

He started flushing again.

"You should feel really rotten, going on about how you loved me—love is something you shouldn't lie over—"

"Wuh—wuh—what about you?"

"What *about* me?"

" 'Oh, Suh-Spence, I'm not what you think,' " he said, imitating her. " 'Oh, Spence, duh-don't you have respect for me.' "

"So?"

"You never tuh-tried pushing me away, did you?"

Pig took the last of her clothes, went to the closet, turned on the single dim bulb.

He turned off the light in the room, started slowly toward her.

"Oh goodie, here comes John Derek now, am I ever excited."

That stopped him. "I thought you luh—luh—luh—"

"Of course I like you, Spence, but—"

"Let me fuh-fuh-finish!"

Pig went back to hanging up her clothes, not all that sure she could control her hands.

Softly he managed, "I thought you liked me a lot."

"I do, but, I don't know, Spence, you're just so inexperienced and immature." She turned to face him now. "I always like my men to be very gentle." She walked slowly toward him. "For example, I prefer a circular motion myself."

"Circular?"

"Sure." She unbuttoned his shirt in the semidarkness. "Like this." She pulled his shirt out of his jeans, spread it, and ran her fingertips around and around his breast. His nipple hardened which fascinated her, but she didn't stare. "Now you, you're more this style—" She grabbed his breast hard and squeezed it roughly.

"Ow—"

"Shut up." She went back to circling her fingertips around his nipple, wondering if it would harden again. "Circular. Gentle and circular." She raised her blouse up over her breasts.

He began tracing circles around her nipple with the tip of his index finger.

Pig could feel her breasts starting to swell. "That's sort of the idea," she told him.

"Gentle and circular," he said. "I get it, I get it," and then he tried to grab her again.

Pig broke free without much trouble. "Beautiful but dumb, Spencer, that's all you'll ever be." She walked to the bed, sat down on it. "Shoo."

He stood there staring at her.

Pig sighed. "Well, you just look so mournful, it's all I can do to keep a straight face. But as long as you're here, I may as well check out your equipment." She gestured for him to walk over.

He took a few steps.

"My arms aren't that long."

He moved up alongside.

She began to unbutton his jeans but her hands were shaking so she could almost not grip the buttons. "Stand still."

"Suh—sorry."

She finally got the jeans open, pulled down his elastic-top jockey shorts, tried not to react as his penis sprang free, at a forty-five degree angle to his body. She had only until then seen her father's and brother's and neither of them hard.

"Huh—how do I do?"

"You mean compared to all the others?"

He nodded.

She was tempted to zap him by saying, Well, I can't tell a thing till you get an erection. "Way above average, Spence. *Way* above."

"Guh-good."

" 'Course I can't really be sure without testing."

He had such a perfect surfer's body and he was good-natured and kind, not really stupid—it was just the awful speech thing that made him seem that way. She lay back on the bed, worked her jeans over her hips, took off her blouse, and when she was naked, so was he, and she reached out for his penis, began to guide it in when he hollered, "Omigod, I think I'm coming," so she quick let go and they lay silently alongside each other for a few minutes until he had control. Then she reached for his penis to try to guide it in but it was soft now.

Pig began to rub his stomach, slowly, in larger and larger circles until she began to graze his penis again, and when he was hard she parted her legs and as she reached for him he said, "Goddamit, shit, here I come," so she quick let go and waited and watched as he went soft and she just wanted to cry, because there was a secret, some trick she didn't know the answer to and *what was it* and then suddenly he was crying out in wild frustration at the top of his considerable voice, *"How the fuh-fuck do you fuh-fuck?"* and Pig yelled right back, *"I don't know, I've never done this either,"* and he said, "Huh?" and she said, "That's right, believe it, people say things, what about you and your cheerleaders?" and with that he grabbed her but not roughly, and kissed her, but with care, and he held her a long time, which was fine as far as Pig was concerned.

Only it didn't quite solve their problem.

There are moments that change the course of history. This wasn't one of them, no apple fell. And probably Pig's action wasn't all that brilliant. But considering that she was young, panicked, desperate, and lost in new and wild terrain, she never felt she had reason to be less than proud.

What she did was this: She turned on the radio.

And Vince Scully said, ". . . ball three to Matthews, and the young lefthander is really struggling now . . ." and Spence said, "Wuh-what the hell are you doing?" and Pig said, "Tell me about Sandy Koufax."

"Tuh-turn that damn thing off."

"Not until you tell me."

". . . he's into the stretch, Matthews waits . . . *ball four,* Matthews goes to first and up comes Mr. Hank Aaron and Sandy is in a jam and he knows it. . . ."

"Go on now about Koufax."

"Well, he's a Jew—"

"—not his religion, dopey—go on about his pitching."

"Well, he's got the great fastball."

"Um-hmm," Pig said, "and how's his curve?" She reached out in the darkness, found his penis, began gently to rub it up and down.

"Puh-Pig, you know more about baseball than anyone, you know about his kuh-curve so—"

"—I want your opinion, Spencer, now just please do what I say."

"Well, the curve is—Oh, Christ, I think I'm gonna come—"

"—you *won't*, not if you concentrate on telling me why his curve is so terrible—"

"—he's got the good curve, Pig, it's just he won't use it under pressure—"

"—now that is really interesting, Spencer, I wonder why, is he stupid do you think?"

"It's juh-just confidence, more'n likely."

". . . Aaron digging in now, taking his time . . . he represents the lead run with Matthews on first, 2–1, nobody out in the top of the eighth. . . ."

"Some say he's got control problems that he never will get over."

"That happens when you got the guh-great fastball."

". . . and here comes Walter Alston out of the dugout . . . he's got Sherry warm in the bullpen but he's not looking out that way. . . ."

Pig said, "I wonder what he'll say to Sandy out on that mound?" Slowly she began to spread her legs wide because he was hard again.

"Oh Jesus, Pig—"

"—probably insult Sandy, call him a fool for walking Eddie Matthews to lead off the inning, you think?"

"No, he'll say, 'How you feel Sandy?' and Sandy'll say, 'Fine' and Walt'll say, 'Not tired or nothing?' and Sandy'll say, 'Rarin' to go' and Walt'll tell him, 'Okay, but we got Sherry ready to take over so don't give that nigger nothing too good' and Sandy'll say, 'Don't you worry, Skipper, I'll fog it by him sure,' and Walt'll say, 'I got faith in you, Sandy, just stay calm.' "

He was inside her now, deep, going deeper, and Vince Scully said, ". . . Alston on the mound now, trying to calm the young lefthander—"

"See?" Spence said. "Just like I told you."

". . . Sandy's clearly upset with himself for letting Matthews get away but Alston's not looking toward the bullpen at all. . . ."

Pig began rocking her hips gently.

"You guh-got to quit that fast or I'll come," Spence said and Pig said, "Stop that talk, I'm plain sick and tired of you all the time talking about how you're going to come, you're not going to come, you won't come, but I think he ought to take Sandy out, I think it's a mistake, what do you think," and Spence said, "Wuh-well, you can ruin a young guy's confidence if you lift him in pressure sut-situations, he's got to get the confidence to go with the fastball, he's got to get the confidence to throw the curve, he's got to steady down and get control and—"

—and Pig cried out.

"Wuh-what?"

She did it again.

"Tuh-tell me what's goin' on?"

"I'm coming," Pig said, both amazed and ecstatic, guilt racked and guilt free, her legs locking around the slim waist of Spencer T. Murtaugh, her hips thrusting up and up and up again as she indeed, for the first but not the last time in her life, came. That was the second thing she learned that night: She wasn't sure about most things, not other girls or fashions or foreign policy, and she wasn't really certain how she felt about boys in general or Spence in particular.

But hey, fucking was really terrific. . . .

Less than a month later, in a summer-league game, Spence made two circus catches in center and creamed a three-run three-hundred-foot homer, driving in his team's only scores in a 4–3 squeaker.

Nobody paid any attention.

Because the Steamer was on the mound that day, the starter and loser, but still, after that afternoon, nothing was ever quite the same.

He was nervous, naturally enough, and he hit the enemy leadoff man in the small of the back with his first delivery. Man on first. The second pitch went *behind* the second hitter, rolled all the way to the backstop. Man on second, count one ball. Third pitch, also wild, man on third, count two balls. In comes Spence all the way from center to calm the young southpaw. He talks to the Steamer, the Steamer nods and nods. Back goes Spence to the outfield. The Steamer delivers, ball three, followed quick by ball four. Men on first and third. The next batter, a twenty-year-old slugger, he hits in the foot. Bases loaded.

A little laughter now from the stands.

Pig, T-shirted and sandaled, hollered for them all to shut the hell up, shouted to her brother to settle the hell down.

The next pitch hit the backstop on the rise, rolled crazily around while the bases emptied. Top of the first, down three zip, nobody out. On the mound the Steamer kicked at the dirt, took the ball in his big hand, went into his motion, and fired. Strike one. Strike two. One down. The next batter went down looking. The third out swung and missed.

In the second inning, two more walked, a double steal and a wild pitch accounted for the fourth run.

From there till the seventh when rain ended things, he allowed no more runs. All in all, he hit five batters, walked eleven more.

He also struck out nineteen.

Sitting in the stands that afternoon was the father of the enemy shortstop, a writer for the *Herald Examiner* who asked Pig curiously where the wild-man pitcher went to college. Pig looked at the guy like he was from Mars, but explained politely that Stan had just finished eighth grade. The reporter, whose name was Rafferty, wasn't in the sports department, but he was acute enough to know a genuine phee-nom when he saw one.

"California Koufax?" was the title of his article.

It was read by many people, among them a scout for the Dodgers who, out of curiosity really, stopped by for the Steamer's next performance.

Again he lost, this time 7–2.

He struck out only seventeen and walked the first six men he faced. But it was his second straight no-hitter and even at summer-league level, that didn't happen every day.

The third start of the summer Steamer began bringing in the crowds. All over Santa Monica, people began meandering over to see this grammar schooler the papers wrote up. He lost again, and he gave up a scratch single. But his reputation was already starting to build with the opposition. *Nobody* dug in against him. Nobody really wanted much to hit against him. He was big and blond, almost as fair as his sister, almost as attractive.

Except he squinted.

Because he had weak eyes. He couldn't really see the plate so God knew where the damn ball was going to come. The only thing for certain was that it was going to come rocketing and if it hit you anywhere at all, it smarted.

Rumors began. Some people said that a few months earlier the Steamer had hit a twisting batter in the nuts and the guy was a permanent soprano. Other people claimed they had seen with their own eyes when the Steamer caught a rich kid from Brentwood in the kneecap and forget about him ever walking without a limp.

Pig arrived early for every game, charted every pitch the Steamer threw, talked with him after about his velocity and moving the fastball around more against righthanders. And she grieved quietly with Spencer who was having a wonderful season—.385 average, flawless in the field— before an indifferent world.

They moved through high school as a trio with the Steamer as the star; even though he was behind them in grade, there was never any question as to who would catch lightning in a bottle. Pig managed quietly to keep her grades high, while neither of the others much cared. All that was important was that they pass and stay eligible and they did.

Steamer signed with the Dodgers amidst a surprising amount of hype and hoopla, and they sent him, age seventeen, to Bakersfield to try and control his talents. Almost as an afterthought they gave Spence a try there too, and Pig spent the summer after graduation up with them. But it was lonely when they were away and she looked almost forward to school again, except when she got to Santa Monica Junior College it wasn't very taxing and more than that, nothing much really interested her, she was far too old to be a tomboy anymore and when she was close to twenty she realized, at least at night she did, especially at night alone, that she was drifting, and worse, drifting badly.

One morning she was jogging along the surf when this weird guy fell in step alongside and Pig didn't even give him a glance, she wasn't in a mood for being hit on, but he asked her *please* before he *expired* to stop because he couldn't keep up with her and the way he talked she knew right off he was gay so she slowed and he told her his name and he was a still photographer at Universal and what about a sitting, he was good, he promised he was and since she had nothing else on in her life right then, she shrugged, made the appointment, and went back to her run.

The pictures turned out all right she thought, but he thought they were a lot more than that and so did *Playboy* when he sent them on and shortly thereafter Pig sailed off to Chicago and not long after that she bared herself and was Playmate of the Month and stayed awhile in Hefner's mansion on North State Parkway.

She was, in that world, a definite sensation, not just

because of her looks; but the Steamer had been called up
by the Dodgers and was getting famous in a small way for
his potential, and they made for a family that was easy to
write about and look at. The *Playboy* people wanted her to
stick around and be a bunny, and Pig tried, but she hated
the hours and the waiting on tables so she headed back
for California where people kept contacting her for more
pictures.

Within two years she was probably the most photographed and certainly the best-known nude model in the
country. The Steamer got her box seats for all the Dodger
home games where the surrounding crowd would always
stand up and cheer when she took her seat, and she dated
a lot of ballplayers, some of them stars, most of them
dumb, but everybody always assumed she was too, so it
never became a problem. And she had her picture taken at
the park with Cary Grant and that got in the papers, and
with Danny Kaye, and that got in the papers too, and she
was mentioned in various columns, usually as being about
to marry someone she'd usually never said hello to. She
smiled a lot and she was, as always, goodhearted and gorgeous, so she never lacked for companionship.

But the drifting was starting to get out of control.

One night when she was twenty-four the Steamer asked
her to be nice to this old fart agent who used to be at
Ashley-Famous but was on his own now and thought the
Steamer had maybe potential for tv endorsements. Pig
didn't much want to but she did it anyway, having an intimate dinner at a terrible Polynesian place south of Malibu.
The guy was a snooze, full of movie stories in which he
was constantly saving situations, but Pig nodded always as
alertly as if the guy were Casey Stengel himself, and when,
over his third mai-tai he said, suddenly, "Can you act?" she
almost answered, "What do you think I'm doing right
now?" but she didn't, only shook her head no.

He got out an initialed notepad, made a few marks.

"What'd you just put down?"

"Reminder is all—I'm putting together a ten-week tour

of *Seven Year Itch*—wanted Tina Louise for the Marilyn Monroe part but it never worked out and—"

"Act in front of *people*?"

"Relax, it ain't *Hamlet;* and anyway, they probably won't take you."

But they did. Not only did they take her, they wanted her. Within two weeks Pig was actually on a stage.

Which was where she met Metzenbaum.

A wild man. A whirlwind. Maybe five feet tall with this huge mop of frizzed black curly hair. Always on the move, chain-smoking, interrupting you before you finished because he knew what you were going to ask and was already into the answer. And dressed immaculately. Brooks Brothers style. Always with the blue oxford cloth button-downs and the navy-blue-striped tie and the dark three-button suits.

Twenty-two, he looked sixteen, and was the hottest young director out of Yale in years. Within six months of graduation he had a hit off-Broadway with an O'Casey revival and within six months after that he had a flop on Broadway but it was enough to get him a contract for a devolpment deal at Warners and he was only directing this stock tour as a favor to the Paul Lynde type who was playing the big role in the play, Tom Ewell's.

He sat them around the rehearsal hall the first morning and they read the play out loud and Pig knew she was embarrassing but nobody at least laughed, and after that Metzenbaum said that today was Monday and the books would be out of their hands by Friday without exception and he looked at Pig when he said that last, the without-exception business, but although a couple of the other actors were upset, she wasn't, because she'd learned her lines already, it wasn't hard, not with her memory. Saying them so that they sounded like they were coming from a human was way beyond her, but at least she knew what the words were. After they did the read-through he blocked the first two scenes and had them break for lunch. Pig had brought her yogurt and wheat germ with her which was mostly all she ever ate in the middle of the day so she sat alone in the hall for an hour, checking out pitching stats in the *Los Angeles Times*.

Everybody sauntered back eventually and the rest of the afternoon was without incident except shortly after four at coffee break when Metzenbaum came over to her and said, between quick inhales, "Listen, I know you're new but you'll do fine. All you have to do for this role is stand there and look desirable and that's something you bring to the party."

Pig stood there, waiting for the other shoe to drop.

Then he said it: "I also want you to know that I know you're talented, and you can go on hiding it if you want to. But just don't think you're fooling anybody."

Talented, Pig thought. Oh, *tishlubb,* and she was amazed at the absurd lies people would say to try to go to bed with her. And just to prove what a liar he was, she decided then and there to let him go to bed with her and afterward to confront him with his falsehood, so after rehearsal, on the way to their cars, she said, "What was the name of that book I heard you talking on about?"

He didn't know.

"Oh, sure, you remember, the one by the guy with the foreign name."

"Stanislavsky?"

Pig nodded. "Him."

"Building A Character. What about it?"

"You think I should maybe check it out? I mean, it couldn't hurt or anything."

"Let me know what you think."

"I will. Only where can I find it, do you know?"

"Not anywhere within five hundred miles of Southern California," he said. Then: "I'm not real crazy about Southern California." Then: "I'll bring you my copy tomorrow." Then: "If you'll promise not to mark up the margins."

"I also don't dog-ear pages," Pig told him. Then: "I

was sort of hoping to read it tonight. I could sure use all the help I can get before disaster strikes."

"I don't live far," Metzenbaum said. "Why don't you follow me?"

"Why don't I just," Pig said, and she did.

Metzenbaum lived in a small rented one-bedroom apartment off Pico not far from Farmer's Market. He unlocked the door and she tried not to notice that he had trouble getting the key in. He finally managed, gestured her inside.

She had never remembered seeing so many books. Pig was about to ask, "You read all these?" but it would have been too dumb, obviously he had, he was that kind of weird figure from the East, they did that back there, read books when the weather was bad. He muttered something about not really being settled in and the books weren't in anything like order so he stooped here, and stood on tiptoe there, and Pig waited for the fiddling to finish, watching him. She was maybe half a foot taller minimum and probably also outweighed him and she knew, as he moved around with his suitcoat still on, shirt still buttoned to the throat, that she could outrun him and probably could beat him in arm wrestling if it ever came to that, but she didn't mind at all, he was going to be the first genius type she'd bedded down with.

But it was obvious, as the hunt for the book dragged on, that no matter how smart he was in some areas, he sure didn't know from fucking, so she joined in the search for the Stanislavsky doing her best, she said, to help, managing to brush his body a time or two, managing to nudge her breasts across his elbow and then when she had his attention she went into her passive-aggressive routine, which she'd gotten pretty damn pat, bringing him forward while it seemed like he was the one doing the leading and it took some time but eventually she got him into the bedroom and out of his clothes and he had a nice enough cock but he didn't know quite what to do with it, and she came to the rescue there too, gently, and when he finally came inside her there was no doubt in her mind that he hadn't been bored.

He lay spent in her arms, his weight not enough to be uncomfortable. Her arms were longer than his, and she was broad in the shoulders too. She reached around and held him and for a moment he seemed like some cherub and she wondered momentarily if she should burp him. "Hey, you were terrific."

"I was just along for the ride and we both know it."

Pig kissed him lightly on the eyes. "Here I'll admit I'm talented," she said, and waited for him to reply. He didn't, so she went right on. "It wouldn't be lying to say that about me here, not like your bullshit before."

"Huh?"

"You know."

"What bullshit?"

"Oh, that thing, that remark, you know, where you went on about how I was this incredibly fantastic performer and couldn't fool you."

"I never said that."

"Talented you said though."

He rolled off, reached for a cigarette, lit it in silence, looked at her.

Pig felt uneasy. "Probably you're going to deny it now."

He smiled, shook his head, continued to inhale rapidly. "I never meant to imply that you were the second coming of Laurence Olivier. But you definitely bring some surprises to the party."

"I don't get that."

"Well, every actor brings what they are, naturally. The way they look, how they move, how they talk. With some that's all. You talk to Rock Hudson fifteen seconds, if you want what he's selling fine, but you better not want any more, because what you see is what you get."

"But not with me?"

"Correct. You come on like some sex bomb with your eyes and coloring and the boobs out to here." He jabbed out his cigarette, lit another.

"What's my surprise though?" Pig asked.

"You're very vulnerable, Pig."

Pig shook her head. "I don't see that."

"Who's bullshitting now?"

Pig shrugged.

"You've got a lot of emotion just inside. You may not want to tap it, but it's there." He looked at her closely in silence. "Why are you embarrassed now?"

"Embarrassed? Shit, why should I be embarrassed, it's just, I can't figure you, what you're after, you're too smart; I mean, you just fucked me, you can't want to fuck me."

"Why are you all of a sudden so vulgar? You didn't swear all day till now."

"Why do you want people calling you 'Metzenbaum'? Why the last name? Your first name's Rick. What's wrong with using that?"

"I choose 'Metzenbaum' as pure affection; it sets me apart from the masses. Just as my Brooks Brothers look sets me apart from the masses in glorious Southern Cal. And why didn't you answer my question about vulgarity; you changed the subject rather awkwardly."

"I'm rather awkward I guess is the thing. Listen, can you find me that Stanislavsky book, I've got a dinner date I'm gonna be late for."

"You said you had nothing on; you wanted the book for tonight."

Pig shrugged, rolled into a sitting position, feet on the floor.

From behind her, Metzenbaum said, "Want to try something, want to experiment around, just for the hell of it?"

"What kind of an experiment?"

"A Sense Memory."

"I don't know what that is."

"Ah, but I do, and soon you will too, if you'll risk it."

"What would I have to do?"

He gestured to the armchair across the room. "Just go get comfortable."

"Like this? With no clothes?"

"Sure, if you want." He smiled again. "I've never done one naked, but there's no reason not to. Besides, it'll read great in my memoirs."

Pig went to the armchair, sat stiffly.

Metzenbaum laughed. "Don't get too relaxed now."

"Well, I'm scared you're gonna make an ass out of me. I'm more used to jocks, not you brainy weirdos."

"You feel more at home with dummies I guess; more closely allied intellectually."

Pig waited.

"*A Sense Memory,*" Metzenbaum said, bounding off the bed, speaking the words very loudly, as he began to walk naked back and forth in front of the armchair, gesturing sharply and constantly with his cigarette. "It is, if you will, a tool, an actor's tool, an exercise that is oftentimes helpful. And it is based, follow me now, the concept of it is based on the firm belief that the five senses—see, hear, touch, taste, smell—these senses have memories of their own, and if properly executed, the performer will often be able to flush out things that were there but that you had not remembered were there. In other words, the senses have memories that are independent of the brain."

"Are you gonna hypnotize me? I don't go for being put in a trance. So if that's it—"

"Just-shut-up-and-relax!"

"Oh, that's really easy with you yelling at me."

Metzenbaum walked behind her, jabbed out his cigarette. Without preparation he began slowly massaging her neck and shoulders.

"Hey I like that."

"Oh close your hole." He continued to knead her shoulders and work the sides of her neck gently. "Sit straight," he whispered. "Position your body properly. Get the stress off."

Pig shifted in the chair, balancing herself easily.

"That's better." The tips of his fingers worked at her

shoulders. "Okay—shake your wrists, really give them a good going-over."

Pig did.

"Feel better?" he aked when she was done.

They did.

He slowly let his fingers slide down from her shoulders until they rested gently on her breasts. Just the tips of his fingers on her breasts. Feathers. Circling. "Now in theory, when I'm seventy-five, the tips of my fingers should be able to retain the exact sense they're getting now, the way your flesh feels to them. Just as in theory, my eyes should be able to see—not remember but *actually see*—the contours of your justly famous body." He lifted his hands, walked around, knelt naked in front of her. "You relaxed?"

"I guess."

"Then we'll begin."

"Do I close my eyes?"

"No, this is acting, remember, and the eyes are kind of a little bit important, dumbhead."

Pig made a smile.

"Don't be insulted, but I'm going to assume that tonight was, well, let's just say you did not lose your virginity this evening; may I assume that?"

"You may definitely assume that."

"But when you did lose your precious maidenhood, morning, afternoon, whenever, was it a pleasant experience or was it fraught with trauma."

"Pleasant, kind of."

"You're how old now?"

"Be twenty-five."

"Good."

"What's good about it?"

"You didn't hesitate; when you answered, you didn't pause or think about lying. That's what's good. 'Cause what we're trying to get at now is in a way truthful. Now when this 'pleasant kind of' experience happened, how old were you?"

Pig closed one eye. "Maybe fifteen."

"Okay. So we're going back ten years give or take. You relaxed?"

"Pretty."

"This is it then." He paused for a long time before he said it: "Hear his voice."

"Whose?"

"The person you first slept with. Hear his voice."

"That would be Spence."

"I don't care about his name. I don't care how long it takes. I just want you to hear his voice."

Pig shut her eyes and started to concentrate—

"—open."

She opened her eyes. "It would be a lot easier for me to remember if I could just close my eyes and think a little."

"I don't want you to *remember* his voice, I want you to *hear* it."

"He stuttered something awful."

"Don't send me reports. Just try very hard to hear."

Pig tried very hard.

"No hurry. . . . All the time in the world. . . ." He was speaking softly now. ". . . just take all the time you want. . . ."

Pig let her arms hang loose, began breathing deeper.

". . . let it happen . . . nice and slow . . . nice and very slow. . . ."

"I think it was early evening—no no, it was later, the Dodgers were playing and I think—"

". . . don't think . . . hear his words . . . and don't be afraid . . . people are either afraid of what will show . . . or what won't show . . . and it doesn't matter . . . the world goes right on . . . so just. . . ." He stopped.

"How the fuh-fuck do you fuh-fuck?" Pig said softly. "How the fuh-fuck do you fuh-fuh. . . ."

Now her voice trailed off.

Her eyes started blinking.

Her face filled with blood.

And she shattered.

She gasped twice for breath, and her arms crossed stiffly in front of her face and she made it out of the chair, trying to beat her tears to the bed, failing. Blinded, she reached for the pillow, felt around for it, brought it full against her face and sobbed.

Metzenbaum was lying alongside her when she got control. "I shouldn't have messed around with this," he said. "I'm sorry."

"No, don't be, it's okay, but see, Spence—his name was Spencer T. for Tracy Murtaugh—and we went together all through high school and after that too, in the minors at Bakersfield, and he was just beautiful and everyone figured we were suited and were gonna make it permanent and we *were* suited, at the start anyway, but he was just so stupid though, and that got clearer and clearer only we'd put in so much time together I couldn't leave him, I couldn't just go and break up with him it wouldn't have been fair, not with him depending on me because it wasn't that he couldn't hit the fastball or the curve, he could, he just couldn't do it often enough to make a living and that was hard for him to take, and that's why we were gonna go through with it, marriage and all, and . . . and *Jesus*," Pig said loud and mortified as the tears took her face again and the pillow was wet so she bolted toward the bathroom and slammed it shut behind her, locking it and turning on the shower full blast.

Metzenbaum was sitting on the bed smoking when she got control. She came out, breathing deeply. "Wow, what is it with me?"

"You're associating to something unpleasant would be my guess, and to put it mildly."

Pig nodded, switched pillows with him, and lay back staring at the cracked ceiling. "He dumped me was what happened," she said evenly. "For a prissy little prim little secretary. I didn't even know he knew her till he told me they were getting married and I thought sure it was a joke and then when I saw it wasn't I remember thinking, 'How can you dump me, I would never have dumped you, and for her, what does she know, where was she when you were batting one ninety-five?' And then he got so mean, just so rotten mean about everybody would want to fuck me, I was good for that, the fucking, but no one ever wanted to be seen with me, not permanently, because I was just a pair of tits and in ten years they'd be drooping to my knees and," and she managed to say "shit" before the emotion had her a final time and she was too whipped to run so she turned away and lay there, red faced and swollen and out of all control.

Metzenbaum rolled alongside her, paralleled his body with hers, and held her. "I've got to admit I was wrong," he said gently as she wept on. "You're not emotional at all." He shook his head as he started to stroke her. "I just don't know how I could have been so mistaken; there's obviously no vulnerability here. . . ."

Pig didn't take the Stanislavsky book with her that night because she didn't leave that night, and after the rest of rehearsal and the ten-week tour following, she moved in with Metzenbaum permanently, at least two years' worth of permanently, and she did subsequent tours, stock sometimes, sometimes dinner theaters. She played the Monroe part in *Bus Stop* and the Mansfield part in *Will Success Spoil Rock Hunter?* and *The Marriage-Go-Round* and *Butterflies Are Free* and *The Girl in the Freudian Slip* and she wore lots of towels and bikinis and dresses that were by no means all cut high, and she lived with a lot of people, not quite top-class directors and not quite top-level executives, and the drifting got to not bother her much at all because she realized that was what she was supposed to be, a drifter. And then at the Reggie Jackson series she met a skinny multimillionaire singer/songwriter on the skids who was really nice but also really weird, a biter given to sending her on bizarre missions, crazy casino bets, or picking up nervous Jews at McCarran Airport on steaming Vegas mornings.

* * *

"A nervous Jew," Schwab the Slob said, hopping up and down in mock fury. "Johnny Small called *me* nervous —I'll trade innards with that no-talent pinko commie fag tomorrow."

Pig laughed as she led him quickly through the airport toward the limousine. "What he actually said was for me to look for a nervous Jew with his shirttail out."

Schwab the Slob grunted, began tucking his shirt back inside his trousers.

"He made me promise to say that," Pig said then.

"I suspected." He looked at her a moment. "How *did* he describe me—nope, changed my mind, don't tell, don't wanna know." They walked out of the airport into the heat. "Probably said something about me having chubby cheeks. I went through my teens with that nickname— 'Chubbycheeks.' The whole world thinks I'm pudgy on account of these." He tweaked himself. "And I'm not. It's a terrible cross to bear."

"Sounds like," Pig said, and then they were to the car. He opened the door and they tumbled in and he put his briefcase on the seat between them as the driver started back to the Grand. She sat back and stared ahead and was aware that he was watching her close but she didn't think anything of it until he went, "Hey you really are amazing," and maybe it was because of the early hour or maybe because he seemed almost cherubic kind of with, like he said, his chubby cheeks, but his remark was a surprise, not the good kind, and she didn't mask it well.

Because suddenly he was going, really fast, "Hey, it's not what you think, I'm not hitting on you, I'm happily married, they allow one happy marriage by law each year in Hollywood and this year is mine, I just meant you look amazingly like you looked, you wouldn't remember, see, but I've met you before."

Pig studied him. "I'm good with faces usually."

"I was a nerd, a schlepper, I crawled out from under rocks in those days; see, I was brand new to out here but

I knew Rickie Metzenbaum from back East and you guys had a house for the summer somewhere I think in Tranchas on the water and there was a party and he invited me."

"We only gave the one party." Pig shook her head and took a breath. "Not one of your high points. You still see him?"

"Not so much; since Rickie won the Oscar he's become convinced his shit smells like perfume. It doesn't much make for two-way conversations."

Pig nodded. "He always had that in him I guess." She looked out the window at the flat land. They were on The Strip now and making good time. "So how come you're here, a remake of *The Magus*?"

Schwab the Slob broke up awhile. Then he said, "Hey, you're funny."

"When I'm desperate."

He opened his briefcase, took out a mimeoed screenplay in a blood-red cover. "Read this and tell me what you think." He handed it over.

Pig looked at it. "What's this *Tinsel* about?"

"If I tell you, there's no point to letting you read it. Just read it."

"Who do you want for it?"

"Please. A cold reading is all I'm after."

"Done."

"How is Johnny," he said then, making the "is" meaningful.

"Good, all things considered."

"He was strung out a few years back."

"I got him off the hard stuff within a month," Pig said. "I'm a health nut and I told him I wouldn't put up with it. Grass naturally is still with us, but he's given up booze except for beer and wine."

"Hey, that's good."

"Yup. What's bad is I've turned him into a compulsive gambler. I'm kind of afraid to get him off that, I'm not sure what the next addiction is."

"You two serious?"

"We get on."

"He's due for a decent marriage."

"I don't see me marrying," Pig said.

"Against your religion?"

"I think I'd be a rotten wife is all." She thought a moment. "I'm better as a hooker without portfolio. . . ."

3

Torn, Pig lay alone in the bedroom, staring out the window. She reached behind her, felt around on the bedspread till she located the script. She looked at the red cover for a long time, as undecided as ever. Should she mention it to Johnny or not? Would he laugh if she did? She wasn't sure; just wasn't sure of a lot of things. Except ohhhhhh, sweet Jesus, did she want the part.

She looked at the bedside clock. After two already. Schwab and Johnny had been jabbering since before eleven, how much was there to talk about, especially since Johnny hadn't even read the script yet.

But she had.

Ohhhhhh, dear sweet sweet sweet Jesus.

Johnny stuck his head in then from the living room. "Listen, we're gonna order up room service, take care of yourself, you don't mind, do you?"

Pig gestured for him to come in.

"What?"

Pig gestured for him to close the door.

"I'm in a meeting, can't it wait?"

Pig bounded off the bed toward him going, "Johnny listen, you've got to please hear me out, this is important or I wouldn't get into it, it's crucial you understand, sure you understand, here's the thing, and I just know what I'm talking about, you've got to have faith when I tell you I know, I mean there isn't any question in my mind at all

—Johnny, don't laugh, swear you won't, I know you won't —Johnny, I'm really embarrassed to even say it because I've never yet used you and I wouldn't if this wasn't, like I said, essential and everything but I can play the shit out of that part so help me God."

"What part?"

"The Monroe part."

"It's cast, Pig."

"Cast?"

"Raquel Welch."

"Listen, she'll be wonderful."

"Apparently there were a whole bunch of meetings involving a whole bunch of people and everything worked out fine."

"I'll just maybe go on down and grab some yogurt in the coffee shop."

"Piglet?"

"Hmmm?"

"I'll order you up some, you eat with us."

"The truth is I'm not hungry, I think I'll call the pro and see if he's free, my serve was crummy yesterday."

"You're welcome."

She blew him a kiss. "Scoot."

He hesitated, finally closed the door again.

Fug.

HOW COULD SHE BE SUCH A WIMP?

She stormed to the window, got bored by the view, went to her bureau, rummaged through the drawers till she found her tennis stuff, threw a blouse and shorts toward the mattress, missed, picked them up, rolled them into a ball, and fired her best fastball toward the center of the bedboard.

Stee-ri-yukkk.

Of course Raquel Welch was cast. You couldn't cast anybody else, not really, so why didn't she ask, casual-like, "Oh, by the by, who's playing the Monroe part, Raquel I assume?"

Of course Welch could always keel over of a stroke.

What a terrible thing to think, Pig admonished herself. Wishing somebody dead. She walked back to the window, thinking. Maybe Welch had fallen madly in love with a wonderful guy and married him a few months back and was pregnant but hadn't quite started to show except by the time of principal photography she'd be out to here, what then?

Or maybe the King of Saudi Arabia was mad for her and was willing to give her the southern half of the country but the hitch was she had to give up her career to get it. Grace Kelly gave up her career for half a country, anything was possible.

Pig picked up the phone, got the pro shop, made the date for the lesson, hung up. Then she lay on the bed and struggled out of her peach slacks, kicked them toward the closet. She stood, unbuttoned her peach blouse, dropped it, unhooked her bra, took off her pantyhose, wandered into the bathroom where she stood naked close to the full length mirror.

It wasn't tishlubb though; she really would have been good in the part. She'd played a bunch of Monroe parts, her coloring wasn't that different. God knew there was nothing wrong with her body.

Pig studied her body in silence. She stood straight, shoulders back, facing the mirror.

No complaints.

She turned left, stood sidewise.

Fine.

Now she turned to study the right profile.

Per—

She moved closer to the mirror.

Now she closed her eyes, shook her head, opened her eyes, looked at herself in silence. Was it her imagination or her humiliation or was she just being hypercritical—

—or was the right one starting just a bit to sag.

I really needed this, Pig thought, especially today. She looked at her right breast for a long time.

Maybe yes, maybe no.

Just to be on the safe side, she brought her arms up in front of her body, pressed her palms hard against each other, released, pressed again, released, over and over. It was the best isometric for the pectorals she knew.

Press, release, press, release. Five hundred times couldn't hurt. She walked out of the bathroom and crossed the large room, exercising in a steady rhythm. Naked, she stopped at the window and stared at the arid land. Press, release, press, release.

Then she looked down at her right breast. "Behave," Pig said.

Press, release, press, release.

Only four hundred and seventy-six repetitions to go. . . .

IV

NOEL

When, during the *F.I.S.T.* screening, he heard his father say, "They didn't catch it in time," Noel was simply incapable of a reply. Julian Garvey was such an elemental power, not just in the world of the family but in the biggie outside as well, that the notion of actually outliving the old man had never really occurred. Noel stood there while his father went quietly on, saying as he blinked back tears, "Don't say anything to your mother, she doesn't know." Noel made no reply, just went on doing what he had been doing, i.e., standing there. Then his father fought for a smile, finishing with, "I believe the other shoe was just dropped."

Noel finally managed, "You'll have to let me think."

"Of course. But Noel? Remember, all I'm after is a week of your life. If I can't intrigue you with Magic Town by then, it's quits."

"My book is very important though, Daddy. I really do have to think."

"It may well be a great book, Noel. But please—don't ruminate too long."

Noel spun and hurried back to the poolhouse/screening room complex, walked around the side and down some steps to the outside entrance to what was now his office. He unlocked the door—God only knew what his Beatle memorabilia was worth, let alone the Dylan stuff—and walked inside.

Upstairs, *F.I.S.T.* trudged into its third hour.

Was it important, his book? Were the Beatles significant?
Would they be Tut's tomb in five thousand years? He
grabbed a stack of Beatles records and stuck them on the
spindle, was about to blast the lyrics when he remembered
the folks above. He took his unattached Sennheiser stereo
headphones and adjusted them for comfort, then plugged
the LED infrared transmitter into his receiver. They were
new gizmos, these unattached jobs, and they were terrific
for listening when you wanted to wander freely and do
some heavy thinking and not be bothered with the mess of
a long curling cord.

> *It's been a Hard Day's Night,*
> *And I've been working like a dog.*
> *It's been a Hard Day's Night,*
> *I should be sleeping like a log.*

Probably that wasn't symbolic, Noel thought. "Log" and
"dog" certainly didn't set up a particularly complicated
rhyme scheme. But the title phrase had reverberations.
He grabbed his remote control module, clicked it, and
paced around the debris-filled room.

> *Yesterday,*
> *al my troubles seemed so far away*
> *Now it looks as though they're here*
>   *to stay*
> *Oh*
> *I believe in yesterday.*

Click.

> *. . . and nothing to get hung about*
> *Strawberry Fields forever.*

Click.

Eleanor Rigby,
died in the church and was buried
along with her name.
nobody came.

Click.

There are places I'll remember
all my life though some have
changed.

Click.

. . . and we lived beneath the waves
in our yellow submarine.

Click.
Click.
Click!

Or were they silly? Were they great and lasting like Schubert and Shakespeare or just Burke and Van Heusen with a mystique wrapped around them?

His father had a way of doing that to him, making it all seem silly, anything Noel's fancy landed on, silly, and Noel was back twenty years before, bursting with his great discovery, because he had been heavily into comic books for two years already since he was barely six, but this was his first inspiration, and he tried it out on Sissy and she thought it was brilliant too, so at dinner he said, "I know who would win in a fight between Superman and Captain Marvel."

His mother sighed. "Noel, must we discuss comic books at every meal?"

"I didn't at breakfast."

"True, but in general, you understand my position."

"Oh, but this is important," Sissy said. She adored Noel and mothered him from her vantage point of one year longer on the trail.

His father said nothing, just ate.

His mother said, "Julian, you might pay mind to this because I've been rereading the Wertham book, you know the psychiatrist Frederic Wertham, *Seduction of the Innocent,* and his conclusions are something any parent should be aware of."

Julian indicated for her to continue.

Estelle chose her words carefully. "Well, if one thinks, one can figure out what Bill Tilden and Leonardo da Vinci and Gide and Proust and Hans Christian Andersen have in common, yes?"

"Was Andersen?" Julian asked, surprised.

"Apparently so. Well, this Doctor Wertham feels the same kind of life-style inherent in Batman and Robin. Or that Gertrude Stein and Alice B. Toklas might very well have enjoyed the company of Shuuna, Queen of the Jungle."

"*Sheena,* Queen of the Jungle, she's beautiful, she can kill leopards, I know she can 'cause that's what she wears all the time, a leopard bathing suit." Noel paused and looked at his parents. "Captain Marvel," he said.

"Captain Marvel what, dear?" his mother said.

"Would win, would win, would win," Noel chanted.

Sissy reached gently across, touched him on the arm. "Just tell them, hon."

"Okay," Noel began. "Superman is Superman and Captain Marvel is really this kid, Billy Batson, until he says SHAZAM! Y'unnerstan?" His mother nodded. "Okay. He says SHAZAM 'cause each letter stands for a guy. *M* is Mercury—that's speed. But Superman's fast. Any guy can leap tall buildings in a single bound you know has gotta be fast. Okay. Now I'm gonna save the *S* for last, but here's the others: *H* is for Hercules' strength, *A* is Atlas' stamina, *Z* is Zoosie's power, *A* is Ack'le's courage. Okay, Superman's the same so far right?"

"Noel," his mother wanted to know, "how much longer will the explanation take?"

"He's getting to it," Sissy said. "He's almost right there."

"Ta-dumn," Noel said, making a fanfare. "The *S* in SHAZAM stands for Solomon's wisdom. Solomon was maybe the smartest guy that ever lived, Bible Comics says. Okay." And now he was getting excited again, fidgeting, his fingers playing the table like a piano. "Superman was a dumbhead. He was just this ordinary baby from Krypton who was shipped here by his father before the doomed planet exploded."

"Put your hands in your lap, Noel," Estelle said. "What doomed planet?"

"Krypton, Mommy. Now don't you see? Superman isn't *really* super, he's only super 'cause he's *here*. On Krypton, probably he'd run a gas station or like that. Well, what chance is a gas-station guy gonna have fighting against the smartest guy in the history of the whole world? Y'unnerstan'? Y'unnerstan'? Captain Marvel would just mop up the floor with him, ta-dumn, *ta-dumn!*"

"Have you the least idea, Noel," Julian said speaking for the first time to his son, "how terribly Sheena of the Jungle must smell? Wearing leopard in that heat?"

"She doesn't smell, Daddy, she swims all the time."

"Do you know how ghastly the smell of wet fur is, Noel?"

"She doesn't smell, Daddy."

"But Superman must."

Noel just looked at his father.

"When does he have his Superman suit dry-cleaned? He wears it every day. Think how your underwear would smell if you wore it year after year after year. He cannot have it dry-cleaned, Noel. Can you imagine him walking into an establishment and saying, 'When can I have my Superman suit back?' He would be giving away his secret, Noel. The dry cleaner would know who he was. And besides, what if his services were needed and he had to let people die because his suit was at the cleaners?"

Noel was playing the piano with his hands again, faster now, a wilder tune. "It doesn't need cleaning, Daddy—it's special material from Krypton."

"Ah, Noel, it couldn't be—you yourself said he came here when he was a baby so I will allow you the possibility of his having a Superman diaper, but he doesn't run around saving the world in a white diaper with an *S* on the side, does he? Of course he doesn't. Therefore he must have had the Superman suit made for him here on earth and therefore he must smell like a Bowery bum—"

"—not a bum, Daddy—"

"—and why doesn't Captain Marvel have short pants?"

"Huh?"

"He grows in size when he says that word—if you were suddenly my size, Noel, your trousers would hit somewhere around my knees. And I would think that therefore—"

"—it's special, they're all special!" Noel shouted as he ran from the table.

But they weren't really. Not special at all. Not when you looked at them that way. What they were was silly. Silly drawings of silly stupid men in silly dumb costumes saying silly stupid dumb words out loud and that night when he was himself again Noel took his collection and gave them the heave, ripped them to bits and stuffed them in the trash, and felt a lot better for it and——*Click.*

> *Hey Jude,*
> *don't make it bad,*

Click. Click. Click.

> *She loves you yeh, yeh, yeh,*
> *She loves you yeh, yeh, yeh.*
> *You think you've lost your love,*
> *Well I saw her yesterday—yi—yay,*
> *It's you she's thinking of,*
> *And she told me what to say—yi—yay.*

Silly. That's really what the Fab Four were when you came right down to it. When you really really pay attention what you end up with is just four jerks from Liverpool who fell into it with their hair styles. And Dylan? Dylan wasn't Dylan, his name was Bob Zimmerman, brought up in Hibbing, Minnesota, with a father named Abe who sold appliances for a living and *where was the symbolism in that*? Noel grabbed for some of his notes and began shredding them, because his father was on the home stretch now, begging for a week, and how could you turn down a request like that?

Noel ripped up a few more pages, then stopped. Maybe he might come back to it later, no point in destroying it all. But no point in leaving it around either. He opened a closet door and started stacking everything inside, clearing the room. Halfway through he stopped, kind of laughing, because the thought struck him that even if it was only for a week, still it was show business, and my God, my God, how would he ever have tried to explain *that* to the other three members of his own and only group of friends, the Flab Four.

They were all of them movie brats, brought up in the industry and unenamored of it. Bratty and bright, outcasts all, and unquestionably all weird. But Noel, proudly, laid claim to being the weirdest of the bunch. Proof?

The Story of the Pulling of the Pud.

Noel, in the fall of 1963, had long since forgotten comic books, and was also over baseball statistics, in which, before he was embarrassed into throwing in the towel, he had become America's leading expert on World Series *fielding* stats. He would drive people crazy asking them Home Run Baker's lifetime series numbers, and then cry, "Nine thirty-two. He fielded .932 in *six* series, thirty-seven putouts, forty-five assists, six errors."

Now he was deeply into television. He knew by heart the entire weekly schedule for every station in Los Angeles, and more than anything, he loved sudden program changes, because that was the kind of thing that kept you alert to what was going on. On September seventeenth he was deeply torn, because at ten the Keefe Brasselle Show was on, and if you knew anything about bad art, you knew instinctively that the Keefe Brasselle Show would never die. But also at ten was the debut of *The Fugitive* created by Huggins, the guy who did *Maverick,* so that was going to be worth at least a look-see.

Upset and unsettled, Noel consoled himself at half past nine by watching *Dogpatch.* The deal his folks had made was no tv till after homework so he made it a practice to bolt dinner and race through his studies, which he could do pretty easily, so that by eight-thirty he was into his pajama bottoms and alone in his room with the color tube for company.

Twelve, closing in on thirteen, he lay there and sometimes he touched his nipples with his fingers and sometimes he scratched his balls and this *Dogpatch* was really dumb, all about how Daisy Mae had bought this ring for Li'l Abner because he obviously was never going to buy one for her, only she dropped it in this muddy area as she was on her way to the Yokum's house and in the low-cut blouse she always wore, Noel watched kind of bored as Dixie Crowder decided that the only way she would ever find it was to clamber around in the mud on all fours and she got all dirty, natch, and you really couldn't see much cleavage, but she had the most fabulous tits and Noel wondered as he lay there what they were made of, no, he knew what they were made of, skin and flesh and like that, but were they firm or saggy like his mother's and how big really, and what were the nipples like, did they kind of swell when you touched them the way his did and if she let you see her tits, if Dixie Crowder would oblige, what did you do with the bra thing, where did it unbutton, or . . . or. . . .

. . . what the fuck was happening?—what?—*what the fuck was going on with his pecker?*—because he had been fondling it, sure, stroking it, sure, but now there was this warm feeling in his nuts and he sensed something starting to surge and he grabbed himself with both hands to try and make it stop but shit, here it came, here this creamy stuff came, this horrid creamy stuff where his pee should have been, and it was coming and coming and his pajamas were soaked with the sticky stuff and wouldn't you know his mother would call "Noel" just then and approach his bedroom down the hall and Noel dove under his covers and lay there while his mother entered and looked at him and said, "Homework all done, you sure?" and he said, "Oh all, yes, absolutely, good night, Mommy," and she left and he peeked down and *aaaahhhhhhhhh*—the sticky stuff was soaking the sheets.

Noel kicked himself clear and ran to his bureau for another pair of pajama bottoms and then he locked himself in the bathroom and looked at himself. His pecker was soft now, redder than he'd ever seen it, and swollen.

Obviously it was going to fall off.

He had somehow broken it, there would be no more pee coming through, and it would fall away from his body in the night, without question.

Noel bit his lip, contemplating his moist pajamas. How could he dispose of them? The outside garbage can. Yes. Terrific. He started out of the bathroom, stopped. What if the garbage man saw and brought them in and gave them to his father and said, "Mr. Garvey, Mr. Garvey, there is this diseased clothing in the garbage can, I think it belongs to your crazy son Noel."

Ah, but if he put the pajamas in a bag and then put the *bag* in the garbage can.

No good. What if the garbage man was a bag collector and—

—but what if he put the bag itself inside a box—

—and what if the garbage man also collected boxes?—

—then what if—

—but what if—

—so what if—

It was a long and very dark night for Noel Garvey.

Swifty brought the light.

Swifty Ballinger (nicknamed not, as stories had it, for the agent, Lazar, but rather for Tom Swift, because Ballinger had, almost from childhood, a phenomenal knack for mechanics and invention) was, at the age of thirteen, the talked-about kid at Harvard, which was the most talked-about private school in L.A. He was already, at thirteen, the biggest head in the vicinity. Flabby in build, with breasts almost like a girl's, he hated exercise in any form, and his excuses to get out of gym class were legendary among the faculty, who enjoyed him for his wit and imagination.

He also had parents with pretty good credentials. His father was a studio head. No point in naming the studio, it kept changing. He would run one place into near bankruptcy, get fired, then turn independent producer until another studio needed him. He never ran either Universal or Columbia, but it was hard to name another that he didn't lose fortunes for. A big, hearty man, broad and powerful with a sense for the jugular, he was also a closet queen known throughout the industry as Attila the Fag.

Mrs. Ballinger had been imported from England. A glorious-looking redheaded actress of limited talent but supplied with a body that just didn't end, she quickly, for services rendered, achieved the appellation of the British Open. How they managed Swifty one could only conjecture, but except for sexual preferences, it seemed a rock-solid Hollywood marriage.

"Horseradish?" Swifty said to Noel later that week. It was after lunch and Noel was starting off toward the gym.

"What?" Noel looked at the other boy who was holding what looked like a root in his hand and was chewing.

"Makes you flushed," Swifty said. "We can bag gym class. I've got some Maui Wowee in my pocket."

"I'm not into all that kinda stuff," Noel said.

"Dumb," Swifty said, and chewed a little more. "Do I look fucking flushed yet?"

Noel studied the other boy. "Reddening a trifle."

"Maui Wowee, Noel. I had some last night. Attila was out with the, you should pardon the expression, boys. I don't know where the Open was. I went out by the pool and partook of my very first Maui Wowee."

"And?" Noel felt obliged to ask.

Swifty stopped chewing long enough to whisper the words, "Ribbons of sperm, Garvey, glorious convoluting patterns of jism. See, I'd never done it in the water before."

"Lemme try some of that horseradish," Noel said. He took a bite, started to chew. "Done what?"

"I was floating in the lounge chair chatting with the stars, Noel, when suddenly it hit me, how glorious it must be to meat-beat in a heated pool. Little did I foresee the difficulty."

"Meat-beat," Noel said quietly.

"The cock doth not harden beneath the waves," Swifty intoned. "It stayeth in a flabby state. Pud-pull as I would, I could not make the cursed thing obey me."

Noel was chewing very hard on his horseradish now, and whether it was suggestion or not, he was feeling very flushed indeed.

"So, necessity being the mother of et cetera, what did I do, Noel?"

"What, what?"

"I stood in the shallow end. By one of the underwater lights. And then just at the crucial moment I bent my numb legs and watched as the come came. Hey, 'come came' is funny."

Noel said nothing. "And it made ribbons?" he asked finally.

Swifty nodded.

Noel stayed silent, but he wanted, if it had been a different world, to embrace the other boy, because sex was not a subject his father ever talked about and God knew it was not the kind of thing you mentioned to Estelle, but now, standing there chewing horseradish to try and skip gym Noel didn't feel so bonkers anymore. No. He was certainly, at least on occasion, bonkers. He just suddenly, at last, wasn't the only weirdo on the block. . . .

* * *

"I thought it would fall off," Noel said, very slowly, watching the sun slooooowly sink. It was the first time he had ever been stoned and he and Swifty were alone by Swifty's pool, while the maids scurried around inside, getting their dinner ready.

"Not . . . possible," Swifty said. "Not in the . . . twentieth century."

". . . well, see . . . it must be . . . 'cause I did . . . think it would fall . . . my father and mom . . . we don't . . . get into sex much . . ."

"Not with each other, I hope," Swifty said, and he cackled with laughter, lying there in his bathing suit, helpless, his breasts jiggling up and down.

". . . sex is a no-no . . . around our house it is. . . ."

On that Swifty rolled off the chair.

"What's funny?"

"Sex ain't no no-no with . . . Julian Garvey. . . ."

"No shit?"

"Didn't I tell?"

"What?"

"Your father fucked my mother."

"No shit."

"Many times."

"How'd you know?"

"I stuck a really good recording machine . . . under the Open's bed . . . a voice-activated job . . . fabulous stuff you learn. . . ."

"Go on."

". . . well, yesterday she was . . . banging this ICM agent . . . and he was in a deal with your dad . . . and the Open said this agent was better than your dad. . . ."

"Hmmm," Noel managed.

"Dinner, Mr. Swifty," the butler called from the main house.

They got up, started in. ". . . 'course the Open . . . she's a very supportive type . . . never fails to tell everybody they're better. . . ."

Noel smiled, shook his head. ". . . my father and your mother. . . ." He stared at the sun awhile. ". . . kind of makes us related. . . ." he said when he was able.

Noel stayed stoned pretty much the entire next week, just grass, but of the highest quality. His mother was pleased at his relaxed attitude about things in general, and delighted that his passion for television was tapering.

He began going to the library on his own afternoons, getting research started for a big paper, he explained, and although Estelle was momentarily perturbed that Harvard might be putting too much academic pressure on her child (long papers at a tender age might prove damaging), she couldn't find it within herself to criticize her son for studying.

Two weeks later, when Swifty nabbed the mescal buttons from Attila's cache, they were both wildly excited, since genuine hallucinogens didn't come along every day. They were alone in Swifty's room, staring at the round, dirt-brown objects. "I hear it tastes like an armpit," Swifty said.

"True," Noel told him, "but according to the books I've studied in the library, one has to put up with the bitter to enjoy the sweet. You see, because of the qualities inherent in the basic substance, it cannot be compressed into ordinary tablet form. No, what we'll have to do is take a couple of them buttons and stick them on our tongue and chew until soft and just endure."

They each put the brown buttons on their tongues. "I don't know if this is gonna be worth it," Swifty said.

"It takes two hours for the hallucinogenic effects to begin," Noel said. "You see, mescaline is a member of the chemical group known as 'amines.' Its proper chemical name is '3,4,5-trimethoxyphenylethylamine.' Didn't know that, did you?"

"I don't know it now," Swifty said.

Noel stretched and chewed his mescaline. There was no doubt about it. He was getting kind of more than a little bit interested in something even better than the tube. . . .

2

The Flab Four actually came about because of Swifty's sudden desire to have a little fruit-salad party, all the rage at most of the better California private schools. To have one, what you did was you went to your parents' medicine chest and without checking out what the prescription bottles contained, you took half a dozen pills or capsules from half a dozen bottles and so did the other partygoers and then you took all the booty and stuck them in a punch bowl and mixed them thoroughly and then everybody grabbed a handful and waited around to see what happened.

The Wertheim twins were all Swifty could manage under last minute conditions, so he and Noel and the other two mixed the pills up down in Swifty's game room and stared, dubiously, wondering who would grab what and in which order. The Wertheims—both of them short and relatively round—were named Diane and Daniel, but because Diane was nicknamed early on "Dee," that transmuted to how they were always referred to now: Tweedledee and Tweedledum. She was fiercely neurotic and already a political activist; he was every bit as disturbed as she, but his interests lay more in the poetry/sex-fiend areas.

They were, needless to say, fabulously wealthy. Their mother had come to America after World War II from Switzerland, just another of those European starlets that Zanuck seemed to be importing then by the gross. She

was lovely and blue eyed but her face seemed frozen whenever a camera came near. Which did not mean she failed
in Southern California because she possessed a talent that
was as much admired as it was genuinely rare: She married magnificently. General feeling was that only Jennifer
Jones was in her class when it came to nuptials. Old
Wertheim, her first and the father of the children, was
well into his sixties when she latched onto him. He was
so thrilled at her pregnancy he left her incredibly well
provided for, cutting out, in the process, an earlier spouse
and their three children. Lawsuits were of course brought,
when Wertheim died, but they were settled amicably, and
the widow Wertheim went on to continuing glories.

"Do you think we can die from this shit?" Tweedledee
asked, dubiously, staring at the punch bowl with its multicolored contents.

Swifty, a little edgy too, looked at Noel. "Ask the professor here."

Noel peered into the bowl. "Since we have no idea what
is involved here, anything I say would be in the realm of
speculation—"

"—just can we kick off or not?" Tweedledee wanted to
know.

"Well, I think those red objects are Seconal and these
green jobs are Dexamyls. . . ." His voice trailed off. "I
think we can get very sick but death I find doubtful."

"Geronimo," Swifty said, and he grabbed a handful,
eased them down with a mouthful of Schweppes.

Noel followed suit. Then Tweedledee and Tweedledum.
Then they all went to various overstuffed chairs in the
game room and sat down to wait.

"Are you children enjoying yourselves?" the British
Open called from upstairs. "Swifty, are we remembering
our manners?"

"We're playing 'I Packed My Grandmother's Trunk,'
Mom," Swifty hollered back, moving quickly to the punch
bowl, getting ready to hide it in the near closet if the
occasion demanded.

"Well, we'll be home early, darling."

"Have fun."

"See you, pal," Attila the Fag called.

"Yup, yup," from Swifty.

"I don't feel shit yet," Tweedledee said when the sound of the front door closing was done.

"Oh I do," Teedledum said. "My God, it's fantastic, the tingling sensations."

"Oh bullshit with you and your tingling sensations," Tweedledee said. They were often violently competitive with each other and she was particularly sour now.

"Do you know why she's mad?" Tweedledum asked. "Do you know why she is in a frenzy of jealousy?"

"Just shut up," from his sister.

"Because I had a nightmare last night," Tweedledum said. "A doozy."

"You lucky shit," Twiddledee replied.

"I don't get it," Noel said. "Why is that good?"

"They go to the same shrink," Swifty explained. "And obviously Tweedledum had a better session today."

"Not only that," Tweedledum cackled. "Not—only—that—Doctor Raymond likes me more than her. *I* am Doctor's favorite."

"Are not, are not!"

"Am am am and go fuck yourself."

Then everybody lapsed into silence and waited for something to happen. When nothing much did, Swifty asked if anyone was interested in a little hashish oil.

"Smash?" Tweedledee said. "You've got real honest-to-Christ smash?"

"Very pure."

"Where do you get that kind of stuff? I can't get that kind of stuff," Tweedledum said.

Swifty put his finger to his lips, got up, beckoned them all to follow. Beyond the game room was a corridor and at the end of it was a large safe door with a dial combination. "Wine cellar," Swifty said, fiddling with the dial. He concentrated briefly, then pulled at the heavy metal handle and the door swung open.

There was wine inside, of course, some of it just fine California, a lot of it rarities. But there was also, labeled carefully and scattered around on the various shelves, dozens of containers of the airtight variety. "Don't you know the secret to Attila's success?" Swifty said, as the twins stared silently at the labels. "He supplies more stuff to more stars and directors than anybody in the business."

"You mean your father's kind of a pusher?" Tweedledum asked.

His sister whirled on him. "So what—a lot of people think our mother is a whore."

"My family all of a sudden seems so normal," Noel said. "I'm almost ashamed."

Swifty moistened some rolling paper with several drops of hashish oil, then prepared a joint. "I think we ought to do this down by the tennis house," he said. "The maids might get nosy." He ushered everyone out of the room, checked to see that it looked precisely as it had before, then turned out the lights and slammed the great metal door shut. "It would not augur well for my future if Attila learns I've got the combo," he said, and led them back to the game room where he emptied the pills into the toilet, flushed it, grabbed some matches, and continued on to the tennis area.

"I wonder if we can die from *this* shit?" Tweedledee asked as they ambled along.

"You and your dying, you and your dying," Tweedledum said.

"The professor knows all," Swifty said.

Noel said, "It's the amount of THC in cannabis that gets us stoned and good grass, even Swifty's, doesn't have more than one or two percent THC. Good hashish oil is thirty percent. So it's maybe fifteen times stronger than what we're used to." They went into the tennis house and smoked the joint, passing it around, taking tokes, keeping it in movement until it was just a roach, which Swifty handled easily by use of a paper clip.

After a few minutes Tweedledee said, "It must be my constitution, but I don't get affected the way other people do." She went out on the tennis court then and started hitting imaginary forehands. "I don't feel shit," she said. "Who wants to play?"

"Wait till I finish conducting," Swifty replied, waving his arms slowly, the paper clip serving as baton.

"Hey, let's *really* play 'I Packed My Grandmother's Trunk,'" Tweedledum said. "I'll start. I packed my grandmother's trunk and in it I put an apple." He looked out toward his sister who was playing net now. "Your turn."

"I packed my grandmother's trunk," Tweedledee said, "and in it I put, lemmesee, lemmesee." She smashed an overhead. "And in it I put an apple."

"No no no," Tweedledum said. *"You* can't put an apple in, *I* put an apple in. You've got to put in something else."

"Oh, right, sorry," Tweedledee said. "Shit, lemmethink. Okay. Got it. I packed my grandmother's trunk and in it I put an apricot."

Noel began to giggle.

"No no no no, how stupid are you," Tweedledum hollered. "A *b*. You've got to start your word with a *b*."

"Oh, right, 'course, gimmeasec," Tweedledee said, and then she said, "I packed my grandmother's trunk and in it I put a bapple."

Now Tweedledum was giggling.

"What's so funny?" Tweedledee wanted to know. "Bapple starts with a *b*." She came into the tennis house and opened the refrigerator and took out some peanuts. She ate a few, stuck a few more up her nose. "This is very good for the complexion," she explained. "No, I guess I mean, peanut *oil* is very good for the complexion. No, that's close though. Peanut oil is good for preventing sunburn." She shook her head, joined the other two in giggling.

"You know what's really sad," Swifty said then.

"What?" Tweedledee asked.

"Well," Swifty said. "Painting makes permanent what you see, but what we could really use on this earth is something that would make permanent what you hear."

"Oh that is a good point," Tweedledum said, not laughing anymore. "That's just such a fucking heavy point I want to cry."

"I know what we could call it if it ever existed. Paintings are what you call what you see, right? You could call what you hear, tell me if you like this, you could call them 'soundings.'"

"'Soundings,'" Tweedledee said. "God, is that a word. What a deep fucking word 'soundings' is."

Then suddenly Noel was shouting, "Hey, hey, listen, *listen* everybody, there *is* something on this earth that makes permanent what you hear, and it's called music."

They all started rolling on the floor then, and the hysteria kept moving from one to the next, like an exploding spantial, just when one was done laughing the next would hit another burst and then the group would be caught up in it and maybe it wasn't funny at all, maybe you had to be there, but whatever the case, by the time they were over the laughter, they were bonded together; the Flab Four was born.

They became, instantly, inseparable. Easier for the boys, since all three attended Harvard, but the full quality of their mesh needed Tweedledee, she had the drive, the social passions, she was the one who forced their interests toward Vietnam, because early in '64 one hundred and one Americans had already been killed there, and later that year, when the bodies of the three civil rights workers were found buried in Mississippi, she was the force behind their sending money to the families of the dead and letters to LBJ.

All the parents were thrilled at the friendship, since not only were they all in the same social sphere, they also didn't have unpopular outcasts to fret about at night. Now they were raising children who if they weren't popular at least had good intimate friends.

So, stoned and together, they bopped their way through the rest of '64, getting arrested for the first time along with 793 others at the conclusion of the Free Speech protests up in Berkeley, hurrying off to Selma in March of '65 for the Montgomery Freedom March. Money was never a problem for them, since the Widow Wertheim never remembered just how much cash she carried in her purse and Swifty could always push stuff from the wine cellar in a crunch.

The summer of '65 they took an apartment in the Haight-Ashbury district for a while and the Fillmore had just opened, so they went to hear the Grateful Dead and Big Brother and the Holding Company and Country Joe and the Fish, and for Noel it was the best time of his entire life, not counting the two contacts he had involving death. Not *his* death. But still, unsettling.

It was a hot July morning when the first incident occurred. The day had begun wonderfully. The beautiful girl who shared the apartment upstairs and who went to Smith in the off-season had been given an amyl nitrite ampule and wanted bad to screw and Noel obliged, the two of them breaking the capsule after considerable foreplay, and Noel rode her into a glorious orgasm and she wasn't unhappy either, and after that he wandered out into the Haight trying to remember what he had left the apartment for in the first place. It was hotter now, and he walked a long while, eventually passing a public pool where he thought why not, so he went in, got a suit, stowed his stuff in a locker, and took a position happily stoned, clinging to the side of the deep end of the pool.

The place was jam-crammed full of children and when the black kid first said, ". . . help . . ." Noel thought it was some kind of joke. The kid had run off the board and jumped in so he must have known how to swim, Noel reasoned.

But the black kid sank under the water.

Noel watched him, waiting for the punchline, was it a practical joke or what, and the pool was very noisy what with everybody screaming so when the black kid struggled to the surface and went, ". . . help . . ." again, no one could possibly have heard.

Noel continued to watch, fascinated.

The child was trying to get his arms above the surface and sometimes he could, sometimes he couldn't, it was at best a fifty-fifty operation, and he said it one more time, very very soft now, ". . . help . . ." and then he was under again.

Noel pushed off, dove down, took the black kid's arm, hauled him to the side of the pool, then lifted him out. "Thanks," the black kid said, and then he was lost, running in the crowd.

Noel clung for a long time to the side of the pool, not sure if he'd saved someone's life or not. That night, during a morphine experiment, the Flab Four discussed the situation. Tweedledee said yeah, it must have been, but Tweedledum said no, it was just a crazy reaction to the sex capsule. Swifty couldn't get the story straight, so he decided not to vote one way or the other.

Noel, then as always, just wondered. . . .

Things began to get strung out in August, especially for Tweedledee, the Watts riot hitting her hard, and she left their place in the Haight and worked some in the riot area, the aftermath leaving her in a state of dazed depression. Tweedledum was madly in love with the dark Smith beauty one floor up but she wouldn't give him a tumble, *even* with amyl nitrite. Swifty took a quick trip to see the home folks and tell them how great summer school was going, but his main purpose was to raid the wine cellar, which he did, bringing back a supply of various goodies that would easily last the remainder of the vacation.

The night of his return he wanted to hit a flick, but the Wertheims did not share his inclination, so Noel kept him company. They each took a little toke of hash and then went off to find *Those Magnificent Men in Their Flying Machines,* which they decided would provide a better sound-and-light show than anything else playing then in the bay area.

Tweedledum was really zonked when they returned, lying sprawled and snoring deeply in the corner. Tweedledee just sat quietly on the bed in the single bedroom and was playing mumbly-peg on the wooden floor with the kitchen knife. Noel stuck his head in, waved, and in reply she grabbed the knife, held it in thrust position, and told him to get the fuck away.

"Little problem," Noel said to Swifty, as he backed into the main room, and Swifty, frowning, went into the bedroom briefly where Tweedledee only said, "I'm warning you, motherfucker," which was enough to send Swifty into a quick confab.

It was eleven at night and they had been gone for well over three hours and their problem as they saw it was simply this: They didn't know what she had taken. Swifty had brought up many samples and trying to go through and figure what was missing was impossible because he hadn't really paid that much mind to what he was bringing, just so it was major league in terms of quality and power.

Just then Tweedledee came running out of the bedroom with the knife and they scattered, Noel and Swifty, keeping her in the middle, except she was doing a crazy thing now, she was rubbing the blade along her body, scraping her clothes with the sharp edge, and then she snarled and pulled her dress off, standing in the dim room fat and pale and scratching the sharp edge of the knife across her skin, saying, "The roaches, shit, it's the fucking roaches," and Noel said, "I don't see any," and Tweedledee said, "Under, under, you dumb cocksucking son of a bitch, *the roaches are under here,*" and she was scraping the knife across her skin now, making herself bleed slightly where she'd made it too raw, and Noel said, "Right, gotcha," and he moved right toward her, unafraid of the knife, and began scratching her skin with both his hands saying, "Don't panic, Dee, we'll get those fuckers out; Swifty, come help get the goddam roaches out from under Dee's skin," and as Swifty moved in Noel said, "Hey, may as well give me that, that's not helping," and Tweedledee surrendered the knife which Noel skidded across the floor toward the corner where Tweedledum was snoring blissfully while the other three worked at his sister's body.

"Snakes!" Tweedledee hollered. "Snakes and roaches," and Noel said, "How heavy has she been into coke?" but Swifty wasn't sure, she'd been away, so had he, so Noel stood and tweaked her nose and she screamed in pain.

"Hey Dee?" Noel said. "You want to know, Dee—pay attention strict attention to me!"

"What?" she managed.

"The name is 'formication' and it's kind of a standard everyday thing, nothing to worry about, you just have this conviction that snakes and bugs and ants are crawling around under your skin and you want them out, am I right? Dee? *Are you paying strict fucking attention to me?*"

"Fornication is fucking," Tweedledee said.

"It certainly is, Dee," Noel went on, running his hands over and over her body, keeping up a steady line of talk for her to concentrate on. "But that's with an 'n,' this is an 'm,' they're different letters—Dee—Dee—tell me about about 'm' and 'n.' "

"Well, they, 're, they're . . . different."

"Bingo. Absolutely. They are certainly different letters," and he gestured to Swifty to flick the lights on and when the room was bright they began walking her, Noel talking about the lights and how lights scared the shit out of snakes and roaches, hell, roaches were like fucking vampires, strictly panicked when things got bright around them, and they kept her walking, Noel filling her in on all kinds of info, like did she know that psychedelic drugs were almost not called psychedelic drugs, and that confused her, but she was interested kind of, so Noel explained that the actual word was coined in 1956 so it was less than ten years old, and it was this early worker in the field, Humphry Osmond, who coined the word, but first they didn't know what to call the mind expanders, and of course, Aldous Huxley was always interested in that particular subject and he and Osmond were in correspondence as to what the fuck to call them, what generic name, and Huxley came up with a name he liked and he sent a couplet containing the word to Osmond, and this is how the couplet went:

> *To make this trivial world sublime,*
> *Take half a Gramme of phanerothyme.*

"Phanerothyme," that was Huxley's choice for the whole bunch, LSD and the rest.

"Pretty," Tweedledee said.

"That's what Osmond thought," Noel told her. "But too pretty." It was four in the morning by now, and his throat was hurting from the constant chitchat, but her paranoia was lessening. "So he decided on psychedelic. End of lecture."

"I didn't take any LSD tonight," Tweedledee said.

"But you had more than just coke?"

She nodded and stretched. "Oh sure."

"I wonder what, exactly."

"Oh you know. A pinch of this, a taste of that." Now she was yawning.

"She's gonna crash soon," Swifty said quietly.

Noel nodded and now Tweedledee was smiling, eyes half closed. They led her back into the bedroom, put her on the old mattress, went back outside, exhausted. They each got their sleeping bags ready, shared a large bottle of paregoric because they were too whipped for anything stronger, rolled up in their bags, and fantasized probably for all of five minutes before they were asleep.

Noel was the first one ready to roll so the next day around noon he got up and made a big pot of coffee and when it was done, he poured a cup for Swifty, then poked him enough times to wake him, went back to the kitchen, repeated the process for Tweedledee who was in rocky shape, still kind of stoned, but clearly on the mend; Tweedledum, it turned out, was the one who was no longer around.

"Jesus shit," Swifty said, pounding on the rotund form, but it remained inert.

"He never pulled this before," Tweedledee said.

"You dumb cunt snap to, he's dead!" Swifty screamed, but Tweedledee just told him, "When we were kids he used to hold his breath till he passed out or close to it, but this is a new one on me."

Noel said, "Check the stuff you brought up again. What the hell could it have been?"

Swiftly took a careful inventory before he said, "The mandrake root is gone. I had it labeled specially because it ain't the kind of shit you mess with. Fuck, he used it all."

"Oh sure that's it," Tweedledee said, kicking her brother lightly in the ribs, whispering, "Come on now," before turning to Noel. "He got all excited because there's this famous poem about getting a kid pregnant with mandrake root and he wondered how it would work on a guy."

Noel quoted, " 'Go and catch a falling star, get with child a mandrake root.' It means gather with a child a mandrake root, not anything about knocking up anybody. At least I think that's what it means."

"Come on now, I'm gonna keep this up till you cut this out," Tweedledee said, poking and poking with her foot. Then she knelt beside him and said, "Okay, no mercy," and started tickling him with both hands. She began under the armpits and she went at it under the chin and finally she knelt and gave him both barrels in the ribs, his most vulnerable area, and when that didn't work she rocked beside his body awhile before folding.

It all got very wild after that, because the cops had to be informed, the Widow Wertheim too, and they decided on her first, so Noel made the call, saying that this terrible thing had happened and get right up here please and I can't put Dee on the phone now, she's kind of in bad shape now, and then they tried after he'd hung up to iris in on a story that might hold, and the best they could come up with was unrequited love, he loved this Smith girl who'd crushed him and by accident he was given this bad stuff on the street, there was a lot of bad shit on the street, that much was sure true, and they repeated the story over and over and hoped it would hold water for the world outside.

It did and it didn't. They weren't jailed or hassled by the cops; they left the Haight the next day free and clear. But the Widow Wertheim knew she had a sick cookie on her hands with Dee who she stuck in a terrific sanitorium south of San Diego. The Garveys and the Ballingers watched their boys a bit more closely the next months too, and Swifty went back into shrinking while Noel started going, with irony noted, to Doctor Raymond who had ministered the Wertheim twins when they were twins and in whom Noel didn't put a whole lot of faith.

By mid '67 they were together again, with a new name now: The Mama and the Papas, and they spent this love summer in the East Village, which was fun except Tweedledee was obsessed with Vietnam now, over six thousand dead, three thousand more than the year previous, and she was panicked that Reagan was going to be governor of California and Nixon might get the big job the year following, and then where would the country be, so in '68 they all went to Chicago for the summer. Noel got arrested and Swifty too while Tweedledee got clubbed bad in the head by a goon cop because who could tell which sex was what anymore and she looked for all the world like an overweight boy.

They were very strung out now, and even if they hadn't been, it was a tough time to look the world straight in the eye and see anything sensible, what with King blown away in April, Bobby in June.

Tweedledee blew herself away just before entering USC. She was, she told them the day she did it, awfully tired. She had planned to fly to Washington and self-immolate herself in front of the Pentagon but halfway to the airport she simply ran out of energy, told the cab driver to pull over to the side of the road, and while he was following her instructions, she sought, successfully, the rest she needed.

Swifty and Noel took a new name, The Odd Couple, and took to calling each other "Oscar" and "Felix," but the fun and games were ending and though they flew east together and spent their three days at Woodstock properly ripped, it wasn't totally fun. Because they both knew a simple thing: One of them was due to die next and who was it going to be?

They went to Stanford together, aging freshmen, but their split was clear. Swifty's brains were scrambling badly while Noel was becoming fascinated with heroes. Where would the next ones be coming from. Malcolm and Martin gone. Rose's boys. LBJ gone, Tricky Dick manning the helm. Dylan with his head fractured somewhere in the East. The Beatles split over greed. Teddy gone with the wind because of Mary Jo. Thirty-three thousand dead in Vietnam and Calley had killed how many in My Lai? Calley and Manson seemed on their way to becoming culture heroes and that seemed, to Noel, somehow wrong, and he didn't give a shit if Paul McCartney's death was a rumor or not, Paul McCartney wasn't a hero anymore.

Swifty's eyes were like piss holes in the snow. He said to Noel, "I've been waiting for good flying weather." It was a stunning Stanford dawn, mid-May, cool, but without the chill of April.

Noel was reading a Patton biography. He put it on his chest and lay there, watching the other man. "What if I call Attila?" he said. "Maybe you could get your old pad back at Menninger's. You loved the view, remember?"

"I'm done with them. I'm just waiting for a little more visibility, then vrroooooooommmmmm."

Noel stood. His room was on the fifth floor. It had a big window with a lovely view of the campus. "I'll drive you to the airport."

"Ah hey, come on."

"I mean it, it's no problem."

"I mean, 'Hey, come on, quit bullshitting me.' "

Noel was very strong, much stronger than Swifty of course, but he wasn't sure what Swifty had taken, how deep or dangerous the resultant frenzy could be.

"Any messages?" Swifty said then.

"To?"

"I said quit the bullshit, you know who, them, them."

"The Wertheims you mean?" He walked casually toward the door, stopped when he was certain he could cut Swifty off.

Swifty was crying, which wasn't unusual, he'd been doing that lately, but usually when he was in some kind of wild aberrational voyage, when walls turn soft and the floor speaks hurtfully. But now it was scary because he just stood there, totally unaware that his eyes were gushing tears. Finally, when they reached his mouth, he wiped the back of his hand across his lips and found out what was going on.

"Hey, you're not really in shape to run the marathon," Noel told him. "Let's go grab some coffee."

Swifty's eyes were bulging now. He wasn't aware of that either. Or the tremor in his left hand. "So Smilin' Jack's about to blow," Swifty said. "And we'll check things out in the wild blue yonder at some later date."

"You're not getting out of the room, Swifty, so cut the aviator shit."

Swifty pulled himself as erect as he could, snapped off a salute, looked at himself in the dresser mirror. "I've always had these tits," he said. "Isn't that the weirdest fucking thing?" That said, he took a step toward the door but Noel was too quick for him, only Swifty laughed because it turned out he was the one who was too quick for Noel after all, and the window was closed but no matter, Swifty dove through and sailed, arms wide now, from sight.

Noel, five floors above, heard the body land. . . .

Although his parents never believed it, Noel's entrance into the Marine Corps that summer was not a sudden decision. He had spent hundreds of hours, literally, deciding which branch of service to enlist in. The Marines were always his choice, he simply wasn't sure if he could measure up. He looked like Yogi Berra, he was strong basically, but he'd never had a physical job, never really done anything physically beyond social tennis. Finally he screwed his courage and in August he was gone, busting his ass at Camp Upshur, praying at night to be able to hold together and survive the next twenty-four-hour ordeal.

It was really that, a day-to-day thing with him, at least at the start. Gradually, halfway through training, he began to realize he was going to succeed and beyond that lay the shot, if only he got shipped to Vietnam, to be, just once, a hero.

When basic was finished he had hoped to get shipped over only instead he was headquartered in San Diego, close enough for his parents to bug him on weekends, driving down, Estelle's brow permanently furrowed, convinced something terrible was going to happen, and Noel tried to explain to her that something terrible had *already* happened and it was called San Diego. Perhaps the happiest day of Noel's life was the following June when he got his shipping orders and then it all blurred, the leave-taking, the long trip across, the move to Thoung Duc in Quang Nam Province, or was it the move to Quang Nam in Thoung Duc Province, all the names seemed totally impenetrable to him and the heat he had been told about but not really prepared for, he had been in high temperatures often, most notably around Palm Springs, but that was desert heat, dry, and here it was as if the air had weight to it, it dragged at you, pulled you to earth so that it was only with concentrated effort you could keep your proper Marine posture. And the suddenness of dawn and dusk surprised him too. Light-switches almost, and that was different, and his first combat moments came close behind dawn, roaring down in a chopper, landing, following his platoon leader on the run, their run becoming a walk as they entered the swamp area, and in less than ten minutes he saw a dead VC with leeches on his eyes and that was not the kind of thing you wanted to dwell on, and Noel didn't, because the explosion came then, that and the sniper fire, and Noel felt himself in the air and then heard his body splash down in the mud and he drank his own blood for a while as the ambush continued and when he managed once to open an eye he saw a leech moving up his shoulder toward his face and Noel thought how humiliating it was, forget the pain, the blood, the leeches, the stink and screaming, it was the humiliation that ripped most, because he had been a Marine for almost a year, a combat soldier for less than half an hour; he would never be brave enough to explain that failure, he knew, and he hoped he would never have the chance to. Please, Noel prayed, as the screams went on around him, please God just this once let me die.

Close only counts, though, in horseshoes, and the many medics and orderlies who cleansed him and supplied him with food and blood and stitched up his wounds in the field and later in Saigon eventually foiled his wish. He was hospitalized for a very long time, and for most of that period what he feared more than anything was not any permanent impairment or the like; no, all he had to do to get his personal panic button ringing was to think about how horrid his homecoming was going to be.

In fact, it was even worse than his imaginings, because they thought, his parents, sister, acquaintances, that what had been miraculously brought back to them was simply this: a hero. There was no convincing them otherwise. Besides, he had the medals to prove it. So what he wanted to be and wasn't he was, at least to those around him, and back in the manse on Sunset, Noel grieved.

He knew returning to Stanford would be a waste, but he tried it, transferring after a semester down to UCLA, a ten-minute drive from home. UCLA was just more of the same, though, what was the point to studying when you didn't know why you were doing it or what you were studying toward. Noel's depression deepened, he was floundering and he knew it. He moved out of the house, rented a small beach house, fucked a lot of girls, jogged some, got into organic foods. Rolfing came then, and then tai-chi. Bioenergetics fascinated him, and so did Esalen and est. Scientology he hung onto for a while too. Primal-scream therapy was helpful, at least for a little but the only time he actually thought he saw sunshine was when he had the guru except the guy turned out to be not from India at all, but Sausalito, a fact Noel didn't bruit about a whole lot.

He took to giving up his visits to Swifty, as guilty as that made him feel. Ordinarily he tried to stop by Swifty's home once a week and read aloud but Swifty's inability to respond became just too depressing and it was after leaving Swifty's one day that he messed around with a little too much LSD and he could tell the way everyone was whispering around him that probably he was into a breakdown. Riggs wasn't bad though, and it was there he began to think a lot about the 60s and their importance to today and then he focused from the decade in general to the Beatles and Dylan in particular and when he got home he enjoyed researching them a lot.

But nothing in his entire life, not anything ever, had been as intriguing as the week he spent with his father watching *Tinsel* start to become a reality. Which was why the news from Harry Brennerman that Welch had changed her mind and wouldn't do the picture hit him so surprisingly hard. . . .

*   *   *

As soon as he heard Brennerman's voice on the phone, Julian knew there was trouble. "Keed," Brennerman began, "we have got to talk. You got five minutes?"

"For you, Harry, six."

"I'll be on over," Brennerman said and as Julian hung up and sat back at his desk, it must have showed in his face, because Noel, seated on the office couch, said, "I haven't seen you look so sad since we lost the Japanese gardener."

"You're mistaking sadness for concern."

"About?"

Julian shook his head. "I fear, my darling, that we will know all too soon."

Brennerman hurried in a few minutes later, smoothing his hair across his skull. He sat in the chair across from Julian, said hello to Noel, took a deep breath and said, "It's nothing that can't be worked out."

"That bad?" Julian replied.

"Men of good will can do miraculous things, keed."

Julian waited.

"She won't do it naked," Harry Brennerman said then.

"I don't see why that's a problem," Julian said with a large smile. "Since only the entire last half of the film hinges on her nudity. *What the fuck do you mean she won't do it naked?*"

"She's never gone bare in her life, and I just got a call from her people saying that her whole career has been based on the fact that in this time of sexual freedom, so called, she's been the world's leading sex symbol and she's always kept her clothes on."

"It was agreed she'd do the part, Brennerman."

"Not naked. Not now. Everybody's been after her to strip for years—she was offered really big bucks to do that Wallace bestseller *The Fan Club* but she wouldn't."

"This is one of your noted ploys to sweeten the pot, isn't it? Up her salary and suddenly the sun is shining."

"I'd tell you to go fuck yourself but you probably do

already. Now, do you want to make a movie or do you want to shout?"

"Finish your spiel, putz."

"I think there's a shot she'll do it in a bra and panties."

"Well that *is* good news," Julian said. He turned to Noel. "Eliza has just been rescued from the ice, child, face Mecca for me, thank you."

"You're an awful person anyway, Julian," Harry Brennerman said. "But trying to deal with you when you're about to get your period is almost too much to bear."

"Brennerman—a bra and panties ruins the aesthetic reality of the film, plus, who the fuck wants to see her in a bra and panties for half a movie?" Suddenly he clapped his hands. "Wait a second—all is not lost—Brennerman, we'll shift the movie to Japan and she can play it in a komono." Garvey stood, smoldering, voice rising as he said, "Even better—*even better*—we'll put the whole thing in Alaska, she's alone in her house, there's a blizzard raging outside and her heater goes on the fritz and she can do the movie in an ankle-length parka! The public will come flocking or I don't know show business." He gestured toward the door. "Miss Welch is out, Mr. Brennerman, and so, may I add, are you."

"You got your financing on her name, prick—don't be in such a rush to play hero—"

"—let *me* worry about producing, I suggest you worry about finding jobs for your clients, assuming you have any."

"Bye, keed," Brennerman said to Noel. "Must be wonderful, having a father who's Hollywood's best-loved man since Harry Cohn."

When they were alone again, Noel said, "Hey, the picture's still on and everything."

"Of course."

"Do you think that was a ploy to get more money?"

"No, darling; Harry doesn't work that way. She's out. Miss Welch is no longer aboard the train."

"But what are we going to do?"

"Smile, baby."

"But what are we going to do? Tell me!"

"Are you really worried?"

"Well, I've just enjoyed—"

"—because you must stop. We are not looking for Atlantis, Noel. We're simply in the market for a lady who is built like a brick shithouse. Believe me when I tell you something."

"What?"

"Such creatures are not totally unknown in Southern California. . . ."

3

THE CASTING SESSION
(Hollywood's Longest-Running One Act Play)

THE TIME:
The Present

THE PLACE:
The office of JULIAN GARVEY, famed film producer.

AT RISE:
THREE MEN are seated around the expensively furnished room. GARVEY, elegantly dressed, tie buttoned, is at his desk with several yellow pads and pencils handy. NOEL, his son, also with pads and pencils, is on the couch. ROBERT SCHWAB, GARVEY'S son-in-law, is in a chair. ALL THREE study various casting guides, film yearbooks, movie magazines. For a moment the only sound is that of pages turning.

SCHWAB

Okay; Andress.

NOEL
(*Looking up from his movie magazine*)

Huh?

SCHWAB

I figured it would be best to go about this logically instead
of just spraying names around. Alphabetically, the first
one I came across was Ursula Andress.

JULIAN

May I say something that is not intended to ruffle feelings?

(*Both SCHWAB AND NOEL nod.*)

It is essential that in this room, here and now, we feel
free to say anything we want, no matter what. We must
not put governors on ourselves, because there are many
people who feel that the fate of a film is settled by the first
day of photography. If you've miscast the crucial roles, no
amount of pasting later on is going to cover the flaw.
Clear so far?

(*Both SCHWAB AND NOEL nod.*)

Then may I say that I think Ursula Andress is one of the
more vomitous ideas I've heard lately.

SCHWAB

"Vomitous" huh? Does that mean you don't like it?

JULIAN

Schwabby, listen: This picture is your baby. You wrote it,
you've got to be on the floor directing the mother. However, it is my memory that this story is rather centered on
the last hours of Marilyn Monroe. If the story were instead centered on the last hours of Ilse Koch, I think Miss
Andress would certainly have rated consideration five
years ago.

SCHWAB

You're saying you don't want a foreigner.

JULIAN

That is one hundred percent correct. I feel this is peculiar-
ly American material, and it would be unbalanced if we
were to cast it otherwise. So in your own alphabetical
way, when you come to Brigitte Bardot, Marthe Keller,
Romy Schneider, Elke Sommer, you can skip on down.
Are we agreed?

SCHWAB

Makes sense to me; okay by you, Noel?

NOEL
(*Looking up from his movie magazine*)
Huh?

JULIAN

Darling, please try to focus a bit more on the proceedings.

NOEL

Right, right; sorry.

SCHWAB

I think we can skip Ann-Margret, unless anyone objects?

JULIAN

Curiosity compels my asking why. She might be wonderful.

SCHWAB

I had a friend who worked *Carnal Knowledge*. The nudity
was very hard for her, and we've had enough trouble with
nudity.

JULIAN
(*Takes a yellow pad, writes.*)
I think we ought to keep a "possibles" list and I'd like to
put her on. If we have to strike her later, we strike her
later.

SCHWAB

Fine. Listen, I meant to say this when you put the slug to foreigners. I have a personal thing against models who try to act, so I'd like to also leave out people like Lauren Hutton, Jennifer O'Neill, Cybill Shepherd. No ex-models, okay?

(*JULIAN nods, indicates for SCHWAB to continue.*)

Lemmesee where I was. Right. Carroll Baker.

JULIAN

Shit, Schwabby, get hold of yourself.

SCHWAB

Sorry, sorry. Diane Baker.

JULIAN

No to her, and I don't want Kenny Baker either, move on.

SCHWAB

Candy Bergen?

JULIAN

She could certainly play the Monroe part. However, she is not now and has never been voluptuous and I do not intend to people our project with flat-chested sex symbols if you don't mind.

SCHWAB

How 'bout Jackie Bisset?

JULIAN
(*Writing on his yellow pad*)
Now *that* intrigues me. A lot.

NOEL

Am I going crazy?—didn't you just say no foreigners? She's English.

JULIAN

Well, that's not really foreign.

NOEL

Shit, Daddy, it's in Europe.

JULIAN

Go back to your comic books, Noel, you're paying far too much attention.

SCHWAB

Karen Black could act it.

JULIAN

Karen Black naked? Get hold of yourself, child.

SCHWAB

Susie Blakely?—nope, another model. Bujold? Good actress.

NOEL

No good, she's Canadian, another foreigner.

JULIAN

(To SCHWAB)

The boy learns quickly, doesn't he?

(To Noel now)

You are most definitely my son. Proceed.

SCHWAB

Burstyn—don't say it, I know she's too old, but God she could have acted the shit out of the part a few years ago, she would have been a goddam dream and—

(Suddenly jumping to his feet tucking in his shirttails)

—I've got it—I've got the killer idea—don't piss on this one, Julian, I mean it—give it a chance to sink in—she's not exactly what we had in mind but *think about it*—will you promise to think about it?

JULIAN

Solemnly sworn.

SCHWAB

Wait for it—wait for it—here it comes: *Ali MacGraw.*

NOEL

I *am* going crazy—Daddy says no foreigners then creams over Bisset, you say absolutely no ex-models and you hit us with Ali MacGraw, who only modeled how many years?

SCHWAB

She was a fashion coordinator for a lot of those years, there's a difference. She was *around* modeling, but she wasn't in front exactly of the camera, there's a difference.

NOEL

I think we all ought to pull up our trousers, it's getting very deep in here.

JULIAN

I happen to be personally fond of the lady, but I defy anyone to name a country she could be the sex symbol of.

SCHWAB

Okay, okay, but can we at least pencil her in on the "possibles" list?

(*JULIAN nods, writes.*)

NOEL
(*Quietly*)

Dixie Crowder.

SCHWAB

Again?

NOEL

She had the best body I ever saw in all my life. Not that I ever saw her for real. But in photographs or the tube, nobody ever came close. Not for me anyway.

SCHWAB
(To JULIAN)

Who's he delirious over?

JULIAN

She was a television star a decade ago. Daisy Mae on *Dogpatch*. She is still—and I have seen her for real, a week ago it was—glorious. She is also happily married and retired for many years so we can proceed briskly, there are twenty-three letters to go.

SCHWAB
(Starts to read from his casting guide, stops.)

My big sister went to school with Ginger Abraham back in New York. Face from the past is what brings her to mind. I had such a crush. Not to be believed. When she was fifteen, I don't think Taylor could have touched her.

JULIAN

I met her when she was twenty-two or three. . . .
(His voice suddenly drifts off. There is a pause.)

NOEL

You worked with her, didn't you, Daddy? You must have known her well.

JULIAN

(For the first time now, he rises, moves to a window, stares out.)
Never as well as I wanted, my babe; not half so well as that. . . .

(LIGHTS quickly fade. In the ensuing darkness, however,

the voices keep right on going: "Blythe Danner." "Cathe-
rine Deneuve." "Sandy Dennis." "Angie Dickinson." "Don-
na Douglas." "Patty Duke."

LIGHTS UP as lunch is ending. GARVEY paces, holding
a cardboard container, his tie now unbuttoned. Suddenly
he whirls.)

JULIAN
(*to SCHWAB, in mock fury; ALL THREE are tired now.*)
Did you just say Lainie Kazan? To a figure of my importance in the industry, Lainie Kazan is suggested?

(to NOEL)

Want any of my peach yogurt, hon?

(Balefully)

I hate fucking peach yogurt.

(*Back to SCHWAB now*)

If you ever ever ever say anything that dumb to me again,
Robert Schwab, I'm going to fix you—I'm going to hire
Abbe Lane for the part and let you get a performance out
of *her*.

NOEL
I think—

JULIAN
—baby, if you're going to say you think we ought to
consider Dixie Crowder again, I would greatly appreciate
it if you wouldn't.

NOEL
Well, you're not coming up with many gems, y'know.

JULIAN

Casting is an art and this is a particular bitch to solve. Consider: She must be glorious to look upon, plus a consummate actress, plus be able to project vulnerability. Plus she must have that sense of past time about her, like Swanson in *Sunset Boulevard*, we need a girl who brings an overpowering reality to the screen.

(He thinks a moment.)

I wonder if Margaret Trudeau is available?

(LIGHTS FADE again. Again, the names never stop. Only now the voices are getting more and more weary. "Jill St. John." "Carly Simon." "Sissy Spacek." "Connie Stevens." "Stella Stevens."

LIGHTS UP and it's late in the day. The office is littered with coffee cups and rolled up yellow pages. GARVEY, sleeves rolled up, sits in a chair, his head in his hands. SCHWAB thumbs through various manuals. NOEL lies on the couch, staring into space.)

SCHWAB

Natalie Wood is the last name alphabetically.
(He drops the manual to the floor.)

JULIAN
(Barely lifting his head)
Not if we can convince Efrem Zimbalist, Jr., to perform in drag.

SCHWAB

I hate your jokes. I really hate your jokes. I hate everybody's jokes just now.

JULIAN

Read us the "possibles," hon.

NOEL

The possible possibles as well as the barelys?

JULIAN

Please.

NOEL

(*Reaching for a sheet of yellow paper, reading tonelessly*)
Ann-Margret, Jacqueline Bisset, Julie Christie, Sue Lyon,
Ali MacGraw, Kim Novak, Valerie Perrine, Tuesday Weld.

SCHWAB

God made the earth in just seven of these; I don't know
how he did it.

JULIAN
(*Rising*)
He didn't have to deal with actors.

(*Rubbing his eyes*)

None of them truly make the hackles rise, do they? Logic
dictates there simply must be those we've overlooked. Let's
get to it.

NOEL

You mean we're not finished?

JULIAN

Hon, believe me, the surface has yet to be scratched. From
the top, Schwabby.

SCHWAB

Ursula Andress.

JULIAN

She wouldn't be bad, who knocked her out of contention?

NOEL

You did.

JULIAN

Oh. I knew it was somebody. . . .

(*LIGHTS START THEIR FINAL FADE. JULIAN,
NOEL and SCHWAB continue as before, except now we
don't hear them. Now what we hear, from speakers all
over, are names, read mechanically, growing louder and
louder in no logical order:* "Joan Collins." "Suzanne
Somers." "Sheree North." "Farrah Fawcett." "Linda Ron-
stadt." "France Nuyen." "Barbara Loden." "Dolly Parton."
"Julie Newmar." "MAMIE VAN DOREN." MONIQUE
VON VOOREN! SANDRA DEEEEEEEE!!!*

CURTAIN

4

"I would like please," Julian Garvey said to his wife, as he walked in after work two days later, "an ice cold vodka stinger on the rocks. Double."

Estelle nodded, began to ring for the maid, then changed her mind and said, "You like it two to one, yes?"

"Remarkable."

"It is, considering not only how many years it's been since you had a double stinger but also how many years more it's been since I ended my bartending career." She went to the bar by the library while Julian collapsed in the leather chair that was his favorite. "Where is the silly Creme de Menthe?" she said, almost to herself.

"Bottom shelf, rear," Julian said, eyes closed, breathing deeply. "In the old days, you'd have gone straight for it."

"In the old days I felt racy mucking about with alcohol," Estelle said. "And I did so like to please my man when he returned home from the wars. But that, my dear, was, as we both know, another country, and that lady has long since passed on."

"Don't be bitchy, I'm not really up for it just now."

Estelle stopped dead, the ice bucket in one hand, the lid in the other. "Was that bitchy? I'm sorry." She turned her attention then back to the drink she was making.

"Query: Noel is where?"

"He'd seen two movies already today but then he read somewhere that Jane Fonda was voluptuous in *Coming*

Home and perhaps you were making a mistake not putting her on the list, so off he went. He's very excited these days, thanks to you."

"I could have saved him the journey—I think I was told that in the love scene with Voight either some or all of the nude shots were done without seeing Fonda's head. They just used a double for the body; standard."

"Such a wondrous business," she said, bringing him the drink in an enormous brandy snifter filled with ice.

"I may live after all," he said, saluting her with the drink, before commencing to down it. "But it's such a different business now, Estelle. There are no such things as secrets anymore, thanks to Mister Xerox."

"Meaning?"

"I got shot down today by Ann-Margret, Valerie Perrine, Jackie Bisset, Julie Christie, and Ali MacGraw. Inconceivable." He drank again. "I hadn't even submitted the script to half of them. I just called their agents and touched base and whap—before I'd said, 'Oh, by the way,' they said, 'Forget it.' I felt like that comic strip character, the one with the dark cloud always over his head."

"Do you know how it happened?"

"Sure. Once a script leaves your little hot hands, it gets Xeroxed. And then the Xerox copies get Xeroxed. This is a very common occurrence. Twenty-four hours after a new script is finished, television's already ripping it for some quickie tv movie."

"What reasons were you given? What did they say?"

"Oh, they'd fumpher up some limp excuse or they'd say it wasn't right for their client or their client wasn't interested or their client wouldn't do it because of the nudity. The more honest ones just said flat out they thought it was a piece of shit."

Estelle answered the phone when it rang then. Covering the receiver she whispered, "Do you want to talk to a Philip Schwartzman?"

"No one *ever* wants to, but since he's *the* money behind *Tinsel* I'd best pay my respects." He took the phone from

his wife and in a booming voice said, "Phil—Phil listen—
you can absolutely relax—I spoke to Edward Bennett Williams myself not more than an hour ago and he promised
me he personally would defend you on the morals charge."

"Hey, guy," Schwartzman said.

"That was a rather convoluted joke, but a joke nonethe-
less."

"I got it, I got it."

"Good," Julian said. "Then we can move on to more
religious matters. The reason I called you was—"

"—did you call me? I called you."

"Another attempt at humor, Phil; go on."

"I just thought I'd check in. Touch base. See how
things were hanging."

"The world is filled with sunlight," Julian said. "Flowers
are on every tree."

"Then it isn't true?"

"You mean about the moon not being made of green
cheese? Don't believe every little rumor that comes along,
Phil."

"About Welch walking our venture."

"Don't believe every little rumor that comes along,
Phil."

"I am told, on very good authority, she won't do *Tinsel.*"

"Since I'm sure that the authority you are resting your
case on comes directly from the playground at the local
kindergarten, may I ask you to please call Harry Brennerman. She is totally willing to do our picture. In point of
fact, she loves it, so Mr. Brennerman says."

"With or without clothes does she love it, Julian?"

"Costume problems have rarely submarined entire pro-
jects, Phil. I admit the lady is a bit squeamish about baring
her boobies, but time has a way of altering thought."

"Perrine means nothing foreign, Julian."

"Why bring up Valerie?"

"Oh, Julian, cut the charade."

"But I was doing so well."

"No you weren't. You're losing a step maybe. Happens to the biggest."

"Cut to the chase, Phil."

"We'll still take Welch and *The Deep* did good foreign, so we'll accept Bisset. Period."

"You son of a bitch, you know they both said no; you knew it when you called, why don't you come out and admit you're backing out?"

"Okay. We're backing out, Julian. You happy?"

"Anything that enables me to terminate a conversation with you fills me with joy."

"Don't blame me 'cause you've lost it, Julian. Listen, we're buddies, I won't tell a soul. But next year when they don't seat you up front at Chasen's, the whole world's gonna know." And he hung up.

"Maybe I have lost a step," Julian said. "Phil Schwartzman got the last word in on me; that never happened before." He looked at the receiver a moment, then slammed it viciously into its cradle. He whirled on his wife. "If you tell me that was a childish action, Estelle, I promise I'll kill you here and now." He picked up his double stinger and chugged it. "I wouldn't mind another," he said, handing the glass to his wife.

She took it and returned to the bar.

Julian sat brooding in his chair. "You know the greatest fear in this racket? It's not going broke or getting fired or producing *Cleopatra*. It's losing a step. Like Billy Wilder now—a giant, Estelle. *The Apartment, Some Like It Hot*, a whole string. But now when people see him they say, 'Oh, he was so wonderful.' He *was* so wonderful. 'Was' is the killer word out here, my sweet. Losing a step is right next door to dying."

Estelle, in a Betty Boop voice, began to sing, "I'm sorry for myself."

Julian brooded silently after that. He finished the second drink and halfway through the third he decided it might be best to take a little nap but he had trouble navigating, so Estelle locked arms with him, led him out of the room and up the stairs and down the hall to his bedroom and then to his bed where he sat, letting her help him unbutton his shirt. "You'll feel better tomorrow," Estelle said. "That's a promise."

Julian shook and shook his head. "You stupid bitch, don't you understand—*the money's gone!*"

"You'll just have to go to a studio, that's all."

"*Been* to the studios. All those peabrains. They won't touch it without a star an' no star will touch it."

"You'll think of something, you always think of something."

Julian shook his head.

Singsong: "Yes you will."

He took her hands and held them tight. "It's dead, Estelle. *Tinsel* is dead as Kelsey's nuts." Then he fell back on the mattress and closed his eyes. "Estelle?"

"Right here."

"Let's not tell Noel till morning. . . ."

At four A.M. Estelle tiptoed into Julian's room carrying a tray. Using the hall light for navigation, she put the tray down on his dressing table, then moved to the bed, gently began to tap him in the shoulder.

He stirred.

She kept on tapping till his eyes fluttered open.

"Shhhhh, now," she whispered, finger to her lips.

He lay back and groaned.

"Shhhhh, I said." She went to the tray, took a damp washcloth, handed it to him. "Rub your eyes." While he was doing that, she got his mug of coffee, exchanged it for the washcloth.

"You're too old to be a stewardess, Estelle, and my head hurts."

"I'd like to go outside where we can talk, Julian; Noel's such a light sleeper. Put on your robe, it's going to be cool."

He was about to argue, but something in her tone told

him it was time to shut up and listen, so he did as he was told, threw his robe about him, tiptoed down the stairs out to the patio by the swimming pool. "I want you not to be flip," Estelle said then. "I want you to consider this as perhaps the most important talk of our lives."

Julian nodded, blew on his coffee, let the steam massage his eyes.

"When Noel came home last night, naturally he wanted to talk to you but I said you were exhausted and had gone to bed so he talked to me as a surrogate, and he hated the movie, didn't like Fonda for *Tinsel* but the main thing was he was just so excited, Julian. Just so full of notions and ideas and I did something then and there."

"You didn't tell him?"

"Of course not. No. I simply excused myself and put in a call to Arthur Bailey-Hall. We talked, I'm afraid, for the better part of an hour." Arthur Bailey-Hall had been their lawyer for over a quarter century. His last name was, of course, a total fabrication, which was one of the reasons Julian picked him in the first place.

"About?"

"*Tinsel.* Julian, I want you to produce it yourself."

"Dear heart, I am producing it myself. I have been producing movies all by my lonesome for lo these many moons. What did you imagine my occupation was?"

"*I asked you not to flip, Julian.*"

"So you did. I erred. Genuine apologies all round. Explain what you mean, Estelle, 'produce it myself.' "

"I mean with your own money."

Julian just stared at her.

"You can do it." She brought some folded pages out of her bathrobe pocket. "Arthur explained ever so much to me."

"Estelle—Estelle, no one except Joe Levine uses his own money to produce films. The whole secret to being a successful producer is *never* to use your own money."

Estelle stared at the pages, covered with tidy notations.
"Now," she said, "what was *Tinsel* to cost?"

"It wasn't totally ascertained. Ballpark figure—four to
five."

"Arthur said four."

"Arthur is a very wise man, which is why he got killed
three times for alimony when one of his specialties is
divorce work."

"And your fee?"

"Half a mill."

"So that's three and a half. Now, Arthur explained
about studio overhead. Anywhere from ten to twenty-five
percent. If you produce it yourself, there is no studio
overhead so we're at least down to three. Arthur also said
that if you really put the blocks to every aspect of the
budget, you could get another couple of hundred thousand
sweated away."

"Assuming that were true, so?"

"Julian, you've got twenty million dollars in the bank,
what the fuck are you going to save it for?"

Julian just sat there in silence. "I can't remember your
having cursed before, not like that anyway," he said finally.

"This is very important to me, please do not subject-
switch, you're very clever, try not being so for the duration."

Julian sipped his coffee in the chill dawn, studying his
wife.

She peered at some figures, getting them straight. "You'll
probably get more than your money back out of television
sales alone."

"An X-rated picture? Absolutely. We can show high-
lights on Captain Kangaroo, drum up advance interest
with the kiddie crowd."

"You'll shoot double coverage like everyone else does—
now dammit, do you want me to guarantee you against
losses? Is that what you need to have the balls to move?"

Julian sighed. "Use my own money. They'll probably

drum me out of the producers' union. Strip me of my epaulettes and illiteracy card."

"Then you'll do it?"

"I have to, don't I?"

"I think this once."

"If it's all right with you then, I'd like some more sleep. We'll all need our energy come morning. I'll start to prepare an announcement and off we go." He stood, started into the house.

"Who'll star?"

"I haven't the foggiest but I can promise you this: If Julian Garvey works for free, ain't nobody gonna make a fortune off this opus."

"Meaning?"

"Fuck it, we'll find an unknown."

When Dixie Kern found the blood-red copy of *Tinsel* in her mailbox the following afternoon, she assumed there had been a mistake. She opened to the title page, saw it was a Julian Garvey production, and still didn't know what to make of it but the best thing was clearly to pitch it, since Mel would never be happy with manuscripts around the house. She started toward the garbage cans in the back when she thought that was dumb, why not check the thing out first, what else did she have on for the afternoon anyway? She took it to her bedroom, read it straight through, lay alone without moving after that, watching the afternoon sun play through the leaves outside. It wasn't till she reached for a cigarette and tried to light it that she realized just how terribly her hands were trembling. . . .

"Julian, it's Dixie Kern."

"My day is officially made," Julian said, shifting his weight in his desk chair. "What can I do for you—name it, you've got it—a five-year subscription to *Liberty*, I'm your boy." He rested the receiver between his chin and shoulder and massaged the other side of his neck.

"Julian? Did you leave a copy of *Tinsel* in my mailbox earlier today?"

"Of course. Why do you ask?"

"What did you do it for?"

"I suppose a sense of tidiness as much as anything. After all, this project kind of began at your house last week. Now that we're gearing up, I thought you might be interested in seeing what it had all been about."

"Who's starring?"

"That will be the secret of the century when unveiled. I promise you, Selznick's search for Vivien Leigh will be forgotten once our talent hunt gets under way."

"Well, good luck with it."

"Thank you, Dixie, it was good of you to call."

"*De nada.*"

"Oh, did you read it?"

"Kind of glanced through."

"What'd you think?"

"Got real pos—possibilities, bye, Julian."

Julian hung up and called, very loudly, "Noel," to his

son, who was working out in the gym adjoining the main office.

Noel, perspiring heavily, stuck his head in. "Yessir?"

"Did you put a copy of *Tinsel* in Dixie Kern's mailbox?"

"I sure did, why?"

"You can't just do that, hon. You must tell Daddy before embarking on adventures like that. We are playing, I hope you understand, with very high-quality explosives."

"Don't get you."

"Query: What studio for years was known as having the best security? Answer: Warners. Query: why? Answer: because one sunny afternoon an actor tried to actually kill Jack Warner because he didn't get a part. I shit you not. He hid in the bushes and when Warner left at the end of the day he jumped him and was strangling him before someone happened to come by and broke it up. But from that day forth, the security at Warners was unparalleled. I'm not saying there will be murder over the Monroe part, but I'll tell you here and now that once word of our venture hits the streets, the number of face-lift procedures in Beverly Hills is going to skyrocket. We're giving a has-been or never-was a chance to be the most sought after thing in the world—a moooooooovie star. And one must not fling scripts around casually."

"I wasn't being casual."

"Now I'm afraid *I'm* the one who doesn't get *you*."

Noel walked into the room, clad only in gym trunks, his bearlike body dark except for the many white scars. "This morning at breakfast—when you told me how you'd decided to flush that asshole Schwartzman and his foreign funding—you said you did it on account of me."

"As God is my witness," Julian said.

"Schwartzman was panicked that there was going to be trouble what with an inexperienced director and an inexperienced producer, me, and he was leaning on you to take over production and you felt that would castrate me so you told him to go stuff it, is that an accurate representation, Daddy?"

"Syllable for syllable."

"Then query: Am I the fucking producer or not?"

"Of course, but—"

"—well I always thought Dixie Crowder would be good for the part, you know that, and I wanted her to have a chance to read it, before I reached any final decision. There was nothing casual about what I did, I hope you see that. I want to be a good producer and I want to make you proud."

"Hon, you can cast Phyllis or Barry Diller for the part if you want, but I'd like to think that before you made such a move you might at least alert me, who has to pay for it, and Schwabby, who has to spend ten weeks on the floor making the performance happen. Now may I please ask: no more surprises. Let's act as a group when we act, all right?"

"Deal." Noel paused. "I wonder how I can try and meet her though."

Julian had to laugh. *"Meet* her? You can fuck her if you want—"

"—don't talk that way, Daddy—"

"—as a matter of fact, considering the way her dental hygienist of a husband humiliated me on the court last week, I would consider it a favor if you did."

"—I'm not interested in that, you don't know what you're talking about—"

"—she couldn't finish saying the word 'possibilities' when I asked what she thought of the script. Believe me, she's more than a little intrigued. Don't you understand yet what this part is, honey? It's catnip raised to the level of the plutonium bomb. This is a *vehicle* role and it's going to an unknown. You know the famous Hollywood dictum? —'Always make the deal before the picture comes out?' Well, if our girl plays it right, she'll have two more contracts signed before we're finished shooting. And once we do come out and we're a smash, it's a decade of fame. All to someone who couldn't quite catch the brass ring the first time round. This is a life changer, Noel."

"I wouldn't know about that. All I know is I sure would like a meeting, if you could arrange for it."

"Christmas just came early," Julian said. "Just make sure you don't."

"Quit that kind of thing!"

Julian raised his right hand high. "Henceforth, a vow of verbal chastity," he said.

When she walked out of Giorgio's the following morning, Dixie cried out, "Julian!" in surprise.

"My day is officially made—oops—I used that same line on you yesterday. Apologies all round." He fell in step beside her. "Listen, as long as we've run into each other, let me walk you where you're going—"

"—just to the parking lot—"

"—fine with me, it saves the bother of calling you later on. Dixie, let me cut to the chase: There is one enormous favor you could do for me."

"Oh, am I not going to like this," Dixie said, walking briskly along Rodeo. "Hit me with it."

"Take a meeting with Noel."

"Huh?" She glanced over at him.

"My son Noel. Chat awhile."

"He can call me on the phone only don't have him call me on the phone okay? If Mel should happen to be there, I would have *mucho* explaining to do."

"How splendid to have such a trusting helpmate."

"Julian, Mel isn't crazy about pictures in general and you in particular. I can't imagine he'd be thrilled to find me talking to your son. Can't we just bag all this?"

"Noel genuinely wants to meet you in person, Dixie."

"What in the name of God for?"

"He wants to prove to himself finally and forever if you're right for the lead or not. He's the producer; his word goes."

"The lead in your picture?"

"The very one. He's convinced you would be perfect."

"Julian, I retired."

"So did Richard Nixon back in sixty-two. 'You won't have me to kick around anymore.' Remember?"

"Julian, listen. I've got a birthday coming up this week, I'm busy as hell, if I met Noel it would best be on the sly and who needs it."

"He's at the Bel-Air Country Club now. All he has to do is drive his Excalibur for five minutes to be at your door."

"The maid's home."

"Send her to Farmer's Market—"

"—Mr. Balducci brings my produce—"

"—then send her to the Pacific for sand dabs. I want this for Noel, Dixie."

"Solly, Cholly."

Julian sighed and stopped. "If you can't, you can't, I understand. Bye, *Scar*lett," he said as he turned away, and Dixie took several steps before she flushed with anger, because her face was flawless, her body too, but there was a tiny scar on her left buttock and Julian used to touch it or tongue it in the old days and call her that, *Scar*lett, emphasis on the first syllable, and now she whirled back saying, "Don't you threaten me, you son of a bitch."

Julian turned too, facing her, saying, "My God, Dixie, you ought to know me better than that—"

"—I don't threaten—"

"—of course you don't—no reason you should—"

"—so don't go on with that '*Scar*lett' crap—"

"—who would I tell?—who would be interested in such trivia?—certainly no one I can think of—"

"—then apologize."

"I do. Fervently."

"Okay," Dixie said. "That's better." She opened her purse, rummaged around for a cigarette. "Listen, if it's really a big favor, what the hell, I can always find five minutes."

"You were always kind," Julian Garvey said.

* * *

It was on the dot one-thirty when Noel spun his Excalibur left off Stone Canyon and into the open garage space, which began to close electrically as soon as he was safely inside.

Dixie stood in the garage beside her Porsche. She was all in tennis white and she was smoking. Noel, in his best Carroll's suit, got nervously out of the car and said, "I want you to know I really appreciate this."

Dixie shrugged. "Just so it won't take long."

"Do we have to stay here in the garage?"

"Look—I'm not into this on-the-sly stuff, and I'm very jumpy just now." She ground out her cigarette, lit another.

"I only wanted to see what you looked like in the light was the reason."

"Looney-tunes," Dixie said, but she gestured for him to follow her, and they started out of the garage, moving down toward the black tennis court in the distance.

Noel's mind was full of his first orgasm.

"Do I pass muster?" Dixie said. "Or did the sun turn me into a pumpkin."

"I know you're doing this because my dad asked—"

"—on the button—"

"—and don't think I don't appreciate the fact that this is an imposition, but you see, I've never been a producer before and I've got to follow my own instincts. Before I get into it, just please know one thing: I'm not at all . . . I'm not like my father."

Dixie shot him a glance.

"I mean, I know his reputation as a womanizer. I'm not like that. This is business—"

"—then why don't we get to it?"

"Fine," Noel said. He stopped and stared at the famous black court. Then he turned to Dixie. "You're physically perfect for the part. I'm the one who's interested in following this through. Not my father or Schwabby, who's going to direct. You are strictly my notion. I've got to know two things though: First, are *you* interested in following this through. If you could get the part, would you want it?"

"Hypothetically or for real? Hypothetically, anybody probably would want the part. Anybody that comes from my corner of the ring. I mean, I told Julian I was retired and I suppose strictly speaking that's true, but there wasn't this wild public outcry when I gave up thesping. It wasn't like when they canceled *Star Trek*, and the mail room had to take on extra personnel to handle the load. So yeah, sure, why not, how many great roles does a girl get a shot at? But for real, forget it."

"Why?"

"(A) My husband would kill me, (B) my husband would kill me, and (C) I don't think my husband would be very pleased about the whole thing."

"I'm not sure my father would be either, but that's for down the line. I mean, *if* this works, and God knows the chances are it won't, we'll find the right time to let the world know. The important thing is you'd like to do it. But that brings up the second point: *Can* you act it? It's a very emotional role. I've never seen you play anything like that and I'm not sure that you're capable of it."

"I don't think I am capable of it. What you saw on the tube—that's all there was. I didn't have all these untapped depths lying around. Frankly, I think I would stink up the joint."

"You're a very honest lady, Mrs. Kern."

"Listen, the dopey show's back on reruns—I can't very well tell you I'm Maggie Smith when the proof is on right after *Brady Bunch*."

Noel nodded and turned, starting back toward the garage. "See, this didn't take long."

"Interview's all over?"

Noel nodded.

Dixie shrugged. "That's about as long as my interviews used to take."

"Frankly, I'm crushed as hell."

"Listen, you don't see me dancing, do you? It was a very flattering notion, even if a little on the weird side."

"See, goddamit, I know you can play it—deep down I'm

totally convinced—you were a kid when you quit, you're
an experienced woman now, you could handle that emotional stuff, you've seen stuff now you didn't know existed
before, you've got to be thirty-two, thirty-three years old,
not some ingenue."

"Thirty-six tomorrow," Dixie said.

"You're a very honest lady, Mrs. Kern."

Dixie broke out laughing. "Thirty-eight tomorrow."

"Listen—please—I know the role, see? I've gone over
it and over it with Schwabby—I know how every line's
supposed to be read. I could tell that all to you. Half an
hour's work together and we'd know—I've got a script in
the car—"

"—no good—I only sent Ethel into Brentwood—"

"—tomorrow then—please—"

"—I know who you inherited your pushiness from—"

"—you owe it to yourself, don't you understand that?—"
and before she could reply he hit her with another argument and another after that and he left the garage with
her consent which was really an exciting thing. Because
this was a terrific lady and if she could learn to do it
right, it wouldn't be a feather in anybody else's cap but
little Noel's, and he wheeled his Excalibur toward Sunset
hoping only that he would not become jaded like his
father, going through the world, attributing immoral behavior to any and all, especially people like Mrs. Kern,
no matter what the prize. . . .

Alone in her oversized kitchen, Mrs. Kern poured herself a cup of coffee and wondered why she'd agreed to let
the kid come back. Probably because he seemed so damn
sincere.

Not like his father.

God, genes were crazy things. Here was Julian, Leslie
Howard back to earth, and here was Noel, Yogi Berra
young. Young and due for a disappointment.

There was no way she could ever play the part. Not
well. Not if she had to read for it. Readings always pan-

icked her, made her voice go all wooden and monotone.

Dixie located a Sweet 'n Low packet, opened it, and stirred it into her cup, thinking that maybe what she'd do tomorrow was take a Librium before he got there.

Bad idea.

All they did was make her want to sleep. Vodka would be better. A couple a' snorts of vodka always loosened her up at parties, maybe it would do the same earlier in the day.

She took her cup and began to wander through the big house. It was a wonderful place, a perfect place almost, except when you were alone in it.

Dixie walked in silence to where she could catch a glimpse of the black court and then she stared at it awhile, wondering what her kids would have been like, hers and Mel's, what kind of surprises their genes would have come up with. It wouldn't have mattered to her much, Mel's looks or hers, either would have suited her fine.

Just so they didn't get her brains.

Because sure Mel loved her and of course she returned it. But what about five years down the line? She was his trinket, no denying that. And so far she'd done well enough. But when he was closing in on fifty and she'd left forty far behind, well, trinkets tend to tarnish when they get old.

But if she was somebody, naturally that'd be a different thing. If she was somebody, it wouldn't matter if a couple a' wrinkles took up permanent residence alongside her eyes. If she was somebody . . . well, there was just no doubt about it.

Mel would be so proud. . . .

Noel was deep inside Dixie the next noontime, the two of them diagonaled across the Kerns' king-sized bed when Mel, from the foyer, shouted "It's me" and Dixie, her tone tinged with joy, shouted "What a fantastic surprise" and grabbed wildly for her robe, on the run toward the foyer, leaving Noel to grab his scattered clothes, which he managed to do and then holed up in the bathroom, doing his best to dress quickly while his mind focused on the black kid in the pool, the little black kid going down that summer in the Haight, and Noel thought, Jesus, somebody come for me, somebody pull me out and I'll never do this again, never anything like this again, I swear, I swear no matter what, *never,* and when clad he stood frozen while the black boy kept sinking, kept sinking until, he had no idea how much later, Dixie opened the bathroom door and Noel whispered "Has he gone?" and she nodded and Noel said "Did he see my car?" and she shook her head, the garage door had been carefully closed and before he could ask anything more she held up diamond earrings and said, "For my birthday, he brought me this for a birthday surprise," and then she was shouting and crying, "What the fuck am I doing with you?—am I crazy?—am I fucking crazy?—who are you, I don't know you—" and Noel just stood there, staring as her hysteria built, her face splotchy, the tears streaking down and she was making terrible sounds, helpless panicked sounds and staring at the two diamonds shaking her head with the jerkiness of a marionette and Noel grabbed her then, roughly, with all his power, and forced her around screaming, "Look—look, don't you see, I was right, don't you see—*look goddamit*—" and for a moment Dixie looked at the wild creature in the bathroom mirror while Noel went on, never letting go, his voice big and building "—you *can* do it—the part, the part—you can and you will, *it's yours,* I swear, so help me Christ, so help me Christ and hope to die!"

V
GINGER

Ginger, from the beginning, had it all.

The Father: Stan Abraham, Phi Beta Kappa, Princeton, Law Review, Virginia Law. Tall, always tanned, gracefully athletic, a scratch golfer. Patient, polite, unfailingly logical, this last a help in the field of tax law, which was the specialty of Abraham and Abraham, the family firm.

The Mother: Phyllis Isaacs, tops at Bennington, knowledgeable about all fields of dance, specialized in modern. Five six, weight never over one ten except when pregnant. Pretty and quick minded and rich.

The house: a duplex at 735 Park, the corner of Seventy-first Street. A master bedroom suite, a bedroom for Ginger, another for two-years-older sister Freddy, a guest room. Downstairs the usual living room, dining room, library, kitchen. Assorted maid's rooms for assorted maids. They never stayed long.

Ginger herself was born the year after *National Velvet* opened; the movie obviously meant not a great deal to her at the time, but it did make Elizabeth Taylor a star, and that marked the start of the endless comparisons. Because Ginger had the same startling dark coloring.

And the violet eyes.

Mentally she had her mother's quickness and her father's sense of logic. She was quiet and rarely rebelled, never if you gave her a sensible reason to do what you wanted her to do. If you told her to clean up her room, she might dawdle, but if you said, "Oh, *Die Grossmutter* is coming today, I hope your room isn't like this when she gets here" Ginger turned instant dervish because now she knew why. Also, *Die Grossmutter*—Grandmother Isaacs—never arrived without presents and wondrous stories and in general did more than most when it came to spreading cheer.

Not that all day every day was spent cheerfully, but how bad could your bringing up be when the one time in your life that your father got mad at you he didn't get mad at you? Explication: the story of the airplane.

"Hey, the piddler wants a plane," Phyllis said to Stan early one fall morning over coffee. Ginger was more than two but less than three at the time, fresh out of diapers but accidents did happen; "piddling" was how Phyllis referred to the act.

Stan, never at his best before seven, nodded.

"What did I just say?" Phyllis asked, and then she broke out laughing because she knew he hadn't been able to concentrate remotely on her words.

"It was about something."

"Close, I'll give you that." She stuck her arms straight out and began making airplane sounds.

Stan finished his coffee, poured himself another cup.

"We were in the park yesterday and she saw an airplane stuck in a tree and ever since then, she has been berserk with desire."

"Airplane," Stan said.

"You're closing in on it," Phyllis told him. "Stop off somewhere why don't you on your way home and bring her one as a surprise."

Stan nodded. "Think Schwarz's'll have one?"

"If they don't, my darling," Phyllis said, rising and embracing her man, "then believe me, the dark ages are already upon us. . . ."

That night, entering the foyer, Stan shouted, "Surprise." He managed to kick the front door closed and put his

briefcase on the mail table. Then he just waited, the enormous wrapped package in his arms. "Surprise!" he shouted
again, louder this time.

Phyllis entered, apron on, from the kitchen. She was an
excellent cook, particularly when it came to gourmet
dishes. She entertained often and beautifully. "What's
that?" she said, nodding toward the package in the F.A.O.
Schwarz paper.

In reply Stan shouted, *"Surprise"* the loudest time of all.

From upstairs now, footsteps. Freddy peered over the
bannister. "We been playing Baby Lion," she said.

"We've," Phyllis said from below.

"That's right," Freddy nodded. "And Baby Lion has
been so bad. Baby Lion cuh-umm," she called then, as
she walked down the stairs.

Ginger came crawling after.

"Baby Lion sit," Freddy said.

Ginger sat promptly on the stairs.

"Better," Freddy said. "What could that be?" she said
then, pointing to the package. She looked at her father.
"For me?"

"You get the next present," Stan said.

" 'Course I do, fair is fair," Freddy said and she hurried
up the stairs past her sitting sister. "Baby Lion open your
present," she finished, then she was gone.

Stan put the package down and Ginger crawled toward
it.

"Baby Lion's over, hon," Phyllis told her. "Walk."

Ginger nodded and stood, moving to her father. "What
ever could be inside there?"

"Beats me," Stan said. "I was hurrying home just a few
minutes ago when this weird-looking delivery guy came
up to me and said, 'It's impossible, it's just impossible, I've
got to get this package to someone and I only know the
name and not the address and where am I gonna find
someone called Ginger Abraham in a city of eight million
people?' "

"*I'm* Ginger Abraham, Daddy."

"I know. 'Course I remember a thing like that. I just had a heckuva time convincing this weirdo delivery guy that you were. He wouldn't believe me, he kept saying I was only after this package and I said, 'I swear on a Bible my daughter's named Ginger Abraham' and he said, 'Okay, do it and I'll believe you' and I said, 'I don't happen to have a Bible on me at the time, I'm a lawyer,' and he said, 'Tougho, no Bible, no present,' and just then this minister walked by reading Genesis and I asked could I borrow his Bible for a sec and he said, 'Of course, my son' and he handed it over and I swore on it and that was that." He put the package on the floor. "I haven't the foggiest idea what could be inside it, what did you order from F.A.O. Schwarz lately, Ginger?"

Ginger rocked back and forth and looked at her mother. "Whatever is he saying?"

"I think he wants you to open the present, baby."

Ginger set to work. There were ribbons to be pulled off and colored wrappings and it took time, because the package wasn't all that much smaller than she was but her daddy watched and her mommy didn't go anywhere either. Ginger kept glancing up at them as she worked away, muttering, "Whatever can be inside of here?" in one variation or another until, at last, she knelt over the box and lifted out the contents. "Heavy," she said, as she put it on the foyer floor and looked at it a while. "Oh, it's an airplane, how wonderful, I got to go tell Mama Lion every little thing," and with that she was up the stairs and gone.

Stan just stood there.

"Don't pop your cork," Phyllis said, gathering up the box and wrappings.

Stan said nothing, simply started going through the mail.

Phyllis was working in the kitchen a few minutes later when the door slam practically shattered the plaster, and she was not without control, but nothing, and they knew it, irritated her more than when they slammed doors because that meant eventually chipped paint and plaster and a few more eventually down the line, workmen, so she took the stairs two at a time and found them in Freddy's room where she began, "How many times must I tell you *never* to slam doors—" but the startled look on their faces told her they hadn't, so she quick excused herself and went to the master bedroom where Stan was undressing. Phyllis quietly closed the door and leaned against it. "Shoot off a howitzer, why don't you?"

Stan, in his shorts said, "I didn't mean for it to be that loud, accident."

"Unlikely. You are simply given, from time to time, alas, to periods of regression."

"I really hate Sigmund Freud," Stan said.

"I'm sure he has yet to penetrate Princeton, but we at Bennington find he often has a certain wisdom."

"She didn't even *play* with it, Phyl."

"Well why did you buy her that monstrosity?"

"Because you fucking well told me to."

"I merely asked you to buy—"

"Phyl, I love you a lot but shut up, you are perilously close to being strangled and I shit you not—you said buy a plane so I left work early and I hit Schwarz's along with half the preteen population of Manhattan and I finally got waited on and he said they had little plywoody things for under a buck and decent-sized things for five to ten and I wanted the kid to really love it, so I got the best, do you understand *best?* That 'monstrosity' cost fifty-nine bucks and all she did was run upstairs to play with her sister."

"The plywood plane was the one you should have gotten."

"It wasn't much bigger than my hands."

"She's a *baby*. She could fly to Cleveland in what's downstairs. Something that size overwhelms her, she can't return the affection, don't you see?"

"I can do without any more Freud too, okay?"

Phyllis nodded and went to him quickly. "It was my fault. *I* should have bought her the plane."

Stan embraced her. Eventually.

"What's the matter with Daddy?" Freddy asked that night at dinner.

"Nothing," Phyllis said.

"Oh yes, oh yes, Mama Lion knows. Daddy is very very very very mad."

"No he isn't," Phyllis said.

"He hasn't said a word all meal, Mama Lion hasn't heard nothing."

"Anything," Phyllis said.

Ginger got up then, quickly, and ran around the table to her father. "I just love my airplane so much," she said. "It's so wonderful and huge."

Stan hugged his daughter and looked at his wife. "So much for Freud," he said.

Probably the biggest thing that wasn't perfect in her growing-up years didn't involve Ginger herself, but rather Freddy. More specifically, the way her parents were picking at her all the time. Ginger adored her older sister, and it wasn't Freddy's fault about being overweight, or not getting better grades in school. She was tubby and broad hipped but always, always kind.

"A bunch of us were talkin'," Freddy said one night at dinner. "About how next year, next year"—she spooned herself a portion of green beans—"we're not gonna turn into members of the snob club just 'cause we're all of a sudden freshmen." She scooped up another spoonful and was about to pass the platter to Ginger on her left.

"Leave some for the rest of the troops," her father said.

Freddy looked at him. "They're beans, for cripes sakes —*beeeeeeeenz*—"

"—your father meant—" Phyllis began.

"—enough left for you?" Freddy asked Ginger.

"Oh yes, more than plenty."

Freddy looked at her father again. "Then why make a thing out of it? If it was chocolate cake and I was liable to for cripes sakes bal*looooooon,* then I'd understand, but when it's *beeeeeeeenz.*" She shook her head.

"You would never be a member of the snob club," Ginger said.

"What's the snob club?" Phyllis said.

"All the freshmen at Hewitt, they sort of automatically become these huge snobs when they get into high school. You never catch them talkin' to anybody younger, even if they were friends the year before."

"Talking is an i-n-g word," Phyllis said.

"I love having dinner with the family," Freddy said. "When I die for cripes sakes, on my tombstone it's gonna say, 'Here lies Freddy Abraham, killed by dinner with the family.'"

"Going is an i-n-g word."

"I know we seem to pick at you, Freddy," Stan said, "but please why don't you stop making it so easy."

"Manners never hurt, did they now?" Phyllis asked. "Can you mention an instance in recorded history where decent manners damaged a person?"

"I love the way Freddy talks," Ginger said. "I understand exactly what she means."

"No one has ever accused an Abraham of being inarticulate," Phyllis explained. "But there are ways and ways."

"Oh, now that is poetic," Freddy said. "Ginger, write that down. 'There are ways and ways.' Tomorrow, when I'm walkin' to school, I'm gonna reduce everyone to tears with that one."

"Walking is an i-n-g word," Phyllis said.

And suddenly Freddy was on her feet, on her feet and screaming, *"Fucking is an i-n-g word!"* And then she ran.

"You must stop being mean to my Freddy," Ginger cried out, and she fled too, chasing her big sister to her room upstairs.

Freddy had put Chuck Berry's "Maybellene" on her little phono and was sitting on her bed, chin in hands, staring at the turning disc. Ginger sat alongside her, took the same position. Next Freddy played "Sixteen Tons" with Ernie Ford singing, and after that her Fats Domino collection.

"I made up my mind on a course of action," Ginger said then.

"Yeah, what'zat?"

Very carefully Ginger said, "I'm walkin' in their big bedroom, see, and then I'm talkin' to the both of 'em, and I'm gonna say 'Fucking fucking fucking fucking fucking' and then I'm comin' back here."

Freddy had to smile. "Oh Ginge, you couldn't do that if you had to. Anyway, you shouldn't. It'll all pass. I'll go in later and put on my sincere face and tell 'em how sorry I am and how much I appreciate all they've done for me and yes I know how lucky I am and I'll promise to be better in the future. Standard apology two-A."

"Nosirreebob, not this time. I'm gonna really give it to 'em."

Freddy took off her blouse and looked at herself in the mirror. "I'm such a pig. I disgust myself sometimes."

"You're gonna be proud of me when I come back," Ginger said.

"Oh baby, I'm proud of you now."

"You just wait right here, you'll see," and Ginger got up, saluted, and marched out of the room down the hall to the big bedroom. The door was closed. She knocked and her mother said. "Is that you, Freddy?" Ginger said no, but could she come in? With the affirmative answer, she opened the door.

Her father was lying on the king-sized bed studying some typed pages. Her mother was in the bathroom, the tub water running. When her mother appeared in the doorway, slender and dark hair pulled back, Ginger looked first at one of them, then the other.

"What's up, babe?" Phyllis said.

Ginger waited.

"Speak," from her father.

Ginger stood awhile longer.

"Sweetie, can this hold till later, my tub's about to overflow?"

Ginger smacked her forehead. "I forgot what I was

going to say, wherever did I put my brains," and she
waved, skipped out into the hall, closing the door behind
her. Then she ran back into Freddy's room, crying, "I
did it, I did it, I said it really loud and everything."

Freddy was standing by her bathroom mirror, pushing
at a blackhead on her cheek. "They musta peed in their
pants."

"Oh they did, they did, and then I said I'm gonna keep
on talkin' like that till they stop bein' so picky on every
little thing you do."

"I bet Dad spanked you."

"Nosirreebob, he started but I said I didn't care if he
went on beatin' me forever, nothin' was gonna make me
change my mind."

"Oh you little dope," Freddy said then. "How do you
expect me to believe a story like that?"

"Every word is true."

"C'mere." Freddy spread her arms.

Ginger sagged into them.

"Bet you didn't say one word."

"I tried though. I really wanted to."

"Ginger, listen, it isn't *in* you; you can't help being
perfect."

"I'm *not*."

Freddy hugged her violet-eyed sister. "The trouble is, I
really think you are. . . ."

She wasn't perfect, of course, but all in all the staff at
Miss Hewitt's had no cause for complaint. From the start
Ginger got easily the best grades in her class. And she
helped the teachers when she could. And she helped the
other girls when they needed it.

More remarkably, none of the other girls resented her.
She was always the most popular kid around, and though
there was some argument among her fellows as to whether
she was really the brightest or just worked hard, nobody
disputed her physical presence. She was this sort of stunning *thing* floating from grade to grade, gathering momen-

tum with the years. The summer before she became a freshman Ginger spent a lot of time preparing and reading, because high school could clip you from behind if you didn't watch it. The result was that her average for the first semester freshman year was between A and A-plus, the highest it had ever been.

And it was shortly after that that her parents told her they were seriously considering switching her to Brearley.

They called her into the library one night after dinner, closed the door, and let her in on their contemplation.

Ginger heard them all the way through before she said, "Query: Why?"

"Because we think it might be good for you."

"But I like it where I am, Daddy—"

"—when he says good for you, what your father means, Ginger—"

"—I'm happy at Miss Hewitt's, I love Miss Hewitt's, I really really really don't want to leave."

"Brearley's the best girl's school academically in all New York," her father said. "I just don't think you're being stretched sufficiently where you are."

"You mean Hewitt's no good?"

"Of course it's good, it's very good, but you're a very special child and you deserve the best."

"I couldn't get into Brearley."

"We've checked. There are openings. They're not disinterested."

Ginger sat on the chair by the window and stared at her parents, sitting close together on the couch, sipping their coffee. "Please," she said finally. "Don't make me."

"Baby," her father said, "nobody's going to *make* you do anything."

"The final decision's yours, that's a promise," her mother agreed.

"They're all so skinny and smart and sophisticated at Brearley—I've met some Brearley kids—I won't get on with them, I just know it."

"Baby," her father said, "if there's one thing in the

world you don't have to worry about, it's getting on with people."

"They'll laugh at me, they do that there—all the Brearley kids I've run into, they're always laughing at you behind their eyes. They think they're superior and they're right, they are, I won't be able to keep up."

Her mother said, "It's natural for you to feel that way, we've sprung this on you rather suddenly. Believe us, if you couldn't keep up, we wouldn't dream of sending you."

"Please," Ginger said. "Can't we forget about this? Never talk about it again? I'm getting almost A-pluses at Hewitt, I thought you were happy with me."

"Hewitt's a second-rate school," her father said.

"Then why did you send me there? Freddy too."

"When I said second rate, I didn't mean 'second rate' exactly, just 'second rate' in comparison to Brearley."

"Why do you want to take me away from all my friends?"

"You'll make new friends," her mother said.

"No I won't, not there; they'll laugh at how I look."

Her parents just stared at each other. Then her father said, "Ginger, obviously you must know you're really very beautiful."

"You have to say that, you're my father, but *they* won't say that, all they'll say is how overweight I am."

Her mother shook her head. "How tall are you, Ginger?"

"Five-five, you know that."

"And how much did you weigh last time you were weighed?"

"A hundred twenty."

"Then how can you think you're overweight?" her mother wanted to know.

"Because—" Ginger began.

"—honey," her father said, "you're almost fifteen, you're supposed to have baby fat when you're that age."

"See? See?"

"See what?"

"You think I'm fat too, you just said so."

"I don't be*lieve* this," her father said, standing suddenly.

"Don't get mad at me, Daddy."

"Honey, I never get mad at you, but do you think we hate you? Of course you don't. Do you think we want to cause you pain? Of course you don't. Then why do we want you to change schools? Because we don't love you? Of course not. It's because we *do* love you and want what you deserve, the best."

"Don't shout at me like that."

Stan turned to Phyllis. "Was I shouting?"

"You seemed a bit agitated," she replied.

"Well Christ, I'm not, not remotely, I just don't want this scene going on into perpetuity, so Ginger, you tell us, do we follow up on the Brearley thing?"

After a long pause: "Query: You really think it's best?"

"We do," Stan said. "Yes, ma'am."

"Then I must go to Brearley."

"Ginger," Phyllis said. "Think about this now—you really do see it's best. And it is your decision."

Ginger thought about it. Then she said, "I'll just have to bust my butt and try and make you proud. . . ."

"*Grossmutter, Grossmutter,* tell me a tale," Ginger said to Grandmother Isaacs on her weekly stop-off for tea. It was late spring and Brearley had just said yes positively and everything could not have been going better. They sat in the old woman's antique-laden Fifth Avenue apartment with the lovely view of the sailboat pond at Seventy-third Street. Ginger sat at the old woman's feet, balancing her tea cup carefully while the maid passed the tray of Scottish shortbread that was *Die Grossmutter*'s fatal weakness.

"About what, Little Rabbit?" Grandmother Isaacs said, plopping four pieces of shortbread on her plate.

"Tell me about Mommy, I love her so," Ginger said, shaking her head politely to the shortbread tray. "Was she beautiful when she was young? I bet she was."

"Not like you." The old lady stared for a moment at Ginger's eyes. "Still violet," she said, something she had been saying ever since Ginger could remember. "If a strange man comes up on the street and says he has some blue eyes would you like to change, what do you say?"

"I say, 'Thank you, *Grossmutter* likes violet.'"

The Ancient took a bite of shortbread. Some crumbs got on her mouth and stayed there. Ginger, in a moment, knelt and dabbed them carefully away. "Good rabbit."

"What did she like to do when she was my age?"

"Eat."

"But she's so thin."

"When I first knew her, she was a fatso."

"Mommy?"

Die Grossmutter nodded, bit sharply into the shortbread piece, licked her lips clear of crumbs. "Chocolate."

"She never eats it now."

The old woman stared for a long time before saying, "Christmas."

Ginger knew about *Die Grossmutter*'s troubles lately concentrating. Most of the others had begun to taper off their visits. She was the only one as faithful as before. Now, as she watched, the old eyes began to glaze. Ginger shook the old woman on the knee just a trifle. "Christmas," she repeated.

"Christmas was checkerboard cookies, Rabbit. No matter how many I had baked, your mother wanted more."

"I wish I had that recipe, I would surprise her this Christmas, *Grossmutter*. Do you remember?"

"A great recipe is like your name; you can't forget."

"Do you remember anything else chocolate Mommy used to love?"

"Fudge. Cakes. Special cocoa. Pudding and cookies and sauce."

"I think maybe next visit I'll bring my notebook and jot a few of those down."

"One each visit is the most I could give away. And I couldn't give that."

"Why not?"

"Because you can only give great recipes to people you love. That's from the Talmud."

"And I thought you loved me."

"Funny looking object like you, who could love you?"

"I'll just have to bring my notebook and hope is all."

The old eyes were glazing again. She rumpled Ginger's long black hair. "Little Rabbit," *Die Grossmutter* said. . . .

Not late into that fall Phyllis called Doctor Benjamin, who was the top, or at least the most expensive pediatrician on the East Side and who had taken care of her children from the beginning. It was close to noon and Phyllis sat in the library, waiting for the good doctor to come on the line. In the meantime, she flicked her long left thumbnail against her front teeth, the sharp click the room's only sound.

When he picked up, the first words he said were, "There's a lot of it going around," and Phyllis, out of affection, laughed. The two things Felix Benjamin wanted to be were either a borscht-circuit comic or a shrink. She chose him for her children because of that latter orientation, but the former had to be put up with. He always began his conversations with either the line he had just used, or, "It's a virus" or, "Take two aspirins every four hours and call back tomorrow." It was his contention that those three phrases were all any medical man had to know to succeed in a long-running career.

"I hear it's a virus," Phyllis replied. And then she said, "You know I wouldn't have bothered you if I didn't think it was important."

"Understood. I assume it has to do with the beautiful Ginger."

"Why do you assume that?" Phyllis asked quickly.

"Because my calendar says it is annual physical time and she is coming in this very afternoon. Will you be accompanying her?"

"She asked not. I think it embarrasses her she's still seeing a baby doctor, if you want to know the truth. Having her mother hold her hand makes it too humiliating."

"Understood." There was a long pause on the line before Doctor Benjamin said, "You did call me."

"Well, it's embarrassing," Phyllis said. "It makes me sound very ego ridden and narcissistic and I haven't told anybody else about it."

"Why don't you just do it quickly."

"Okay, here's the thing—I'm five six and I weigh a hundred ten, which isn't so terrible when you're going to hit the big four-oh next year. When I graduated Bennington, I weighed the same. Ever since I stopped growing, I've weighed one ten."

She could hear him snoring experimentally on the other end of the line.

"Dammit Felix, don't laugh at me, I'm serious about this."

"About what?"

"Well . . . it's weird but . . . well see, Ginger's been cooking me things."

"I am lost," Doctor Benjamin said.

"She got all these recipes out of my mother; stuff I was nuts about when I was a tubby little kid. Chocolate recipes. And she surprises me with them at night sometimes. She comes in all proud and beaming because she's busted her hump for hours in the kitchen making some goddam torte or nut fudge."

"And that's it?"

"I guess."

"Take two aspirin every four hours and call me tomorrow."

"Please, Felix, I asked you not to laugh."

"It just doesn't sound like such a much, Phyllis. Leukemia I'll fret over, but I can't get worked up over chocolate cake."

"Stan feels just the same as you do—"

"—tell me, is it good, if it's good have her bake me some, I'm queer for chocolate."

"Yes it's good, it's very good, it's delicious, that's not the point."

"What is?"

Finally Phyllis said it: "I'm gaining weight."

He waited for her to continue.

"It's not just that she makes the stuff, see, I don't know if you'll understand this, but she makes me eat it too. Emotionally she forces me. If I don't stuff my face, she gets whipped. It's like trauma time if I don't finish my plate. And I want to tell her to stop, but she's only doing it for me, and I want her to like cooking, I love cooking, and she never did till kind of recently, so I don't want to kill her interest, but I weighed one thirteen this morning and *it's not funny.*"

"And you want me to head her off at the pass, is that it?"

"I don't know what I want except for it to stop and you're her doctor and she cares for you and trusts you."

"Well, I don't know how I'll bring the subject *casually* into our conversational flow, but I'll do my best. Phyllis?"

"What?"

"There's *not* a lot of this going around. . . ."

Ginger sat alone on the examining table waiting for Doctor Benjamin to arrive. Her blue Brearley uniform was hung neatly over the hanger in the corner and she got up and walked around the bare room, wearing only her bra and panties. The room was a little chilly so she rubbed her arms to get the circulation going better, then sat back on the table again, legs dangling.

Doctor Benjamin, stout and brisk, hurried in saying, "Now let me see, how many months pregnant are you— oops, wrong chart."

Ginger smiled. "Hey Zeppo," she said, her name for him since she'd discovered that he was collecting material for the definitive biography of not Harpo, Chico, or Groucho, but Zeppo Marx.

"I get my hug?"

"I brought one along." She embraced him quickly, then

he moved away and looked at her. "What's wrong?" she asked then.

Doctor Benjamin shook his head. "My God, Ginger, does that horrible Brearley insist on blue underwear too?"

Ginger nodded. "Isn't it obscene?"

He sighed and moved across the room, sitting on the small stool beside the scale. "May I be serious?"

"Query: Why are you looking at me funny?"

"That's what I wanted to be serious about—you're going to leave me, Ginger, and dammit, that's the only sad thing about my life. You all grow up and don't get measles anymore and it's bye-bye Benjamin." He shook his head. "Okay, end of feeling sorry for myself, hop aboard." He thumbed toward the scale.

Ginger moved across the room and onto the scale, standing very straight, her back to it, which was the way Doctor Benjamin always measured you, so he could make jokes without your seeing the actual results. "You certainly don't look six four," he said, after he'd done her height.

"I slump I think is why," Ginger told him.

"Um-hmm," he said, quickly getting her weight, gesturing her back to the table. She sat as before, and as he reached for a tongue depressor, he asked how she'd been feeling in general, any complaints. Ginger stuck out her tongue, said, "Ahhh" on cue, then as he started with the flashlight in her ears, she replied she felt great, really terrific.

Then he said casually, "No problems with food or like that?"

Ginger thought a moment. "Food?" She thought again. "Nossir. None at all. Why do you ask that?"

Doctor Benjamin said, "Primarily because you're down to ninety-seven pounds and that's a considerable drop and—"

"—ninety-*two*!" Ginger screamed, and she jumped off the table and ran to the scale and weighed herself again. "See? Do-you-see-what-it-says?"

"Easy—"

"—I worked for those fucking pounds."

"My mistake, I'm sorry."

"I worked hard!" she said, glaring at him in the sterile room. And she could not stop shaking with anger. . . .

Ginger was still angry when she got home at half past four. She went straight to her room, undressed, put her uniform away neatly, got her books arranged in the order she planned to study them. 4:35.

She threw on a robe and went downstairs for a snack.

Damn.

Some days nothing went right—there was only iceberg lettuce in the refrigerator. Romaine was so much better. A pound of iceberg was fifty-six calories while Romaine was only fifty-two. Four calories with the same nutritional value so *why wasn't there any Romaine?*

She took the largest leaf from the iceberg head, went to the sink, and washed is carefully. Then she got a plate and spread the lettuce leaf on top. She reached for a butterknife on her way to the condiment shelf, which she quickly opened. And there it was.

French's yellow mustard.

It had only been the week preceding that she discovered that Gulden's brown, which she had been using, was two calories per tablespoon higher than French's yellow. This was the six-ounce jar she was opening now, and carefully she took out one third of the contents with the butterknife. Ordinarily she didn't need quite that much, but she was angry and that always did crazy things to her appetite. Two ounces was what—? Forty-four calories. Plus one for the lettuce leaf made forty-five.

What the hell, what the hell.

With a sculptor's calm, she spread the glorious yellow condiment on the lettuce, making totally sure that every spot on the leaf was equally coated. It took her probably five minutes to get it absolutely right. When finally she was satisfied she reached for the knife and fork and slowly began to cut into her creation. She was always kind of dainty with a knife and fork and she took her time now, making equal ladylike bite-sized segments. She chewed each bite slowly, savoring the wondrous mixture of flavors. By the time it was gone she felt stuffed, and being careful to put everything away, she went upstairs to tackle geometry. . . .

Stan was steaming when he got to Doctor Benjamin's office. Of course you couldn't tell it unless you knew him well. He seemed, in his Brooks Brothers costume, as quietly well turned-out as ever. The ideal barrister, forever placid, logical, calm.

Phyllis, of course, knew better, so her first words to him as he entered were, "Just don't take it out on me, I didn't insist you be here. Blame Felix."

"What's it about, do you know?"

"Not the slightest. He just said it was crucial for us to come."

"It better be," Stan said softly.

They waited fifteen minutes, till after six and the last child had gone, before Doctor Benjamin called them into his private office and they sat. "As you know I saw Ginger last week. I didn't call you in then because I wanted to get all her test data in before we spoke. I have it now."

"Did anything come up?"

"Her *tests* are fine," Doctor Benjamin said. "One hundred percent. Notice I emphasized 'tests.' "

"The point being?" Stan said.

Doctor Benjamin took his time before saying, "I think we're into a dangerous and complicated situation."

Phyllis began to get upset then. "There *was* something in the tests."

"Not at all. But that doesn't mean I don't think that Ginger is a very very very sick girl."

"Sick?" Stan said. "In what way?"

"She feels better now that she ever has—that's the truth, isn't it, Stan? The child is in just the most wonderful mood, she can't be sick."

"Phyllis," Doctor Benjamin said. "The child has lost twenty-eight pounds."

"I don't believe this," Stan said. "Did I leave work early to be told my daughter's lost weight? Doc, she's been dieting. She wanted to lose so she lost. Period."

"Almost a quarter of her body weight?"

"Children overdo things," Phyllis said. "You're a baby doctor, I don't have to tell that to you."

Benjamin rubbed his eyes. "This is where it gets complicated, please don't take offense. Stan, you're what, six feet, one sixty?"

"One fifty-eight approximately."

"All right, what I'm telling you is you don't see what's happening, either of you. Hear me out—I get a call a week ago from Phyllis and she's upset. About? Not the fact that her child has *lost* almost thirty pounds but that *she* has gained *three*."

"I have to watch it every second," Phyllis said. "If I don't I balloon."

"Ginger could be a fashion model tomorrow if she wanted," Stan said. "People come up to her all the time. Two months ago someone from the Ford agency saw her at school and talked to her."

Doctor Benjamin started talking more quickly now. "I have been in this line of work a quarter century and I have never seen a child as beautiful as Ginger Abraham. From the beginning. Remember Phyllis? People used to stop her in the office here? Ask who she was? Black hair, the white skin, those eyes. Well I'm telling you, no, I'm asking you, begging you *please*, that child is disappearing in the mists and if we want to get her back we're going to have to *do* something."

"I don't understand what you mean. What would we do?"

"I'm not expert in these fields; take her to someone who

is. But the first step is going to be yours—you've both got to realize how dangerous this is. Look—when she was in here I was shocked at her appearance so I did something —when I told her her weight, I added five pounds to see if there was any reaction."

"And?" Phyllis said. "Was there?"

"I would say between eight and nine on the Richter scale. She swore, she got incredibly hostile, she shook with rage."

Phyllis looked at her husband. "I find that very hard to believe."

Stan smiled. "I've got a kid who looks like a Vogue model only better, who's gone into a new school and knocked them dead—ninety-fives at *Brearley*—the phone rings off the wall with kids her age asking her places. Sounds like we're clearly in a situation of incredible danger."

"You don't see anything at all?" Doctor Benjamin asked.

"I'm a lawyer," Stan told him. "I see what's there."

2

Ginger began to run.

Out of boredom at first. She'd been waking by five since the end of October and an hour of going over the past night's homework still only made it six and breakfast wasn't for an hour so that six to seven, time hung heavy. For a while she tried poetry memorization, Dickinson and Poe, but that didn't work off her energy needs.

So she started running. At first her lack of endurance was embarrassing. She could make it from Seventy-first and Park down to Fifty-ninth but never all the way back. Not without stopping. That damn hill at Sixty-seventh Street beat her every time.

She decided to switch routes and the first time she ran into Central Park itself there was no doubt she was frightened, it being dark and all. But there were other runners too and that helped. So she would enter the park at Seventy-second and Fifth and kind of wave up at *Die Grossmutter*'s dark windows and then head around in the big western circle, curving down along Central Park West to Central Park South, then up to Seventy-second again. It was a good run and beautiful even if cold, but she was cold all the time anyway so what difference.

By Thanksgiving she could make it twice around the circle easily and she was proud of that. Then back home, a good hot shower, throw on a robe, and zoom down to the kitchen to make breakfast for the family, scrambled eggs for Phyllis, fried for Stan and Freddy. She'd sit with them, watch them eat, munch on a carrot or something, then back up to dress and off to school.

Just before Christmas vacation began, she cornered her father after dinner. "Query: Could I please possibly do you think have my main present early?"

"The point being?"

Ginger handed him a small ad she'd clipped from the back of the *Saturday Review*. "I'm wasting so much of my time and I feel so energetic and all, that what I'd like to do is take speed-reading. There's this special cram course that's given now." She pointed to the ad. "I think I could really knock 'em dead if I could speed-read. You'd be so proud and I swear you wouldn't be throwing your money away."

"How fast do you read now?"

Ginger shrugged. "Not fast enough. You should see what I'm up against at school. If I do five hundred words a minute I'm losing retention. But with this course, I could easily triple that and if I bust my butt, maybe five times as fast."

"It doesn't seem terribly festive."

"It would be for me, though."

"You're doing wonderfully as it is so how—"

"—I want to be valedictorian—and I'm not smart enough—but with this I can be—don't you want that for me? My God, this can make the difference between being fifth in my class and being first. Why do you want to deprive me of the chance to be valedictorian?"

"Easy, baby."

"I want it so is all."

"Okay," Stan said. "When have I ever turned you down . . . ?"

It was almost a perfect Christmas vacation. Ginger got up as usual at five and practiced speed-reading till half past six then ran till eight when it was time to shower and go to the cram course itself, which ran nine to eleven.

Then home again and more practicing—it was incredible how quickly you improved if you only practiced the techniques, if you really concentrated hard—and then to top off the day, a twilight run.

The colors were so vivid in the park for her then; everything was more vivid for her, tastes and smells too, and she kept her mind busy memorizing calories. Frozen asparagus tips were good, twenty-two per three and a half ounces, but bamboo shoots were better, just twenty-seven calories for three quarters of a cup. Raw snap green beans were better yet, a whole cup barely thirty-two. And seven eighths of a cup of drained cooked cauliflower were twenty-two, so there was a pal when you needed one. Celery and chickory and lettuce and chard, they were nice to have around too. So many wonderful things to eat, so many friends.

Nights she and Freddy or sometimes the whole family had orgies of movie- and theatergoing. *A Taste of Honey* and *Becket* with Olivier himself and *Gypsy* with Merman and *Irma La Douce* with Elizabeth Seal. And *Bye Bye Birdie* and *Music Man* again, and the movie of *West Side Story* and *The Hustler* and *Breakfast at Tiffany's* with Audrey Hepburn who was super but starting to get fat.

Christmas Day spoiled it all, when it should have been so wonderful. *Die Grossmutter* came over for the opening of the presents and Ginger got exactly what she wanted, a three-sided mirror, full length, like they have in clothing stores, with one main mirror and two more hinged on either side so you can really see what you really look like. And Freddy seemed happy with all the Broadway show albums Ginger got her, since Freddy was determined now to become Frank Loesser or die in the attempt.

Then, after every present but one was opened and "ahhed" over, Ginger quickly left the room, returned with a large, beautifully wrapped and ribboned object, handed it to her mother, and said, "It's kind of fragile."

Phyllis loved opening presents. She did it in a childlike fashion, not carefully, but just ripping anything that stood in her way. She yanked at the ribbons and pulled the paper loose and then when she saw the old cookie jar she said, "Oh, Ginger, it's beautiful."

"I got it in the Village. He swore it was antique. I just think it's kind of old. Open it."

Phyllis lifted the lid.

"Your favorites," *Die Grossmutter* said, looking at the dozens of checkerboard cookies filling the jar to the top.

Phyllis opened her arms. "That's just so sweet of you."

Ginger gave her a hug. "Try one," Ginger said.

"It's not even noon yet. Later. With the turkey."

"Oh I can't wait that long, Mommy."

"I'm still full from the brioche at breakfast, sorry."

"One little cookie can't hurt you," Ginger said.

"I'll have several, but later."

"But Mommy, I was up half the night making them—I threw away the first three batches because they weren't perfect."

"Don't start getting all worked up," Phyllis said.

"Grossmutter," Ginger said. *"You* tell me." She took the jar and held it for the old woman. "Are they like from childhood? I worked so hard."

Grandmother Isaacs reached a shaking hand toward the jar. Ginger steadied her, guided the cookie to her mouth.

Ginger waited as the old woman chewed.

"Almost as good as Scotch shortbread," *Die Grossmutter* said. She turned to her daughter on the couch. "You're *mashuganeh* not to have any."

"Lemme try one," Stan said then. Ginger took the jar to her father. "Freddy, you can have a couple if you want."

Ginger took the jar to Freddy.

"One more wouldn't kill me," *Die Grossmutter* said, and Ginger filled her request.

"Hey Phyl, try one huh?" Stan said. Then: "Toss me another."

"Me too," from Freddy.

"I remember those Christmases," *Die Grossmutter* said. "In those days, always snow. Not like today." She looked at Phyllis. "I would pull you through the park and you would holler, 'Faster faster.' You don't remember."

"Not that," Phyllis said.

"Please," Ginger said.

"Everybody else is stuffing their faces, I should think you'd be satisfied."

"But I made them for *you*, Mommy."

"Ginger, we've played these games too often, now stop it."

"All night long till I got them right."

"Stop it, Ginger."

"You could at least eat one it won't kill you—" Ginger began.

"—I don't want the goddamned things," Phyllis finished.

Ginger grabbed the cookies, ran from the room, came back shortly after, put the jar down empty by her mother. "I threw them all in the garbage," Ginger said.

Phyllis left the room.

"The jar was the real present anyhow," Ginger hollered after. . . .

That night at one Phyllis quietly opened Ginger's door. "All work and no play," she said.

Ginger looked up in bed from her speed-reading. "I was just testing myself. I'm at seventeen hundred words a minute without losing comprehension."

"Wonderful," Phyllis said softly. Then, "Ginger, what's happening? That was so horrible today with the cookies. Turn out the light, please?"

"I'm not tired, Mommy."

"I want to hold you," Phyllis said.

Ginger turned out the light.

Phyllis climbed onto the bed and cradled her daughter. "Not such a baby anymore."

"I'm growing up is the cause of the trouble, I think. Give me a few more years and I'll be fine. Adolescence is really the pits, Mommy."

"Are you happy?"

"Oh yes. Everything's so wonderful, I feel so good and strong and there's just a glow around everything."

Phyllis began to sob.

"Hey, come on," Ginger said, patting her mother. "Poor Mommy," Ginger said then, over and over, till Phyllis gained control. . . .

Spring cleaning for Phyllis always began March first regardless. She did the bulk of it alone because it was one chore she relished, a trait inherited from her mother. You really could feel good about yourself if *you* did the housework, not a bunch of maids.

Phyllis made it a habit to begin with Ginger because she was the neatest. That way you were through the first room almost before you knew it. She came in lugging the vacuum and a mop and pail and then she brought in a second load of cleaning aids. She examined Ginger's curtains which were not the newest but still had maybe another year's life left in them. The bathroom was in good shape and before Phyllis really got down to the heavy stuff, she took a quick look-see in the closet and it was neat and Ginger didn't need many clothes, not when all she wore was the blue school uniform. High on a shelf was Ginger's suitcase and Phyllis stopped and looked at it because, no question, it was frayed and maybe a whole luggage set would make a swell birthday present when the time came. She reached up to flick the suitcase down but it was heavier than she remembered, so she brought in Ginger's desk chair and stood on it. She brought the case down and it wasn't really backbreaking, but it wasn't all that light either. She moved off the chair, put it back, stuck the suitcase on Ginger's bed, and idly opened it to see dozens and dozens of cans and tubes and jars and bottles of liquids and powders and pills, all of them either laxatives or diuretics or enemas or suppositories.

Phyllis felt suddenly so cold. . . .

* * *

Stan was sitting in Ginger's room when she hopped up the stairs from school. "Hey, fancy meeting you—" Ginger began, stopping when she saw all her medication lined up in rows on her desk. "Boy, some snoop you turned out to be." She headed for the closet, took off her shoes.

"What's this one?" Stan said, holding up a bottle.

"Agoral? That's a laxative."

"And Metamucil?"

"Another laxative."

"And these Senekot tablets?"

"Sometimes one works better for me than another. I never told you guys about the constipation because Mom worries."

"And these diuretics? You can't pee either and you didn't want to worry us about that too?"

"Don't be sarcastic."

"Ginger, I'm a rational, quiet-spoken fellow as a rule. I would like very much to remain that way. Where'd you get these prescription diet pills?"

"I gave some gobbledegook story to *Die Grossmutter.*"

"How often do you give yourself enemas?"

Ginger shrugged. "When you have to, you have to." She got out her sweat suit and running shoes.

"No," Stan said quietly.

"Hmm?"

"We're both of us sticking together till this is over."

"What's the matter with you, Daddy? Till *what's* over?"

Stan rubbed his eyes. "Ginger, how much do you weigh?"

She shrugged again. "You mean morning or night?"

Stan stood. "Of course you understand I'm pitching all this stuff."

"That's a lot of money you're wasting."

"I can afford it. Come on."

"Where?"

"I want you on my doctor's scale. I've got to know precisely what I'm dealing with."

"Are you crazy? I'm not getting on any scale with these clothes on. They'll add *pounds*."

"Strip then."

"Get naked? In front of you? I will not."

"Goddamit Ginger—"

"—you're scary when you get like that."

"I don't like losing my temper. I rarely do. I think you know that. But I promise you I am going to put you on a scale before five minutes more elapse. I suggest you bring your terrycloth robe with you and we'll weigh that and then you can take off what you're wearing and slip on the robe and I'll weigh you and subtract the robe from the total, thereby arriving at *your* exact weight. Now, if that doesn't suit you, I'll carry you down there myself right now. Which is it to be?"

Ginger got her robe. It weighed two pounds. She weighed eighty-six with it on.

Eighty-four without.

They went immediately to the kitchen, Stan silently pulling Ginger along, and after a moment Phyllis joined them. Ginger tried running to her mother but Stan held tight, forced her down onto a stool by the kitchen table in the center of the room, where Ginger slumped and muttered, "Don't let him hurt me, Mommy."

"What's in the icebox?" Stan said.

"Please, Mommy."

"Be quiet; if anybody's done any hurting, Ginger, it's what you've done to your mother. What's in there?"

Phyllis took out some ground beef.

"Cook some," Stan told her.

Phyllis asked how much.

"Don't bother me with questions, Phyl—cook the damn stuff, I don't care, a hamburger's worth."

"I need to run," Ginger said. "I'll just go twice around the park and straight back here, I promise."

"Nobody's doing any more running," from Stan.

Phyllis asked should she grill it or broil it or what.

"Just—cook—it—Phyl—*now*."

Phyllis got out a frying pan and sculpted a large hamburger patty with her hands.

"I'm not eating that," Ginger said.

"Oh are you wrong."

"I don't care how bad you hurt me, Daddy, I'm not putting that poison inside me."

"Wrong."

"Why are you *doing* this to me? Mommy, my God, why are you helping him? Tell me."

Phyllis carefully kept her back turned by the stove.

Ginger turned to her father. "That's twelve hundred ninety-six calories a pound that stuff."

"I don't care what it is, it's good for you—"

"—I don't understand anything, I thought you loved me, Daddy—"

"—just shut up—"

"—I really thought you did—Mommy, I thought Daddy loved me—"

Back still turned, Phyllis said, "He does, baby, he truly does."

"Then why is he trying to make me fat?"

Stan just stared at his daughter. Quietly, after a pause, he said, "Ginger, you are almost five foot six and you weigh eighty-four pounds. Now you're a bright girl. Surely, you cannot logically consider yourself fat."

"I will be if I eat *that*." She made a face and pointed toward the stove.

"Have we got any ice cream in the freezer?" Stan asked.

"Häagen-Dazs chocolate maybe," Phyllis said.

"Get it out so it'll soften," Stan told her.

"You must both get hold of yourselves," Ginger told them.

Phyllis put the ice cream pint on the kitchen table.

Ginger stared at it. "Wonderful," she said. "That's only 182 calories for each two point nine ounces. Mom? Why don't you see if we have any good old-fashioned lard around the house somewhere." She looked at her father.

"Lard's one hundred seventeen per tablespoon, you should like that a lot."

"Is that what we spent money on speed-reading for?" Stan asked. "So you could quick-memorize calorie charts?"

"We spent it," Ginger answered, voice rising, "so I could try and be the best in the best school in the city and my grades have never been as high. Have they, Mom. Tell him I got ninety-seven and nine on my last two tests."

"She did," Phyllis said.

"All I've done all my life is try to please you, Daddy, so *why are you doing this to me?*"

"It's for your own good," Stan said quietly, then turned toward the stove. "Is that damn thing at least warm, we're not entering in a goddam gourmet contest you know."

"It's warm!"

"Then bring it over!"

Phyllis slammed the patty on a plate and stuck it on the kitchen table along with a knife and fork. Then she got a napkin and handed it to her daughter.

"What's all this for?" Ginger asked, looking up from one of them to the other.

"Do you want salt?" Phyllis asked. "I didn't salt it much."

"It doesn't matter, I'm not going to eat it."

"You know you *are* going to, now get started," Stan said.

"Aren't we all being kind of on the juvenile side?" Ginger asked.

"Ginger; Ginger baby, try and understand me—I'm a logical man. I've run my life that way. It would not have been logical to cook the hamburger without having someone in mind to partake. It is five o'clock in the afternoon. I am having my dinner at seven. So is your mother. That leaves you. So please start."

"I'll make a deal with you. I'll eat it at seven."

"It'll be cold by then."

"I love cold burgers." She looked at her mother. "Tell him that."

"I don't know where she gets it, but she does."

"She will eat it now."

"I won't eat it now," Ginger told him. "Which kind of puts us at an impasse."

"There is no impasse," her father told her. "I am quite a lot bigger and stronger than you are and more than capable of feeding you."

Ginger started laughing.

"It's not funny, baby. I can force-feed you."

"Let's just bag this till dinner," Ginger said, and she started to stand.

Stan shoved her down. "Eat the meat, Ginger."

"Don't be rough on her," Phyllis said.

"Shut up, Phyl. Eat the goddam meat, Ginger."

"Mommy, he's scaring me."

"Then eat the hamburger right now goddamit!"

"Query: How long does this game go on?"

"I'll tell you," Stan said. "It goes on till I say it's over. This is just the start. Because I can't stand over you at lunch, but I sure can the other meals, and tomorrow for breakfast you're having a nice glass of fresh-squeezed orange juice and a rasher of bacon and fried eggs and two pieces of buttered rye-toast and all the milk you want and tomorrow—"

"—that's eight hundred sixty-nine calories—that's more than I eat all day—that's crazy—"

"—and tomorrow for dinner we're having roast beef and mashed potatoes and gravy and—"

Ginger bolted for the door.

Stan brought her back, shoved her on the stool.

"Don't hurt the child," Phyllis said, getting louder. "That's not going to accomplish a goddamned thing—"

Ginger grabbed for her mother's hands. "Why does he want me to be fat, Mommy—why does he want to destroy me?"

"He doesn't—he really truly doesn't—"

Stan forked a bite-sized piece of hamburger toward Ginger's mouth. She turned her head away. He grabbed her chin, forced her back to face him. Ginger clenched her teeth tight together. Stan let go of her chin and made her mouth open by pressing his strong hands into her cheeks and her mouth opened but she turned her head away again and when he grabbed her chin a second time, she got her teeth back clenched and Stan shouted, "Hold her head still!" to Phyllis who just stood immobile until Stan roared, "Do what I fucking well tell you!" so Phyllis took her daughter's head and held it straight and Stan forced his daughter's mouth open and shoved the fork full of hamburger inside.

Ginger spit it all out.

Stan slapped her in the mouth.

Phyllis began to cry.

Stan shoved another fork of meat into his daughter's mouth and again she spit it out, screaming, "Poison! Poison!" until he slapped her twice, forehand and back and now he was crying too as he blindly got another forkful of meat, shoved it into her mouth, held her jaws tight shut until she had to gag or chew and swallow so she chewed and swallowed and five minutes later, snack time was finally done. . . .

Breakfast the next morning was more of the same, only worse at the start because the fried eggs were, of course, much messier than the hamburger plus Freddy's being present only added to the hysteria. But by the end of the meal Ginger seemed at last to realize that her father was deadly serious and she finished the remainder of her food without being fed. She gulped down the last of her milk, shot him a look that was not friendly, and got ready for school.

The roast beef dinner was ready when she joined her family that night in the dining room. She watched him carve a large slice of red meat and put it on her plate. Then he gave her a large helping of mashed potatoes. "How much gravy?" he asked her then.

"Make a lake," she said finally, and watched as he made the depression in the middle of the potatoes with the bottom of the gravy spoon, filled it up. He added a few string beans and brought the plate to her, stood alongside.

Ginger hesitated a long time. Then she said, staring at the wall across, "If I eat this can I go or do I have to watch you stuff yourselves?"

"When you've finished every bite, we'll discuss that," Stan told her.

"No," Ginger said. "No. Because I don't care if you tie me down I won't touch this if I have to watch you eat. You make me fucking sick, Daddy, if you want to know the truth."

Phyllis poured Ginger a large glass of milk, set it by her plate.

Stan sighed. "You're not going to sidetrack me, Ginger, by trying to use foul language. We're only interested in your food. Your company isn't so fucking glorious just now either, if you want to know the truth."

"Can't we all just please have dinner?" Freddy asked.

"You may leave as soon as your plate is empty," Stan said.

With that, Ginger grabbed her knife and fork and cut up all her roast beef. Then, chewing as fast as she could, she ate the meat, mixing bites with the potatoes and gravy, swallowing quickly before shoving in some more. She ate in total silence and when her plate was empty she gulped down her milk and was gone before the others had finished serving themselves, shooting a sullen look toward her father as she fled.

She had that same look for him before bed when she came in to be weighed. She stepped on the scale in her terrycloth robe and watched as he moved the weights.

Eighty-six and a quarter.

She left in anger and silence. Stan tried a Scotch and soda before trying to tackle his briefs. He had hoped for more than a quarter pound gain, had planned on getting the kid up into the nineties inside a week at most. No. A week was optimistic. Ten days though for sure.

Only it went so slowly. The next night she was still the same, eighty-six and a goddam quarter and she seemed almost glad about it just as, the night after that, she seemed ticked that she was almost eighty-seven. She made eighty-seven even the next night which, taking off the two for the robe, meant five pounds to go.

Except would his relationship with his daughter survive the course?

She was so filled with hostility, so reluctant to even look at him much less talk, and her silence filled the big apartment. He and Phyllis tried to get Freddy to act in their behalf, to explain that they did really still love her, their Ginger, and she'd see that someday.

Ginger called Freddy a Judas and told her to fuck off.

It was as if the child were becoming possessed by a new and vile demon. She was swearing and instead of being neat, her room took to looking like a shambles. She appeared each morning, wolfed her breakfast, gulped her milk, went back to her room alone till school time. And at night the same.

But son of a bitch, at last her weight started to climb.

It took a week for it to begin to show any signs of steadiness but then it came. Eighty-eight, really eighty-six, took six days, but eighty-nine only half that long. Ginger was eating more now, and maybe even more slowly. She hit ninety in two days, then hung there on a plateau for a while, then ninety-one and finally ninety-two, an honest ninety without the robe, and Stan really felt he at last began to sense a thawing in his relationship with his daughter. Not that she had smiled at him since he beat her in the kitchen. Or even initiated a conversation. But her swearing subsided, she said how sorry she was to Freddy. And if they were a going item again, could he be far behind?

It was a bitch of a time for help, because their old maid —old meaning she'd stayed for more than six months— left because she couldn't stand the atmosphere in the house and besides, Phyllis had yelled at her several times because of the tension Ginger was causing. There followed a bunch of live-ins, some who couldn't boil water, a few who could. They'd last a day at the least, usually four or five times that long; most of them couldn't speak English at all, just the semiliterate Spanish they got by on.

Alicia was the first girl they were rooting could last the course because she was fat and sunny-dispositioned, even if a natural-born klutz. Her first night she broke a china platter, the day after that two Baccarat wine goblets. But she was so sorry and Phyllis felt the need then of a smiling face around the house.

But even Phyllis had to throw in the sponge when Alicia came running in to her, babbling in broken Spanish that something terrible had happened to the washing machine. Phyllis followed the frightened maid to the pantry where, indeed, the machine was making sounds like it was a refugee from Cape Canaveral, but Phyllis quickly silenced it by pulling out the plug. She was not noticeably inclined mechanically but she opened the lid of the machine and saw that Alicia had way overloaded it.

"Dir-tee dir-tee," Alicia said, still scared, pointing to the terrycloth robe that took up most of the washer, and Phyllis nodded as she lifted the robe out.

It was then that she felt the first stone.

Not big and it was slender, carefully sewn in the bottom hem of the thick, fluffy-when-dry material. Phyllis got a scissors, ripped it out, felt around, found the next, and the next, and the one after that, and then she ran to the kitchen and grabbed the meat scale and brought it in and in a frenzy now began slicing the robe to pieces as she found more and more stones and put them in the scale and the scale needle kept going up and up as Phyllis kept on, not stopping until the truth had dawned, that being that Ginger was probably seventy-nine pounds now.

And dropping fast.

3

"Hey, Zep," Ginger said, waving as Doctor Benjamin walked into her hospital room. "Welcome to the cube."

He looked around the totally barren place, said, "It's only yours for as long as you want it." Then he seated himself in the chair beside the bed. "I know you just got here and that it's all discombobulating, but we haven't got time to waste and this is going to be a very hard conversation."

"I'll just put on my thinking cap," Ginger said, "and off we go."

"You're a very sick girl, my darling."

"Race you round the block, let's see who wins."

"You've got a terrifying disease about which we know not remotely enough except that it is named *anorexia nervosa* and it is fatal possibly twenty percent of the time."

"That to scare me?"

"Ginger, I am your doctor, not a parent, so I don't have to play games with you, as you did with them, gulping down food and vomiting it after and enacting your charade with the stones. I just want you to know what we're into and the future is yours and yours alone."

Ginger closed her eyes and lay back.

"When I said your illness was named *anorexia nervosa,* I was, in point of fact wrong. It is *mis*named that, since the word *anorexia* means a lack of appetite and my guess is that you are and have been since the onset, consumed with hunger and thoughts of food. My guess is also that you have not had your period for many months."

"Darn," Ginger said. "And all this time I was sure I'd conceived." She looked at him then. "Immaculately natch."

"I can't really tell you a whole lot more about it, because we're all still groping in the dark. But it does seem to always attack perfect young ladies like yourself."

"I sure feel perfect in this place right now, Zeppo. Maybe even 'divine.' "

"This 'place' as you very well know is Lexington Hospital, not six blocks from your home. This is predominantly the children's section, more particularly the experimental part."

"I get to play guinea pig? Wonderful."

"I'd like to get to the terrifying part of the sickness, if you don't mind."

"Query: Who's stopping you?"

"Okay, here it is: You don't think you're thin."

Ginger sat quickly up. "I'm not thin. I'm not saying I'm fat, understand, but I'm sure a long way from skinny."

"You're telling the truth, I know that. You don't perceive of yourself, when you examine your body in a mirror—"

"—don't bullshit me, Zeppo—I've got a three-way job and I study myself sometimes, so I *know* what I look like. And I'm sure as hell not thin."

Doctor Benjamin took her hand. "It must be very scary for you, I know. You must think I'm telling you the world is round when you're just positive it's flat."

"I'm not, goddamit, thin, so change the record."

"Try to believe this: To the world at large you look like an escapee from Buchenwald. You're a skeleton with skin on, period. Seventy-eight and a quarter pounds."

"You're all out to fatten me up for the slaughter, every fucking one of you!"

Doctor Benjamin stood. "I'll be back in a couple of days."

"What—what happens till then?"

"Nothing. You just lie here. No visitors, phones, mail, tv. You're not allowed to read or get out of bed. Everything you do burns up calories and you haven't any extra. We're trying to modify your behavior. The dietician will be in shortly. You select your own meals. If your weight stays the same or goes down, you stay in your cube as you call it. And stare. If your weight starts to go up, we restore privileges. We'll weigh you each morning and night. Good-bye."

"Wait—how long have I got to stay?"

"Up to you."

"Why have you turned against me? What did my folks say to you?"

"Don't try manipulating me."

"Why are you doing this to me?"

"You know."

"But I don't."

Doctor Benjamin paused. "Child, I wish you joy," he said, and he was gone.

A black lady came in a little later with a clipboard. "I am your friendly neighborhood dietician," she said. "Name of Aaron like the baseball star. What would your preferences be for lunch today?"

"Can I have anything I want?"

"We're running a little short of beluga caviar, but you can pretty much pick." She got her clipboard into position to write.

"I'd like some cottage cheese then."

"Large curd or small?"

"Doesn't matter calorically."

"Fine. What else?"

"Mustard?"

"We got Heinz."

"It'll have to do."

"What else?"

"Nothing."

"Okay. How about dinner tonight."

"Same."

"Fine. Now how about breakfast tomorrow?"

"Same."

"Easy to remember," Miss Aaron said. "Bye."

That night she weighed the same, seventy-eight and a quarter, and she asked the nurse who weighed her if she could have a tv set, it was dull in the room and the nurse was as nice as could be but she went the night without television.

Miss Aaron arrived again the next morning after breakfast, clipboard in hand. "Would you do me a favor," Ginger asked.

"Here to please."

"I'm sure my mother has a note for me outside somewhere. Reception or whatever. And my sister too. And probably a present from my grandmother. No one's delivered them and I don't want anything getting lost in the shuffle."

"Didn't the doctor explain? Sure he did, he must have. Nothing, no mail, no contact. It's up to you for how long it stays that way."

"Well I'm going fucking crazy!"

"Must be awful," Miss Aaron said, clipboard in position. "Now about meals."

"Are you always so fucking cheerful?"

"No, just in here. I beat the crap out of my boyfriend when I'm off duty. Cottage cheese again?"

Ginger rolled over and looked away.

"I got to put down something so I'll just ditto what you had yesterday."

"Put down what you want, I'm not going to eat it."

"Fine with me," Miss Aaron said. "See you tomorrow."

The next day Ginger said, "Listen, you've got to get me something to read," to Miss Aaron.

"Oh honey, come on, don't be silly."

"I'll pay you."

"That makes it swell. Deal. How much?"

"As soon as I get out I'll make it ten dollars a book."

"No deal. I'm strictly a cash person."

"You were bullshitting me, weren't you?"

"Just trying to get along with the patients, honey. I think we should switch to a different food today, you must be getting bored not eating the cottage cheese. Why don't you not eat green beans for a change? Might up your spirits."

Ginger began to giggle. "That's really clever," she said.

"Just trying to get along with the patients, honey. What do you want to drink?"

"Tea."

"Progress. String beans and tea all three meals?"

Ginger nodded.

"Easy to remember. See you tomorrow."

That night Ginger decided they could find someone else to fiddle around with so she got up and holding to the wall, made her way out of the room into the corridor where the old night nurse sat alone and gray, reading at a desk. When the nurse looked up Ginger said "I'm going home now," and moved on past toward the elevator.

"Shhh," the night nurse said. "Others are sleeping."

"Don't come near me," Ginger whispered as the old woman approached. "I'm very strong."

"Of course you are," the nurse whispered and she took Ginger by the arm and Ginger struggled and it was like fighting *Die Grossmutter,* it should have been that simple, only there was no strength somehow in her body.

"I'm a powerhouse," Ginger said. "I'm not going to give you another warning."

Then the old woman did this incredible thing: She lifted Ginger up, cradled her in her arms whispering, "Oh child, there's just nothing to you," and as she was placed back in bed, the covers pulled up tight, Ginger, silently, began at last to cry. . . .

Did that happen? Any of it? The next morning when she woke Ginger wasn't sure. Her throat was dry and her eyes felt funny but that could have been from anything.

Except she was weak. Her arms were really a disappointment to her. No strength at all. She moved her legs under the blanket and even that took effort. When her beans and tea came she just pushed the tray aside and lay there. What month was it? April? Something like April. "What month is it?" she asked Doctor Benjamin when he came in.

"I hope April," he told her. "How are things in Glocca Morra?"

Ginger shrugged. "Hey Zeppo, please, I want to get out of here."

"Isn't it funny; that's what I want too."

"Do it then. You can."

"When you're strong."

"Why are you against me?"

He pulled a chair close to her bed. "Let's talk about that. Why would I be? You must have some ideas. Here you're fine and I'm keeping you in this place. Why am I torturing you?"

"You've always hated me, Zeppo."

"Why didn't you tell Phyllis? I'm sure she would have found a different doctor."

"Maybe you don't hate me, you just want to see me fat."

"Let's talk about that too—why would I? To put you in a circus as the fat lady? I could be your agent maybe. But ten percent of a fat lady's salary probably isn't enough to live on."

Now Ginger did begin to weep. "I dunno . . . I just dunno . . . everybody wants me fat and I can't figure why. . . ."

"Ginger—Ginger listen—I've known you since womb time and I'm going to ask the hardest thing I ever asked anybody before, but just consider it before you say no: Consider the possibility that *you* might be the one that's out of step. What if the mirror's misleading you?"

She was dreamy now. "My three-sided mirror? It would never lie. . . ."

"Make believe the earth is round, kid. It could be."

"I'm so gross."

"What if you're not?"

"Oh I am though. . . ."

"What if you're not?"

". . . I dunno. . . ."

"I think you're not so sure anymore."

". . . I don't wanna be fat, Zeppo. . . ."

"I don't want you to be."

She was crying harder now. ". . . oh Zeppo, I'm just so hungry . . ."

"I know, baby."

". . . I just think about food all the time. . . ."

"Must get kind of dull."

". . . it does, oh, it does, but what can I do . . . ?"

"Eat some food."

". . . I hate food. . . ."

"You just said you thought about it all the time."

". . . I hate cottage cheese . . . I hate goddam beans. . . ."

"I've got an idea—why not try a chicken leg for lunch?"

". . . a chicken leg? . . . do you know how many calories that is? . . ."

"No, but I'll bet you do."

She made a nod.

"Okay? Want me to order it up for you?"

Now she was beginning to break apart with sobs. ". . . is . . . is . . ."

"Just let it happen, Ginger; take your time."

". . . there something . . . wrong . . . with me . . . ?"

"I think there might be. What do you think?"

". . . I dunno . . . I guess . . . maybe . . . but . . . but Freddy gets the . . . legs. . . ."

"Come again?"

". . . home . . . Freddy eats the chicken legs . . . I like the . . . the wings are my favorite, could I have the wings . . . would it be okay . . . ?" She was crawling toward him now and he opened his arms till she was comfortable and drifting.

"I think it can be arranged," Zeppo Benjamin said.

* * *

She ate sparingly those next few days, but once she was in the habit, her appetite began a quick return. Her weight came in plateaus, and after a week she could have visitors, and she and Freddy chattered like birds, and the week after that she had total privileges, a tv set, a radio, mail, and freedom to walk the corridors, freedom to read and even start exercising once her weight hit ninety. When it was over that mark for ten days straight, she went home and Brearley couldn't have been more understanding about her absence and letting her make up work at her own more than good speed. She finished the year with one of the top five averages in her grade which was an improvement over the first semester in spite of the difficulties, and all was quiet on the Abraham front until the Saturday afternoon in early June when *Die Grossmutter* came for a visit, and she was weakening, the grand old lady, her mind starting to play tricks, but Ginger enjoyed her visits anyway. Then about three o'clock Ginger excused herself and, because she felt chilly, went to bed.

The coughing began before four and when her mother took her temperature it was already over a hundred and two and by the time she called Doctor Benjamin and found he was out of town it was closer to two degrees higher and the cough was dreadful. Phyllis tracked the doctor by six and he said he would be back in town before eight and would stop by and not to worry, but Phyllis couldn't help saying, "What if it's pneumonia?" and he said, "Pneumonia in June, when will Ginger stop doing things the hard way?" and hung up on what was clearly meant to be a note of reassurance.

Ginger lay groggily in bed, covered with perspiration, the cough deepening, really ripping now, forcing her body to jackknife with its power and Freddy was scared and even Stan seemed more than a little shaky. Phyllis stood by him and whispered, "I just pray it isn't what I think" and Stan whispered that pneumonia wasn't that big a deal anymore, nothing like it used to be, and *Die Grossmutter*

put cool compresses on Ginger's forehead and said how
wonderful it was this didn't happen before, if it had been
pneumonia before the hospital, it could have been bad,
and Ginger coughed and drifted and when she wanted to
sleep they left her alone.

She lay trembling in bed, waiting for Zeppo to come.
She'd seen a whole lot of him since she'd faked him into
the nickel seats with her Barbara Stanwyck crying act over
the chicken wing. Now, burning with fever, she kicked off
the blankets and pulled at her nightgown awhile before
she managed to get it off.

Naked, she advanced toward the three-sided mirror and
studied herself from all angles. Disgusting she was. A
cow, a ninety-two-pound ugly. But if this was pneumonia
—if this was really pneumonia, what a break that would
be. The pounds just fell off when you had pneumonia.
With luck, if it was a really decent case, there was no
telling how far she might go. The seventies were a cinch,
and maybe even better. Sixty-nine pounds. Sixty-eight.
Really at glorious last, thin. Teeth chattering and losing
strength, she gripped the friendly mirror for support and
prayed, as the coughs wracked her again, that pneumonia
it would be. Oh yes, oh yes, please.

God knew she was due for a lucky day. . . .

4

To the Assistant Manager of the Mauna Kea Hotel, on the Big Island of Hawaii, Harry Brennerman said, "Who is the one with the eyes?"

"You'll have to be a little more specific, Mr. Brennerman."

"Oh come on, come on, you have to know, she eats alone, dark hair, stacked, runs along the beach sometimes at dusk. The stunner's who I'm talking about."

"That would be Miss Abraham," the Assistant Manager said.

"What can you tell me?"

The Assistant Manager hesitated.

"Oh stop it," Brennerman said. "I've only been coming here how many Februarys now? I'm a grandfather, rape is not on my mind this morning."

The Assistant Manager consulted a card. "Miss Ginger Abraham. Twenty-four Central Park South. She's been here ten days, she'll be here four more." He put the card back. "And she is alone."

Harry slipped a sawbuck into the guy's coat pocket and sauntered down to the beach. He spotted his quarry standing ankle deep in the surf, wading out in the direction of the raft maybe seventy-five yards away. Harry hurried toward her, decided to give it his best shot right off, said, "Keed, have you ever considered a career in pictures?" In the two-piece white suit she was wearing, she looked even better close. Five six. Curves. 120.

She looked at him and broke out laughing. "I can't believe anyone would use a line like that in the twentieth century," she said, and dove into the water, swimming strongly toward the distant raft.

"Fug," Harry said, watching her. He hated swimming because among other things, he parted his long hair direct-ly above his left ear and combed it straight across his bald skull, and neither wind nor water added much to his beauty. But there was a heat about this one. When she stared at him with the violet eyes for that flash, he knew he was on to something. So, taking off his Hawaiian shirt which he hated a lot but his wife had given it to him for this trip, so what are you gonna do, he moved carefully into the Pacific and began his slow breaststroke into deep water, cursing as an occasional wave broke over his shoul-ders, doing God only knew what to his hair.

Panting, he reached the raft finally and gripped the ladder for a while, summoning the energy to climb aboard. "Miss Abraham," he managed to the girl lying eyes-closed facing the sun. "At risk of limb and life, I have pursued you. Harry Brennerman is my name."

Ginger rolled over on one elbow.

"I am an agent. An independent agent and not unsuc-cessful. Because, primarily, I like to think, there are only George Chasin and I who are also gentlemen."

"I've heard of his restaurant," Ginger said.

"The restaurant of which you speak is Chasen's with an 'e.' I can tell you are not totally familiar with Southern California."

"Mr. Brennerman, this is certainly very flattering, but I must tell you that my only interest in the picture business has been to someday be nibbled to death slowly by Roger Monaghan," Ginger said, naming a star of around forty who had eyes like Robert Mitchum and the body of a young Errol Flynn.

"I can arrange for you to meet the Rajah," Brennerman said. "I leave nibbling to the lawyers."

"Query: Will this make a better story than Ava Gardner?"

"What about her?"

"Well, here I am being discovered on a raft in the, shall we call it slate-gray Pacific. She was discovered in the Walgreen Drug Store."

"(A)," Harry Brennerman said, "it was Lana Turner, not Miss Gardner. (B) it was Schwab's, not Walgreen's. And anyway, (C) the whole thing was press-agent bullshit in the first place."

"You couldn't be an agent," Ginger said. "You're not nearly greasy enough," and with that she smiled, thanked him, and swam back in toward shore.

The best lunches in all of Hawaii are those served at the Mauna Kea Beach Hotel, and as Ginger was about to tackle her large buffet plate filled with cold mahi-mahi and sliced turkey and various salads, a very tall gray-haired woman stopped by her table. "I come as an emissary from Mr. Brennerman. I am Mrs. Brennerman and I am to plead his case. He wants me to tell you that he is indeed an agent, he asks that you join us for coffee, and hopeful of a positive response, he told me to tell you he has already covered his entire body with a coating of bear grease."

"That may be the sweetest invitation I've ever had," Ginger said. "I shall be by."

Which she was, maybe half an hour later, and from the start she hit it off with the Brennermans. They were all very open with each other, telling her all about their three kids and eight grandchildren, two of whom were brain damaged and the mother was pregnant again and what could you do but cross your fingers. She told them about how her folks were split and how this trip was a treat from her father for finishing Sarah Lawrence a semester ahead of schedule. She was going to hang around his office from February till fall when she was accepted at

Virginia Law, only she wasn't sure what she really ought to do was maybe get a doctorate from Yale and teach English lit somewhere because more than anything probably she loved to read.

And no, thank you very much, she didn't want to be a movie star. Primarily, Ginger explained, because she disliked the idea of acting plus she was devoid of talent. Harry pursued but Ginger was firm, and they settled, since she had to head back through L.A. anyway, for dinner at Chasen's. The one with the "e."

He also arranged, she discovered when she visited his offices, quick get-togethers with Wyler, Wise, and Wilder, all of whom were in one form of preparation or another. The day after the meetings Ginger was offered a small part in *Star!*

She asked to read the script.

Harry Brennerman had apoplexy in front of her as he tried to explain that people in her position (A) usually didn't get offered parts right off and (B) if they did, they bowed toward Mecca and said thanks.

Ginger held firm.

Harry snuck her a copy of the screenplay and then watched, stunned, as she read it. She read crazy, this one, with her index finger zigzagging down the print. She finished the whole goddam hundred fifty plus pages in six minutes and then said, No, she thought it was a silly story, she didn't want to do it.

News like that didn't take too long to seep around.

After all, Bobby Wise's two previous musicals had only been *West Side Story* and *Sound of Music* and here was this unknown saying no.

It was the start of Ginger's legend.

The next day Wyler called in about *Funny Girl* and Ginger read the script and was delighted to play the role, that of the Ziegfeld dancer who had the hots for Omar Sharif. She moved directly into *Charly* in the part of the factory sex-pot who got interested in Cliff Robertson after he stopped being stupid. Jewison grabbed her next, where

she was the rich-bitch tease Steve McQueen dropped for
Faye Dunaway.

Three movies made, none released, but the publicity
drums were pounding. This *creature* had come to town and
taken up residence in a small suite at the Beverly Wilshire
Hotel, which she was paying for *herself*, before she went
off to for Christ's sakes law school. She gave horrendously
frank interviews, made all the improper social moves, and
directors were standing in line to get a chance at her.
"Hepburn with tits" was the general appraisal, and no one
who met her denied that once the violet eyes were on
you, you started getting crazy thoughts in the middle of
the night.

"So this is the hot girl," Julian Garvey said.

"I wouldn't know about that," Ginger said.

Harry Brennerman said nothing, just took a seat in a
corner of Garvey's office and flicked his eyes, back and
forth, one to the other.

" 'The Hot Girl' is a phrase of mine, Miss Abraham. If
one lives in this Mecca of culture long enough, one realizes
that there is always, always, a 'Hot Girl.' Right now it is
you." He turned to Brennerman. "You gave her a copy of
Pioneer Courage?"

Brennerman nodded.

Garvey smiled at Ginger. "This habit of yours of reading scripts is something you must break, Miss Abraham.
Take a leaf from the pages of Liz Taylor, who only reads
her own roles. That's just a suggestion."

Ginger nodded and smiled back.

"Now of course, the two leads in *Pioneer Courage* are
cast, as you know, with Heston and MacLaine, but I think
the role of the discontented dance hall queen could be
terribly important with the right actress. Which is, of
course, why we are here. You see, Miss Abraham, I think
we're closing in on a classic here. *Pioneer Courage* can
make a powerful statement for these times about the core
of the American character, don't you agree?"

"I thought it was prepubescent bullshit," Ginger said.

"Don't fence-straddle with me, child; did you like the script or not?" He turned to Brennerman again. "This one's got a mouth on her, Harry."

"Wait, you don't know the half."

Garvey looked at Ginger for a moment. "It is a dreadful script, Miss Abraham. It is bilge piled high. But I think it would not be unwise for you to appear in it."

"Why?"

"Because it is, to coin a phrase, commercial. And a lot of people are going to see it. How old are you?"

"Twenty-three."

"Then you're old enough certainly to remember Camilla Sparv."

"Who was she?"

"She was the Hot Girl two years ago, Miss Abraham. And two years before that, everyone was after Maria Perschy. Shall I go back through the decade? Sandra Church. Pamela Tiffin. Diane McBain. Luanna Patten. Hot Girls all."

"Query: Why is he telling me all this?"

"Idle banter is all, Miss Abraham. But the calendar tells us that here we are in the summer of sixty-eight. And here you are, all steaming and pursued. With, of course, no released picture yet smiling down at us from the silver screen. Summer has a way of turning into autumn. One doesn't notice it here in lotusland, but this is a tough town, especially on glories such as yourself. And twenty-three is not necessarily, in Hollywood, young."

Ginger nervously bit on a fingernail. "And you think that if I take the dance hall hostess, it could maybe help?"

Garvey nodded and sat forward at his desk. "There is a poem by Emily Dickinson, Miss Abraham, which tells us that our ardor doesn't last forever, that when glimpsed at a later time, the object of our affection seems less imposing."

Ginger turned to Harry Brennerman and said, "I can't believe this asshole."

Harry Brennerman held his head.

Ginger whirled back to Garvey now. "You ought to be recorded and stuffed and stuck in Disneyland. Jesus, you sit there in your tailor-made clothes and you favor me with your best Leslie Howard angle, oozing smarmy charm from every pore, and telling me if I don't play this tits-and-ass role I'm going to be forgotten, and to clinch your case you dazzle me with poetic erudition. In the first place, putz, the poem is by Dorothy Parker, not Dickinson —my God, the only things they have in common is they were both women and they both wrote short—and the name of the poem is 'Healed' and it goes like this:

> *Oh, when I flung my heart away,*
> *The year was at its fall.*
> *I saw my dear, the other day,*
> *Beside a flowering wall;*
> *And this was all I had to say:*
> *'I thought that he was tall!'*

Ginger stood then. "I'm sorry, Harry, but I didn't want this meeting in the first place," and turning, she left the room.

Garvey turned to Brennerman. "Interesting child," he said.

"Not exactly run of the mill."

Julian stroked his chin and stared at the open office door. "I think I may bed down with her for a time. Bring her properly to heel."

Brennerman stood. "She may just be too quick for you."

"In matters of the heart, Harry," Julian Garvey said, "I make it a practice never to bet against Julian Garvey. . . ."

Ginger lay sprawled across the bed, eyes half closed, the third Chivas and soda on the table beside her. The Beverly Hills Hotel bungalow was almost completely dark, the chief source of light being the bathroom where Garvey sang softly to himself. Ginger, still in her bra and panties, shifted her body slowly, peering toward the sound. Eventually Garvey emerged, wearing a dark paisley silk robe. "Why don't we all just get comfortable," he said, reaching to unhook her bra.

"Justa minnut," Ginger said, her words slurred badly. "I jes wanna go over the facks one lass time."

"I am here but to elucidate," Garvey said, moving for the Chivas bottle, walking around to her side of the bed, filling her glass again.

"You meen that yer gonna get rid of Shur-lee Mac-whatzis and star me."

"If you've no objections, of course."

"An' the fack that I'm about to have sexual innercourse with you has nothin' to do with nothin'?"

"I would never damage a project as close to my heart as *Pioneer Courage* for something as mundane as sex."

"An' Shur-lee didden mind?"

"She hasn't officially been informed."

"But she's gonna be?"

"In the morning."

"Query: Can I truss—"

"Where did you get that 'query' business? It's very color-ful. You don't mind if I start using it. I shall give you credit at every opportunity."

Ginger kind of blinked and just lay sprawled.

Garvey bent toward her again. "Now I really think we owe it to ourselves to get comfortable."

"You first."

Garvey smiled and stood and slipped out of the paisley robe, draped it over the end of the bed. He was already erect and hard as he straddled her body.

Ginger looked at his penis and shook her head sadly. "Oh you poor man," she said.

Garvey said, "What?"

"Couldn't plastic surgery help?" Ginger asked. "Or may-be a dildo?"

Garvey was shriveling rapidly by now.

Ginger scooted out from under and started getting dressed.

Garvey threw his robe around him, covering himself, and said, "You really are a world-class cunt."

"Praise from Caesar." She zipped up her skirt, began buttoning her blouse. "You needn't see me home."

"You've been planning this from the start, haven't you?"

Ginger stopped dead. "How could *I* be planning anything when *you* were the one who called earlier and said it was crucial we meet here."

"Why did you come?"

"Obviously, I thought to screw. I mean, you're a very famous cocksman, Mr. Three-by-Five and all that; how often does a girl get a chance to hump a Flynn or a Mitchum or a Monaghan. But I thought it was going to be thrilling, Julian. Distant violins, good conversation, subtle seemingly accidental body contact. And what happens? You try to get me smashed on Chivas and give me a line that Moe of the Three Stooges wouldn't swallow."

"We're awfully sober all of a sudden."

"That's because we were quite surreptitious as to where we deposited our Scotch. I promise you, several plants will be dead in the morning." She slipped into her sandals, grabbed her purse, headed for the door.

"My dear, you cannot begin to fathom the depth of the grave you've just dug for yourself."

Ginger whirled in the doorway. "Hey, putz—I had a rich grandmother."

"Meaning?"

"I've got my fuck-you money, Mr. Garvey; go scare your secretary, you'll do better."

The next morning Harry Brennerman's phone call woke her at seven. "I just heard from your friend Julian."

"I don't want to know," Ginger told him.

"You might just. He's offered you a three-picture exclusive deal at five-oh per."

"*Whaaaat?*"

"I swear."

"It's some kind of crazy revenge, tell him no," Ginger said, and she rolled over into sleep.

The next day Garvey sweetened the pot and Ginger, of course, said no again, and the day after that UA snuck *Thomas Crown Affair* in San Diego, a very successful sneak, Dunaway proving she wasn't a one-shot after *Bonnie and Clyde,* a good change-of-pace caper role for McQueen. But the one they came out talking about was the violet-eyed brunette, who was that rich-bitch McQueen dumped halfway through the picture?

"Listen, we really ought to meet and talk some things through," Brennerman said the following morning. "It's getting to be crazy time and a little sorting wouldn't hurt." He told her he'd stop by her suite at the Wilshire at noon and they'd skip across to the Derby for the Cobb Salad, which suited Ginger well enough, and she was really in a good mood when Harry knocked on her door, because it was a crazy game, Hollywood, but as long as you kept enough sanity to know that when a hot streak ended you had to walk away from the table, how could you get hurt?

She thought he'd had a stroke, he looked that ashen, and at the same time she said, "What?" he said, "Have you seen it?" and at the same time she said, "Seen what?" he said, "Here," and handed it over.

It was a rag, a nothing sheet, *The National Enquirer.* And on its tabloid-sized front page was the headline, THIS IS A SEX BOMB? and a few words explaining that a certain Ginger Abraham had three pictures in the can and already they were saying "Monroe" in movieland.

The rest of the page was one giant photo. It was Ginger in her junior year at Brearley, standing there facing the camera, just before her fourth and final hospitalization, when she was at her weakest, barely sixty-five pounds. There were a dozen other pictures inside the centerfold, all from that terrible anorexic time and now Ginger stood grief stricken as she stared at the skeleton with the dead skin and the deader eyes. "I. . . ." she started to say, don't like to think about those days. "I. . . ." she started to say, I really thought I was fat, I didn't know, I didn't know.

"Oh, Harry," she finally said and followed with a helpless gesture of her hands. "The things we do to ourselves. . . ."

And then the press descended. It was dog-day time, and suddenly here was this present for them, this story of the hottest unknown girl in the business, this girl who everybody said was built like a brick shithouse with the face of a Vivien Leigh, and my God, look at the used-to-be. It was like the Christine Jorgensen story only without the sex change. Not only was she a beauty, she was smart, not only smart, rich, a distinguished family, old Jewish money, the works.

Every paper in the country began working on it, and stories about the disease began appearing with every expert they could dredge up, and articles about Brearley and interviews with her classmates at Sarah Lawrence, and they tried nailing her at the Wilshire so she moved to Brennerman's house, but they found her there quick enough, and everywhere Ginger went, there were people taking her picture, and asking questions, the same crazy questions over and over, and then the rest of the media began crawling over her, frenzied maggots, raping her of her privacy. *Time* ran an article about the possibilities of the disease's returning, called "The Abraham Syndrome: Will the Beauty Last?" And *Newsweek*, not to be outdone, did a story condemning Ginger for not speaking freely with the press, because think of the thousands of anorexics who might be helped if she would only just tell how she whipped it. Then the local CBS station in L.A. got hold of some *Thomas Crown* footage and contrasted it with the still shots from her anorexic days, while the anchorman chastised both *Time* and *Newsweek* for giving such undue publicity to a performer who hadn't yet done anything, thereby giving additional undue publicity to a performer who hadn't yet done anything.

Ginger fled.

She took the red-eye to New York where her father met her at the gate, limousine waiting outside, but when he got to his place on Central Park South eleven reporters and photographers were already camped out under the awning. Ginger stayed with her father a couple of days, then at night slipped up to the duplex on Park where Phyllis still lived, alone in the enormous duplex with nothing but the maids for company. It was, of course, an enormously posh building, and when the press found her there, the management of the apartment house phoned Phyllis and said listen, you must really do something about this, people do not purchase quarter of a million dollar apartments in order to be pestered by newsmen every time they go in or out. Ginger phoned Freddy, who was of course friendly, but she was also the mother now of a girl, one Ginger Isaacs Friedman, Freddy's husband being a brilliant young Bostonian who had decided after one year at Harvard Law that what he really wanted to be was a rabbi, and they were living near Cambridge, but their apartment was small and probably a circus wasn't the best thing in the world for the baby.

Ginger flew to London, where things, if not good, were at least better; after that she spent a day in Paris where all she did really was rent a car. Holland was flat and hot and uneventful, but they left her alone there, and in Belgium too, and Ginger drove and saw what sights there were to see, falling naturally in love with Bruges, which was probably where she decided that she didn't know for sure what she wanted to do with her life but going to Virginia Law sure as hell wasn't it, so she wired them from Brussels withdrawing at least for now, and when she snuck back into the country late in August, the Democratic Convention had exploded in Chicago and nobody cared quite so much just now for the story of a rich kid who once upon a time had been underweight.

Brennerman caught her at her father's late on the end of a steaming Friday, with the news that the delayed Garvey picture was now called *Fortune Favors the Brave* and that Heston was out because of a schedule conflict and MacLaine had to leave for Japan when shooting was to

begin so did Ginger want the lead or didn't she. One picture, no strings, one two five flat. It was starting in mid-
September and was headquartering mainly in Denver,
shooting in the boonies an hour outside town. And oh yes,
the Rajah was now in the lead, for a mill plus ten percent
of the gross from two and a half times negative. Roger
Monaghan himself.

"The ball, you should pardon my vulgarity, is in your
court," Brennerman said, and Ginger could picture him,
seated hunched at his desk, running his hands from the
part just above his ear all the way across his skull, smoothing, smoothing. She held the phone in silence and did
some figuring. Certainly a lot of bread; maybe in the hills
outside Denver, even a little quiet. Not to mention Mister
Monaghan.

Shortly after Labor Day she left for Colorado. . . .

"Nibble me some more," Ginger said as she lay naked
on the large bed in the largest suite in the Brown Palace
Hotel.

Roger Monaghan got up, rummaged through his trouser
pockets till he found a decently rolled joint, lit it, and took
a couple of tokes. He held it out to Ginger who shook her
head. "Let me have a few minutes to refuel," the Rajah
said. "I ain't no chicken no more." He was a big man,
probably six foot three, a 1930s-type movie star, Gable
sized, Flynn sized, not like the ones today.

"You're just about the best fuck I ever had," Ginger
told him.

He shrugged. "It's what I do. God knows I ain't no
actor." He walked naked to the windows and stared out
at Denver in the night. "Hey? You're not one of those
nutcakes who has to boff her leading man to feel secure?"

"Hmm?"

"Well, you'd be amazed how common that is. When I
first started out, I'm going maybe twenty years back now,
I figured my leading ladies were all over me on account of
I was so blockbuster irresistible. Now I know better. It's

not such a nutcake question when you consider we only met this afternoon."

"You remember back when you rescued Jean Simmons from the rapids and fell in love with her even though she was married, the two of you just couldn't help it, but at the end you pretended you were a coward and left her so she could have her good name?"

"That piece of shit? Sure."

"That sleeping bag scene where you kissed her. It was really me you were kissing. I was thirteen and saw it seven times."

He inhaled again on the joint, ran his hands through his trademarked red hair, looked at Denver again, then gave it the finger.

"What was that about?"

"You know why I took this piece of shit that starts tomorrow?"

"Certainly not the money."

"I don't work for money, Chubby, I *get* the money. If this had shot in Montana I'd have said 'fuck no' but I was born in the outskirts of this shitburg and I never cut it here. I skied great and I played football okay but I never could cut it. Well I'm here now, and fuck them."

"Fuck *me*," Ginger said and she opened her arms.

He came back to the bed and lay alongside her.

"And you are too an actor," Ginger said. "Before when you said you weren't, you were wrong and I know it, because I never felt this way about Troy Donahue."

"Sorry, Chub, but I know my limitations. Acting is Olivier. Acting is Brando. I just happen to photograph well from certain angles. I'm a starlet. That's my occupation. Whenever I go to Europe and they give you those cards to fill out, you know, name and address and passport number and occupation? I always print 'starlet' in the occupation line."

Ginger kissed him.

"And I'm very married," the Rajah said then.

"The point being?"

"We're gonna have to spend the next couple months together. I've got a great body, use it, then pack up your tent and steal away."

"Why the sermon?"

" 'Cause you're a nutcake and I sense things and there's no point getting into it with me. I'm married all my goddam life to a schizo Catholic lady who isn't quite sure if the Pope is quite devout enough."

"Why'd you get started with a love match like that in the first place?"

"It was spring and the rubber broke."

Ginger hugged him, then lay back. "I won't get involved, I promise." She closed her eyes and inhaled deeply. "Now goddamit—*nibble*."

"And people think it's easy being a movie star," the Rajah said. . . .

5

"Here comes goddam Garvey," Monaghan muttered, glancing out the window of his trailer caravan. He and Ginger were having lunch alone at the table in the rear, the caravan parked near the ghost town they were using most of that, the third, week of *Fortune Favors the Brave*.

"Why do you hate him?" Ginger asked, cutting herself a piece of roast chicken, scraping away the skin.

"I hate his jeans," the Rajah said. "Anybody who wears two-hundred-dollar custom-made blue jeans earns my enmity. I also am not crazy about the way he hovers around you." Suddenly he got excited and said, "Quick, duck out of sight and be quiet," and as Ginger obeyed, across the table he did the same. Then, as Garvey was very near the caravan, Monaghan began to groan passionately, "Oh Jesus, Ginger, don't stop, don't stop—"

"—hey cut this," Ginger interrupted.

"—shut up, shut up," the Rajah told her, and then he began making the caravan shake slightly as he raised his voice and said, "Oh yes, all of it darling, take it all, all the way, oh please, my Christ, shit *ahhhhhhhh*."

Garvey knocked on the caravan door. " 'Tis I."

"One sec Julian old buddy," the Rajah said, trying to sound frantic. He moved to the caravan door and zipped and unzipped his trousers as loudly as he could. Then, mussing his red hair, he opened the door, panting lightly. "How they hangin?"

Garvey moved inside the trailer and nodded the length of it to Ginger who was seated eating the chicken, drinking iced tea. "I know you've got a short attention span," he said to Monaghan, "so I shall attempt succinctness." He paused, then said it: "The news is getting around and we cannot keep it any longer under control."

"What news?" the Rajah said.

Garvey gestured toward the two of them. "Word of your alliance, the way you two are, shall we say, dallying, is building. Wilson had a blind item yesterday. But I think Haber is getting ready to blast it wide open."

"Who gives a shit?" Monaghan said.

"The American public will not be uninterested, I think. I frankly don't give a fuck about you, Monaghan, you're an old warhorse, you've been busted for drugs and you've boffed more fifteen-year-olds than Fatty Arbuckle ever dreamed of. But Ginger's new to the trade, and I think it's splendid of you to damage her the way you're about to." He turned. "Good day."

The Rajah returned to the table and just sat staring. "I do not believe what just happened," he said finally.

"The point being?"

"That's the first time anyone outside my beloved wife gave me any crap in five years. It's eventually what makes it all shitty when you're a star—everybody agrees with you all day long, because they think they can make money off you. I've been a hot hunk of meat for a long time. I'm used to smiles."

"Do you good," Ginger told him.

"You know why he did it, don't you? On account of you. I don't think he cares for anything in the world. Except maybe he does for you." He reached out and gently touched her breasts. "But'll he'll have to get in line behind the Rajah, won't he?"

Ginger took his hand, held it to her cheek. "Best go easy."

"Explain that."

"Well, you told me not to get involved with you and I'm

doing my best. Now don't you go getting involved with me."

"I am involved with you, you dumb Jew."

From outside the caravan now, the second assistant director said, "Ten minutes, Mr. Monaghan."

"You got it!" the Rajah shouted back. He looked at Ginger. "You getting bored with me already?"

"Probably I love you," Ginger said. "Or at least I'm sure as hell smitten. But just go easy, that's all."

"Give me a reason."

"Because I do crazy things. I react in crazy ways."

"Such as?"

"Just believe it!" Ginger said sharply. Then she got up and left him there. . . .

Ginger watched nervously with the rest of the crew as, across the street, the Rajah was getting ready to take his fall from the second-story window of the house they'd built down to the muddy street below. He was famous for that, doing his own stunts; he and Lancaster were the only ones who did and probably it was stupid, because most of the time you couldn't really tell. But he did them. A stunt co-ordinator set them up, of course, but when the cameras came to roll, it was the Rajah's body that was on the line.

Garvey appeared, stood at the back of the crew, looking like death.

Ginger left her chair and moved to him. "What's the matter?"

"Nothing to concern you."

"Well do you mind if I stand with you? Because frankly I've never been around when he does one of these and I'm just the least bit panicked."

"He's a pro, he'll be fine. He could make a living as a stunt man more than likely." He looked at Ginger then. "My son's in jail again, Ginger, and I don't know what in the name of Sweet Jesus to do."

"Drugs?"

Garvey shook his head. "Not this time. No, he caused

a commotion at a Nixon rally in Texas. Why doesn't he cause a commotion at a Nixon rally in Massachusetts, they'd more than likely pin a medal on him. Noel does things the hard way. He got his head busted at the Democratic Convention in August."

"He sounds like a very political kid."

On the street below the window now through which the Rajah was to fall, the stunt coordinator began piling up large, six-foot-long empty cardboard boxes. Monaghan stood with him, the two of them deep in conversation.

"That's what's so frustrating," Garvey said. "I have a brilliant son who I love perhaps more than life, except, of course, how can he know that since all I tend to do is yell at him and in general find fault all the day long. And I promise you that a year from now he won't be able to read about politics without falling asleep. He has been insane about Willie Mays, about *Dogpatch* on television, about any number of things. He wrings them more than dry, then leaves them. Totally obsessive behavior."

"I know a little about obsessive behavior myself. Have you tried getting him shrunk?"

"It hasn't particularly taken." He looked at her. "Is that what helped you finally?"

"You mean the *anorexia*?"

Garvey nodded.

"It didn't hurt, but it's not what cured me."

"What did?"

Ginger stared at the street now. They were starting to cover the cardboard boxes with a large piece of burlap and piled burlap bags all around, to make it seem like a loading area.

"We changed the arena," Ginger said then.

Garvey shook his head.

Ginger began to explain. "I'm sorry, that's shrink talk. You must understand, I didn't know when I got sick that I was sick or why, and I don't know really when I started getting over it. At least not at the time. I guess the thing came on me when I was about to change schools and I wanted to look as thin and good as possible and without my knowing it, the sickness came on. It lasted, oh, a couple of years. They'd stick me in the hospital to make me eat and I'd eat to get out of the hospital and then starve again and then back to the hospital and then out and more self-starvation, in and out, in and out; when it got really bad I was deep into bingeing."

Monaghan and the stunt coordinator were peering out of the second-story-building window down toward the burlap area below. It was probably a ten-foot fall. Maybe twelve.

More nervous now, Ginger began talking very quickly. "That's when you're insane with hunger and you go down and stuff really inhuman amounts of food down your throat to kill it and run back upstairs and vomit, so you'll stay the same weight. You feel so guilty it's a bad scene, I'm here to tell you."

"But eventually you started to eat."

Ginger nodded. "When *Die Grossmutter* came to stay."

"Just about set," the stunt coordinator said to the director and cameraman.

"Let's get to it then," the director said.

"The who?" Garvey asked.

"My grandmother, the family matriarch. A great lady, really, but going senile, and see, I'd always tried to be perfect but I knew I was nothing special, and then the weight loss, the beating hunger, holding out against a thing like that and bringing it to heel, well suddenly I *was* special, and I was controlling the household, people were going to pieces over would I eat a carrot stick or not and then my folks started fighting. It was about my grandmother. See, my father wanted to put her in a home but Phyllis, my mother, she wouldn't have her mother in a home and they really began to go at it. Terrible terrible fights. Here was this senile old woman in the guest room and my sister was away at Wellesley by then so there were

just the four of us in the place, and the fighting between
my folks got shitty, and I'd sit there at dinner and eat and
watch them battle."

"Why were you eating though?"

"This is all *post facto* thinking, you understand. And
super oversimplified. But suddenly, as my shrink said, the
arena had shifted. Nobody gave a rat's ass if little Ginger
ate or not, now my perfect parents were killing each other
over this old lady who needed twenty-four hour nurses to
not hurt herself. Bottom line: I started feeding my face."

Ginger shut up then, because there is always tension before a take but never as much as when physical jeopardy
is involved, and now everyone seemed to be scurrying to
position and the Rajah waved to Ginger from the window,
waved and made a circle with his thumb and index finger,
and she waved back and then they were rolling until the
sun went behind a cloud and no sooner had the director
shouted, "Action" than he shouted, "Shit, cut it, hold it,
son of a bitch," and then there was not a hell of a lot to
do but wait, the silence terrible as the small cloud finally
passed beneath the sun and then it was "Action" again,
and the Rajah was framed in the window, for just an
instant before the villain threw the punch and out Monaghan came, trying to grab hold, failing, suddenly spinning
down a dozen feet, landing flat as a cloud of dust rose from
all the burlap.

Only the Rajah didn't rise too.

He lay where he had fallen and suddenly everybody was
screaming and running forward toward the burlap area
and when they were almost on him, up he jumped, smiling
and shouting, "And still the fucking champeen!" breaking
into laughter at all the technicians he had suckered.

Ginger was in a cluster with Garvey and the script girl,
an elderly marvel of a woman who could make her Olivetti
obey her even in a windstorm. Monaghan dusted himself
off good, talked quietly with the stunt coordinator, then
started in Ginger's direction, pausing only momentarily at

the card table the script girl had set up, complete with notes and paper and schedules and typewriter.

"Dammit," the script girl said softly to Garvey then; "my husband gave that to me," and Garvey very quickly said back to her, "Put in for a new one, I'll see you're reimbursed," and the script girl said, "It's not the money, Mr. Garvey, it was a *gift*," and Garvey said, "Well, there's not much we can do about it is there?" and Ginger didn't understand what was going on at all, what the hell they were talking about, until she saw, as the Rajah ambled smiling toward her, that he took a pipe from the base of the camera that belonged to the camera operator and stuck it in his shirt pocket without really breaking stride.

"Did your heart go pitty-pat while I was layin' there?" he asked Ginger.

Ginger nodded, and he threw an arm around her shoulder, started herding her toward his caravan to await the next shot only Ginger wasn't budging. "Since when do you smoke a pipe?" she said.

He gave her a look. "What're you talking about?"

"You've got a pipe in your shirt pocket."

"So? Big deal."

"So it isn't yours," Ginger said, and she reached for his pocket.

He knocked her hand away.

Now a few members of the crew were starting to look at them.

"This is crazy," Ginger said. "Give the guy back his pipe."

"Just shut your face, okay?"

"What did you take from the script girl's table?"

He moved up very close to her and dropped his voice. "Do you want to get a whole lot of people in trouble? If you do, just keep yapping."

"You mean do I want to get *you* in trouble."

"Hey nutcake—ain't nothin' gets the Rajah in trouble. Don't ever forget that."

Ginger whispered, "Are you on something?"

"No, lady, but I could be off you awfully fucking quick you don't shut up."

Now everybody on the crew was watching them.

"You can't just steal stuff," Ginger whispered.

"Honey, I can do whatever I fucking want, don't you get that? I can take what I want when I want and nothing is said, because I make money for people, they'll eat any shit I choose to serve. I just risked my ass for this piece of cinema history, now don't *please* make me lose my temper."

Ginger stood her ground, starting to reach again for his shirt pocket.

Monaghan took out the pipe and shouted, "Hey Barney, this yours?" to the camera operator.

"I was pitching it, Raj—it's no good."

"That's what I thought," Monaghan answered, and, staring dead at Ginger, broke the pipe in two. Then he went back into his pocket again, took out a Mark Cross pen. "You want this, Sally?" he shouted to the script girl.

"I've got plenty more," came the quick reply.

"She *does* want it," Ginger said, and she surprised him, ripped the pen loose from his hand. "It was a gift."

He slapped her in the mouth.

"It was *special*," Ginger said, still not backing away, even when he raised his hand to slap her again.

The moment froze. Ginger stood her ground.

Finally the Rajah said, "Sal, I needed to take some notes on the next scene, but I remember now, I got a ball-point in the caravan." He took the ball-point, carried it past a dozen people, handed it back to the script girl. "Sorry."

"Whenever you need it, it's always here, Raj."

"Sure, sure," he said, and turned then, hurrying alone toward his caravan.

There was not the least doubt in any of the crew's mind that something approaching true love had descended on *Fortune Favors the Brave.* . . .

* * *

The second Friday in November, over Ginger's protestations, the Rajah took off for L.A. to begin discussions with his wife about divorce. All, he said, when he returned, seemed amicable enough, and in the long haul, he figured it had to work. The Wednesday following his return to Denver, however, Mrs. Monaghan attempted suicide via sleeping pills, and if her maid had not happened to walk in at half past six in the morning and been able to get the ambulance in time, it would have been over.

She also left a note which hit the *Los Angeles Herald-Examiner* that afternoon. Written in a weak hand, it got quickly to the point:

> *Dear Miss Ginger Abraham;*
> *I do not, of course, hate you. I only hope you can give Roger what I have tried to over our twenty years of marriage, beginning when he was an out of work actor and I was working and pregnant with our first-born. I only hope you do not hate me for taking this, the coward's way out. Believe me, I would have lived without him if I could.*
>
> *Rose Monaghan*

"Fucking religious cunt," the Rajah raged, storming around his suite in the Brown Palace.

Ginger, hysterical on the sofa, pulled herself together enough to scream, "Jesus, she loved you, how can you say that? If the maid hadn't happened to come in at half past six—"

And now he was screaming back, "—don't give me any *happened* shit—the maid *always* comes in at half past six —it's her fucking *job* to come in at half past six, to get the Jesus freak ready for Mass—she's killed herself three, four times the last ten years. She knows to the hundredth of a fucking ounce how many Nembutals make her drowsy, how many make her sick—this is all a goddam *ploy*, that's all it fucking is."

Whether it was or not, the gossip industry of America

could have cared less. Mrs. Monaghan's timing could not have been better. Nixon had just edged Humphrey not two weeks before and the country was ready for a different kind of comedy. Hungering for it, as they proved less than a month before that when they went crazy buying everything in sight about the Kennedy-Onassis nuptials.

Now the columnists—personality journalists as they liked to be referred to—descended on Denver. They hung around the hotel, buttonholed the crew, the more important came to location when possible, came to the area when not. Long-range lenses took pictures of the principals. And tens of thousands of words went out. Rose was deeply and unfairly wounded; Roger a flawed and confused fellow sinking dangerously toward middle age.

Easy prey for a villainess like Ginger.

Slowly Ginger began to come apart. An unexpected snowstorm crippled shooting and she was stuck in the suite, not able to go anywhere because if the weather cleared they would be shooting again immediately. There were knocks on her door, at any and all hours; strange people who turned out to be reporters delivered her room-service meals. The phone would not stop ringing.

The Rajah claimed he was going to tell the truth about the maid, but he couldn't very well with his wife still recovering in the hospital. His PR guy begged him to pay a reconciliatory visit to Los Angeles but Roger told him to fuck off; he'd hunkered down before, he could do it again. He took to drinking heavily and didn't give a fuck who knew.

Garvey was wonderful with Ginger. Not that there was much he could do. But he was there during the day frequently to see if he could help, he chatted with her, told her stories of the old days, saw to it that she was alone when she wanted to be, when she desired company, he was always there.

But she was being vilified and it was not a happy time. She couldn't stand her suite but she wasn't free to leave it and face the mob downstairs. She couldn't go to the win-

dow and watch the mountains because photographers had
taken positions across the street and she had to keep the
blinds down once she knew. She wasn't hungry but she ate,
was exhausted but couldn't sleep, and if she didn't get
some release soon, she told the Rajah one night, she knew
she was going to snap.

He came for her at three that morning. By half past they
were roaring out of town alone, having service-elevatored
to the basement, snuck from there to the car Roger had
arranged for. He was drinking heavily as he drove, which
would have scared Ginger under ordinary conditions, but
these sure weren't those. He loved to drink and drive too
fast, he said, it put an edge to dull time, and he liked
always to have an edge around.

Where are we headed? she wondered.

To where it's private, he replied. To where it was always
private if you knew how to maneuver things. If you ever
really need privacy bad, this is where you come.

Vail? Ginger said, stunned when he told her. Is that
any quieter than Grand Central?

The Rajah took a long pull on his bottle of Jack Daniel's,
told her that just because he loved her didn't mean he
couldn't belt her for being a wise ass. Ginger made a smile,
snuggled up beside him, and almost went to sleep.

B.J. was waiting for them in the living room of her small
house near what in summer passed for a golf course. The
Rajah had given her a quick rundown on the girl before
they arrived, saying briefly that B.J. Thornton was out of
New England and so far was the only American ever to
win the Olympic women's downhill. She'd got married
soon after that to a rich guy from Chile and they'd had a
kid but the marriage didn't take. B.J. got a good enough
settlement but he kept the baby and she made her living
now, and a good one too, as the highest-paid woman ski
instructor in Vail.

Ginger had expected, naturally enough, a powerful
woman, because even though she really didn't ski, she'd
watched them enough on television to know they needed

muscles like wrestlers. But B.J. Thornton couldn't have stood much over five two and was slender. She was also very pretty in a freckled redheaded way and couldn't have been more than thirty years old. She ran right into Roger's arms, and he didn't seem to mind that a bit so Ginger was understandably a little distant when he finally got around to making intros.

The next piece of business didn't warm anybody's heart either, because at first light Ginger found herself on the snow-covered golf course being given a quick lesson in cross-country skiing by B.J. while Roger stood off to one side watching. They were all clad in ski clothes B.J. had assembled for them after Roger had called to alert her of their arrival. Ginger kept falling down and felt like the fool of all the world but B.J. was full of encouragement, helping her quickly up, explaining again how you pushed off and took a long easy stride and pretty soon anyone could be an expert.

Ginger kept, for the most part, falling down.

"Let's hit it," Roger said finally. "Lift'll open soon."

"Where are we going?" Ginger asked.

"Me and the champ here are going, you're going to stay close to the house here and practice."

"Maybe a few other people will be doing the same," B.J. said, "but they'll be concentrating on what they're doing, the same as you, so don't worry about being recognized. Key's under the mat. Go inside when you're tired. Don't overdo, okay?"

Ginger looked at the Rajah. "You're leaving me here?"

"You wanted privacy, right? You're getting it. Cross-country bores the piss out of me, so we're gonna take the lift to the top and ski the back bowls. That way I'll enjoy myself, you'll enjoy yourself once you get the hang of it, and there's steaks in the freezer for supper. If you've got any objections, say so now, but I sure didn't come here to hide in the fucking house, I could have done that back in Denver."

"You go," Ginger said quickly.

"I'm sorry, this seems fair to me," the Rajah said.

"It is. Scoot. Have fun."

"Right," he said, and then they left her alone.

Ginger seethed. She hated snow, hated skiing, hated movie stars—and she kept on falling down! After an hour she went inside, decided to poke around the house, praying fervently the place would be a tasteless pigsty.

It couldn't have been lovelier. Dark wood and picture windows and simply done. Small, but a good kitchen, a large sauna. A few trophies on one wall of the living room, but nothing ostentatious.

Shit, Ginger thought, and she went back outside to practice some more, determined to knock their eyes out when they saw her next. It was hard, damn hard, and she did fall some more, but by eleven, when she broke for something to eat, she was beginning to get it. She made herself a BLT on white toast and brewed a pot of coffee. She was tired and her muscles ached but by one she was back on the golf course again, slowly moving along the open white area, gliding nicely now, starting to actually ski down the gentle hills that must have been bunkers in springtime. Then, at close to three, she went back into the house and undressed, took a warm bath, found a book by Ross Macdonald she hadn't read, went into the small second bedroom, and slid between the sheets.

It was dark when she jerked awake.

From somewhere, now, came laughter.

Ginger got up, shivered, grabbed for the knitted quilt at the foot of the bed, and moved out into the main part of the house, and since it was small it didn't take her long to track the sound. B.J. and Roger were seated across from each other, looking at each other, talking and laughing, and there wasn't much unusual in that, nothing to get excited about, except for the fact that they were seated in the sauna and were both naked.

Ginger stared briefly through the glass window, spun away, stumbled, ran for the bedroom, frantically groped around for the light switch while Roger called, "Hey

Chubby? Ginge? You awake?" She finally found the switch and when the room was lit she started looking around, trying to remember did she hang things in closets or put them in drawers and then Roger was shivering naked in the doorway, saying, "You were sure zonked."

Ginger said nothing.

"I'm freezing my nuts off," he said, and he made a gesture toward her.

"Roger, what the hell is going on?"

"Hey, you're upset."

"Upset? *Upset?* I just left hysteria far far behind—"

"I don't get this."

"Don't—gaslight—me!"

"Ginger, goddamit—"

"—shit—I mean shit, Roger—here I am with most of America thinking I'm Lucrezia Borgia on account of you and I wake up to find you humping another girl in the sauna."

He started laughing. "If you think that's humping, we're in deep trouble."

"Well you practically were; you were naked."

"It's a sauna. You're supposed to be naked. We were fucking freezing when we got back; it was blue murder in the back bowls when we started losing the sun."

"I don't give a fuck about the temperature; you can skip the weather reports please."

"B.J. and I were pals in the past, that's all."

" 'Pals.' Oh that's a really 'neat' word; you mean, like we're 'pals' now?"

"No, Ginger, not at all like that, and please quit doing your Jewish American Princess number before I really get pissed. Now come on."

"Come on where?"

"Oh shit," he said, and he moved suddenly toward her, ripped the quilt away, hoisted her up, and carried her into the sauna, putting her down on the bench beside him but he was between her and the door so there wasn't much she could do.

"Did you get the hang of it finally?" B.J. asked.

Ginger looked at the other woman briefly, and she saw where the power came from; it was like a swimmer's body, the muscles long and smooth and the breasts were larger than Ginger had thought from seeing her in clothes. She looked quickly away, feeling like a milk sow.

"The first day is always miserable," B.J. went on.

"Hey this is terrific," the Rajah said. "Me and my ladies. B.J., get us a joint."

B.J. nodded and hurried out of the sauna.

"I am just not into kinky sex," Ginger whispered when they were alone.

He broke out laughing. "This isn't kinky, Chub." Now he made a Groucho Marx leer. "That's for later."

"I'm embarrassed. I don't know her."

"Beautiful, isn't she?"

Ginger agreed.

"She'll be wrinkled when she's eighty."

"We'll *all* be wrinkled when we're eighty," Ginger said.

"I ain't gettin' that far," the Rajah said, and then B.J. was back with the lit cigarette. She handed it to Roger who inhaled deeply a couple of times, passed it to B.J. who did the same, then gave it to Ginger who shook her head, changed her mind, fumbled with the thing, inhaled tentatively once, strongly a second time, handed it back to B.J.

Their bodies were starting to glisten now.

The Rajah pulled Ginger to him for a moment, reached out a hand toward B.J. "Being a famous and sought-after movie star is really the pits sometimes." Then he started to laugh stupidly. "Hey, that's strong," he said to B.J., then laughed some more.

He looked so dumb laughing like that, Ginger started laughing too.

"Tomorrow, Ginger?" B.J. said. "We'll try getting you to take a few of those little hills."

"I can do them now," Ginger said proudly.

B.J. chalked one up.

"Let's all go take a bath," the Rajah said, and they tried,

but the tub was too small, so they showered instead, and then they cooked the steaks and had another joint and a couple of bottles of red wine and then Rajah took Ginger to bed and was more ardent than he had ever been which was pretty fucking ardent indeed, and the next day they all felt great and spent a lot of time together doing cross-country and Ginger liked B.J. by that time and didn't even care when the Rajah kissed her a long-time good-bye that evening before they started down to Denver.

The weather cleared, the movie resumed, the Rajah gave a mass interview about his wife's other phony over-doses, and how the maid was due to wake her anyway, and that had impact, public opinion slowly turning back toward Ginger. *Fortune Favors the Brave* wrapped in early December and the Rajah's PR guy persuaded him to go through the charade of a reconciliation, at least for the duration of the Christmas holidays, and Ginger went back to her suite at the Wilshire.

So the press left her alone till the first of the year when the rumor, which was false, hit, that she was pregnant with Roger's child, and then Roger himself hit a Porsche on the Pacific Coast Highway and died of fire. No star since Jimmy Dean had died at the peak and the press geared up for one final go-round. The Widow Monaghan added fuel by getting publicly hysterical at the mortician's and screaming that "that woman" would never be allowed to the funeral, that she herself would die before allowing such a thing.

Ginger, for her part, tried very hard to hold it together, she resisted sedation, took another name and another suite but that subterfuge lasted as long as it took to grease a few appropriate palms, and when she was exposed and the ringing and the flashbulbs got too much, she met Harry Brennerman in his office-building garage and he was ready with a cheap brown wig which she adjusted while he drove her to Burbank Airport where he'd rented the plane which was ready when Ginger got there. Ginger kissed him and asked, Why, why did the press have it in for her, what

was it about her that was so special, and Harry said,
You're not Henry Fonda or Jimmy Stewart, you're more
Garbo, more Sinatra, and Ginger said, What do you mean
exactly, and he hugged her a final time because he cared
and she was in such rotten shape, dangerously so maybe,
and finally he said, There's secrets about you, strange
things; you're mysterious, Ginger, and she smiled and
said, Funny, all my life I've wanted to be, now I don't feel
so hot about it.

B.J. met her at the Denver Airport in early evening and
drove slowly up to Vail.

"I'll do something for you sometime," Ginger promised
as they got underway.

"He was a friend," B.J. said.

"I just had to get away was the thing."

"You're away now, relax."

"Would that it were that easy," Ginger said, staring at
the night.

"Who does your wigs, Frederick's of Hollywood?" B.J.
wanted to know.

"Oh shit," Ginger said, ripping it off. "I forgot the goddam thing was there." She rolled down the window and
sailed it into the night.

"The Colorado State Police will now go mad trying to
locate the body," B.J. said.

Ginger almost laughed.

B.J. drove quickly up route seventy.

"He was sober, you know," Ginger said after a while.

"Raj? I won't tell anybody, it would ruin his reputation."

"He wasn't even driving all that fast."

"Bite your tongue."

Ginger almost laughed that time too.

The first thing B.J. did when they were inside her house
was to go to the medicine chest, and return with two
yellow pills. Ginger was dubious.

"Valium is all," B.J. said. "Once you get to sleep, you'll
be gone for days. The trick is to get you there."

"You sure?"

B.J. nodded and poured some red wine to wash them down. Then she started the bath water running nice and hot, and left Ginger to have a good soak. By the time Ginger was done, B.J. had covered the bed in the small bedroom with a large white towel; she indicated for Ginger to lie down, gave her another long white towel to cover herself. "I've been doing this for years, just have faith, all right?"

Ginger, almost starting to relax, nodded and lay back.

B.J. took two very large wads of cotton and got them sopping wet. "Witch hazel," she explained, "just close your eyes." Ginger did and B.J. rested the cotton carefully in place. "If you feel like sleeping, sleep," B.J. said. "You don't have to make conversation."

Ginger nodded and lay there.

B.J. took her right arm and began slowly massaging her fingers. "With any luck at all, by the time I finish your second arm, you should be out."

"You're a lot cheaper than Elizabeth Arden," Ginger said softly.

"Don't talk. Let me know if I'm being too strong." She rubbed from the tips of the fingers up, then, when she was done with that, she worked at the back of the palm. Then the wrist. "Too strong?"

Ginger shook her head. She began to breathe more deeply as she lay there with the cool cotton on her eyes, the fingers working the tension out of her forearm now, now up, the biceps, the shoulders, the neck, and she was drifting, barely able to speak and say, ". . . I'm not. . . ." as B.J. began to kiss her nipples.

". . . shh . . . of course you're not, neither am I. . . ."

". . . you must . . . stop . . ." Ginger managed, as B.J. lifted the towel away from her body, began slowly to trail her tongue from Ginger's breasts down toward her vagina.

". . . and I will stop," B.J. said. ". . . I promise you . . . but not now. . . ."

". . . no . . . not now. . . ." She could feel B.J. on the

bed kneeling above her. Blindly Ginger reached out until she found B.J.'s breasts.

". . . you're so beautiful . . ." B.J. whispered.

". . . we're all so beautiful . . ." said Ginger.

She never really left Vail.

Oh, she went to New York City when Stan had his first stroke, and she wept her eyes out in Boston at poor Freddy's funeral. And she became a wonderful skier, and learned the mountains of Chile as well as Switzerland, and she helicoptered several times into the Canadian Bugaboos.

But as far as show business was concerned, she never left Vail. For a short period she was news, but that interest faded with the change of decades, and when Richard Lamparski contacted her for his "Whatever Became Of . . . ?" series, Ginger was genuinely amused and pleased.

Which was why she was so astonished, on Monday, the seventeenth of April, 1978, to open her front door and find Julian Garvey standing there, with a blood-red copy of *Tinsel* in his hands.

VI

FINAL CASTING

Monday

1

"Aw hey, what a thing," Ginger said, going swiftly into Julian's arms, holding him a moment. When they broke, she studied his face before she said, "My God, you still look like Leslie Howard on a good day. I guess the Devil hasn't picked up your option."

"Very show-biz talk coming from a ski bum."

"That was one part of it I liked—the chitchat. There was an old foreign art director on our flick—"

"—*Fortune Favors the Brave* deserves better than simply being termed 'our flick.' My personal take almost hit seven figures. Ergo: art."

"Anyway, this old foreign guy, we were eating at a restaurant one night and he cut into his steak, looked at it, and shook his head. Then he said, 'Definitely second-unit meat.' I never forgot that." She hooked her arms in his, led him through the entrance.

The house was small, beautifully appointed. Vaulted ceilings, wood paneled, giant picture windows overlooking the mountains. "It's lovely, if you go in for breathtaking views."

Ginger made a little bow, said, "Coffee?"

Garvey nodded, followed her into the small kitchen. "Live by yourself?"

Now she nodded. "Just me and my shadow."

"Query: Don't you get, on occasion, lonely?"

"In your lexicon, I suppose that's a euphemism for 'horny.'"

"Well, that too."

Ginger turned and faced him. "Julian, I know it's a bit early on for deep philosophical discussions, but baby, the fall of Western civilization as we know it is not, repeat not, going to be caused by the bomb. It's going to happen when enough women realize that fucking a man is not such a terrific thing in and of itself. Most men couldn't pass Intercourse One. They weigh a ton, they've got next to no control, they've got absolutely no interest in pleasuring their partner, they've usually been drinking which does terrific things for their breath, and they are not particularly panicked about getting themselves pregnant. The plain fact is that a vibrator is at least as good a conversationalist besides being much easier to clean. Once that word spreads, men will slip to the level of occasional curios. The cordless vibrator, my friend, will soon render you extinct."

Julian clapped lightly and said, "Callas never sang a finer aria." He fell silent then, studying her, riffling the pages of *Tinsel* as she measured out coffee and dumped it into a paper holder, poured in water, plugged the coffee-maker into the socket. "You have, as they say, kept your figure."

"Skiing does that."

"Is that truly all you've been doing?"

She turned, faced him with her violet eyes. "I'm embarrassed to say this, but I'm kind of slowly edging up on the world's longest doctorate."

"Wonderful. On what?"

"Oh, I don't know what to call it, mainly Dorothy Parker and her miseries."

"Why take so long?"

"Well, I guess because once I get the damn degree I'll feel obliged to *do* something with it, get a job maybe; maybe do articles for learned journals. That just sounds so dreary I can't face it."

"You may be the only creature yet spawned, my beloved, to reach the age of, what are you, thirty-three—without ever having any even brief contact with rational behavior." He riffled the pages of *Tinsel* again. "Vail seems reasonably dreary all by itself. Teaching could only improve things."

"Maybe to you. I came here first though with Roger, when we needed quiet and he'd once had an affair with this famous lady-type skier, B.J. Thornton—"

"—oh sure, the Olympics."

"That's right. She lives just next door as a matter of fact. Anyway, he said Vail was for hiding and during the circus after the funeral, B.J. put me up. See, Vail's very transient. Nobody's ever here to bug you for long."

"Like I am now?"

"You're a friend. You were the most decent one during those crazy times. I have to admit, however, that since you do nothing for nothing, there must be some purpose to your being here. I assume it has to do with that red thing you keep riffling in my ear."

Julian put the script down. "Just thought you might like to read it."

"And?"

Julian shrugged, said nothing.

Ginger broke out laughing. "Don't tell me, don't tell me—if I put out you'll offer me a part." She threw her head back and howled. "I can see us fifty years down the line. You'll be senile and not able to get it up—"

"—what makes you think I can get it up now?"

"The day you can't, *Daily Variety* will be ringed in black. Anyway, you'll be senile like I said and I'll have left menopause far behind and with trembling hands you'll still be trying to figure out some way to grapple me to the mattress."

"A lovely future awaits us both."

"Julian—Julian listen: I'm not that great a lay."

"Such talk only inflames me—"

"—hey listen," came from outside the kitchen door then, and as it opened and a redheaded woman of forty entered, saying, "About tonight—" Ginger said quickly, "—what are you short of this time, sugar or flour?" She smiled, extended her hands to the other two. "B.J. Thornton, I'd like you to meet Julian Garvey."

"Sorry I interrupted—"

"—listen, no problem," Ginger said, again quickly. She turned to Julian. "B.J. is the local galloping gourmet, only she forgets crucial ingredients and is all the time borrowing. What is it this time?"

"Would you believe salt?"

Ginger went quickly to a cabinet, got out a large container of Morton's, handed it over. "What are you calling tonight's gathering?" She smiled at Julian, explaining. "Kind of an end-of-season banquet. Vail sucks in April."

"Sorry to have interrupted," B.J. said, turning toward the back door. "Big fan of your pictures, Mr. Garvey."

"And I of your skills, Miss Thornton. Perhaps someday fate will throw us together for an even longer period of time."

B.J. laughed quickly and was gone.

"Seems lovely," Julian said then.

Ginger shrugged. "Good fences make good neighbors." The coffee was done then; she poured them both double mugsful, led him to the living room. "Hey? There's really not much point to my reading that red thing."

"As a favor to me I hardly see how it can harm you."

"Julian, you've gotten on pretty good so far without my literary opinion and besides, it is one of my life's ambitions to be the only girl under sixty who's not written up on one of your three-by-five cards—"

"—don't embarrass me."

"I never understood—why did a man like you who thrives on conniving and secrecy, spread the word about those goddam cards in the first place."

"You don't think *I* spread the word? May we change the subject? I don't want to talk about it."

"Make you a deal. I'll read the script if you'll tell. Those are my only terms. I think you know I'm nutty enough to mean it."

Julian sighed. "In the first place, I cannot explain why I started doing it except perhaps I thought it might make interesting reading for my dotage. And in the second place, it is inexcusable that I have continued the practice. But it was all secret. Always. And then I had this bubble-breasted secretary and I made the inconceivable mistake of getting involved. When we terminated, she took it badly, and thank Christ I caught her *trying to take the cards out of my desk.* I stopped her, naturally, from that, but I could hardly stop her from talking to a few knights of the keyboard. I was a blind item for several weeks and by then the jig was, as they say, up." He sipped from his coffee mug, watching her across the room.

"You want me to start reading this now?"

"No. After I'm gone." He glanced at his watch. "Which will be shortly; I've got a car waiting to take me back to the airport. My office is reasonably chaotic without me."

"I don't get it—why didn't you just send me the script and then call me?"

"You'll understand once you've read it. I had to see for myself what you looked like. Did you still look well."

"You could have asked me that on the phone."

"Yes, child. But considering your past history of psychoses, you might have honestly said you looked well when you weighed anywhere from seventy-five to two hundred and seventy-five pounds."

Ginger smiled. "True."

"Suite eighty-four," Julian said then.

Ginger waited.

"The Bel-Air Hotel. I've booked it for tomorrow evening. I'll be there at eight. No one need see you. You go up Stone Canyon, take a left just short of the hotel, circle around behind it. You can walk in from there and suite eighty-four is dead ahead. If you're not there by nine, I'll go home. Don't call me about the script. If you're interested, just be there." He got up then, walked across the room, kissed her gently on the forehead. "You are still, may I say, something."

"Query: Whatever is going on in your brain?"

Julian made a smile. "Don't make me be sincere," he said then. "I do it so badly. . . ."

When she was alone a little later, Ginger poured herself another mug of coffee, speed-read the script, then dialed L.A. information for Harry Brennerman's office number and when she got it, dialed him. "This is the ghost of Christmas past," she said when he came on the line, and she envisioned him sitting at his desk, smoothing his hair from the part just above his ear all across his skull. "When you're done smoothing, I'd like your opinion on something."

"Keed, that you can have for free, but my love costs. Throw me a kiss or I hang up as of now."

Ginger obeyed.

"Tell me how you are. Good? Say you're good, Ginger; I swear, everyone I know is having strokes, root canal, spinal fusions. It's shit growing old."

"How would you know?"

"Now *that's* my girl. I've missed you plenty."

"That situation may be alleviated," Ginger told him.

"You coming down? You wanna stay with us? I'll book you into the Wilshire, whatever. When and for how long?"

"This is when I want your opinion, Harry. Candid."

"I am crossing my heart as we speak."

"Well Harry, my fan clubs all across the country are deluging me with so much mail I figured what the hell, why not come back and please the masses."

Dead silence.

"I'm talking about resuming my career, in case you missed the thread."

"My candid opinion consists of one word: disaster."

"But—"

"—Ginger, you're not right for here. I got you into it, let me even things up and keep you out."

"I didn't stink up the joint did I?"

"Keed—hear me good—MacGraw stayed away four years and the word is *Convoy*'s a major-league bagel. Three big hits she had behind her till then. Audrey Hepburn stayed away seven years and she died at the BO. And God knows how many hits she had behind her. You had three bits and one lead and sure it was a hit, but the Rajah carried most of it on his shoulders. And that was ten years ago. There's no market for Ginger Abraham no more; God's truth. The best I might get you maybe is a cameo on something like *Starsky and Hutch* and that would mainly be for nostalgia freaks—"

"—but what if I had a lead—"

"—you won't get a lead—"

"—but what if—"

"I thought you were going to school—you're the brightest actress they ever let in the union—stay at school, teach, write, it's death for you down here, remember what it was like?"

"I was a kid."

"You were never a kid."

"Harry—"

"—I'm begging—out of, and you know I mean it, undying affection—"

"—but if I got a lead, would you handle me?—"

"—Ginger, you *won't*—"

"—but *if if if*, would you handle me?"

There was a long pause. Then, sadly, "It would break my heart. It would just break my heart. But I would do it. . . ."

"I saw him leave," B.J. said, coming in through the kitchen again. "I gave him plenty of time to make sure he didn't pop back." She poured herself some coffee, moved into the living room where Ginger was still sipping at her second cup, staring off at the mountains.

"I'm waiting for a third thing to happen," Ginger said.

"How so?"

"Well, things happen in threes, isn't that what they say? Julian appears, that's one. And no sooner is he gone than out of God knows what blue, my old agent got me on the horn and asked if I'd consider a quick trip to L.A. Universal's got something in mind I guess." She took a drink of coffee.

B.J. broke out laughing. "As we used to say in high school, you lie like a rug."

Ginger nodded.

"Was that red thing Garvey had a script?"

"Entitled *Tinsel*."

"And you liked it?"

"The lead's pretty sensational."

"Did he offer it to you?"

"He didn't say boo. That's the way Julian operates. He never says anything specifically. He just suggested we might chat a bit tomorrow night at the Bel-Air. Suite eighty-four."

"So you'll screw him to get the part."

"More likely what'll happen is I'll screw him and *not* get the part."

"Doesn't that prospect bother you?"

" 'Course it bothers me."

"Then why do it?"

Ginger shrugged. "Curiosity maybe. Playing out the string. Vail's boring just now. Millions of reasons."

"Got to be a better one than any of those."

Finally Ginger said, "Okay. Heat."

"Hmm?"

"Heat," Ginger said again. "Being closest to the fire. All those people reaching toward you because they're caught in the cold and you, you're special. What I was sitting here realizing when you came in was that I hadn't known it was an addiction. But I guess it's like AA. You're never cured. And *you* know what I'm talking about, don't deny it. What would you give right now to be the fastest in the world again downhill?"

"Anything."

"Well then?"

"Except the logic doesn't hold—"

"—screw logic, I do crazy things, I've proved that often enough—"

"—I *loved* to ski. The same cannot be said of you and California."

"Too much fell in my lap. I couldn't handle it then."

"And you're saying now you can?"

Ginger shook her head. "Probably I'll just find a different way to destroy myself. . . ."

2

"Did he have to pick *now* to go to Vail?" Schwab the Slob said across the room to Noel. "It couldn't have waited?" He looked at his watch. "Shit. Eleven and not a goddam thing accomplished." He spread his arms wide and said to Johnny Small on the sofa, *"Ce n'est pas ma faute."*

"What's that mean?" Johnny asked.

"It means the fucking phone won't stop ringing," Schwab the Slob answered, sitting at Julian's desk, looking up as Matilda Brown entered, as always calm in the midst of maelstroms, and said, "These are the new pages you wanted, Mr. Schwab."

"Thanks, thanks," Schwab said.

"Four copies?"

"Right. Can you hold calls, Matty?"

"Mr. Garvey as a rule takes anything from his A list."

"Well, I'm just a poor schlepper from the tube," Schwab said. "I don't even know what the A list is, and I've got my composer here and I've got to try to get something accomplished."

"Calls will be held," Matty said, and she left the room, pausing only to check to see if anyone needed more coffee. Satisfied that they did not, she went back outside.

"Who goes skiing in April?" Schwab said sourly to Noel.

"Come on, Schwabby, he'll be back midafternoon and anyway he wasn't skiing, it's that a condominium came up near where the ex-president stays and Daddy thought he had to take a look-see. What if Ford makes a comeback? The price'll triple easy."

"Which will, of course, rescue your father from the poorhouse." He shook his head, stood, handed copies of the new pages to both Noel and Small. "Lemme explain these while you look 'em over, okay?"

"Are you changing the main character or anything?" Noel asked.

"I said I'd explain—"

"—I just want to be in synch with you on every comma, every line of dialogue is all, Schwabby. I want to be sure I understand just how everything should go, how you see it in your head."

"You shall, you shall."

"Good. I'm sorry I interrupted. Go ahead."

"Okay. Right. Now—"

"—it's Mr. Kamen on two, Mr. Schwab," Matty said then, just her head appearing beyond the door. "He would very much like to discuss a client of his, his secretary says."

"Who's Mr. Kamen?" Johnny wondered.

"The Morris office," Schwab told him. "Stan Kamen is the real Sue Mengers." He hesitated. "Explain that Julian isn't here please and—wait—wait, I've got it—tell him that Julian said specifically no son-in-laws were allowed to talk on the phone, it's against Guild regulations, okay?"

"I'll give it a try," Matty said, gone again.

"Shit, where was I?" Schwab said.

"The nature of the changes," Noel prompted.

Schwab took a deep breath. "Thanks, Noel." He went back to Julian's desk and sat. "All right, we all remember my killer idea about the music—about how when the Monroe part moves from room to room she's got these control modules so she changes channels when she wants. And we also remember that there were to be different kinds of music so that each room she wandered dazedly into had a different kind of character—hard rock here, Sinatra middle-of-the-road stuff there, yes?"

"Go on," Noel said.

"Well, what this is, these new pages, what I've done is I've made specific the kind of Sinatra stuff I want Johnny to come up with. I mean, there's all kinds of Sinatra, he did 'Somethin' Stupid' as well as 'Nancy with the Laughing Face' as well as 'My Way.' Well, I've indicated the specific song types needed to underscore her psychological deterioration, if you dig. I mean, I definitely want her to try to get the fucking president on the horn in the hard-rock room, and while she's waiting and waiting I want the module to be something she fiddles with, almost unconsciously, so that when things are going good, when she thinks she's gonna get through, the music is still hard but it's soft, and when she realizes she's liable to get flushed, it gets louder and louder so that it's almost kind of her own craziness bansheeing back at her."

"I could easy come up with a Kiss-type number," Johnny said. "No group around drives me as crazy as those guys."

"Fine, fine, but lemme go through all of what I want before we get into the specifics, okay?" And as Noel and Johnny nodded, Schwab stood and began to pace, tucking in his shirt, going through each page, explaining each room and how it would alter as the character's madness built, and Johnny nodded, lying back on the couch, eyes half closed while Noel took frantic notes, jotting down whatever he could, nodding to himself, sometimes grunting little asides.

Noel looked at his watch when it was 11:37, muttered, "Duty calls," and went into the adjoining gym, closing the door behind him. At precisely 11:40 he picked up the phone and dialed, knowing it would be answered on the first ring because that was their signal, when he absolutely had to call it would be at precisely that time, 11:40, and one ring later, when he heard the hesitant "Yes?" he said, quickly, his voice at a whisper, "I better be over at one."

"But why?"

"There's new pages. A bunch of 'em."

"You said the part was mine though; what do new pages have to do with it?"

"It *is* yours, Dixie, but Christ, understand this please, I can't spring you on everybody like you jumped out of some cake at a stag dinner. *They've* got to want you too. Daddy and Schwab. And they will. There's gonna be a bunch of screen tests later on. And I'll insist on that—they both know I think you'd be terrific so they'll humor me. But then—*then*—when you test and do it *perfect*—perfect because you'll know *exactly* what the director wants for every comma, then it'll be easy sailing."

Noel could hear the striking of a match, the following inhale of tobacco smoke.

He closed his eyes and said, *"I am not my father*—but if you think that, if you think I'm using you, if you think I'm not serious about this, if you think anything like that, that what we're doing isn't important, then let's bag it now and I promise you you'll get your screen test anyway—but I want this to be just so wonderful, Dixie. I swear."

"What would I tell Ethel though?"

"I don't care about maids, there's a million maids, all I care about right now in this world is this picture and you being wonderful, now how much do you care?"

Another inhale. Sharper. Then: "There's a million maids, be here at one," and then they both hung up.

Noel went into the bathroom, left the door wide open, flushed the toilet, waited a moment, turned both spigots on full at the sink, hurried back into the main office then, saying, "I buzzed home but no one there's heard from Dad, so that means he'll be back on schedule. If he's ever late, he calls ahead."

"Good," Schwab the Slob said. "We're about to start over on these new pages in a more detailed way." He looked at Johnny. "Let's eat in, all right? You mind? Saves a lot of time. I'll have Matty order whatever you want."

"Couple extra packs of Camels'll do me fine."

Schwab buzzed Matty on the intercom, looked at Noel for his lunch order.

"I don't think I should be here," Noel said. "It's going to be intricate musical stuff and I think I'd ask so many questions trying to understand, I'd just be in the way."

"Probably right," Schwab said. He spoke briefly to Matty, then began pacing again.

"One thing before we begin?" Johnny Small said.

Schwab nodded, tucked in his shirt, kept moving.

"I'm embarrassed to even get into this but I said I would so I am: My lady is eating me alive about our picture."

Schwab stopped. "Huh?"

"Pig. The blonde. She picked you up in Vegas."

"Oh right, sure. What about her now?"

"Don't laugh—she wouldn't mind a whole lot playing the lead."

"I've got to think the odds are kind of small," Noel said.

Schwab went back to Julian's desk and collapsed in the chair. "It's like I'm under siege," he said. He looked at Noel. "I took your sister to a big 'do' yesterday at Allen Carr's? Now I have I hope a reasonable grip on reality. I mean, okay, I'm a writer, that automatically makes me insane, but within those limits, I'm all in all not bad. I'm kind of short, my shirt comes out a lot, I'm cursed with these fucking chubby cheeks that only a grandma could love. The best I can give me is 'cute.' On certain days, in the dusk with the light behind me, you could legitimately say Robert Schwab was a 'cute' guy. I'm keeping you all awake thus far, grunt somebody."

Noel looked at Johnny and said, "He actually thinks he has a grip on reality."

"Well, at this party, you'd have thought I was hung like Johnny Wadd with Ty Power's profile and the bankroll of a Pritzker from Chicago. They were coming out of the woodwork. Every chick between twenty and fifty with tits was finding every remark I made hilarious. I'd say, 'Which way is the bar?' and some hunk would melt, the victim of my irresistible charm." He looked at Small. "You're getting my point?"

"She would settle happily for a screen test, Pig would. If I could tell her that, she'd stop bugging me."

"I'm gonna test a bunch of people in maybe a month, six weeks, it's the crucial role, no sense rushing it. But shit, there's a limit to how many people I can honorably put through that torment. Tests cost money and it's Julian's now, not the Bank of America's."

"Pig claims she's talented. I should slip that in to you casually."

"Fine. Tell you what. Let me see some recent footage of her and if there's a chance, we'll test her, okay?"

"Except there isn't any recent footage."

"Okay. I can't tell as much, but let me see some old stuff, then."

"There's no old footage either."

"I don't *believe* this," Schwab said.

"She understands movies though—her old man did the blood for *Psycho*. She was kind of brought up around flicks."

"Hey Johnny, please can't we drop this? Pretty please I'll send her a present from Gucci, can we get off this now."

"I goddam knew this was gonna be awful," Johnny said. "Look. All she asks is would you please give a call to Rickie Metzenbaum and ask him for a rundown. He's worked with her and he'll tell you all about how talented she is."

"I'm not calling Rickie Metzenbaum. I hate Rickie Metzenbaum. He doesn't speak to me hardly anymore. We were almost buddies once but now he's such an 'industry figure,' we are ships that pass in the night. If she's serious about this—"

"—believe me, she's *very* serious about this—"

"—fine—*she* should get Rickie on the phone and have the bastard call me. Okay? If he says she's Duse, I'll pay attention. Otherwise, next case."

Johnny stood. "Fair enough. I'll go call her now." He gestured toward the gym room. "I wouldn't mind a little privacy, all right? It'll take a certain amount of explaining."

"Talk all you want, just be brief." He considered that a moment. "Hey, was that funny? I'm so punchy, I can't tell if anything's funny anymore."

Noel smiled, looked at his watch, got up to go. "I'll come back maybe two-thirty." He started for the door.

"Hey Noel?" Schwab the Slob said.

"Speak."

"That party scene I described? That was true."

"So?"

"Well, I happen to be monogamous by nature but you're free. You can just pluck it off the tree, man."

"Use people, you mean. Take advantage and dump 'em."

"That's very cold ass. I just mean. . . ." he shrugged. ". . . well, it's there, that's all."

"You've got the wrong Garvey."

"Julian's not so terrible."

"Depends what corner of the ring you're coming from," Noel said.

3

"Rickie Metzenbaum please," Pig said.

The secretary's voice sounded muffled. "Mr. Metzenbaum's in a meeting right now."

"Right, right." Pig cradled the phone and glanced at her watch. Five past twelve. "You have any idea how long he'll be?"

"No."

"You couldn't maybe slip him a note or anything?"

"No."

"No problem, just would you please leave him a message? Tell him Pig called and—"

"—I'm sorry, who?"

"He'll understand. It's a nickname sort of thing. Just say Pig wanted to talk to him and that it was very very very very important and wouldn't take more than at the most, a minute of his time."

"Thank you, I'll see—"

"—would you mind reading it back to me, please? I want to make sure the four 'verys' are in the right order."

There was a pause. "Was that a joke or something?"

"Hopefully, I guess."

"I'm a very good secretary or I wouldn't be working for someone like Mr. Metzenbaum, Miss Pig, and I don't need any jokes since I've got a tooth dying on me. I'll read you the message back. 'Pig called. Call her.' Okay?"

"Sorry about your tooth," Pig said. "Thank you." She

hung up and stood, staring for a moment around Johnny's Malibu place. Anywhere else in the world, what you would call it was a dump. It was narrow and rickety and damp and the walls were thin enough so you could catch all the neighbors' fights without half trying. Not only that, when the waves started building, you just knew the whole house was going out to sea. Still, Johnny had paid an even six hundred thou cash for it a year before and it was worth half again more than that now. If you had a place in the Colony, you could name your own price and there was always someone looney enough to meet it. Some comedy director was supposed to have bought a place that the garbage man didn't like to go to and paid seven figures.

Pig started out to the upstairs terrace then spun back to the phone and dialed Fox again, 277–2211. When the operator answered she asked for Mr. Metzenbaum's office and when Rickie's secretary said, "Mr. Metzenbaum's office" Pig said, "Don't hit me, I'm sorry, it's Pig again."

"He's still in the meeting."

" 'Course he is, but I forgot something—listen, can I have your name, I hate just talking to a voice."

"Hennessey."

"Hennessey. Right. Now what's your last name?"

"Was that another joke because—"

"—I know, I know, your tooth. I'm embarrassed, Miss Hennessey, but I'm so stupid I forgot that Mr. Metzenbaum doesn't have my number. Not only that, if he did have it, it wouldn't do anybody much good since I'm not there, mainly because I'm living in the Colony now."

"Is that in Los Angeles?"

Tishlubb you bitch, Pig thought, because it was against the law to work in movies and not know what the Colony was. "Malibu is sort of Los Angeles, I suppose. The number's 456-9999. Shall I run that by you again just to make sure?"

"456-9999. Good-bye."

Pig hung up again thinking God had done some rotten things in His time but maybe nothing worse than creating secretaries. They had this Mafia mentality; who waited for who? Who got put on hold longest? It was your honor if you goofed and she glanced at her watch, saw that it was now 12:14 and probably 12:30 would be when they'd break for lunch, so this time she took the phone and pulled it as close as she could to the upstairs sundeck and placed it on the floor. She was wearing the white bikini Johnny liked and now she unhooked the top piece, dropped it beside the phone, took a towel to cover herself until she was safely lying on the floor of the sundeck. Then she pulled off the towel and bared her breasts to the sun.

She had been gradually getting them tan since Welch exited, because when screen-test time rolled around, wouldn't it knock them dead to see her body all one bronzed color. Not to mention what it said about the character of the Monroe part, that she worshipped her body, turned it naked to the sun for sustenance.

The problem of course was that the area was sensitive, and it wouldn't be all that hysterical if she showed up for the screen test with boobs peeling but what the hell, maybe they wouldn't even do the tests naked. Either way, she was ready.

Pig opened one eye and got a glimpse of the time. 12:18. Snooze. Twelve minutes till the meeting logically should end. Did Rickie still wear those funny Brooks Brothers clothes with the rep ties and the blue button-down shirts? And the frizzy hair? And what could she count on him to say to this Schwab guy?—it was important that he not lay it on too heavy, but enough to be impressive, considering the two of them had this terrific mutual hate on for each other. Pig shrugged. If there was one thing about Rickie, he could talk pretty good, she had a lot of things to fret over, but how he'd handle the call really wasn't one of them.

12:20.

12:21.

And thirty seconds.

Pig rolled over on her back and crawled off the sundeck

like a jerk, but what the hell, you never knew who was gonna be on the beach and she didn't want to shock anyone, but once she was safely inside, she stood and meandered down to the kitchen, got out the carrot juice and the wheat germ and two organic raw eggs and mixed them in the blender, then downed it for lunch.

Why did health food have to taste so crappy?

12:27.

She went to the living room, flicked on the tube, caught the end of one soap, the start of another, then got Hennessey back on the line for round three. "Anbesol," Pig said, as soon as the secretary had said who she worked for.

"Pardon?"

"This is a nonbusiness call," Pig said. "I just hate it when I have tooth trouble and I wondered if you've tried Anbesol, it works miracles for me and pain isn't something I'm all that happy to deal with. A-n-b-e-s-o-l."

"Thank you very much."

Casually, Pig said, "Welcome, bye, oh one sec, I did tell you my business with Rickie wouldn't take long, I said that, didn't I?"

"Look." The voice was stern. "You are not the only phone caller of this nature Mr. Metzenbaum receives, you are simply among the most consistent—"

"—hold the phone, what 'nature' are you implying?— we were at one time very close personal friends and I want you to know that—"

"—well I want *you* to know that Mr. Metzenbaum is leaving for location scouting—"

"—when location?—"

"—that's not really your affair I'm afraid—all you need remember is he is very busy, the man is swamped—"

"—he's not going on location right away?—not for a long time or anything?—because what's crucial is—"

"—*please* don't call again—not with pseudo dental cures or anything else. We will, as the expression goes, call you."

Pig slammed the phone down, but too late, Hennessey's

click beat her action, and she stood trembling over the phone wondering if she should report to Rickie the kind of secretary he had working for him, a Transylvanian cunt.

Naw, Pig decided. She had never made trouble for anyone, never gone out of her way to harm a soul and maybe Hennessey couldn't help it, probably she was a dog and anyway, she was in pain, nobody's pal. When Rickie called she'd summon up what charm she had lying around, hit him with the request to call Bobby Schwab, wish him well, thank him, and exit dancing.

If Hennessey ever gave him the message in the first place.

That thought first crossed her mind at 12:45 and she couldn't shake it. She tried to sun, tried to work up a little interest in the fact that Burt Reynolds was going to be on the *Dinah Shore Show* coming up.

No good.

She lasted till 1:02 when she dialed 277–2211 again and there was, this time, no answer at all in the Metzenbaum office. Pig let it ring and ring and then finally a voice came on and identified itself as the message desk and whom did she wish to speak to.

"Mr. Metzenbaum asked me to call at one."

"There's no one in the office just at present. Perhaps he's in the commissary."

"Could you switch me over please?"

"Certainly. Please hold."

Pig held for all the good it did. Mr. Metzenbaum wasn't in the commissary. Pig got the message operator back, gave a detailed report because that way, Hennessey couldn't ruin her permanently.

Unless the message desk simply reported to Hennessey. *It shouldn't be this hard!* Just to call a guy you slept with and talked with and lived with and he cared for you, or said he cared for you, sure, years ago, but years ago counts for something.

Pig paced. 1:10. If he'd gone off the lot to eat, no way

he'd be back much before half past two. The walls of the house were closing in too fast for her to survive eighty more minutes alone, so she dialed Johnny's service and told them very precisely that if a Mr. Metzenbaum called please for chrissakes get the number and say she'll call back soon.

Then she put on a tight bra, threw a sweat shirt on over it, and went outside for a jog. The beach was empty pretty much, April being April, but the smog was heavy, L.A. being L.A., and there was no way in this world to spot Catalina. Pig walked down to the water and when she reached it, took a few steps into the surf.

She jumped back fast, surprised by the intensity of the cold, and she wondered how in the world she could have loved the surf so when she was growing up in Santa Monica, not so far away. They used to go in the water then at fifteen, her and the Steamer and Spencer T. Murtaugh, and it hadn't been that great a trip she'd taken, these last twenty years.

She began to run, gracefully and fast but even with the tight bra, she could feel them bouncing almost painfully, and God only knew the last thing she needed was for them to lose any more firmness than they already had. Johnny said she was crazy when she worried that way but she knew what she looked like once, she had been there to see.

Pig walked briskly, forcing herself to stay just inside the edge of the water; it was good for the thighs, kept them firm and tight. You could never be too kind to your thighs.

The phone was ringing when she got back close to the house at 2:06. Naturally. Naturally. It would be Rickie about to catch a plane and buzzing from the airport and Pig bolted across the last yards of beach and into the house only by the time she got there, it was dead.

Naturally, naturally.

It's a goddam *plot,* Pig thought as she quick dialed the service and asked if a Mr. Metzenbaum had tried to contact her.

"No messages whatsoever."

"I just heard the phone ringing so there's got to be *some*thing."

"Oh yes. That was a mistake. Someone Spanish asking for Conchita."

"Did he leave a number?" Pig asked, because sometimes Rickie would do that kind of thing, practical jokes. When the moon was full.

"It was a *mistake*," the service lady said. "More often than not, they don't leave forwarding instructions."

Everyone's a comedian, Pig thought, hanging up. But then, who wanted to spend your life as a service answerer? Probably this one came out here to make it in show biz and look where she ended up, but every so often she tried out new material on the customers—

—the phone rang again.

"Yes!" Pig said, too loud, betraying too much, but what the hell, she was nervous.

"Blah blah blah blah blah blah blah Conchita," a man's voice said in some kind of frantic Spanish.

It was definitely not Rickie being clever. "Sorry, you have the wrong number again," Pig said.

Faster now: "Blah-blah-blah-*blahblah* Conchita?"

"Ees no Conchita," Pig tried slowly. "Wrongo numbero, okay?"

"Blah-Conchita, blahblahblah *Conchita*?"

"There's no fucking Conchita here now quit tying up the line!" Pig screamed and slammed the phone down hard into its cradle.

Before he could call back again, Pig dialed Fox and when she got through, a voice other than Hennessey's said, "Good afternoon, Mr. Metzenbaum's office."

"Tell him it's Pig, please."

"Mr. Metzenbaum isn't here."

"Fine. Will you be sure to tell him that P-i-g called when he gets in from lunch."

"Mr. Metzenbaum isn't coming back from lunch. He has appointments out of the office the rest of the afternoon."

"Let's go back to square one, all right? I gave the other girl a bunch of messages—"

"—that's Miss Hennessey. She's at the dentist and won't be back until at least Wednesday."

Maybe there was a God, Pig thought.

"Did she give those messages to Mr. Metzenbaum?"

"I couldn't swear to it."

"Could you contact him now then for me please and just say that I called, and I'm waiting at 456-9999."

"I'm just temporary and I can't bother him. I was given very strict instructions about that. I don't want to get into trouble."

"Well, if he calls in," Pig said.

"I'll be sure and tell him, Mrs. Pig."

A dumbhead, Pig thought as she hung up. Her future was in the hands of not just a nerd, but a temporary one at that.

Maybe there wasn't a God too.

At 2:35, when it was clear that she wasn't going to come close to making it through the rest of the day while at the same time retaining her sanity, Pig put in what she knew would be her final call to Fox, because when she toured dinner theaters a few years back in *There's a Girl in My Soup* it turned out she had a better ear than anyone had ever given her credit for and so, when she was through to the office, she took a deep breath, crossed her fingers and, as haughtily as possible said, in a deep English tone, "Yes, this is Mrs. E.C. Humboldt-Frith here, and it is imperative that you deliver a message to Mr. Metzenburg."

"Mr. Metzen*baum* you mean," the temporary said. "What message?"

"Well, the meeting is simply off and that is that."

"Meeting?"

"Child, you must pay heed, yes, the meeting, the meeting between your Mr. Metzen-whatever and my husband, Mr. E.C. Humboldt-Frith, who, as he constantly reminds me, is film editor and critic for the London *Sunday Times*. Now, if you will give me your solemn word that you will *immediately* call your employer and deliver all that is pertinent, I shall let you go."

"He's not my employer, I'm just a temporary. And I don't want to get in trouble. Mr. Metzenbaum doesn't like interruptions when something important's going on. If *you* called the Polo Lounge and spoke to him though, he couldn't get upset about that."

"The Polo Lounge, oh, it's just too dreary," Pig sighed. "Ah, but if I must, I must, good-bye, child," and she hung up, hollered, "Hot Shit!" with everything she had, quick zoomed upstairs, switching into her lucky peach outfit that Johnny loved so, and then she was out the door and into her beloved Corvair—Nader was just another nerd when you stripped the frills away—and gunned her way, on a note of triumph, toward Rickie Metzenbaum. . . .

She almost missed him. He came out of the Polo Lounge at half past four, surrounded by three guys talking kraut, and he was still only a bare five feet, Rickie, so they all three towered, but why she almost blew it was he was in sandals now, and a ton of gold chains around his open-down-to-the-naval shirt, and his hair was shoulder length easy, and Pig, getting up from the chair by the entrance said, soft, "Rickie?" but he didn't hear, just kept on moving on with the kraut guys, past the house phones and the booths and around the corner by the cashier into where the lobby opened up and she said, "Rickie" there again, as she went alongside them now, in the center of the place, bellboys shooting all around, people checking in, checking out, but it was bedlam in the place, or at least no one was hearing her or paying her mind so finally she almost ran so that she was ahead of them and then she said his name again, "—Rickie—"

"—yes, Pig, what is it?"

"—well at least you remember my name—"

"—of course I remember your name, now what is it?—" and he walked almost to the main door of the hotel.

"You keep moving away from me, Rickie."

"That's because I'm in something of a hurry, Pig—"

"—well I've really just for a second got to talk—"

"—I keep asking you 'what is it?' but you never say—"

"—that's 'cause you keep moving, if you'd stay still—"

"—Jerry Ford learned to walk and chew gum at once, I'm sure a bright girl like you can learn to walk and talk—" and now one of the krauts opened the door for him and they all spilled from the lobby out under the famous green stripes toward the portico.

"—well there's a guy named Bobby Schwab—"

"—yes I know all about him, he's a fool who's in the son-in-law business now and lucky to be there—"

"—well he's written this movie—Julian Garvey's the producer and—"

"—I don't need the *dramatis personae,* just tell me for Christ's sake what it is you're after—"

"—the lead's wide open, Rickie, and they're gonna be testing a bunch of people and a word from you would mean just one hell of a lot—"

Menzenbaum raised his hand then and one of the younger car hops shouted, nodded, and started running, and then Metzenbaum turned on Pig, moving in close saying, "Is that what all this is about? Is that what all the goddam phone calls to my office were about?" And now he pointed to the three Germans saying, "—those men? do you know who those men happen to be? They just happen to be in charge of the Berlin Film Festival and we're meeting about a retrospective of my films for their festival, I've never had a European retrospective, I'm a serious film maker, now how do you think it looks when some fucking creature with these udders sticking out comes roaring up and butts in—"

"—I didn't know, how could I know, if you had answered any of my calls—"

"—I didn't *want* to answer any of your calls—"

"—I need this boost, Rickie, it would just mean so much, one quick call, how much can it cost you, just call and say I've got talent like you always told me—"

"—what talent?—"

"—but you always said—"

"—all your talent's in your tits, Pig—"

"—Rickie, Jesus, don't—"

"—all your talent's in your tits, Pig—"

"—quit with that—"

"—all your talent—"

"—*you got to stop that Rickie!*—" she got out, and then she wanted to say, "I was kind to you once," but the words wouldn't come and, "I took care of you once, good care of you once when you needed someone to take good care," but there wasn't a chance for that either, and then a Ferrari was waiting and he got in and after a wave to the krauts he was gone, leaving Pig in not the best shape in the world all things considered. . . .

4

"It just bushwhacked me," Dixie said as she and Mel were finishing dinner.

Mel grunted, refilled his wine glass with the Zinfandel, held the bottle out to his wife.

"I can't risk the calories," she said.

"Suit yourself. But this self-improvement course is sure awful sudden."

"I told you, I just finished telling you if you'd only listen that I was bushwhacked. Who cares about turning thirty-eight? Right? It's a nothing birthday. Thirty-nine, sure, you can begin getting edgy about forty looming on the horizon, but thirty-eight? Ridic. But there it is."

Ethel stuck her head in then to see if anyone wanted any more fish.

"Thanks no," Mel said. "I think the same goes for Mrs. Kern. She can't risk the calories."

Ethel returned to the kitchen.

"Don't make fun."

"Sorry I guess, but it is a little weird."

"Okay, maybe it is, but don't embarrass me in front of the hired hands, is that asking too much?"

"No. But would it be asking too much if I pleaded with you to get off this fish kick a little? Since you had your birthday last week, I'm growing gills."

"Don't you think it's good fish?—I think it's delicious—

I send Ethel to hell and back to get it—she loves getting away for an hour and I love what she brings back."

"This place doesn't deliver?"

"Mel, it's practically beyond the Colony, how can they make a profit being that far out? It's a local place and I think we're damn lucky I heard of it."

Mel sipped his wine.

"You seem so moody lately," Dixie said into the silence.

"You too."

"Well you know why I do—age. I'm just so blue about the whole thing."

"Baby, short of suicide, there's not a whole lot you can do to improve things."

"There is though!" Dixie said then. *"Minden."*

Mel waited.

"If you zap me about this I promise I'll kill you, will you promise you won't zap me?"

Mel crossed his heart.

"Well, here's the thing—I've been doing some little secret research. Since I went into this terrible depression about my age and my looks and my general attitude and I decided what I needed, what was absolutely going to turn my life around was a new outlook; I need to get my vigor back, Mel."

Mel finished his glass of wine quickly, emptied the bottle for his refill.

"Now La Costa, everybody knows everybody else's business at La Costa. Then I checked out The Greenhouse, you know the Neiman-Marcus spot, but in the first place, who wants to go to Texas and besides, I hear it's very dilettantey there."

Mel crossed his eyes and made a strangling sound. Then he slumped over the dining table and lay still.

"I asked you please not to do this, if I remember," Dixie said.

He raised his Robert Duvall face and looked at her. "I'm sorry, Dix, but I cannot take the idea of an intellectual fat farm terribly seriously."

"Well that's because you haven't heard about Minden."

"Oh of course, I swear I'm getting senile. Minden. Yes. Right. Minden. Nabokov wrote *Lolita* there. I also have it in my head that Count Leo did the galley proofs of *War and Peace* on the premises."

"Minden is a mansion in Long Island and it's a very serious place. It's got jogging paths and everything."

"You're very sweet," Mel said. "I must marry you sometime."

"I'm ignoring you because I want this very badly, Mel— I mean, my God, if I crump when I'm thirty-eight, I could be in very sad shape at forty. Minden would replenish me in mind and body. They exercise you and massage you and put you on a three-hundred-calorie-a-day diet if you want, which would do wonders for my waistline."

"But would the price do wonders for my wallet?"

Dixie made a face and said, "It isn't exactly cheap."

Mel got up and walked around the dining room table and stood by her. "One condition and you can go."

She raised her face to him.

"Never ever tell me what it costs." Then he smiled and kissed her lightly and went into the library. A minute later the Brandenburgs were blasting. . . .

In her sleep she began to hear the sound. Distant and repetitive, a popping sound. Dixie turned over, snorted, reached out for Mel's body, and turned the light on when she found she was alone.

3:15?

Again, the popping sound.

"Mel?" she said in the direction of the bathroom, but the room was dark. She got up, moved into the corridor. "Mel?" she said more loudly, but the library was dark too. The whole house was dark.

Dixie blinked. If the whole house was dark, where was all that *light* coming from? She was good at some things, bad at others, but no one alive was worse than she was when it came to waking up.

She went back to the bathroom and put some cold water on her face, slapped at herself a little to get the circulation going.

Again that stupid popping sound.

Suddenly she realized what it was: The tennis lights were on and someone was hitting a ball. Hard. Every so often. For just a minute, Dixie was scared because there was that one Bel-Air horror story which was true about the prowler that lived in one of the big estate's tennis houses. And when you chased him he hid in the ravines. And when you were gone he came back and no matter how early you got up the next morning, the tennis house had been slept in but was empty again.

"Mel," Dixie called, almost a yell, and she wondered if she should call the Bel-Air patrol. Not without checking things, she decided. She wasn't brave by nature but she didn't want to get the cops or someone up there and find out there was some kind of doubles match going on—

—*doubles match?* At almost half past three?

Crazy.

She took a sweater and threw it over her nightgown and then went to the kitchen and got a carving knife in case it was the prowler. Slowly she went outside, silently staying in the shadows of the house until she could catch a glimpse of the court.

"Mel!" she cried then, breaking into a run toward where he stood in his tennis whites, alone on the court, serving, his racquet making a great popping sound when it collided with the yellow ball. He had brought a card table out from the tennis house and as she ran, Dixie could see wine bottles and a glass and God knows what else.

He waved when he saw her, waved and smiled and got another ball out of the enormous filled bucket beside him. Then he hit another blistering serve.

"You scared me," Dixie said. "What are you doing out here?"

"Serving."

She stopped across the court from him, almost angry.

"I know you're serving, when I say what are you doing out here I can see what you're doing out here, what I mean is *why* are you out here *now?*"

He just shrugged.

Dixie hurried to him now, put the carving knife down on the table. "I thought you were the Prowler, Mel; you gave me a fit." She saw the rolled joints on the table then. "Hey, are you stoned?"

"The Prowler?" he answered, and began to laugh. "Me? The famous Bel-Air Prowler. Why would I sleep in the tennis house when I own the regular house too? The *Prowler.*" He laughed till he cried.

"How stoned are you anyway?"

"Oh my dear, almost beyond recognition. We Prowlers are very into grass." He wiped his eyes, murdered another serve.

"Come on to bed now. If you touch a patient tomorrow in this condition, the malpractice suits will bust us for sure."

"That's why God made lawyers, don't you fret."

"Mel, this is crazy, now come on the hell inside."

He took a joint, lit it, inhaled deeply, then again, then held it out for her.

She shook her head sharply.

"A little of the old vino?" He raised his glass off the card table.

Another shake.

He shrugged, drained the glass, filled it to the top again.

"I am simply freezing out here, so must you be, let's hit the sack."

"You have to pass a rigorous course in survival fitness to get your Prowler's merit badge." That struck him funny too.

Dixie was shivering now. "What the hell is going on?"

He blasted another serve. "You know."

"No, I do not know."

"Well I do."

"Know what? Make some sense."

"I know."

"Know *what*?"

"I saw the Excalibur when I brought you your birthday surprise. I've done some checking since. I'm not unaware of the situation, that's what I know."

After a while Dixie decided not to say anything.

Mel served three balls, one harder than the next. "I thought it would fragment or something. Then tonight when you started that dumb way of getting the conversation around to could you get your body toned up I realized, 'My God, she really thinks she's gonna be a star, it's not going away.' So I am." He gestured around to the court. "I really enjoyed this place and I thought I'd hit a few before I left." He gestured now to the shadows beneath the card table and the small bags resting there. "Packed enough to get through the day." He inhaled again, hit another serve.

"How can you just stand there and smile?"

"It's a whole lot better than killing somebody, which is what I thought I was gonna do when I first found out. But what's the point, what good would that do anybody? Better getting stoned. Smooths everything."

"Jesus, Mel, aren't we going to talk about this?"

"I sort of thought we were."

"Not with you like this. Aren't we even going to see somebody, we must know fifty shrinks; my God, aren't we even going to fight?—"

"—Dixie—"

"—*it's not so fucking terrible to want to be in the movies*—"

"—are *you* mad at *me*?—" He started laughing. "I got to think that's funny—I mean shit, I didn't do anything, I'm not walking around playing town pump, I'm just an innocent dentist drilling his way through the world and *you're* the one gets pissed." He shook his head. "Oh God, we Prowlers lead a tough life, no question," and now he was roaring.

"—quit that!—"

Mel turned his back and tried to get control.

"—quit it!—"

"—I'm trying, Jesus, go easy—" He turned back, took another inhale from what was left of the joint. When he was able to talk he said, "No, you're right, it's not so fucking terrible but you know what is?"

Dixie stood her ground.

"What's terrible is how unfair it is in this world to be pretty. I mean, if your nose were a little bit longer or your ass a little bit bigger around, not any of this would have happened." Mel shrugged then. " 'Course, I probably never would have married you either, so what the hell."

Dixie turned then and hurried toward the house. She was cold and there wasn't any point in talking further anyway, not with him in that condition. And even if he hadn't been in that condition, there still wouldn't have been much point, it was something simply beyond him.

Goddam civilians, they never understood.

Tuesday

1

Noel was always the first one into the office. He was there before Matty or Schwab and long before Julian. He had a routine set—make the coffee, read the trades, check out the *Times*. Then he would set to work on the cinematographers. He had made lists of all the good ones and pored over guides to find their credits so if you, say, mentioned Gordie Willis he could flip to the Willis page and tell you sure, *Godfather* was great, sure *Annie Hall* was brilliant, but don't forget *Drowning Pool*. Willis was the best when it came to shadows, but did *Tinsel* need that dark a look? Wasn't the material itself dark psychologically? So would Willis add?

Noel also had lists of sound men although he wasn't really sure exactly who contributed what when it came to sound. And he was working on his production designers when the phone rang. "Yuh," Noel answered into the receiver.

A guy said, "Gimme Schwab."

"He's not in yet. Try back in an hour, I know he'll be in then."

"Would you take a message?"

"Who is this?"

"Rick Metzenbaum and—"

"—hey, my dad's almost worked with you a couple times. I'm Noel Garvey."

"You got a pencil?"

Noel flipped his yellow pad to a clean page, titled it *Rick Metzenbaum, 9:05*. "Shoot."

"He's got a project casting, right?"

"Couldn't be more."

"I'm punchy, I wanted to be sure we were on the same wavelength."

"What's the message?"

"It's complicated—shit—wait, tell you what—let me kind of explain what I want and then you can put it down so it makes sense."

"Anything you say, Rick."

"There's this girl, Pig is what everyone calls her—and she wanted kind of a recommendation from me to Schwab because we knew each other from back East. This all has to do with getting her a screen test. Am I making sense?"

"I think the part you may be talking about is probably pretty much set. Nothing official but—"

"—look, that's not my province, I was asked for a recommendation and see, well, she caught me off guard, at kind of a busy time, and I didn't handle the whole situation as gracefully as some—"

"—is this part of what the message is?"

"No. Just tell Schwab I don't know the project, I don't know what's needed, I don't intend this to be anything more than what it is. Understand?"

"Yes I do."

"Well, this is a very inexperienced performer, Pig. I don't know if she's done film, even tv shit."

"'Inexperienced.' Shall I write that down?"

"Yes. But also this. She is talented. You may underline that. She is terribly emotional, she brings a lot to the party. She doesn't know that, she's never tapped it, but it's there."

"'Inexperienced and underlined talented and emotional.' That about it?"

"Vulnerable add. What I guess I'm telling you is this: If Pig wants it, underline the if, but if she does, she could go all the way."

Pig sat very still, trying not to show her panic, as the guy with the dirty-old-man's face looked at her bare breasts. He had the red-flecked eyes of a drunk or at least of someone who had had a lot too much a lot too long ago. And under the eyes were the telltale bags of the boozer.

Now he reached his soft hands out toward them.

Pig didn't want to flinch, but there wasn't a whole lot she could do about it.

". . . hey . . . easy. . . ."

Pig bit her lip, nodded.

Now here came his hands again.

Pig looked away and shut her eyes as suddenly his fingertips were all over the right one, pressing and kneading. Then they were gone. She was about to sigh with relief when they were back again, this time landing on her nipple, and she was embarrassed to feel it getting firm.

It took all she had not to bolt.

His fingertips shifted to the left one. Again they went all over, touching and prodding. Then they all convened on the nipple and this one got firm too.

Then the tips went away.

Pig looked back at the guy. His hands were crossed now on his chest as he looked at them. His eyes just bore into first her right, then her left, then her right, then her left.

Pig knew she couldn't take it too much longer.

But he would not stop studying them.

Now he moved a step to one side and stared. Now back to dead center, still staring. Now a step left. Now another left. Now he was moving in close again, almost at the left profile. Before she could prepare herself, his left hand was at her nipple, then away. Then it was back.

One really good scream would make me feel a lot better, Pig thought.

She looked at the dirty old man hard as he was in front of her again, his baggy-eyed face revealing nothing. But he could not take his eyes off them. Still staring, his voice husky and low, he said, "Miss Higgins, what in the world are you doing here?"

"Isn't that kind of obvious?"

"Not to me it isn't."

"Well I don't want to go through it again. I told you once, if I told you again, I'd just be repeating myself, so what's the point."

"Miss Higgins, I obviously don't know you very well but please believe me, I'm an old man and not entirely stupid: This is crazy of you, Miss Higgins. One hundred percent off the wall." He started toward her again, his eyes flicking from one nipple to the other, back and forth.

Pig couldn't help flinching.

He looked in her eyes a moment. "Your breasts mean a great deal to you, I suspect."

"No more than to anybody else."

"I think perhaps that's not entirely true."

Pig shrugged. "You could be right. In a way, I guess they've supported me over the years."

"You almost jump when I touch you, do you realize that?"

"How could I not, I'm the one jumping."

"You'll be pleased to know I'm done. I was just checking for Schimmelbusch."

Pig cocked her head and looked at him.

He smiled. "I was making sure you weren't cystic. That's what Schimmelbusch's disease is."

"I haven't got it, do I? Shit, that's what I need just now,

a case of Schimmelbusch." She looked at him. "I say that right?"

He nodded.

"What happens now?" Pig said.

The old guy moved away and sat in a chair across from the examination table. "One of the biggest problems facing people in my profession is this, Miss Higgins: unreal expectation. Patients come in with hopes that we simply have no way of satisfying."

"I'm not asking that big a deal."

He sighed and rubbed his eyes. "You are. In a weird way you most definitely are. If we were allowed to advertise, which is, of course, not ethical, but *if* we were, and if we used the standard before-and-after-type photographs, to show what we were capable of, Miss Higgins, right now as you sit there, you are *already* the after. Women come to me from all across the country and when they tell me what they want, more often than not it's breasts like yours are right now."

"Like they used to be, maybe."

"No. Now. Right now. You have a perfect body, Miss Higgins, what in the world do you want to tamper with it for?"

"Because it's important."

"Well, I don't want to proceed further."

"Then I'll find somebody else."

"That is certainly your privilege."

Pig started to stand, then sat back down because she could feel herself starting to lose control. "I don't want to, though. I want you, Doctor Michaels, because when I was here in Vegas a couple weeks back with my boyfriend, your name came up and everybody said how Vegas is practically the plastic surgery capital of the world—"

"—I'm afraid Brazil has captured that honor—"

"—but there's lots here, am I right?"

Doctor Michaels nodded. "Because of the showgirls, of course, and because a lot of husbands when they win need things to spend the money on, and what better gift than a new body to their wives or whoever. One learns not to ask a lot of questions in this business."

"Well, you're the one I was told was tops and I'm here. I drove the desert all night with you in my head. I mean it. I just took off. No one knows where I am or why but you. So you've got to help me."

"I didn't say I wouldn't, I said I didn't want to."

"Then you will?"

"Miss Higgins—mastopexy is not called for in your case. It's a complicated and expensive operation, and in my view absolutely unnecessary."

"I thought it was like an everyday thing."

"Well you're wrong. You asked for a breast lift and it's not an everyday thing. Do you know what mastopexy involves?"

"Not the foggiest."

"Well, first of all we have to remove the nipple—"

"Remove my nipple?" She threw her arms across her stomach and went "Yuccccch."

"And then we have to replace it, being careful that the site of the new nipple location is—"

"—I'm very squeamish, Doctor Michaels, you gotta stop this kinda talk."

"I could get to like you," Doctor Michaels said, and he got up from the chair, went to a shelf, took down a carousel projector, and plugged it in. He aimed it across the examination room toward a blank wall. "Want to turn off the lights?" he said.

Pig pulled the white robe around her, reached over, flicked the room into semidarkness.

"Mastopexy is a hospital operation. Many thousands of dollars. Recuperative period that can be difficult. You're talking close to two hours per breast. I just want you to know all this going in. And the hardest part of all, from the point of view of the surgeon, is that the nipples match when it's all over. You don't want one slightly higher than the other or, God forbid, pointing off the wrong way. Now this first photograph is of a woman about your age, but in a marked condition of ptosis." He showed the first slide.

"Oh the poor bitch," Pig said. "They're way below her navel."

"Now this is after the operation," Doctor Michaels said.

Pig looked at the new photograph. It was the same angle as the first, the head cut off for personal privacy. Just the breasts themselves. "You got any more?"

"Many. Here's the before." He showed another slide.

"Can I see the after please?" Pig said.

He showed it.

Pig walked to the wall and pointed. "What about that?" she said, indicating a scar that circled the nipples, then ran down the breasts, ending in a kind of inverted T.

"Can you be a little more specific?"

"I can be a lot more specific. When will it go away?"

"Never."

Pig stared at him.

"In a bathing suit or clothes, of course, they're incapable of being detected, and in the dark, who cares."

"I gotta be *photographed*," Pig said. "They'll think I'm trying out for Quasimodo with breasts like that." She turned to the doctor. "Why can't you just give me a shot of that liquid stuff they did to Carol Doda?"

"Because liquid silicone is now illegal. It moves. It leaves the breast area and goes wandering."

"*Yucccch*," Pig said again, and then she said, "Sweet Jesus, somebody, give me a break," and after that she was in tears. "Look. Please. There's this part—they're gonna test a lot of people for it, and I'm gonna be one of them —nobody knows that yet but me, but I'm gonna bust people's chops till they give in and let me test and I wanna look so sensational when that happens, I want to *know* I look so great I'll just feel so confident I'll knock 'em dead —but I don't feel all that terrific about myself just now. . . ."

Doctor Michaels turned off the projector, turned on the lights, gave her some Kleenex. "All right, here's what I can do," he said quietly. "I'll make as small an incision as possible on the inframammary line—that's where the lower part of your breast comes in contact with your body—and I can insert a gel-filled mammary prosthesis—it's like an envelope—the gel is enclosed—and the prosthesis is positioned between your chest wall and your natural breast tissue. The scar is slight to begin with and eventually becomes all but invisible."

"Is this as big a deal as the other?"

"No. I do it either in the hospital or here in my office with my nurses. It's cheaper, of course, here, but that's up to you. Where are you staying?"

"Little motel on the Henderson side of town."

"Better the hospital then."

"How long will it take?"

"Maybe forty-five minutes per. It's not a general anesthetic operation. Novocain and Valium take care of everything pretty well."

"I'll be conscious?"

"The whole time."

"Doesn't sound like that much. I'll stay at the motel."

"It's a very happy operation, Miss Higgins. Of course, in a third of the cases there's what we call the 'firmness' problem."

"Maybe you better explain that to me."

"Certainly. Three months from now you may wake up one fine morning possessing breasts with all the texture and allure of sixteen-pound shot puts."

"Three months down the line will take care of itself. When can we do it?"

"Tomorrow afternoon at five I have a free appointment."

"Deal," Pig said, and they shook hands. "What is what I'm about to have called?"

"Augmentation mammaplasty."

"Augmen . . ." Pig's voice trailed off for a moment. Then she looked at Doctor Michaels. "You mean in order to make them perkier, you've got to make them *bigger*?"

"I know it's not exactly what you had in mind when you came in here."

Pig just sighed. "I guess nothing worthwhile is ever easy," she said. . . .

3

Ginger sat in her rented car behind the Bel-Air Hotel, staring at the clock. It was ten of nine now, and she'd been there, just sitting and figuring, for over half an hour. Garvey was shrewder than she was and no point debating that. And he had something she wanted, which increased his edge.

But if she arrived just late enough to make him think she wasn't arriving, that had to at least a little deflate his ego, increase his nerves. And she had something he wanted too, had wanted for years, that part of her. So she wasn't totally without weaponry.

At five of, she left the car, went running toward suite eighty-four, knocked wildly at the door, and when he opened it she said, "Goddam plane, we circled and circled," and he said, "I was almost leaving, I thought it was done," and she said, "I don't know what 'it' is exactly, but it hasn't even started." And then she went into his arms.

He held her for a moment, then let her go, walked to the phone, and asked for room service. "What are we drinking?"

"Something alcoholic if they stock any," Ginger said.

Julian nodded and ordered ice and Perrier and Chivas Royal Salute.

From across the room Ginger watched him and the receiver was shaking ever so slightly in his hand. Not at all displeased, she excused herself, took her little case into

the bedroom, hung up her few clothes, came back after
the liquor had been delivered. Julian made them each
drinks, stiff ones, and then they sat together on the sofa.
Or started to. But when she was down, he shifted his position, moved across the room to the stiff desk chair, got
comfortable. It was a good move, Ginger decided; he kept
you off balance, made you a little less sure of yourself.
She raised her glass into toast position, then drank.

"Let me put this in as maudlin a manner as possible,"
he said then. "I am closing rapidly in on my sixtieth year,
and my life, all in all, at least when viewed from inside my
skin, has been almost entirely shit."

Ginger nodded. "I can see that. Fame, success, and fortune; sounds awful tough to me. Amazing you've survived."

"I thought a few months back I wasn't going to—I had
a cancer scare—nothing to worry about, all was benign—
however, before that was ascertained I had some moments
of reflection and I reached certain conclusions. Chief
among them was that if my future was going to be the past
repeated, I was not particularly intrigued."

"So you decided to make a nudie movie; sound and
logical."

"Please don't attempt humor when I'm trying to be
serious."

Ginger took another swallow of Scotch. "I told you I
was a lousy lay."

Garvey looked at her for a moment. "How does that
follow?"

"This, what we're doing now, it's all part of the sex act.
You know it and so do I. It's foreplay. Well, I'm sorry,
but things strike me funny. I laugh sometimes just before
climax. I'm probably not gonna change all that much,
Julian."

"Query: Why in the world would I want you to? The
whole basis of my infatuation is your quirks. You're a
bright human being and you're also a performer. Do you
realize how rare that is? There's a famous line Mike

Nichols said. Somebody asked him how many bright—not
shrewd mind you but intellectually sound—how many
bright actors had he ever met and Nichols thought for a
long time and then replied, 'One and a half. Anthony
Perkins is smart and Richard Burton is something.' You,
my dear, are also something."

Ginger drank a little more.

So did Garvey.

Why was he so edgy, Ginger wondered.

"I'm thinking, obviously, of altering the cast of characters in my life—"

"—I've been a homewrecker with the Rajah, remember?
Didn't care a whole lot for the role."

"Dear heart, my particular home has been devastated for
well over a quarter century now. Nothing you could do
could possibly increase the shambles."

They finished their drinks then.

Garvey made them each another. His hands shaking
worse.

"I've never—" he began then as he handed the drink to
Ginger "—seen my wife's face during intercourse. I always had to conjure images. Often you."

"Tonight you'll probably think of her."

"Oh, God, that's a terrifying thought," Julian said, and
he broke out laughing.

Ginger sipped her drink, wondering why he was pushing
the laugh so hard. Why was *he* the nervous one? She took
another sip. It was good Scotch. Not that it mattered.

"I've never dealt very well with joy," Julian said then.
"I suppose I've always been afraid of it. I don't know that
I'd mind it so much now."

"You hustled too much maybe. Probably you thought
the world would end *splat* if anybody came along that
could work the streets better than you." She drank again.

Julian took a long swallow of his drink. "Probably I
was born at the wrong time—*droit de seigneur?*—wasn't
that when the lord of the manor could do what he wanted
and not have to worry? I would have liked to be lord of

the manor." He came over and sat beside her on the couch.

Ginger broke out laughing.

"That's delicate of you," Julian said. "Guaranteed to make the American male feel wanted."

"I'm sorry . . . but I told you I crack up when it's not opportune." She got hold of herself finally and said, "But, see, you put me in mind of a thing in grad school, we were in this seminar and talking about Dorothy Parker and would *she* have been happier being born at a different time, say like now, when it's easier for women to survive in a man's world on their own terms, and this teacher, he said, 'When would each of you most like to have been born?' and I blurted out, 'Anytime after Tampax.'"

They both roared then, and after that Julian made them each a third Scotch and they moved into the bedroom and got ready, Ginger lying naked under the sheets first and when Garvey joined her she made all the right moves, quivered when he touched her in the places that were supposed to make her quiver, stroked him and flattered him and tongued him skillfully.

But nothing much happened, he stayed soft.

No hurry, she told herself, booze does that to people, throws them off their game, and he'd respond, all she had to do was not rush it and keep active and eventually she began to get some response.

Not a whole lot though.

He was tense, and she was afraid she was starting to get that way because men had never been a problem for her, when she had her figure, they came running—

"—why were you looking at the phone," Ginger said then.

"—I wasn't—"

"—yes you were—I could tell you were—"

"—you're wrong—"

"—were you going to make a business call or what?—"

"—shhhh—" He tried to kiss her.

She rolled away, panicked, because right then she realized that he didn't even know she was there, probably didn't care, wasn't even thinking of her, she wasn't attractive for him, not anymore, and then suddenly she realized why.

"What have you heard about me?"

"Heard?"

"Yeah—like weird stories—people have always spread weird stories about me—oh, say, like maybe I was this crazed nympho or maybe some kind of dyke—"

"—nothing—"

"—good, because they're not true, I'm just a plain ordinary garden variety woman, Julian, with plain old garden variety needs" and with that she set out to prove her point, because she was a brilliant and resourceful girl, and when she wanted something she went after it, time was on her side, always, always, and slowly she got him to begin to relax and his body became spreadeagled on the bed and she knelt above him, touching him gently, whispering that there was no need to conjure an image, not this night, because the image was there, hovering and passionate, tonguing and touching and flattering and it took a while, it took a long while, but time was on her side, always, always, and when he was finally rock hard and able to penetrate and explode, he clung to her with what she thought, if it hadn't been Julian Garvey, was genuine affection.

At eleven he said, "Asleep?"

"Drunk yes, asleep, no."

"You never mentioned the part."

"I figured it wasn't big enough for me. I mean, I'd only be on camera alone the last half of the flick. That first half needs a lot of rewriting, Julian, before it can interest someone with my clout at the box office."

"You stars always have to be convinced to play the parts that make you famous. Gable fought like hell against *Gone With the Wind.*"

"Query: True?"

"Absolutely. Plus *It Happened One Night*. Plus *Mogambo*. You name it, he was agin it."

"Maybe you'll talk me into it, you're good at persuasion."

"Let's hope so. Dragons have yet to be dealt with."

"What's that mean?"

"Nothing to bother you with just now. Harry Brennerman still your agent?"

"I haven't contacted him or anything, but I would start with him, sure."

Julian rubbed his eyes. "Where are we now, Tuesday night? I'll need a couple of days to set things in order. Have Harry call me Friday. And tell him not to kill me on the deal."

"I would never do a thing like that to you, Julian, and I resent your thinking I would. Hell, whatever Jane Fonda gets, I'll be perfectly satisfied with twice that."

No reaction.

Julian lay still, staring at the dark ceiling, trying to figure how the next day was going to work. For he dreaded many things in life: surely death; surely pain.

And surely Estelle in the morning. . . .

Wednesday

1

Click-click.

Stitch.

Click-click.

Stitch.

Estelle sat knitting alone by the pool house, a large green umbrella shielding her from the late morning sun.

"Indeed she is a vision," Garvey called out, waving, walking toward her.

Click-click.

Stitch.

Estelle continued to knit. "And the sneak?"

Julian sat across from her under the umbrella. "I don't know why Paramount used San Francisco. It's such a chic audience. Half the people there must have been gays and I don't want to even think what the other half were." He sighed. "Still, if they ask me as a favor to come up and opinion-give, how can I turn them down?"

"You work so hard, Julian. Truly."

"All to keep the wolf from the door, my sweet." He stretched. "I assume the boy producer is already off producing."

Estelle smiled. "I've never seen Noel so happy as these days. He loves the business. I think we can both feel proud of him."

"No question we've successfully launched him. And I

think we owe it to ourselves to turn our minds to other situations."

Click-click.

Stitch.

"I feel we're not as stimulating to each other as we might be, Estelle. There's a certain staleness I detect creeping into our relationship, I'm sure you do too. And I think, therefore, that if we spent a bit of time apart, it could only benefit us both."

She considered his words for a time. Then she pursed her lips and, in her best schoolteacherish tone said, "You mean a seperation?"

"Nothing legal, of course. But perhaps something along those lines."

"Ah well, I don't think I embrace that notion." She returned her attention to her knitting.

Click-click.

Stitch.

"You perhaps didn't give it quite enough thought, Estelle."

"It would be such a wrench at my age, Julian, I think I'd rather not. Besides, what would we tell people?"

"We could always use the Jack Warner line."

"I'm afraid I don't know that one."

"Well, he had an aide for, oh, I don't know, a long time, maybe twenty years or so. Really close aide. Right-hand man, that sort of thing. Inseparable. And one day, the community was genuinely shocked to learn that Warner had fired him. And I think it was Dick Zanuck who went up to Warner and said, 'My God, Jack, after twenty years, what happened?' And Warner shrugged his shoulders and said, 'It just didn't work out.' "

Estelle laughed. "That *is* a funny story. I love the way you tell stories, darling. Actually, I'm really rather happy with you, so why don't we separate some other decade, all right?"

Click-click.

Stitch.

"I don't think you quite gauge the level of my serious-ness, Estelle."

"Aren't we the civilized pair?" She imitated Julian. " 'You don't quite gauge the level of my seriousness.' "

He smiled and clapped lightly. "Rich Little I'm sure is breathing easier without you as competition."

She said nothing.

Click-click.

Stitch.

A maid appeared and asked did Mr. Garvey want some-thing.

Mr. Garvey said he indeed did want something, but nothing the maid could supply.

Confused, the girl retreated.

"Is she new?"

"The Mexicans don't last like the old days, Julian, and that's the truth. Today she's new, tomorrow I'm sure she'll be gone."

Click-click.

Stitch.

"I could concentrate ever so much better, I think, if you would please for Christ's sake put your fucking knit-ting down."

"Mustn't get roiled." The schoolteacherish tone again. She looked across at him. "Was 'roiled' used properly?"

"Estelle, grammar is not the subject under discussion. I'm moving into the Bel-Air for a while. We ought to cen-ter our attention on that point. I don't want this to turn into anything ugly. I'm sure you share those feelings. Now—"

"—who is she I wonder?"

"You mean is there somebody else? There isn't. This is a decision I've reached on my own."

"And pigs have wings," Estelle said. "Who is she I wonder?"

"Estelle, I swear on my mother's grave, there's nobody. *My* happiness is what I'm considering. Mine quite alone."

"Oh my sweet darling, hogs don't leave the comfort of one mudhole without knowing where the next one is—"

"—a very adroit image for so early in the day—"

"—thank you, thank you, but flatter me not, just answer before the question becomes the Chinese water torture, *who is she, I wonder?*"

"Ginger Abraham."

"Ah yes, the famous skiing lesbian. How glorious."

"It's strange, but she out of the blue contacted me about *Tinsel*. She'd heard about it up in Vail, and she read for the part and I don't have to tell you, she was fabulous—"

"—better and better. You replace me with this aberration and then proceed to make her a star."

"You have every reason not to be overjoyed, I admit that, but it's going to be that way—"

"—I think not—"

"—it's fruitless to argue—"

"—I think not—"

"—Estelle—"

"—*I will not be publicly humiliated, Julian—I am not about to be turned in in exchange for the mannish Miss Abraham*—"

"—call her what you want, I don't give much of a shit, Estelle, because she makes my cock work and that carries a good deal of weight when you get to be my age—"

"—that and your tongue are all that have ever worked for you, Julian—"

Click-click.

Stitch.

Julian started to rise. "We could both turn very ugly but why don't we not? Of course we'll keep in contact. . . ."

Estelle broke out laughing. "He actually thinks he's going to leave me."

"There's no way you can stop me, I'm afraid."

Estelle put down her knitting and smiled. "Oh baby, oh you poor poor baby, just you wait right here." And then she stood and hurried off to the main house.

Julian sat still.

The pool man appeared then, an ex-surfer type. He said, "Morning, Mr. Garvey" and put down his chemicals, looked around for the aluminum net to clear the leaves from the surface of the pool.

"It's quite clean enough," Julian said.

"As long as I'm here, though," the pool man said.

Julian smiled. "Why don't you just give us a visit on Friday."

"Good morning, Mrs. Garvey," the pool man said.

"Chester," from Estelle. She was carrying a sheaf of white typing paper.

"Chester was just leaving now," Julian said.

Chester left.

Estelle said, "Now that didn't take long, did it." She got out her spectacles and glanced at some of the pages. Julian could not see what was written on them so he just waited for Estelle to begin. "Shall we play a game?"

"I don't care, Estelle. Fire your barrage and I'm off."

"This won't take long, I promise."

"Fine, fine."

Estelle was getting animated now. "Here's how we'll do it. I'll read the description, you guess the person involved. All right? Here's an opener: 'A bit long in the tooth but still the most terrifying encounter of my life. I thought I was going to end up devoured. Bones on a plate.' " Estelle looked at her husband. "Who?"

Julian shook his head. "I can't begin to fathom where you are, Estelle."

"Bankhead, Tallulah," Estelle said. "Now try this: 'Very very bright. A big surprise. A bigger one: The breasts themselves are not of a stature one might have expected. It is the size of the rib cage that makes them seem enormous.' Give up, Julian?"

Julian started to rise again. "What the hell have you got your hands on—?"

"—that last was Miss Mansfield, Jayne. Now—"

"—give me those, please—"

"—sit the fuck down you son of a bitch!"

Julian sat down.

Estelle put back her schoolteacherish tone. "This *is* rather fun. Here's another: 'Titless and plain, humorless and dreary. *May God have mercy on my soul.*' That was Estelle Claiborne. Here's another one—"

"—where did you get those?"

"Your wonderful Miss Bumpstead sold them to me."

"That's not possible. I caught her taking them out of my drawer."

"No, you old fool, you only thought she was taking them out—in point of fact, you caught her putting them back, all your wonderful three-by-five cards—after she'd Xeroxed them, three to a page, and gotten them to me." She waved the sheaf of typing papers. "You see? You may be Mr. Three-by-Five, but I am just as certainly Mrs. Eight-by-Eleven. Shall we continue? Holliday, Maxwell, Miranda." She shook her head. "Really, Julian, Carmen Miranda, where are our standards."

"And this is supposed to keep me attached to you, Estelle?"

"I rather thought it was intriguing information you wouldn't want bruited about. Did I use 'bruited' correctly?"

"Poor Estelle—all of that is ten years old at least—and those ladies, alas, are dead. In today's world, I'm afraid even the *Enquirer* wouldn't care." This time he did stand.

"Of course not. This was just the nostalgia section. The good stuff I saved for now."

"I don't know what you mean by 'good stuff.' And in truth, I don't much care."

"The wives of the studio executives I mean, Julian." She picked up her knitting again.

Click-click.

Stitch.

Julian stopped dead.

Estelle concentrated on her work. "It's amazing how many top movie and tv executives end up marrying performers. I think your total at the present time is two studio heads, and eleven top executives. And seven more ladies now married to network vice presidents."

Julian grabbed the pages, started racing through.

"Oh they're not there, silly. The good stuff is in my vault."

Click-click.

Stitch.

"Remember how they blackballed that actor, Eddie what's-his-name, Julian? It's amazing what a provincial community it is out here. Remember how he couldn't work for ten years because they caught him screwing the wife of a studio head and no other studio head would use him. Think how popular you'd be. *Two* studio heads' wives. *Eleven* top executives' wives. Oh, they'd love making deals with you, yes they would. Ten years in the wilderness, Julian, that's what they gave that Eddie fellow. What do you think they'd give you. And how old will you be when they let you back inside."

"You haven't got the stomach for the scandal."

Click-click.

Stitch.

"Estelle, you'd be in every paper right along with me and I don't think you'd like that a whole lot."

"I'd love it, you stupid cunt!"

"You'd fold—"

"—fold? *Fold?* Look at you, you weak whoremaster, you're folding before my eyes and we haven't started skirmishing—I would be so brave for the media—I would wring the hearts of America—'I don't know where those terrible cards came from but yes, they are my husband's handwriting, but who could want to destroy such a wonderful man.' I would dig your grave, my love, and help to shovel in the dirt. Believe it."

Click-click.

Stitch.

"And do say good-bye to Miss Abraham for me."

Julian just stared at her.

"Don't look so shocked. I've always been stronger than you and we both know it. I'm afraid, my sweet, that the rest of your days will be spent with none other than plain old dreary titless me."

Julian spun, fled.

"I wouldn't count on a great deal of mercy," Estelle called after him. "Not if I were you."

Click-click.

Click-click.

Stitch. . . .

2

It was drizzling hard when Noel parked his Excalibur in
the empty lot across from Ferguson's ice cream place.
Noel turned off the lights, checked his watch. Not even
nine yet, plenty of time before the place closed.

He got out and jogged across the asphalt to the sidewalk,
checked for traffic, then jaywalked fast, opened the parlor
door and damp, stepped inside. It was hard to concentrate
on which flavors to pick, because for God only knew what
reasons, his father had disappeared. His mother said he'd
come by late in the morning and they'd chatted and then
he left, she assumed, for his office.

Only he never got there.

Where the hell was Julian?

"Lemme have a triple dish of . . . of. . . ."

"—make a pick, huh?" the kid said. "I hate surprises."

Noel glanced across the counter. The kid looked like an
ex-surfer—but that was state law, you had to look like an
ex-surfer to get a work permit in L.A.—but more than
that, you knew he wanted to make it in pictures. Just on
a wild guess, Noel said, "Who do you study with?"

"I'm trying to get in to see Strasberg, but he's only here
six months a year. And he costs; man, it's goddam illegal
what that sucker charges."

"Triple dish of Dutch chocolate and chocolate chip and
toss in some fudge brownie while you're at it."

"Terrific mix," the kid said, as he set to work filling the order.

Noel got out his wallet, stuck some bills on the counter, took his dish when it was ready, waited for the change. He took a bite of each of the three before he went outside, because it wasn't just enough to order great ice cream, you had to orchestrate it too or you would never get full value. The fudge brownie tasted best of the three, which meant it would be the last to go. The Dutch chocolate seemed kind of bland so there he had it, first the Dutch, then the chip, then the brownie for the climax, and saying so long, he went back out into the drizzle which was turning cold and mean. Noel ran across toward the deserted parking lot and when he got to his Excalibur he couldn't have been more surprised to see Robert Duvall waiting for him and the first punch came so fast he was spinning back against his car before he realized who it was that was after him, and Noel turned but as he did, another punch landed, this one in his gut and he doubled over, dropping his triple dish onto the asphalt and the next punch crashed against the side of his mouth, bloodying it immediately, straightening him up, and Noel tried to cover but the blows kept landing, deep into his stomach, again to his stomach, again to his stomach and he gasped and lowered his arms until the punches came at his face again and now the bleeding was getting very bad, blood streaming down from his mouth to his shirt and he threw a hook and it landed but didn't seem to have any effect and now here came a punch toward his eyes and Noel managed to duck his head in time for the blow to land on top of his head and he thought he heard something breaking, fingers maybe, and that was good, but not good enough to stop the punches from tearing into his stomach again.

Noel could feel himself starting to black out.

He lunged forward, grabbed Kern around the neck, hung on, tried to gouge the dentist's eyes out, but it was slippery going, the eyes were wet, either from tears or the rain, and then Kern shoved him back against the Excalibur and launched another attack.

But not so hard this time.

The guy was beginning to tire.

Noel covered himself as best he could, took the punches on the top of his head or his arms, and there was no more, Kern was almost punched out.

But Noel's eyes were starting to slide up into his head.

He fell against Kern, holding him in a bear hug, trying to get his brain working again, and now Kern's punches were very weak, no problem at all.

Noel's knees began to cave.

Kern, chest heaving, pushed him back toward the car again, and threw a wild roundhouse right that landed and Noel spun along the car, off balance more than hurt, and when he faced Kern again, the guy tried the same thing, another roundhouse, and Noel saw it a mile away and watched it come closer and closer until it exploded against his jaw.

He fell back helpless as Kern staggered toward him, banging him in the ribs as best he could, crying terribly now, great audible sobs, and there was no question in that part of Noel's mind that was still clear that the guy was insane.

Another punch to the mouth.

Another punch to the mouth.

Again Noel's eyes started sliding up.

Another punch to the mouth.

He wants to kill me, Noel thought. He wants to kill me and with everything he had remaining, he drew back his right leg and kicked it as hard as he could, catching Kern coming in, square in the nuts.

Another punch in the mouth.

Noel slid down to the asphalt.

Kern began one more punch, then brought his hands together over his groin. Then he drained and fell to the wet ground, landing in the remnants of the ice cream.

The two of them remained on the ground, drained and

gasping, covered with chocolate, covered with rain, covered with blood. They stayed that way, less than five feet away from each other, neither able to move.

In a minute or two a crowd began to gather. Not much of a crowd, just some kids on bicycles, a few grown-ups coming out of the movies. They stood circled around the two men, kind of talking quietly among themselves.

Finally Noel and Kern were able to stand and when they could they each staggered slowly to their cars, driving off in opposite directions. . . .

Except for the fact that the *Charlie's Angels* she was watching was a real bummer, Pig couldn't have been in a more terrific mood.

Not that there wasn't discomfort or that they weren't a little on the black-and-blue side. But all in all, it was better than having a cavity filled. The Valium was given intravenously and there really wasn't much to worry about because Doctor Michaels kept the chatter going, and the two nurses were terrific too, funny and experienced and calm. It was a springtime operation, augmentation mammaplasty, the doc said, and when Pig asked why, he told her, "Bathing suits." You wouldn't think of operations as being seasonal like white sales, but when you came right down to it, it made sense.

He'd shown her the prosthesis, a cellophane-looking packet of thick soft gel, and he'd made the incisions and the insertions before she was really sure he'd even started.

Then, when it was all done, he put her in a one-size-fits-all bra and told her not to lift her hands over her head for a while, and to take it easy and come back in a couple of days.

And that was it. He gave her antibiotics to take every six hours, and pain killers too, and gave her a kiss on the cheek, and sent her on her way.

Kate Jackson was about to get captured.

Unless Cheryl Ladd could warn Jackie Smith in time to effect a rescue.

Snooze.

Pig lay back in bed and stared around her room in Lucky John's Motel. What a dump. If this was what John built when he was lucky, God forbid you would have to stay in his place when he was on the skids.

At least no bugs, Pig told herself.

And the tv worked.

On the table by the bed she reached for her pain-pill bottle. "If necessary," Michaels had cautioned. She wasn't really sure what he meant by that. Pig had never been big on pills, hated putting impure or strange things into her body.

But she also knew she wanted to sleep all through the night.

You didn't get your strength back without complete rest. Exercise was out for a while. She couldn't get them wet, so there went swimming, couldn't raise her arms, so forget tennis or golf. How much pain did she have to have before she could legitimately dope herself?

Cheryl Ladd was too late; Kate Jackson was in the clutches of the villains.

What if they killed Kate Jackson, Pig thought. What a trauma that would cause the youth of America. Because right now all those millions of birdbrains were sitting there *knowing* that no matter how great the peril, old Kate was gonna make it to sell more products next week.

What a great thing though. Pig began to laugh. It hurt, but she couldn't help it. Here would be Cheryl and Jackie roaring down the highway saying to each other, "Hurry, hurry, my God, if we don't make it in time, Kate's a goner" and "Oh I hope they haven't hurt her, faster, faster."

And then they'd get there and zap—on the floor dead would be Kate Jackson.

"Shit," Cheryl Ladd would say, "we didn't make it."

"Fug," Jackie Smith would say, "Charlie will have a bird when he learns she died."

"Wait wait," Cheryl would say.

"You mean you think she's alive?" Jackie would say.

"No, but I think she's got a kid sister who wants to enter the business," Cheryl would say.

Close up on dead Kate.

Fade out.

Half the country would have cardiac arrest.

Pig smiled, slowly got up, moved in more pain to the bathroom, got a glass of water, brushed her teeth. She looked at herself in the mirror. She looked pretty much like Pig. Now, drowsy, she went back to bed, sat, took a couple of pain pills, turned off the tv set, and slept.

Her lips felt thick when she woke, her eyes heavy. The pain pills had done a terrific job—a really one hundred percent marvelous job—

—so why was she hurting?

Was she?

Hurting?

She started to get her feet to the floor in the dark but it was too much for her. She was panting now. Something was crazy, haywire.

She fought to her feet.

The bathroom light? Pig felt around.

Where was it?

Where was the fucking thing?

Finally, finally she found the switch, flicked it on.

The brightness made her dizzy, or something made her dizzy, maybe the pain pills, but she felt lightheaded and had to hold tight to the doorknob before she could steady herself enough to look in the mirror, and what she saw didn't help things a whole lot because her left breast, her poor left breast, it had swollen in the night and over-flowed the bra cup and what was worse wasn't the pain or the terrible tightness of the skin around it. What was worse was that as she watched, she could actually see it getting bigger and bigger and the pain got much worse.

Her breast was swelling hideously now, up toward the area of her clavicle, and watching was like watching what happens to liquid rushing out of a broken bottle.

The liquid in this case, although Pig had no reason to know it, was blood. Nor did she know that a large vessel had come untied and the whole area was engorged, hemorrhaging, turning poisonously black and blue, and Pig couldn't think of anything to do besides stand there and scream as her left breast ballooned before her eyes. . . .

Thursday

1

Estelle spent Thursday in a terrible state of uncertainty. Upstairs Noél was still swollen from some dreadful encounter he had had the night before with a gang of delinquents in Beverly Hills. He didn't want to talk about it, wouldn't in fact, talk about it. And he refused to see anybody, because he said that would have meant talking about it and getting attacked by a kid gang in Beverly Hills wasn't the kind of thing you wanted to remember, he said. And as long as nothing was broken, and he assured her nothing was, Estelle's options were limited.

Besides, she had Julian to fret about.

He had been gone since their encounter the previous late morning, and she could not, simply could not find out where he was. He never showed up in the office, never called in. And he never phoned anybody else either, not his doctor or lawyer or Indian chief.

He had been so frenzied when they'd parted that she thought it must have been an automobile accident, but that was simply silly, because as the hours rolled by, and as the day changed and Thursday rolled into its afternoon, no hospital had called. And they would have if there'd been an accident. A hospital or the police or somebody.

But the phone remained silent.

When he finally did appear, at close to seven Thursday night, he looked like she had never seen him look before. Gone the immaculate man. Perfectly shaven, every Leslie

Howard hair in place. The tailored English suit unwrinkled. This Julian who got out of his car looked like he hadn't slept in don't even think how many hours. And his hair was mussed, his clothes rumpled.

And he was flying.

"Were you worried?" he said to Estelle at the front door. She said she was.

He kissed her on the forehead and said, "What a sweet thing." Then they walked inside. "Noel?"

"In his room."

"Get him, would you? I have news." He walked into the library then, collapsed into his favorite chair, shut his eyes resting until the other joined him. When he saw his son he asked what happened but Noel simply shrugged and said, "I'll tell you later, what's your news?"

"I would love a vodka stinger, Estelle."

She hesitated.

"Daddy's home. Never fear. Now be a darling."

She started into the adjoining bar. "Talk loudly so I can hear."

"The world will hear," Julian said.

"What's your news?" Noel said impatiently.

"If I were an arrogant man, I would likely say that I have just finished thirty-six hours of consecutive marathon negotiations which ended with my making the best deal in the history of film. But being more modest, I will say only that I just concluded the best deal in the history of Julian Garvey."

Estelle stuck her head in. "You do have a way of dragging things out rather maddeningly."

"You never had much sense of climax, Estelle. All right. Here it is without more ado. *Tinsel* has been cast. Finally and forever and done."

Noel waited, watching his father.

"Barbra Streisand will play the lead—"

Noel started shouting. *"You cast Barbra Streisand as a sex symbol?"*

"I said 'the lead,' child—we're changing things around

here and there to fit her talents. There will be no nudity anymore. She will be beautifully and tastefully dressed in lingerie throughout the last hour of the picture. She will not be a fading sex star, she will be a fading singing star—"

"—shit, she played that already in *Star Is Born.*"

Julian smiled, took the drink from Estelle, thanked her silently. "You are only one hundred percent wrong, Noel. Wrong and crucially wrong. She played a *rising* singing star in that and everyone in the world knows that the reason there was so much trouble on the picture was that basically she wanted to have the Kristofferson part because no matter how you slice it, baby, that's where the sympathy lies. And now she will get to play what she's always wanted to play. And instead of being on screen alone for the last seven minutes, as she was in *Star Is Born,* here she will be alone on screen for perhaps an hour. And all those rooms she wanders into? Well all those record players and radios will be playing songs sung by Miss Streisand. And Daddy shares in the record revenue from the start, just as Daddy is in on the picture from the start. On a straight gross deal, darling, no deductions. She will, of course, have control. I'm delighted for her, too. Because if *Tinsel* does half of what *Star Is Born* did—and it will do a good deal better than that—I just made myself eleven million dollars." He took a long drink of his stinger. "Excellent," he said to Estelle. "Why don't you make one for Noel, he looks like he could use a bit of refreshment."

Estelle left them alone.

"I don't think I deserve that look," Julian said then.

"You don't, huh. Not with all the people you screwed?"

"Myself among others, cherub, never forget that."

"You suck, you know that?"

"Do I? Personally, from having people whisper that I've lost a step, I have just signed the biggest star in the world —the *only* star in the world who's a star everywhere— records, clubs, tv, films—no one else is close. Not only did I sign her, I killed them on the deal because they wanted it so badly. So perhaps people will say I've gained a step, which will be closer to the truth. And as for you? Well, I can't feel sorry for you."

"I didn't ask it."

"Poor wounded baby, it's all over your face. Think about it. Less than a month ago you were trying to average the birth dates of the Beatles for some cosmic reason. And now you are almost a formidable figure. You outfaked Harry Brennerman, which I can't do. And you fucked the girl of your dreams many happy times. No. Sorry. My eyes are dry. You've loved this month and you know it and you're good and you'll get better and we know that too."

Estelle brought the drink back then, and Noel drank it in silence for a while. "I'll go see about dinner," Estelle said then. "For the longest time today, I wasn't sure the family was going to be together this evening."

"And many evenings to come," Julian said.

"That's always such a pleasure to me," Estelle replied, and she left her men alone.

"The eleven million?" Noel said finally.

"Yes, child?"

"Is that before or after taxes . . . ?"

Friday

1

That morning, in Harry Brennerman's breakfast room, Ginger was terribly excited. "It's crazy," she said, "but I just don't even know what to begin to ask for."

"It's not crazy," Brennerman said. "It's something that hasn't happened before, ten years away and then bango, a star again."

"You think a hundred thousand?"

"People you never heard of are getting a hundred thousand. People *I* never heard of are getting it. Two fifty's more like a reasonable starting point."

"Julian will just have a bird."

"Let him." Harry finished his coffee, looked at her cup. "Want more?"

"Maybe a speck."

"Waitress!" he called out. Then to Ginger he said, "Drives her crazy when I call her that." He stood. " 'Scuse. I got to rouse the wife to action." He padded out of the room in his slippers, smoothing his hair across his skull.

His wife was making waffles in the kitchen when he got there. "These are just about ready," she began, but stopped when she saw his face. "What?"

"She doesn't know," Harry said. "It's all over town, the barbers in the Beverly Hills Hotel know, the hookers in Hollywood know. The only person in town who hasn't heard about Streisand is interested in a little more of your coffee."

"Son of a bitching bastard shit," Mrs. Brennerman said. Harry nodded.

"Well?"

"Don't 'well' me. I can't tell her. I won't be the one."

"Maybe I'll just go upstairs," Mrs. Brennerman said.

"Don't make the bed," Harry told her. "I'm crawling right back in when she's gone and pulling the covers over my head." He grabbed the coffee pot and went back to the breakfast room roaring, "God hates a coward, let's demand half a million."

Ginger looked at him. "You think?"

"Why not? Plus a percentage. I mean, you said you were resuming your career, right?"

"All the way, this time. This time I stay put right here in Magictown."

"Sure you don't want to go back to Vail?"

"Nothing for me there anymore."

Harry rubbed his hands together and smiled. "Seven hundred and fifty thousand," he said then. "And we don't budge. You got the guts for it?"

Ginger gave him a hug. "Fortune favors the brave," she said. . . .

2

Dixie was daydreaming alone in the tennis house at noon when the phone buzzed. It was Ethel. "He's here," the maid said. "Doctor Kern. He just drove up. He's in your bedroom right now."

Dixie made a sound that meant thanks, and hung up, sitting still, staring at the famous black court. Since she had heard the news an hour or so before, she had felt just so stupid and humiliated. She had had it all, a decent man who cared, and tossed it away.

She lit another cigarette from the one still burning in the ashtray. If only she had the guts to face Mel, or the brains to come up with some kind of halfway clever opener. Maybe it would smooth itself from there.

Then again, maybe not.

She stood up and walked out onto the court, grabbing her racquet as she went. Maybe it would be good to practice ground strokes. Really try and get her mind grooved on that, a good looping backhand or—

—the phone buzzed again.

Dixie walked to it, said, "Yes?"

It was Ethel again, terribly excited now. "Didn't you hear me? The man is in the house. He's packing his clothes. You got to get here. You got to talk. Be kind to the man. Tell him things."

"What things would I tell him," Dixie said, and then

she thought, *omichrist,* I'm asking advice-to-the-lovelorn questions to my maid.

"Jes' get here and be quick," Ethel said, and then was gone.

Dixie stood over the dead phone. Then she sighed and put it down, sat, stood, lit another cigarette, put it out, lit one more before breaking into a run toward the house.

He was in their bedroom, several large suitcases open, and he was tossing his clothes into them as quickly as possible.

"Let me have Ethel do that," Dixie said from the doorway.

Mel shrugged.

"Your stuff'll get all wrinkled."

"It'll hang out."

"Anything I can do?"

"I'll let you know if there is."

"You heard?"

"About Streisand?"

"Um-hmmm."

"I heard."

"I feel just like—"

"—rather not hear."

"Right." She watched him as he got the first suitcase stuffed, zipped it shut. Two more to go, one of them already halfway ready. He kept hurrying to his walk-in closet, grabbing clothes, dumping them into the cases, back and forth fast. "How 'bout if I came crawling and—"

"—look—it's very simple—I need my clothes—I called and Ethel said you were on the court, I figured what the hell, in and out and gone you wouldn't mind. The last thing we need is to talk."

"Why?"

"Because I have a lot of anger. A *lot.* And I don't want to turn it against you. We'll have what they call a 'Creative Divorce.' " Mel shook his head. "If *ever* there was a phrase that had to originate in Hollywood, that's it."

"You don't want, like, to try a reconciliation or anything?"

"I don't want."

"Hey?"

"What?"

"You're full of shit and I can prove it."

He started back into the closet again but she ran at him, blocked his way, going, "You lying bastard, you *said* you called Ethel, you *knew* I was here—why does a man come to a house when he knows someone is there he doesn't want to see? Answer? He doesn't. You called her to see if I *was* here and you did that because you *want* to try again, admit it, I'm right, you're full of shit."

He tried to push by her.

She stood very still.

"It won't work," he said.

"I'll risk it."

"It will get very ugly."

"So will you if you live long enough."

"What do you want, Dixie?"

"To fuck you."

"My nuts are black and blue."

"Aren't you the thoughtful one," she said as her arms went around him. "My favorite colors. . . ."

3

Late that afternoon Johnny brought Pig the news personally and her first reaction was to shriek, "With whose body is she gonna play it?" But then he explained the changes and she began to settle down. He was soothing and so kind —she was in the fanciest room in the Sunrise Hospital and he had put her there after she'd called him half hysterical from the emergency ward.

That was before Doctor Michaels had arrived to reopen the incision, evacuate the blood clot, remove the prosthesis, clean out the area, put it back, and sew her up again. The whole thing hadn't taken an hour and probably she could have gone back to Lucky John's Motel, but her Johnny was having none of it. He had put her in the corner room on the top floor of Sunrise and no arguments, please.

"You'll go back to Malibu when you can," Johnny told her. "I spoke to this Michaels. He said soon."

"We'll do a lot of beach walking," Pig said. "I'd like that."

"I've got to go to the Springs for a while," Johnny said. "The house is absolutely yours, though. As long as you want it."

"What's in Palm Springs?"

"Well, I don't have to tell you what a thing it would be for me to do this *Tinsel* score, especially now."

"That I understand."

"Well, Streisand's people think maybe I'm past it—"

"—well screw them—"

"—no, no, they may have a point—I haven't gone platinum in quite a while, we got to admit that. Well, they've got this kid lyricist that lives in the Springs they think I might make beautiful music with. We've met a little and I'm willing to take the chance."

"Oh you dog," Pig said.

He smiled.

"You feeble fart—how old is this lyricist?"

"Twenty-one maybe."

"Um-hmmm. And how pretty?"

"B-plus maybe."

"We've had a good run, don't end it lying."

"Well, I wouldn't have, but you've been awful good to me, Pig, and you've been through a lot."

"I can take a lot," she said, which was true, and she meant it, which was why, when she was alone the moments after he was gone it surprised her that she started to moisten up. She reached for a Kleenex but too fast, the sharp movement made her gasp and her hands went to her tender breasts until everything was bearable again. Then she carefully took the phone and put it alongside her body and got long distance. She put in a call to Lightning Louis, which was what she called the agent who booked all the dinner theater tours she'd done lately. When he answered, she said, "This is your lucky late afternoon."

"I would appreciate knowing why."

"Because even though Lynn Fontanne is unavailable and Laurette Taylor's dead, I am interested in a bit of summer occupation. I assume you're sending Scofield out in *Hamlet*. He's been after me to do Ophelia; tell him I'll give him a break."

"*California Suite* is what we're assembling."

"Hey, terrific, I can play either of the girls' parts."

"Britt Eckland," Lightning Louis said. "She is very hot since living with Rod Stewart. Everyone knows how much she spends on clothes. There's a genuine interest in seeing her in the flesh. Plus we're negotiating now with Virginia Mayo."

"Sounds like a fabulous dramatic showcase you're putting together there. And hey? If either of them fall out, you can always bring back Irish McCalla."

She hung up and turned off the overhead light, lying very still, staring out at the Vegas neon. She tried forcing her mind toward Rod Carew and what were the odds of his hitting four hundred this year, when only last year he'd come in with a resounding three eighty-eight and—

—no good. Too many things needed sorting. Johnny and no job and dealing with her present pain. She pulled the bedsheet down, revealing the crummy one-size-fits-all bra. Slowly, she cupped hands gently around them.

"Poor babies," Pig said. . . .

Saturday Week

1

Ethel looked through the glass windows of the back door and shook her head several times, but the tiny man with the blue cap just stayed there, smiling at her.

Ethel gave in finally, turned the knob. "Nobody home," she managed.

"When'za gonna be?" Mr. Balducci asked.

"The Kerns is gone. Split. Pffft, you understand?"

Mr. Balducci turned his blue cap in his hands.

"Divorcing, get me. It was bad here and it's gonna get real bad."

"Anna house?"

"Oh," Ethel shrugged. "Doctor Kern's renting it out till after everything's settled."

"Who to?"

She shook her head. "Some rock group. I'm just doing a last clean-up now. They move in Monday."

"I be here," Mr. Balducci said . . .

April–August 1978
New York City